THE ASIATICS

D0360792

7 $\frac{50}{4/20}$ ·

THE
Asiatics

A NOVEL BY

FREDERIC PROKOSCH

WITH AN INTRODUCTION BY PICO IYER

FARRAR, STRAUS AND GIROUX

NEW YORK

Farrar, Straus and Giroux
19 Union Square West, New York 10003

Copyright © 1935, renewed 1962 by Frederic Prokosch
Introduction copyright © 2005 by Pico Iyer
All rights reserved
Distributed in Canada by Douglas & McIntyre Ltd.
Printed in the United States of America
Originally published in 1935 by Harper & Brothers
First Farrar, Straus and Giroux paperback edition, 1983
This paperback edition, 2005

Library of Congress Cataloging-in-Publication Data
Prokosch, Frederic, 1908–
     The Asiatics : a novel / by Frederic Prokosch ; with an introduction
by Pico Iyer.
     p. cm.
     ISBN-13: 978-0-374-52924-6
     ISBN-10: 0-374-52924-8 (pbk. : alk. paper)
     1. Americans—Asia—Fiction. 2. Hitchhiking—Fiction.
3. Young men—Fiction. 4. Travelers—Fiction. 5. Asia—
Fiction.   I. Title.

PS3531.R78A7 2004
813'.52—dc22

                                        2004047132

www.fsgbooks.com

3   5   7   9   10   8   6   4   2

INTRODUCTION

OF YOUTH AND WANDERING

BY PICO IYER

WHEN Frederic Prokosch described, in such vivid and glittering detail, lying in a hammock among the casuarina trees in Malaya, journeying across the snowy passes of the Himalayas, meeting princes and wily traders in the deserts of Central Asia, and watching the play of moonlight on cobblestones as travelers take off across the hills for the valleys of Kashmir, he had not seen a single one of them. In truth, he was a twenty-nine-year-old research fellow at Yale, sitting in his apartment on Elm Street in New Haven and re-creating, with a bravura that only a young man can summon, places he had never seen except in atlases and travel diaries. He had spent a year in Germany and Austria with his professor father, and he had been lucky enough to absorb the cosmopolitan flavors of his father's friends, but in terms of his own exotic travel, the nearest thing he had to show was a recently completed doctoral thesis on "The Chaucerian Apocrypha."

Yet as he sat in Elm Street, as he recalled almost fifty years later in his memoirs, suddenly he found himself walking through the rain along the road beyond Ba'albek. "Day by day," he remembered, "this vision of a continent grew more vivid in my mind. It kept growing in the darkness, it seeped into my dreams. I'd wake up in the night with a sudden glimpse of a tropical city, a shabby old hotel, a picnic by the Brahmaputra, and I'd turn on the light and jot it down quickly."* The continent possessed him, and so powerfully that to visit any of the places he describes today is to find them uncannily like the ones he conjured up.

Almost as soon as *The Asiatics* came out, in 1935, it became an international success, translated in time into seventeen languages and acclaimed by Thomas Mann, Prokosch's father's friend, as well as by André Gide and Albert Camus. One of the first congratulatory telegrams the hitherto unpublished author received came from a London publishing house—signed by T. S. Eliot. Wise beyond his years and clearly dauntless in his imaginings, the young romancer seemed set to be a defining force in American letters.

What all these distinguished writers were responding to was, I think, a rare ability to catch the sense of possibility that travel awakens, the spirit of movement and not knowing where one is going next and being able to take, with equal equanimity, being set upon by brigands and by languid beauties. *The Asiatics* is as much about youth as about the Asia it purports to describe, and it contrives somehow to make youthfulness and wandering seem synonymous. To an extraordinary degree, to read it is to feel young again, and to remember (in my case) traveling across the Atlantic alone at nine years old, a movie star in front of me in line, the man beside me claiming to be a friend of Cassius Clay's.

The book moves, you very quickly see, with the rhythm of a river, not a bus; it meanders this way and that, picking up a new passenger here, taking in the light across the mountains, letting off a passenger there. And things happen—as they do abroad—without a discernible sense

*Prokosch, Frederic. *Voices*. New York: Farrar, Straus and Giroux, 1983, p. 57.

of cause and effect. One of the things Prokosch catches, intuitively, it seems, is the sense that travel puts us into a realm of fairy tale, in which (in the case of this book) one is almost instantly in the company of guardians of harems and opium smugglers and one passes from jeweled scene to jeweled scene as through chambers in *The Arabian Nights*. Anything could happen next: one could be in the arms of a young woman, or in a Turkish prison. Prokosch is, among other things, a connoisseur of anticipation, and the reader going along with him never knows what will appear around the corner.

Reading his book now, I feel I can recognize all the places he visits—he not only captures the clatter of an Indian road, its bullock carts and trucks and bicycles, as well as anyone writing in the twenty-first century, he also throws off the observation that in India roads are more gathering places than thoroughfares (and so explains why my parents' homeland is so exasperating for those who want to get somewhere, and so enchanting for those who like the dallying en route). He sees, in 1935, that Cambodia is "a haunted country, full of shadows, full of ambiguous little hints of the past," as if to say (correctly, I think) that the Khmer Rouge atrocities of forty years on are not just a function of Pol Pot and his henchmen but also reflect something in their country's soil and spirit.

But more than that, he catches the peculiar logic that makes travel a kind of alternative reality, a foreign state in itself that is an intoxication. A Moslem says that America has no gods and, on the next page, asks the American visitor to take him back to New York (turning murderous when refused). Someone else asks the young narrator if he's an American Indian, or wonders, "Have you many concubines, sahib, when you go back to America?" The person last seen in a Turkish prison suddenly appears again in Peshawar, along the Afghan border—every traveler surely knows this kind of encounter—and exclaims, "By God! This is a fairy tale."

It's easy to forget now that the thirties were a golden age of private exploration. World War I and the Crash were beginning to fade from memory, and plane travel was beginning to make the whole world seem open in a way it had never been before. Peter Fleming, Robert Byron, Evelyn Waugh, and Graham Greene were on their way to Kashmir, Oxiana, Africa, and Mexico, and in fiction James Hilton's *Lost Horizon* (with which *The Asiatics* shares more than a plane crash and some lamaseries) was exulting in the fact that suddenly, out of nowhere, as it seemed, the Westerner could find himself in a Himalayan kingdom that had been cut off from the world for all of history. Prokosch himself, always a highly cultured man, would write of being influenced by Malraux and by Colette's *La Vagabonde*, and place his book in the picaresque tradition of Voltaire and Swift and Fielding; but to the reader today, it's very hard not to see him as a precursor of all the young travelers who set up an actual trail across Asia, from Istanbul to Kathmandu, in the sixties.

This is not mere coincidence. Prokosch saw that a new kind of world was coming to light. One of the striking achievements of his book is to depict an Asia in which all kinds of foreigners are traveling without a fixed sense of purpose: aristocrats, adventurers, priests, and what we would call "bums" were moving in every direction, as if in the caravans of old, trading not silks but stories and pieces of disenchanted wisdom. Prokosch's specific hope was to be part of a new world in which borders were as much a thing of the past in life as in art (one of the more forceful characters his narrator meets, in prison no less, is a "patriot-hater"). His "greatest desire," he later said, "is to take part, however humbly, in the resurrection and growth of a truly international literature—an approach to writing which exceeds national limitations, both in matter and mentality."

The beauty of the book lies clearly in its descriptions of lanterned streets and the sound of bells in the night, dusk "dripping like grey moss from the trees" in Malaya and the "labyrinth of sunlight and shadow" in a Tehran bazaar; but this is all spiked by its narrator's keen sense of squalor and suffering, his noting that a Buddhist resthouse is "a foul hut" and that many of the people he sees are "coarse-featured, thick-lipped, savage-eyed." Prokosch's description of locals as "tomcats" and "filthy, secretive creatures" may alarm readers today—he was unable to gauge the idiom of seventy years on—and his generalizations about Asia ("A true Asiatic is never very happy"; "In Asia we believe that selfishness is the only way to gain peace") make no sense at all. He writes with a young man's ruthlessness as well as his sense of adventure, and he seems eager to show himself no fool and not taken in by everyone he sees. In that sense, he is the opposite of Hermann Hesse or Jack Kerouac, say, the other talismans of youth whom at first he seems to recall. If his protagonist is like Odysseus in his readiness to be detained and to forget his destination, his encounters with Circes and sirens and goddesses bathing in a stream, his seeing great caravans of corpses passing across the plains, he is also like Homer's protagonist in realizing that the main story of travel is the conflict between enthusiasm and real life.

As the book goes on, though, I think Prokosch begins to tire, as many a traveler does: some of the freshness begins to fade, and the narrator seems less full of wonder than he was. One of its mounting patterns is for the main character to meet again people he has seen at an earlier stage of his journey, and in every case he finds them changed, though really, we feel, the change is in himself. An object of romantic longing is found to be a hard-headed adventuress; a charming companion turns out to be a con man. It is almost as if one can see Prokosch turning into a different kind of writer as he proceeds, and the glow of early scenes begins to subside. What began as an ode to youth comes to seem more a book about its loss, its passage into something else.

In real life, Prokosch would write more than twenty books after *The Asiatics*, and would in time go to Damascus and Isfahan and the Taj, many of the places he had evoked so magically while sitting in New Haven. He lived for stints in Portugal and Stockholm, in Italy and Hong Kong, and in later life settled down in Grasse, in southern France, where he collected butterflies and put out handmade editions of poems he loved, while continuing to turn out novels that mixed classical allusions and Arabic settings and countesses who seemed to have stepped out of the pages of Somerset Maugham. A little like his young protagonist, he even went around the world collecting pieces of wisdom from great characters; he would come to know Auden and Nabokov and Maugham himself and Woolf, even as he had sought out Gertrude Stein and James Joyce when a teenager in Paris.

Yet one senses that he saw, at some point, that the lack of driving purpose and overarching theme that was the very charm of his first book might become a limitation in the end; and perhaps, like his unnamed narrator, he was always better at listening than at pushing himself forward, more suited to disappearing inside the glow of vivid others than to being a star himself. In all his subsequent books he was never able to match the sense of discovery (of himself, of his voice, and of the world) that he revealed so powerfully in *The Asiatics*, and the world was never to repeat its discovery of him. When he died in 1989, he was one of those melancholy writers best remembered for his first book, of fifty-four years before.

Yet when you turn to his memoirs, published just five years before his death, you will find they end exactly where his writing life began. "The yearning for meanings was the essential yearning of my childhood," Prokosch recalls. "Like a child I saw an inexhaustible amazement in the air, in the blueness of the sky or the wild excitement of the birds." His ability to catch that excitement, to bring those blue skies and birds into a small room in New Haven, and then into small rooms everywhere, meant that his first book was sure to live on long after he did. The memoirs end with their author, in his seventies, in a hammock, paging through a copy of *Around the World in Eighty Days* and wondering, with the eagerness of old, "what strange new excitement the day will hold for me."

Beirut, January 2004

PICO IYER is the author of several books of travel and fiction, including the pan-Asian book of adventures *Video Night in Kathmandu*, written while he was in his twenties. He lives now in suburban Japan.

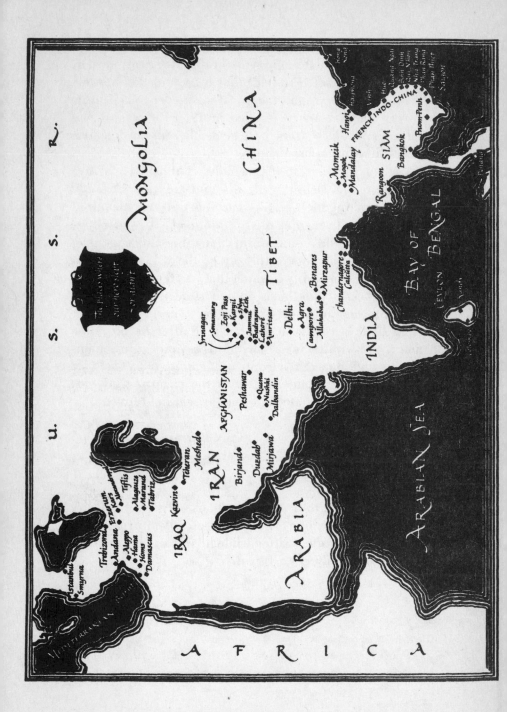

R.

S.

S.

U.

MONGOLIA

CHINA

The place where SID DIED NAZE "ᕍ HAUT"

TIBET

Srinagar
Zoji Pass
Somamarg
Kargil
Jammu
Srya
Leh.
Badrapur
Lahore
Amritsar
Delhi
Agra
Cawnpore
Allahabad
Benares
Mirzapur

AFGHANISTAN

Peshawar
Quetta
Nushki
Dalbandin

Tehran
Meshed
Birjand
Dusdab
Mirjawa

IRAN

INDIA

Chandernagore
Calcutta

Momcik
Mogok
Mandalay
FRENCH INDO-CHINA
Hanoi
Hue
Rangoon
SIAM
Bangkok
Phom-Penh
Saigon

BAY OF BENGAL

CEYLON

Kazvin
IRAQ

ARABIA

Trebizond
Andaan
Aleppo
Hama
Homs
Damascus

Erzerum
Kars
Alaguez
Marand
Tabriz

Tiflis

ARABIAN SEA

Istanbul
Smyrna

MEDITERRANEAN

AFRICA

1

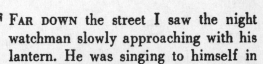

FAR DOWN the street I saw the night watchman slowly approaching with his lantern. He was singing to himself in a soft grief-stricken voice. When he saw me he grew silent, his wrinkled-apple face grew intent and solemn. He passed me quietly. And then when he reached the corner he began singing again, chanting, I should have gathered from his tone, about the coming of disasters, the grief of old men, the end of love.

The air was full of mosquitoes, everything was wet and warm after the autumn rain. Night had covered the ugliness of the city—the signboards, the telegraph poles, the shabby Ford cars, and above all the many daylight noises. All I could hear was the whining of the mosquitoes, and a block away, where the lights were brighter, the lower whining of a radio in a café. There were some girls standing on an outdoor staircase on the other side of the street. I could see their dark skin glimmering in the soft lamplight. But they were quiet, they weren't saying a word. Now and then one of them would turn her head slowly, but that was all.

Outside the café a little old man was standing, gazing at the ray of light that fell through the decorated pane. He knew immediately that I was watching him. Loneliness had sharpened his instincts. So he walked up to me and looked into my face. His own face was in shadow, but I could see his eyes peering through the heat and the darkness like little lanterns, glassy and persevering, full of experience. "You are a stranger to Beirut?" he said in a broken French. "Isn't that so?"

I nodded.

"Beirut is not a good city," he went on. "I've been here four days. It is a hard and ugly city. I see nothing good in Beirut."

I nodded again.

"Take care, young man, of your money. They will rob you like magpies."

"I don't have very much money," said I with caution.

"Ah, but some!" he replied quickly. "More than many of us!"

So he followed me into the café and we sat down at a table together. We asked the boy to bring us some coffee. There was a great noise in the room, the radio blaring and three great Senegambians roaring with laughter and lewdness. Upstairs I could hear some more men laughing and the quick tripping footsteps of the women.

"So you don't like Beirut?" said I.

The old man shook his head earnestly. "No."

"What cities do you like, then?"

"I like Cairo."

"Yes, but that's in Egypt. I mean here in Syria, in this part of the world."

"Cairo isn't so very far away."

"Have you traveled much?"

He nodded absently. He was sipping his coffee with a slow sobbing noise, and his eyes grew soft and reflective.

"Have you been in Istanbul?"

He nodded. "But Istanbul is a dying city."

"You have been in Damascus, of course?"

He nodded again. "Damascus is a good city. Ancient

◇◇◇

and beautiful." He paused. "But I tell you, young man, every beautiful city in the world is growing uglier year by year. You from Europe have done it. You've been ruining beautiful ancient Asia. You ought to be ashamed of your wickedness." He was speaking with a great personal anxiety, as if he too were intimately involved in all this.

"But you look like a European yourself," said I.

"Yes," he said, eyes mild with reproach. "I am a Greek by blood. My name is Papadopoulos. But I was born in Damascus and I am an Asian at heart."

Soon we left the café and walked down toward the water. The waves were lapping gently against the warm white pebbles. Overhead shone a foggy moon, and along the shore a rippling edge of foam.

"I have had three sons like you," said Papadopoulos. "Of your age, that is. Strongly built like you. I am an old man, you see, and at last I'm alone in the world."

I looked out toward the sailboats in the harbor, a litter of Arab sailing-craft, their wet sails loosened and crumpled. "Old," he went on, "but not too old. I visited a brothel last night. I slept there with the girls all night long." His voice was growing a little bit boastful.

"Have you ever been in a Syrian brothel?" he asked in a thick voice.

"No," I replied.

"Some of them are very fine," he said. There was no one in sight, but in spite of that his voice had faded into a cloying little whisper. "You walk along the corridor. Some doors are open, some doors are closed. If the door is open you look in. A girl will be there, sitting or standing or lying, waiting for you. If she pleases you then you enter and make love."

"Why did you come to Beirut, M. Papadopoulos?"

He wasn't listening. "They have kind hearts, those girls.

They laugh easily and they are willing to forgive a good deal. Most of the brothels are new."

"Why is that?" said I involuntarily. I didn't enjoy hearing wrinkled old Papadopoulos talking like this. But still, it seemed to make him happy, so I didn't interrupt.

"Since the French came, you see."

"But why since the French came?"

"Oh, Moslems do not like brothels. They believe that brothels are immoral. They think Beirut a wicked Western city."

"I didn't know that the Moslems were so virtuous."

"Oh," said Papadopoulos with a sly laugh, "they aren't! It is only that their tastes are a little bit different!"

The moon was growing clearer. A slant of moonlight fell suddenly, like a happy little sigh, upon a tuft of moss at my side. The shore grew close and confiding and the pebbles shone like silver.

"My sons have not been kind," said the old man. "They are brave, strong and handsome. Yes. But who made them so? From whose loins did they spring? I don't understand them at all." He sighed with self-pity. He was watching me carefully, and I noticed that his hands were trembling a little. "They are rich, all three of them. But they no longer love me. When they see me they don't appear to be in the least happy about it. So I no longer go to them. They refuse to give me money, or even food. Yes. And from whose loins did they spring? To whom do they owe their strength and virility? Ah, they have made me very unhappy."

Presently I rose and said good night to the old man. I left him sitting beside the shore, thinking a foolish old man's thoughts, feeling cold and isolated.

I left Beirut the next morning. I rode through the town on a truck that was going to Damascus, and watched the young Syrians in their cheap American suits, students, some of them, others conceited idlers, gossiping in the streets. We passed two or three young men who had come down from the hills, wearing turban and cloak. They looked handsome and graceful and preoccupied. But not the city youths; these looked empty and conceited; they mocked the gentler ones in the old costumes, the old bearded men and the strong graceful men from the hills. Bullies and misers, so they seemed.

Beyond the red roofs we could see the Lebanon hills rising straight up, a wisp of snow on the top. We rode through the refugee quarter as we left the city. Houses built of tins and boxes, hideous things, hotbeds of epidemic beyond a doubt, places where breeding went on at a terrific rate, all the more since the poverty-stricken and the diseased have little else to do. Some of the children, beautiful little Armenians, were digging at roots, nibbling at little bits of this and that which they extracted from the earth. But the strange thing was how the older people had already grown reconciled, how their faces had grown smug again, how their eyes shone with a sleek look and they seemed glad of their misery.

Then the road climbed steeply up into the fierce country to the southeast. Great rocks and gorges, cedars and pines, desolate stretches without life. We passed once or twice through bare little villages that were sitting among the cactus plants in the desert. As soon as we entered them we could feel the air of sullenness, of secrecy and resentment. And also the scent of urine that hangs over the cities and villages of Asia like a veil. Then out into the bare odorless country again.

Up on the hills beyond, the French driver told me, were

caves, a regular honeycomb of them, all filled with outcast families. Very lazy these people were, and completely resigned to possessing nothing, nothing at all. They ate anything they could find. Frogs, turtles, roots, grasshoppers. Very few people ever visited them, and they had grown to detest all strangers. When some one did appear they hid with great swiftness and skill, and nowadays no one ever saw them any more.

2

THE APRICOT trees stood empty of fruit in Damascus and the little streams were brown and sluggish with the autumn leaves that had fallen. The whole city seemed very quiet and very sad. The lands which we had passed outside the city were covered with locusts, the fields were desolate and spotted, the country roads were overgrown. Like a great desert, waiting and waiting, year after year and century after century for forty centuries, waiting to enter the city and bring its antiquity to an end.

But it was a pathetic sort of antiquity. Without dignity, cheap with age. Perhaps it should really have died long ago. A shabby Frenchman stood at the entry to the chief hotel, leering and accosting. Further down the street a girl in red slippers was sitting under a pistachio tree. In the alley stood casks of ripe olives, stained and lichenous, and a load of green almonds, and a hamper of lemons. All of them spoiled, waiting for the winter to rot them beyond recognition.

One of the passengers on the bus from Beirut began to chat with me in French. He was a small timid-looking man, but persisted in talking to me and grew very friendly. "Are you planning to go to a hotel?" he asked as we entered the city. I nodded. "No, no," he said with great politeness, "you must stay the night at my house."

So I did. We passed pilgrims who were coming from Transcaucasia, so he said, on their way to Mecca. They were lying in the courtyards and around the public fountains, and here and there a woman would slyly lift her veil and show her dark licentious face to me.

M. Aractingi's home was very lovely. Orange trees and jasmine were growing in the courtyard and the arches were covered with vines. In the center stood a fine tiled octagonal fountain full of fat fish in the lily-green water. Beside the pool sat two girls. One was very beautiful, dressed in blue silk and silver-heeled slippers, with huge silver earrings. She was playing the zither. The other one was a little bit older, a tiny mouselike creature weaving away at a small carpet. Indoors we met an old man eating an oily dish of hors d'œuvre, eyes closed serenely, and an old woman in a black hood, extremely fat, eating a chicken that had been daubed in honey and cheese. "My mother and father," said M. Aractingi in a tone of faint apology. The old woman drew her hood over the lower part of her face perfunctorily and the old man opened his eyes for a moment. Then M. Aractingi led me upstairs.

☙☙☙ The little room where I slept overlooked the courtyard. I could see the stars reflected in the pool and the orange trees slowly shedding their leaves. A little lantern hung in the corner among the vines, and by its light I could see the great sphinx moths wheeling swiftly in and out among the creepers.

I was about to get into bed when there was a knock at the door and M. Aractingi entered. He was dressed in a dressing-gown of green silk. He sat down near the window and began to talk. "You must forgive this intrusion," he said shyly. "It is ill-mannered and inhospitable of me." I expected him to continue, but he sat quietly for a minute or two and gazed into the garden with a preoccupied air.

"I am traveling to Turkey tomorrow," he said finally. "Would you wish to accompany me?"

"Yes," I replied. "Yes, very much."

"We shall go by motor."

"You are very kind."

"It is expensive, but I can afford it. It is the best way to travel."

"Are you going to travel much in Turkey?" I asked politely.

He glanced away. "Possibly," he said. "Possibly."

"I am very eager to see Turkey."

He looked at me again. His face was timid and embarrassed, but I thought I saw the faint beginning of a smile there. "Good," he said. "Then I shall drive you there."

"You are most generous, M. Aractingi." I was growing a little bit nervous now. But when I looked at Aractingi again I felt reassured. He was clearly a harmless wisp of a man, rabbit-eyed and very absent-minded. But still, there was something elusive about him that was really quite puzzling.

"Why have you come to Asia, young man?"

"You see," I began politely, "I lost my money in Port Said, where I was going to take a boat for Japan . . ."

"*All* your money, young man?"

"Oh, no, not quite all . . ."

"It was stolen from you?"

I nodded my head. He stared at me dimly with insipid timorous rabbit eyes; and yet there was a very alert look about him now; I couldn't quite understand it at first.

Then I understood. As soon as I said anything whatsoever a little aureole of alertness sprang out all over him. What he saw didn't seem to matter. But what he heard, that was what played on his nerves so strongly. What he heard and what he deduced. A strange sort of intuition was hiding in that repellent little body. A listener, a subtle and profound sort of eavesdropper, that's what he was. His ears were delicate like a cat's, dark and yet almost transparent; they gave his face a quaint, terrified look.

"But that is not the only reason that you are here, is it? You are here, young man, because you wished to be!"

He was right. "Yes," I confessed, "all my life I have longed to see Asia. The mere sound of the word—Asia— has always made my heart beat more quickly. . . ." It was really against my will that I was saying these things. Something about him, his child-like listening quality, drew them all out of me, and now that I had said them they sounded pompous and silly.

"Yes. But you must take care, young man!" His voice grew caressing; he came closer and leaned gently over me. His eyes were still pallid and remote.

"I know," said I earnestly, "one must take care." I tried to cover my embarrassment by appearing deeply concerned.

"Many things in Asia, if you watch her closely, will puzzle you. But don't let them frighten you, young man."

I waited quietly, hoping he would leave me.

"Yes," he added. And then, after a pause: "You are a very lucky young man. Yes. Very lucky. You will never understand how lucky. No. Never."

He sat quietly for a while longer. I could hear the water in the fountain singing gently. Finally he rose and said good night.

"You are very kind to me," he said solemnly as he left me.

"It is you who are kind, M. Aractingi," I replied. I stayed awake for a long time, wondering about him, wondering what his little secret was, wondering why he should be so afraid and yet so eager for company.

10 ◇◆◇

∷∷∷ We had trouble with the car and had to stop in Ba'albek. It grew later and later. M. Aractingi was becoming very nervous. Finally he said, "It grieves me, my friend, but we shall have to sleep here in Ba'albek tonight."

I walked out among the huge ruins and sat down. It had been a very warm day. Dry bits of maidenhair fern were crawling over the tremendous pillars. Here and there among the colonnades stood the black Moroccan guards, evil-looking, thick-lipped, insolent, their bodies strong and supple as tigers.

An odd little thing happened while I was sitting here. Two amiable-looking spinsters with white parasols passed by. One of them was tall and distinguished-looking, the other one short and plump. They sat down in a shady spot not far away from me.

"Incredible," the tall one was saying in French, "isn't it? Sennacherib passed here on his way to Egypt. And the merchants to Bagdad and Ispahan, and the Hittites no doubt, and the Philistines, and the Egyptians I suppose, and the terrible Assyrians I feel sure. Discouraging, isn't it? First there is peace and order and luxury, slowly built up after years of labor. Then come the strangers, the destroyers, the killers. Always. It never fails. The land becomes a desert, the people grow weak and die off."

"Yes, the world changes," said the fat one sadly.

"You think it is change, my dear, but no, it isn't change really. It keeps on and on, it prevents any true change. As soon as human nature seems about to take a turn for the better, along comes war and so on. . . ." Her voice trailed wearily into silence.

Presently they rose and walked on. I was sorry to see them go. I had taken a liking to the tall one; I liked the sharp, cool look on her face.

Soon I rose, too. But as I was about to enter the path

again I saw a small object glittering at the foot of the bench where the two middle-aged ladies had been sitting. I picked it up. A brooch, studded with little red and green stones. Quickly I ran after them. I could still see them hovering and pausing nervously among the pillars like two great birds, one a flamingo and the other a pelican.

I called. "Pardon me!" I cried. "Have you lost something, madame?" I ran up to them and held out the brooch.

"Well, well!" said the small lady. "But what an accident!"

The tall one said nothing, but looked at me. Slowly I could see the expression on her face changing. She smiled, a very genuine and heart-warming smile. Then she reached out her hand and took the brooch.

"You are my friend, young man," she said. And I believed her. I felt sure that it wasn't the brooch that she was thinking of. There was something very secure and Occidental about this kind woman.

She was hesitating, trying to think of something else to say. Finally she drew a slip of paper out of her purse and scribbled something on it with a little red pencil. Then she gave it to me. "I have written my name there for you. I live in Teheran. Visit me if you ever can; I shall always be happy to see you, and I shall certainly remember you." She blushed—a momentary freshness on that dry severe face. I felt happy and reassured.

I looked at the little note and slipped it into my pocket. "Thank you, Mme de Chamellis," I said. She coughed primly and disappeared among the pagan columns with her stout companion.

≈≈≈ For some reason M. Aractingi had changed his mind. "The car has been repaired," he announced as I arrived at the inn again, "and we shall try to reach Homs tonight."

"Good," said I, but I couldn't help noticing how nervous his voice was and how his little eyes moved from side to side.

So on we rode through the dusk toward Homs. We'd been driving for almost two hours—in fact, we'd almost reached Homs—when the car came to a stop again. Aractingi turned toward me and moaned faintly. There were little tears of exasperation in his eyes.

"Well?" said I.

"The car has stopped!"

"Yes," I said.

"It will go no farther!" He looked incongruously frightened.

"Well?"

"I must leave you."

"But why, M. Aractingi?"

"Alas!" he wailed, "it is better for us to part now. You are not safe with me, my lad. They would arrest you, too, if they captured me. . . ." His eyes were watering with excitement. He looked very weak and incompetent.

I wanted to ask some more questions, but I didn't dare. So when he whispered farewell to me, I answered, "Thank you, M. Aractingi, and good luck," and the last I saw of him was when he whisked a slender portfolio out of the car and ran across the field toward the east.

I sat down and began to wonder. A spy, perhaps? A very strange man in any case. But then just as I was about to doze off there beside the road it began to rain. So I rose and walked along the road toward Homs.

I'd hardly gone a hundred yards, though, when I saw the flash of headlights coming from behind me. I turned and looked. Another motor-car was slowing down and coming to a stop beside Aractingi's deserted car. I slid into a clump of shrubs and watched. Two men in big dark coats stepped out of the car and crossed the road. They looked carefully into the deserted car, climbed in and out again, looked around, hesitated, scrutinized the footsteps in the road. My heart was beating uneasily.

Then one of them beckoned to the other and they entered the field across which Aractingi had gone running half an hour ago. Now and again they came to a halt and stooped down, and one of them would flash his light upon the ground. Then they disappeared among the bushes.

I waited for five or ten minutes. Then I saw them come back. For a moment I thought that they had a third man between them. But when I looked again I saw that it was merely one of them carrying his coat over his arm. It was still raining gently.

They crossed the road again, stepped back into their car, turned around in the wet-hissing mud, and drove quickly back toward Ba'albek. And that was all. For a few moments I could see the glow from their headlamps fall on the wet and hideous little trees, turning them into silver. Then they were gone.

I walked on for another mile or so through the rain. Then I saw a small hut standing on a hillock beside the road. There was no light in the hut, but I observed that the roof sloped far beyond the walls, so I walked across the stones up to the doorway and knocked. For a moment I stood waiting. There wasn't a sound. Then I looked through a window, but could see nothing except blackness. So I walked around to the side of the hovel and sat down under the protecting eaves. I leaned my head against the wall and soon I was asleep.

But not for long. Half in dream I felt the warm palm of a hand placed gently upon my forehead. I opened my eyes and looked up. An old fat peasant was standing above me, a candle in his hand, smiling. I stared at him blankly. Then he beckoned to me and I rose. It had stopped raining and I could see the trunks of the fig trees shining like glass in the candle-light.

I could understand nothing that he said, but he was very hospitable. But also incredibly round and shabby. His clothes were falling apart and his old dark flesh fell through in little pincushions of fat. Eloquent bits of food and drink were sprinkled over his shirt and his pants. He wore no shoes at all.

But the eyes that looked forth at me underneath those vast white eyebrows were full of humor and amiability. He chuckled now and then as he chatted, indifferent to whether I understood or not. I lay down on a mat near the window and tried hard to look pleased and attentive. But I was very sleepy, and finally my eyes closed and I knew no more until I saw the familiar gray light that precedes dawn falling through the window across my body.

3

I SAID good-by to the hospitable peasant at dawn and walked along the road toward Homs. I could see the city two or three miles away, just emerging from night, sleepy and innocent in the gray light. Below me I could see the Orontes flowing swiftly among the rocks. Already I could feel the air growing warmer and the clouds on my right growing light and distinct.

I sat down on a stone at the side of the road and looked around. There was something very lovable about this half-world, this world between night and day when nothing was real and recollections of the past were more potent than anything in the present. This is when one sees clearly, I thought to myself; one isn't disturbed by reality; this touch of the fanciful brings us closer to the true nature of life than any number of commonplace objects seen by the light of the sun. Far away I could see the cattle moving slowly out to pasture, and in the valley beside the silver river I could see the Syrian farmhouses and the thin columns of smoke rising here and there.

I looked back toward Ba'albek. Far down the road I could see a man walking in my direction. A tall, powerful fellow, swinging along vigorously. I grew worried for a moment. Then I heard him singing, first faintly and then more loudly as he came closer. Soon I was able to hear the words. It was an old French ditty. Then he observed me sitting beside the road and grew silent.

I could see him staring at me through the dim gray dawn as he approached. He stopped beside me and smiled. "Good morning," I said to him in French.

"Good morning," he replied. He looked down at me wonderingly, legs spread far apart and a warm smile on his lips. "Good morning, fine morning, beautiful morning. What are you doing here, my attractive fellow?"

I told him that I was on my way into Homs.

"And so am I," he said cheerfully. "We'll walk together."

"Good," said I.

"And I'll buy you a fine breakfast when we get there."

"Fine," said I.

He laughed with pleasure and ran his huge fingers through his hair.

So we walked on toward the river together. He told me that his name was Antoine Samazeuilh, that he'd lived in Rouen all his life and that he, for one, was sick of Europe. "If life has no intention of doing you any special favors," he said, "I'd rather go out where I can't be expecting any. Don't you agree? Asia's the place. All my life I've wanted to see Asia."

"Yes," said I. I was rather surprised to hear him say that, it sounded so nearly like what I myself had said to that pathetic fellow, Aractingi. "I want to see Asia too."

"Asia's a big place, of course."

"Yes, it's very big."

"But that doesn't matter. All the better."

"Yes, I see what you mean."

He looked at me slyly. He was a wonderfully handsome man. Twenty-six or twenty-seven, and strong as an ox, with rich blond curls all over his head. He needed a shave badly. But he would have looked well under any condition. He was the sort that is born lucky.

Soon the sun began peering over the foothills and we reached the river Orontes. Both of us were hot and dusty already. "It's going to be terribly hot," said I. "Look. I'm hot already. And it's hardly day."

"I too," said Samazeuilh. "Come. We'll go swimming." So we did. Far up the river great rocks were hanging over the water, and on toward Homs we could see the thin naked boys playing silently in the shallows beside a water wheel, some of them diving in and out and others trying to catch the fish with their bare hands.

The water was cold. But the sun was already hot and as soon as we stepped out on the shore again we felt fine and warm.

Samazeuilh plunged in and out like a trout. Finally he climbed upon a tall rock and slapped his thighs and sat down in the sun. He had a clear strong body, a regular Apollo, hard as a statue and flowing metallic muscles. His wet skin shone like marble as he sat there.

The body of an Apollo but the face of a satyr. There were little pock marks in his cheeks. I could see in his laughing face how sure he felt of himself, how confident of his power and his own good looks. The hero, the survivor, the true male. Self-sufficient and indifferent to the suffering of the rest of the world, with the unquestioning straightforward glance of an animal.

Two bearded old men came to the river's edge with great yellow jugs. They filled their jugs and then stood on the shore and watched us curiously.

So we stepped into our trousers again and marched on into Homs.

There was a small café beside the river and here we sat down in the shade of the hedge. Through the hedge we could see into the kitchen and watch the olive-skinned girls pull the loaves out of the oven and grind the coffee. A fine smell of freshly baked bread and coffee floated through the hedge. And on the hedge itself we could see the bees among the flowers, brilliant hovering bits of gold in the morning sun.

One of the Syrian girls came out and brought us break-fast. "This isn't much of a breakfast," cried Samazeuilh, grinning up at her plump young face; "maybe we'll have to eat you up, too!" He laughed lasciviously. The girl laughed too, rather oddly. I could see her gazing at him through her eyelashes, timid and amorous.

But Samazeuilh didn't even look at her again. "What," he asked me, after she'd brought us our coffee and disappeared into the kitchen again—"what do you think of women? Frankly?"

I shrugged my shoulders. "Sometimes they are very necessary, I think. I need them very much, now and then."

"Yes. I too. About twice a week! But that's all."

"You wouldn't wish to marry?"

"No, by God! I despise women. I'll never fall in love. I never have and I never will."

I looked at his handsome rough face, the big lips, the bright curls, the reddish hair springing up out of his open shirt toward his huge neck. "You never feel lonely, then?"

He ran his hand over his bearded cheek. "No. One can't afford to waste time being lonely. It gets one's mind off the main thing. Don't you agree?"

"What is the main thing, Samazeuilh?"

"Life. The struggle for existence, shall we say? If you feel lonely you're apt to get thinking about death. And that's unnatural, I say."

"Some people just can't help it, though."

"Well," he said thoughtfully, "they're the unlucky ones, that's all. They haven't started off the right way. It's all a matter of luck and habit."

"Do you really think so?" said I.

"Absolutely," he said. He was growing very cocky, his voice was full of conceit. "Happiness is the thing we want, isn't it? Well then, don't deceive yourself, that's my maxim. Make a habit of happiness, no matter what you really believe underneath it all. Pretend to be happy and you'll be all right. It's as reasonable a habit as any other, at that. There are more than enough reasons for anything you choose to be—happy, unhappy, vicious, saintly, hopeful, despairing, benevolent, hateful, earnest, happy-go-lucky—anything you please. Well, take your pick. Pick the one that'll make you happiest. Make your choice first and think up your reasons afterwards. They'll make good enough sense in any case, I dare say."

"Have you discovered all this yourself, Samazeuilh?"

"Oh yes."

"Have you ever been unhappy?"

"Yes, surely."

"When?"

"Well, once I was very sick. I thought I'd die. I almost did. I was a sickly child, you see."

"Was that the unhappiest you've ever been?"

He reflected. "Not quite. The unhappiest I've ever been was when the boys on the streets of Rouen used to tease me. 'Pretty-face,' they'd call me, and jump out from behind the walls and throw me down into the gutter and pull my curls. They told me that I looked like a girl."

"You've changed very much since then, it seems to me."

"A good deal. I had to. I got to hate myself. So very slowly I built myself up as I longed to be—strong, callous. I took exercises, I tried to make myself ugly, I shaved the hair off my head, I made faces into the mirror, I stuck pins into my face and learned to endure pain."

"Yes?"

"And so I grew stronger than all the rest, the very ones from whom I learned how to get along. Be stronger than the next fellow. Don't be afraid of hurting him. The weak ones have no business surviving in this world."

"But you were weak yourself once!"

"Yes, and if I'd kept on being weak I'd have gone down in the flood."

I felt a little bit depressed. "Look here, Samazeuilh," said I anxiously. "I don't know whether you're quite right. After all, we're living in a civilized world, you know. The weak ones ought to have a chance, too."

"Well," he said, "I've never noticed that pity was one of the laws of nature, I must confess. Look at Asia. Africa's a place of sunlight and certainty compared with Asia. Asia touched bottom long ago; it's been sleepwalking ever since, back and forth, this way and that. And why? Because it's given up trying to be strong. It's given up wanting to be alive. There's only one thing it's waiting for, and you know what that is."

"I don't know whether I can quite agree, Samazcuilh," I began. "You see . . ."

"Nonsense!" he cried laughingly. "I'm right; you're wrong. I'm paying for your breakfast, isn't that so? Let's not argue, my friend."

We stayed at the inn all day. "You'll have to pay me now, sir," said the fat innkeeper after dinner when the candles on the table were beginning to flicker.

"We're staying here for the night," said Samazeuilh in a loud voice. "We'll pay you in the morning."

But we slipped out through the second-story windows before dawn and made our way toward the highway that led to Hama. A truck picked us up at dawn and drove us into Hama in the afternoon. The driver was a slender long-haired fellow who wore an embroidered vest and great bulging trousers and a big felt hat. Beside him sat a Bedouin girl, unveiled and very pretty. Antoine tried to catch her eye, but she paid no attention to him whatever. She looked intent and unhappy, and the boy-faced driver kept singing in a soft melodious voice. The two of them never exchanged a word.

☙☙☙ Hama lay hidden beneath the high banks and gorges of the Orontes. Everywhere along the swift-running river we saw water wheels and naked men and boys swimming in the pools. Other men came down with their goatskin water-bags and lay for a moment in the shade before stepping back into the blazing sunlight. Everything looked very sleepy, full of soft, droning, rippling sounds. The brittle leaves on the trees tinkled gently like little china cups and saucers.

We slept beside the river for an hour or two, Antoine and I, and then walked into a hotel garden and sat down at a table. Fat pimple-faced servants were lying around, shooting dice, and through the windows we could look into the dirty rooms and see the torn mosquito netting, the unclean sheets, the faded damask hangings, the distorted mirrors. Outside the walls we could hear the mules shuffling and the cheap Ford cars rushing hysterically up and down the narrow street.

While we were sitting there a woman entered the garden and sat down at another table. She was dressed in Western clothes, in a high skirt and a red blouse and red slippers with high French heels. Her eyes were too heavily darkened with kohl and her legs were a shade too fat. But in spite of this she wasn't at all bad-looking. Lovely big eyes and hair that shone like water under moonlight. She looked sulky and lonely until she glimpsed Antoine. I could see her gradually growing more and more aware of him, casting nervous little glances in his direction, putting a light, carefree expression on her face.

Finally she caught his eye. He rose and sat down at her table without any more ado. I watched him chatting glibly, and her halting replies. She clearly didn't know French very well. But I could see her smiling more and more confidently, a certain richness growing and blossoming in her flesh, little beads of moisture forming on her temples, her voice growing soft and caressing. Her hands began to move gracefully up and down, past her breasts and her neck, toying with her hair, playing with the spoon and the fork.

After a while they rose and disappeared. Antoine smiled and winked his eye at me as they entered the hotel, but he didn't say a word.

※※※ It was growing darker now and cooler in the hotel garden. Far away it seemed to me I could hear the nightingales singing above the gorges of the Orontes. The servants were still shooting dice under the mulberry tree in a ray of lamplight that fell through the fly-speckled window.

I'd been waiting almost an hour when they returned. "By God!" cried Samazeuilh, "I've been damned rude to keep you waiting. Well. Here we are." They sat down at the table, both of them smiling, he rather sheepishly, she softly and secretly. Her voice had a soft purring sound. She looked happy and gentle, and I began to like her.

※※※ A young Turk drove the three of us—Antoine and the girl and myself—into Aleppo the next day. He wore a strange-looking hat, since the fez was now forbidden, and drove with an unbelievable recklessness. Once he ran over a chicken and an old harridan in a wet dirty dress rushed out from the hut, holding a bit of sacking across her face and cursing us violently.

He was very energetic, very much interested in public affairs. He told us how the Turks hated the English for the treaty they had made after the war; and the French for the Senegambians they had stationed in Asia Minor; and the Greeks for their invasion and dishonesty; and the Armenians on general principles of decency; and the Jews for their exploitations. And how they still suspected Mussolini of trying to annex Anatolia, and the Germans of trying to monopolize the factories and the airplane service, and the Belgians of trying to control the railways, and the Americans of trying to govern the whole world. He seemed very angry about it all. War was inevitable, he said, if Europe behaved like that.

The road wound northward in and out among the rocks. Then we passed through rolling hills spotted, rather surprisingly, with little orchards and groves of birch-trees, their snowy bark peeling in dark lines across the trunk, their canary-colored leaves fluttering from the twigs. Then the land grew wasted and flat and open again, great flocks pasturing among the stones, desolate walled villages with cone-shaped huts shivering in the sunlight.

4

ALEPPO was a large and terrifying town, full of Frenchmen and Armenians and cripples. Not a blade of grass, streets white and dry and hollow like tunnels, little spirals of dust moving nervously along the curbs like ghosts.

Zara and Antoine and I walked through the city toward a tiny park beside a mosque. Heavy paunch-ridden Syrians were sitting drowsily on rugs, and high on the cornices pigeons were cooing and cooing without cease. There was a rich almond smell in the air, peculiar and oppressive. Three Syrian harlots passed us and smiled, and for a moment Zara's face grew shadowy and uncertain.

We sat down under a fig tree beside a broken statue. It was a statue of Adonis, his arms gone, his beautiful face dented by the years, little odds and ends of him broken off by statue-lovers. He looked peculiarly depraved and melancholy, there in the shadow of the great fig tree, his great white breasts and empty loins spotted by birds.

We ate chocolates and dried dates and watched the surly-looking passers-by. Turkey was only a stone's throw to the north and things looked restless and resentful.

"Everything looks very restless here, doesn't it?" said I. They nodded absently.

"But very old at the same time," I continued. "Very ancient. The crusaders stopped here, and before them many others, I dare say. . . ." But I saw that I was boring them.

"What interests me is the women," said Antoine, clearing his throat. "They're the ones that look really restless. Women are strange. I remember how they struck me during the war, for example. I was very young then, hardly more than a boy, but I remember clearly how the pretty young whores looked eager and happy, delighted with the disorder and lack of control everywhere, with the advent of new, lusty blood, the casting away of old ties, the secrecy, the viciousness, the degeneracy. They reveled in it, absolutely. They loved the thought of fine young men killing each other. I don't know why. But I remember how they behaved. If a man looked soft or frightened they hissed. They were willing to give themselves to any soldier who had the smell of blood on him. War made them passionate, actually."

There was a dark look on his face and he looked younger suddenly, almost like a boy. "Love's a strange thing," he went on. "Love's cruel; it does mischief at every turn. It saps our ambition and vitality. That's a fact. Lucky the one who can laugh at the whole thing."

"How do you know, Antoine?" said I softly. "Have you ever been in love? Has love ever made you wretched and feeble?"

"No," he answered quickly. "But it would if I'd dare to let it. Have you ever noticed how a creature passionately in love likes to see his own beloved one degraded, hurt, made hideous, everything but killed? And why? Because it gives him back his power; or so he hopes. We're all frightened, self-distrusting beings at heart. We suspect that we're really ugly and weak and stupid at the bottom, even the most conceited of us. So it consoles us to see the beautiful ones whom we love being humiliated. A distressing case of eczema on the cheeks of my proud sweetheart, my best friend falling ridiculously down a stairway or losing his last cent—oh, we sympathize, yes, but secretly we rejoice. I'm sure of it. You see, it makes us just a bit more capable of bearing things, of struggling and surviving."

"You're very cynical, Antoine."

He looked straight ahead, very earnestly. "I'm hungry," he said. "Let's have something to eat."

So I went and bought some biscuits and sausages and wine, and brought them back to the little park. Antoine and Zara were still sitting there, under the beautiful frustrated statue of Adonis. But rather quietly, I thought. Something was wrong. Perhaps they'd been quarreling.

It grew dark and presently the moon appeared from the east. The dome of the mosque looked glittering and suggestive, the autumn leaves cast blue shadows on the naked snow-white god. Below us we could see the wavelets in the river growing bright, like restless little knives suddenly springing into life.

Antoine leaned his head against the smooth trunk of the fig tree and closed his eyes. I looked up at the sky and began to feel dizzy. The Syrian wine was sweet and ill-tasting, but very strong.

I saw Zara glancing at me furtively. "Where are you bound for, mademoiselle?" I asked amiably, wishing to make polite talk.

"Where am I going, is that what you mean?"

"Yes."

"I do not know."

"Are you all alone?"

"Yes." Her voice sounded rich and velvety.

"But you must be going somewhere!"

"Yes. But I do not know where."

"To Istanbul, possibly?"

"Possibly." I could see that she was trying to copy the way I pronounced the word.

"Or Angora?"

"Possibly."

"How will you earn enough to eat, if you are all alone?"

She smiled at me as if I were a child. "I will not hunger," she said softly. I was feeling a little bit drunk and she was looking very beautiful. Her eyes looked sweet and profound, her hair was glimmering like the flowing river.

"You are very pretty," I observed.

She didn't answer, but raised her eyebrows. She kept looking at me as if I were a silly boy. I suspected that she too was a little bit drunk. A faint ironical smile remained hovering upon her lips.

Then I saw her drawing closer to me. She glanced again instinctively at Samazeuilh. His head had slipped down upon the ground and his nose was pointing toward the moon.

"You are very pretty also," she said tenderly to me. I felt annoyed.

She placed her hand upon my hair and caressed it softly. I began to feel happy and affectionate. Then she ran her hand along my neck and down under my shirt along my shoulder blades. I leaned back and rested my head against her breast. I could feel her heart beating. "You are very lovely, Mademoiselle Zara," I said. "You also," she replied. But this time I didn't mind her saying it. She ran her hand under my chin and across my forehead. With her other hand she began to play with my fingers. My heart melted, I closed my eyes, I thought that the world was an undeniably sweet and tender place.

"Come," she said. So I rose, rather shamefacedly, and we walked two blocks toward the river. We climbed down an old mossy stairway that led to the river. The smell of moss and fish and male-smelling water rose up gently from the shore. She led me on along the littered slope, past shattered china and bits of wire and broken springs and rusty pipes, all glimmering grotesquely in the moonlight.

Then we came to a wall, and under the wall grew some sweet-smelling yellowish vines. We lay down on the vines and made love. I could tell that she was far more experienced in this than I, she was so responsive, so considerate and maternal. I felt very grateful, naturally.

When we returned to the little park Antoine was gone. The wine bottle was still there, and the paper wrappings. But not a trace of Samazeuilh. We looked in every direction, but he'd gone. So we walked to a near-by inn and slept in a shabby bed till late in the morning.

"Where has he gone?" she asked me as soon as I woke up.

"I don't know," I answered dimly. "How shall I know?"

"You were his friend! You must know."

"Well, I don't know." I turned over and closed my eyes.

Several minutes later she tapped me lightly on the shoulder. "You must know! We must find him. Perhaps he was angry at us."

"Perhaps." I felt disconcerted and hazy. "Does it matter?" Actually it did, very much. I was very unhappy that Antoine should have left me. I felt ashamed and lonely. Besides, I realized that I wasn't in love with Zara after all, not in the least. She looked rather plump and ordinary in the morning light. There was too much richness in her skin and I could see strange little soft places on her arm, unnecessary bits of fat. Her legs were absurdly round and her hair looked merely oily, no longer like the dark mysterious river.

She put her hand to her face. "We must find him," she repeated timidly. "Quickly." Poor unlucky girl. Nobody had ever been very kind to her, I was sure. Nobody had ever really loved her, that was the sad part about it all.

"Why must we find him?"

She was sobbing now. She pressed her face into the pillow. "Oh," she murmured brokenly, "I love him, I love him, I long for him." She raised her head and stared at me through her tears. "And as for you, you are cruel and full of ingratitude!" Then she pressed her sorrowful stupid face into the spotted pillow again and continued to sob wildly.

So I left her and proceeded into Turkey to Andana, a foul and filthy city full of beggars. There was trouble at Médain Ekhèse and again at Islahiya about passport papers and so on. But I was lucky and got through. I had to pay a little bit, but that was all.

Nothing seemed to flourish in Andana except mud and the autumn heat and the mosquitoes. And when I finally got into the blue-cushioned train again, I found that I had just enough money to take me to Smyrna.

Smyrna was full of autumn, full of red leaves on the scattered trees and dark broken leaves on the ground. I walked toward the shore and looked across the Ægean, out toward the great peninsula far away. There were boats down in the bay and bronze-skinned bare-breasted sailors carrying the cargo, and great brown sacks and vegetables and pineapples, and the smell of tar and salt and sweat.

A little curly-headed girl near by dropped a basket of limes on the cobblestones. Away they rolled down the sloping pavement toward the water, skipping, leaping, lurching, suddenly alive, like a brood of mischievous ducklings. Down across the wooden walk, up over the shallow wooden sea-wall and down into the water. The little girl ran after them, and I with her. Together we picked up two, three, four, five. But the rest of them were down below, floating peacefully in the sea.

So I leaned far over the edge and tried to reach them. One I reached easily, and another and then another. Two more were out there, one of them hopelessly beyond reach, but the other I could just barely touch with the tip of my finger. And then . . .

Yes, precisely. I felt the salty water springing up into my eyes and nose, and my trousers billowing up my legs. So finally I reached one of the stakes and hoisted myself up along the side. I tore my shirt and ran a splinter deep into the palm of my hand, but at last I was in the dry sunlight again, bewildered and exhilarated.

The little girl had disappeared. Under a mulberry tree near by stood a young lady, watching me. I glanced toward her and she smiled, very sweetly. I could hardly believe my eyes. She was a genteel sort of lady, English-looking, with a parasol and a huge straw hat covered with blue flowers. I felt very awkward and began to pull at the splinter in my hand. My heart was beating violently.

I peered furtively at her again and my hopes fell, for she was raising her parasol over her head and beginning to move away. I sat down on the ground and licked gently at my sore palm.

Then I heard a soft voice just over my shoulder. "Excuse me. May I help you?" I didn't dare look up; I was panic-stricken with joy. "Did you hurt your hand?"

I nodded my head.

"Are you an American?"

I nodded my head again.

"It was generous of you to gather up the lemons for the little girl."

"They were limes," I said hoarsely, "not lemons."

"Were they?" She had a wonderful voice, very yielding and yet responsive, too. "You tore your shirt," she said.

"Yes; it doesn't matter."

She stood silently for a moment. Clearly and distinctly I could feel her thinking about me, guessing things, trying to decide.

Then she said, "Can you run a motor-boat?"

"Yes," I said, rather surprised, "I think I can."

"Will you take us out to the island this afternoon?"

"Whom?"

"My father, my cousin, and me?"

I nodded my head once more, eagerly. I grew afraid I might not have heard correctly, or that she might change her mind. "Yes, yes! Where is the island?"

She pointed down toward the great inlet to the south, and in the middle of the inlet was a small island, jutting out of the water like an ornamental flower-pot, overflowing with feathery trees and fringed by scallops of sand.

5

HER FATHER, Mr. Bariton, was a brittle, hothouse sort of creature, unbelievably tidy and precise, almost like a puppet. And still, underneath it all, underneath all this grace and restraint, there was something else. I couldn't quite decide what it was. A rarefied and subtle quality, a sort of despair, a sort of depravity, a feeling of decay and uselessness. And yet exactly in this there was something superb and full of dignity.

Her cousin I didn't like at all, and I could see that it annoyed him to have me along in the boat. His name was Timothy. He was plump and soft, and he too had a mild little touch of hopelessness about him. He looked very stupid. But he was much less stupid than he appeared, I felt sure. Everything he said had a quick tang of sarcasm about it, not really cutting, but just enough to give one a glimpse into his bleak and comfortless interior.

There they lay in the shade, the two Englishmen, while the butler laid out the cushions and the tea-basket. She and I sat on the sand, watching the shore of Asia Minor all around us and the boat rocking gently to and fro beside the beach.

"What are you doing in Smyrna?" she asked.

"Nothing. I am on my way to Istanbul."

"Really! We just came from Istanbul."

"That is a coincidence, isn't it?"

"Well, where are you going from Istanbul?"

"From Istanbul? Well, perhaps to Japan."

"Japan?"

"Perhaps."

"Why Japan?"

"I have an uncle in Japan."

"Oh." She grew silent for a moment. "Is that all?" She looked sharply at me with her clear intelligent eyes.

I began to feel sick at heart and lonely. "Yes," I said. "I have always longed to travel."

"How old are you?"

"Twenty-two."

"Really?"

"Yes."

"In a way you look older. And in another way you look younger. First one and then the other."

I smiled eagerly and waited for her to continue.

She lowered her eyes. "Also," she said, "I think you are somewhat vain."

I didn't know what to say. I was surprised, not at what she said, but at the sudden intimacy of her voice. "Yes," I replied, "I think you may be right. It gives me pleasure to think about myself."

She took off her hat and ran her fingers through her hair. It was fine silvery blond hair, straight and smooth as taffy, nothing wispy or prettified about it. She looked lovely and clean with her hair falling softly behind her ears and over the nape of her neck.

"What is your aim in life?" she asked. "Tell me. Are you ambitious? Do you wish to be famous?"

"A little bit," I said thoughtfully. "Somewhat. But not very much."

"What do you want most in the world?"

I reflected. "Freedom," I said finally.

"Why?"

"Freedom makes me happy, without freedom I should be unhappy."

"Nonsense. You could be happy without freedom if you only were willing to resign yourself to it."

"Tea?" cried her father from amongst the trees. She didn't answer.

"Tea!" shouted Timothy mockingly.

"No," she called back.

I looked at her. There was something curious about the way she spoke to me. She leaned back upon the sand and closed her eyes. The sunlight fell on her face and her hair. Beautiful, flawlessly so; and for that very reason perhaps so remote and unfleshly. Her features were straight and exact, her voice was low and throaty, her limbs were long and slender. More like a boy than a beautiful woman. The wind blew her hair gently across her cheeks, and I could see the rise and fall of her breast and the tremor in her white throat. My heart grew big, not precisely with desire nor precisely with affection—rather with the longing for something distant and unattainable.

"Perhaps," I said finally. But I didn't know what I meant; my mind wasn't working at all, and I'd completely forgotten what we were talking about.

"Do you expect, for example, to marry?"

"It depends," I said with energy. "How should I know? I am poor, though, and I wish very much to move from place to place."

"Have you ever been in love?"

I remembered how I had asked Antoine that. "A little bit," I replied, "now and then. Never desperately, I think."

"Would you like to be desperately in love?"

"No, I think not."

"Because you are afraid?"

"Perhaps."

"For your freedom?"

"Yes, that is it."

"Then," she said half-humorously, half-reproachfully, "you are immature."

"Yes, I know."

"Not physically, perhaps, but emotionally."

"Yes, Miss Bariton, I think that I understand your reasons for saying that. But I don't quite agree."

"Why not?"

"Because I lied, and misled you."

She smiled. Her eyes were still closed, and it was a quick, secretive, delighted, malicious smile. "Really!"

"Yes. Because none of the things that I said are true."

"Really?"

"There are things I desire more than freedom."

"Yes?"

"And I've been desperately in love, to be perfectly truthful about it."

"Indeed!"

"And I long to be a great man."

"Well." Her voice was mild and ironical. But there was something triumphant in it, too. She seemed to be pleased about something, a little victory of some kind or other.

"My trouble," I said, "is, you see, that I'm shy. I'm full of hesitations. I can never quite make up my mind."

"Like Hamlet?"

"No, not quite like Hamlet. . . ." I leaned over her. My heart was beating like mad. "Miss Bariton, Miss Bariton, you are extremely kind and beautiful. . . ." My voice must have sounded very absurd.

I could see a quick flush of color coming to her cheeks. Then they grew pale again. She smiled and opened her cool gray eyes. "You know," she said, "you are a little bit like a child, and a little bit like a woman, and a little bit like an old man. The rest of you is very masculine. It is the rest of you that I see in front of me. But I can feel the others, too." She laughed softly.

Suddenly I felt that I had made a pathetic mistake. I felt that I had lost, that I had ventured into some sort of game and lost. My heart felt heavy and full of longing. I stood up and looked toward the Ægean. The sun was ready to set, three minutes more and it would touch the water.

"Where are you going, Miss Bariton?" My voice was thick and tremulous with disappointment.

"To India, and then to Ceylon."

"Ceylon?"

"Yes, Kandy."

"Really! Ceylon is very beautiful, isn't it?"

"I've never been there."

"But it is!"

"If you ever come to Kandy," she said with a sly smile, "you may visit us."

"Thank you very much, I shall be very eager to see you if I ever come to Kandy."

The sun was sinking now. One last bit of red high on the autumn ferns, the melancholy branches, the bits of seaweed and sea shell upon the sand. The littered fragments on the shore, slowly drawing closer to the rising tide, were full of secrets, ancient half-hearted things, uncertain and discarded recollections.

"What is your first name, Miss Bariton?" I felt ashamed as soon as I had asked it.

"Hermione," she answered, walking slowly through the twilight up toward the rest of them. The tea-basket had been packed again; they were all ready to go.

"Hermione?" The name sounded odd and distant, here on the seashore, Smyrna and Asia Minor in front of us and the Ægean and Lesbos far out to the west and the north.

🙙🙙🙙 Generous Mr. Bariton had given me enough to get to Istanbul. Why indeed I should have wished to go to Istanbul I don't know. All night I rode through Anatolia and I arrived in the great gray city early the next morning. All day I walked through the city, and in the afternoon I found myself sitting in a café above the Bosporus, brooding.

Autumn was heavy on Istanbul. There lay the city beside me, looking across the channel into Asia; plant-like, inert, moribund. A dying city. Everywhere were dogs; the place was full of forsaken and starving dogs. All along the shore stood hideous, empty, unpainted houses. I could hear the radio blaring in the hotel next door.

A hundred fat little bootblacks were hovering noisily out on the street. One of them entered the café with a bell in his hand and an unwashed smile on his lips. He mumbled something. I shook my head. He mumbled something else. I shook my head again. He tittered nastily and ran back into the street.

The door of the café opened again. A tall pale man in a light felt jacket entered. He was very fat, softly and indigestibly so, unpleasant looking. His eyes were black, but they created a paradoxical impression of colorlessness, as if the blackness were only a cosmetic hiding the real insipid emptiness beneath.

He walked up to the waiter and muttered something. He was undoubtedly a Turk, I could see, but his clothes were expensively European and his manner was cultivated in a European way.

Presently the waiter returned with a little jar of red jam in his hand. The stranger nodded and paid. Then he sat down on a table and got out a little leather notebook. He seemed to be adding figures.

It was then that he saw me. He glanced at me perfunctorily, then again, more warily. There was a mildly frightened look in his face for a moment. Then it vanished and he looked at my clothes and my face. I needed a shave badly.

He turned his back once more and made little marks in his notebook. I was beginning to feel uneasy. I knew that Turkey was a strict land, intolerant of foreigners, very particular about passports and very suspicious of spies.

But it wasn't that. He turned toward me once more with an oily little smile and said, "Are you an American?" His voice was amazingly high.

I nodded half-heartedly.

"Yes, I suspected. You have an eager look that is highly American. It stamps you. I recognized it immediately."

I felt reassured. He wasn't a police agent after all, that was certain. He rose and with a questioning smile sat down at my table.

"I like Americans. I have known many, several of them almost with intimacy. They are all eager, full with energy, full with laughter. Yes! I can see the laughter in your eyes, too."

He appeared quite intelligent. But also very soft, very petty and heartless. Incomplete, somehow. I mistrusted him instinctively.

But I needn't have done so. He meant well. "You are without money," he went on, still smiling amicably. "I can see it. You wish money. That is clear. Do you wish a job?"

The last word rolled out between his lips like a little surprise, rotund and bubbling.

I thought for a moment. Then I looked quickly into his eyes. Then I nodded.

"Excellent. I am pleased," he said. "I shall proceed to explain. Come, will you motor with me?"

So we stepped out of the café together. Beside the walk a small open Fiat car was parked. In the back sat a woman, quite dark, also dressed in fine European clothes.

"My name is Mr. Suleiman," said the fat man. "This is Mrs. Suleiman." She nodded but did not smile. We got in.

There was a small blue bear on the radiator of Mr. Suleiman's car. "What is that blue bear?" I asked him, to make talk.

"That is to avert the evil eye," he replied. "With that I never have troubles."

We drove through the sad neglected streets of the decaying city, on along the shore and out into the open country. Mr. Suleiman told me all about himself as we rode. He was surprisingly intimate. "Mrs. Suleiman," he asserted in a high, whispering voice, "was once in the Sultan's harem. That was when she was young and beautiful." I turned back involuntarily and glanced at Mrs. Suleiman. She was quite fat and there was a bit of a mustache on her upper lip. She stared back at me without expression.

"She was very beautiful then," Mr. Suleiman continued. "Eyes like coals, a body graceful and limber like a gazelle. She is growing a little heavy now from eating too many biscuits and too much honey. But she was beautiful once, and I loved her with great devotion."

The last word surprised me a little. But then I glanced at him again and it seemed the most natural possible word. "Where did you first know her?" I asked innocently.

"I was a guardian in the harem," he replied. "I saw her every day, I loved her and she loved me. So after the end of the Empire we married. We have been very happy."

He lit a cigarette and blew three fine smoke rings. "We have traveled much," he went on. "To Paris, Vienna, Budapest, Sicily. Also to Cairo and Alexandria. Mrs. Suleiman has enjoyed it. It has made her modern.

"But times change," he continued sadly. "We are free, yes. But we regret the old days. Both of us were deeply attached to the harem. Both of us feel homesick for the days of the Sultan and the harem. They were full with leisure. We could relax. We could have all that we requested. But now everything is so uncertain and troublesome. I have much money but still I feel uncertain and troubled with life. These are such restless years!"

 Mr. and Mrs. Suleiman and I had dinner at a little inn that overlooked the Bosporus. Below us we could see the lights reflected in the water. "Now I shall tell you my proposal for a job," said Mr. Suleiman with great affability. "I shall be frank. You need money?"

I nodded.

"Would you be willing to travel by ship to the city of Trebizond?"

I paused, then nodded.

"Very well. I shall give you a package of small tins wrapped in water-proof cloth. These I shall place in a small satchel. The satchel I give to you. You take the satchel upon the ship. You sail tomorrow evening. The next morning you approach Trebizond. As you approach Trebizond, opposite the peak of a hill, you will look at the water with great care. You will observe a certain floating buoy. Near this buoy you drop the satchel into the water. That is all."

"That is all?"

"Yes, that is all. Soon after dawn a fisherman's boat will come and get the satchel."

"What will the fisherman do with it?"

"He will bury it near the shore."

"Yes?"

"He will leave it there for a week, or two weeks, or three weeks."

"And then?"

"He will give it to a stranger from Cairo."

"He will?"

"Yes. The stranger from Cairo will take care of it and he will distribute it as he desires."

I knew, of course, what would be in the little tins, infinitely precious and secret. Opium. I was sure of it. But I couldn't resist asking Mr. Suleiman, "What will be inside the little tins, Mr. Suleiman?"

Mr. Suleiman smiled patiently, paternally. "You must be loyal and brave, my young American. Be careful. Remember to be afraid."

🙞🙞🙞 The *Gandolfo* departed on the following evening for Trebizond. Mr. Suleiman left me standing on the deck with the satchel beside me. I was wearing a new suit and in my vest pocket I felt a little roll of bills—not many, but enough for me.

"Farewell to you, my young American," cried Mr. Suleiman in his high soft voice. "Remember to be loyal and wise."

I watched his great fat shape waddling down the deck and disappearing. Suddenly I felt very much afraid. I leaned over the railing and watched the green waters of the Bosporus lapping peacefully below me. Soon the boat began to move. I felt sick at heart. Life seemed all of a sudden to have become something quite new. Everything about me—voices, faces, the sky, the sea, my own body, my fears and loathings—all had become full of significances, heavy with meaning, dangerous.

6

SLOWLY the *Gandolfo* passed the ports of northern Turkey. All night I stayed up, watching the waves of the Euxine flow past me. Black; bottomless, perhaps? Glowing with a deeper light inside that glassy blackness? There's an indefinable sea terror that always seizes me on the water at nights, no matter whether it's near or far, no matter how close to home or how familiar. If I'd been skirting the Straits of Magellan I couldn't have felt more remote, surely, and more mystified by the dream-like powers of geography. Now and then a blanket of mist passed landward across the water and then left it glittering black again.

Leaning across the same railing a few yards away stood a small man in a fawn-colored hat. He glanced toward me once, twice, three times. Then he came up to me and addressed me in French. "You are bound for Trebizond, monsieur?"

"Yes." I could see his eyes shining in the darkness, but I couldn't have said whether he was young or old. "Are you French or Turkish?" I tried to be pleasant, but actually I didn't feel in the least like making conversation.

"Neither," he said. "I am Russian." This startled me somewhat, for I had supposed that Russians kept clear of Turkey, and Turks clear of Russia. He looked at me for a moment. "You too don't belong on this boat, I suspect," he said musingly. But that was all he said about it, and

I didn't know what he was hinting at, I didn't know what to say in reply. I was a bit worried, naturally. There was something intimate in his voice, like a finger reaching into my pocket. "You'll see more of me," it seemed to say.

He stood by my side for a long time. "We passed Ineboli some time ago," he said. "Now we are passing Samsun." He pointed southward across the sea. Far, far to the south I could see a glowing spot in the blackness, no bigger than a grain of sand. "And after that we will pass Kerasund. And after that we reach Trebizond, in the early morning."

And at last came the early morning, and the *Gandolfo* went puffing and panting through the fog toward the invisible city on the eastern shore. The sea was quiet, there was only a slowly moving deep-sea swell, rising from far, far below. But gradually as the fog grew less a breeze came up and the waves grew higher, capped with foam. Out of a gray nowhere came creeping suddenly the great gray waves. Wall after glassy wall. And then one or two came carrying on their foamy peaks the merest glint of light, though there still wasn't any sunlight to be seen in the sky. And then came the very gradual parting of the veil, a flicker of foam displaying itself for an instant farther off, a high wave flashing briefly, a change in the sky overhead. And then, in less than a minute, sunlight came gliding swiftly across the huge sea, the clouds fled over the water behind us, and the real sun emerged marvelously over the black line to the east, Transcaucasia. The eastward water began to sparkle. Five minutes of sheer magic, they were; the sort of thing that makes you suspect for a little while that there's something hiding behind the cloak, after all.

At last the great rocks came into view. Huge black fists jutting madly into the sea, for no manifest reason other than to shatter the waves, to hurl up great parabolas of foam. Beyond these rose the land, an abandoned land it seemed from where I stood, wild and exciting.

When the white walls of Trebizond were only a mile or so away I glimpsed the purple buoy. Nervously I dropped my leather handbag overboard. It splashed. It floated. It rocked in the long shining wake and grew tiny. I sighed with relief and wiped my hands gingerly on the railing.

Then I looked up again. The small man in the fawn-colored hat was watching me. He smiled obliquely, puck-ishly.

But I shook him off when we landed in Trebizond. I was glad to be walking the sloping streets alone, free again, burdenless. The sunlight came flickering and sparkling across the cobblestones, lighting up little tufts of autumn grass, and I felt very happy and light-hearted. I wanted to skip along the paving and laugh. I took in the fine morning air in long deep breaths.

The town was waking up. Scattered people were walking across the clean and sunny market-place. Fat Turkish cooks were buying their morning supplies, bickering mildly and lazily. A little boy skipped past me, selling white hyacinths with the morning dew still on them. Almost I bought one. I don't know why I didn't.

Perhaps it was because, slowly, my light-heartedness was leaving me again. I walked under the mimosa trees that shaded the street toward the Hotel Stefany, a pleasant gray house tucked behind a brambled wall. The people I passed seemed oddly indifferent, almost weary, sophisti-cated in some out-of-the-way manner. There were both Frenchmen and Italians here, and all sorts of in-between things, neither Turkish nor anything else.

I walked into the hotel courtyard. Late yellow roses

were shedding their petals, bougainvillæas were hanging over the pergola. Suddenly I felt oppressed again, uneasy. "Don't go any farther," said the blue finger-like flowers hanging lifelessly over the trellis; "Don't stay here," said the bright sunlight that rippled over the cobblestones like a shallow wave passing over the sand.

I walked in through the front door. It was a clean and orderly house. A demure lady in black smiled toothily at me and led me to a little room on the second floor that opened onto the street. She stood for a moment with her back to the window and smiled at me. Her face was wrinkled, but her hair was still richly black, and she wore a pince-nez with a wide green ribbon hanging from the edge. "I am Madame Stefany," she said, and turned toward the door. "If anything is not quite in order, you must tell me." She walked out, but turned nervously back again in the hallway. "How long will you stay, monsieur?"

"Oh, only a day or two."

She nodded and walked down the narrow stairway with small mincing steps.

❁❁❁ I had breakfast. I walked through the main streets, staring at the shops, listening to the men. I walked into a bookshop and looked at the yellowish magazines and papers. I sat on the edge of the square beside a little fountain and drank a cup of coffee. "What shall I do now?" I wondered. But I didn't decide. I rolled my decision about as if it were a sweet cordial on my tongue, not yet quite ready to swallow it, wishing to enjoy it a little bit longer.

It was midafternoon when I ambled back to the hotel and entered the garden.

I sat down beside a leafless acacia. It was growing cooler. Red autumn leaves were lying on the ground, hungry sparrows on their way down from the Ukraine and the

Caucasus were hopping about on the pergola and in the bare branches. A hawk passed overhead. A child was crying in the distance, beyond the stucco wall. A little girl came out of the kitchen door with a yellow kitten in her arms, stared at me curiously, and ran in again.

I began to feel drowsy. Somewhere a clock struck five.

Then the gate opened, and under the iron gateway, with a newspaper in one hand and a handkerchief in the other, stood my companion of the ship. His fawn-colored hat was pushed back from his forehead and I saw his face more plainly now; that is to say, I really saw his face for the first time. But there was no doubt about it. This was the man.

My heart felt sick and heavy, like an overripe fruit. My finger tips began to tingle.

But without reason, for he came up to me in the friend-liest possible way. "I saw you stop here this morning," he said, apologetically, "and I thought, as I passed by just now, that I might see you again. . . . I was feeling lonely." His smile was really quite charming. It seemed absurd to feel uneasy about him. He was a slight man, delicately built but not soft. On the contrary, one could almost see the hardness beneath that dark-brown serge, the nervous taut muscles, the spring in his legs, the arch of the back.

"May I sit down?" He sat on the bench beside me and placed the paper on the weatherbeaten table. I glanced at it: it was in Russian. "Wine?" he said.

Then he called in Turkish, and presently a darkish woman with a scar on her face appeared. He spoke to her, rather archly. I couldn't understand what he was saying, of course. A smile spread across her face, so that the scar faded into her smile and she looked almost pretty. Then she went back into the kitchen and reappeared directly with a pot of coffee and a bottle of Kakhetian wine.

"You're traveling?" he said, after she had left again. He took out his handkerchief and wiped his forehead. I couldn't help liking his face. It was hard and not precisely handsome, and the gray eyes had something peculiarly penetrating about them, something I had never seen before and difficult to describe. As if, perhaps, he were gazing inside me and reflecting playfully on what he saw there. As I say, there was something disturbing about him, and yet something magnetic and likable, too. Something intimate, something almost alluring. But, lest that be misconstrued, it should be added that he was a very masculine and metallic person in his way. And in spite of the immediacy of his presence his eyes shone with a real loneliness, not sorrowful but haughty.

"Yes," I answered. "I'm only stopping in Trebizond a day or two."

"Oh, you are leaving! Well, so am I." He seemed to be pleased. "And where are you going, may I ask?" He was playing with his silken handkerchief, wrapping it around his thumb, trailing it across his knees.

I was stumped. I didn't know. I hadn't even thought about it, oddly enough. So I said so. "I haven't quite decided."

"Well," he said slowly, "to be frank with you, my plans are almost as uncertain as yours." He was speaking in French, as before, and it was a very fluent and musical French, much better than mine. "Are you going north or south? Or east?"

I confessed that I didn't even know that. I hadn't quite regained my bearings, to tell the truth. Possibly I'd go northeastward to the Caspian and sail from Baku down to some Persian port. Was that, I asked, practicable? Or had I best keep out of Russia?

"Oh yes," he said, "that can be done. But of course it depends on what you want to do. Have you the necessary papers and all that?" He slipped the handkerchief into his sleeve.

"Some of them," I said. "I could get the rest, couldn't I? What would I need?"

He didn't answer. Suddenly he turned to me. "Look," he said. "You are coming with me. To Tiflis." He said it flatly, as if the decision had already been made. "And you won't need any papers. You'll like it, I promise." He leaned back and took a sip of the Kakhetian wine from his coffee-cup.

❧❧❧ After dinner I walked along the dark street again, eastward, upward, away from the harbor. There was a dark cedar grove in an empty square near the outskirts of the city, and here I sat down. The smell of autumn rising from the sea, the city, the earth, the trees, was sweet and hypnotic. I felt very calm. A decision had been made for me. I felt like a boat being tossed gently down the stream at twilight, hearing the leaves fall to the ground in the neighboring park, feeling the tender wind against my skin.

When I returned to the hotel there were some fat Turks sitting on the red divans in the big room, playing tric-trac, smoking cigarettes and nargilehs, drinking coffee. I never saw a Turk drink alcohol, even wine; it was always coffee. They were talking noisily, but quieted down as soon as I entered the room. They were very self-conscious. They had oily skins and very long eyelashes, all of them, and there was an effeminate sweaty smell in the room.

Later, as I lay in bed, I could hear footsteps passing to and fro beneath my room, one man shouting to another, a third one making water in nervous little spasms upon the flagstones directly below my window, a fourth one singing a song in rich low tones, over and over again till his voice died away among the trees. Then I fell asleep.

At midnight I woke up again. I could hear the velvety sound of camels' feet along the highway a block away. A caravan was starting eastward. I felt excited, terribly so; the future was such a dark and boundless thing; life was so limitless, the world was so unfathomably deep and wide. Tears came to my eyes and I ran to the window and looked out. There was a moon shining, the paving looked like water and the trees like plants rising out of the flood. At first I saw nothing. And then, between two houses deep in shadow, a narrow strip through which the lighter shadows were passing from left to right. But I couldn't recognize any shapes. I could only hear the little bells ringing and the sound of the camels' feet.

I heard these nocturnal bells tinkling away as I fell asleep again. They were traveling from the shores of the Euxine to the shores of the Caspian, and they became symbols to me, emblems of mystery, of the past, of the future. Time and space spread in echoing circles like waves from the sound of the little bells. It might have been the Antarctic circle which spread outside my room, it might have been the year one thousand that was rolling around the earth. In fact, as I lay in bed I felt sure that it *was*, that time and space flowed together like waters into a sea, that everything existed forever and everywhere. I was beginning to understand Asia.

And the next thing I heard was the clock striking seven. *Bing-bing. Bing-bing. Bing-bing. Bing.*

◇◇◇ 51

The road toward Erzerum entered a thick dark spruce wood, and in the midst of the wood we three— Krusnayaskov, I and the little Turk who was driving his truckful of canned foods to Erivan—we three stopped at an inn and drank hot coffee. For it was growing cooler. The other two chatted with the innkeeper. "There are brigands in the hills," Krusnayaskov told me later, "and the innkeeper jokingly told us that we'd surely be killed." He seemed to be amiably chagrined that not a single brigand had crossed our way.

We met a horse caravan whose leader was ringing a bell as big as his hat. "Klam-a-bang," it went, "Klam-a-bang," in a dreadful deep religious tone, frightening the crows away. We passed some fields with oxen plowing, and dromedaries grazing on a pasture. Perhaps these were the very ones I had heard last night, I thought. But they seemed much less mysterious in the sunlight.

We crossed range after range, and crossed several rivers. There were tremendous views of the Pontic Chain, high, cold and clear, staring down over the huge empty valley. There were many waterfalls and brooklets edging the road, and innumerable ravines, cliffs and glens. Now and then Krusnayaskov and I got out and walked, for the roads were steep and the little German truck was sadly overloaded. Time and again we passed a band of uniformed Turks repairing or extending the road, or laying telegraph wires, or storing ammunition, or building government stations along the way.

"Things certainly are getting better," said the little Turk.

"Yes," said Krusnayaskov softly, "things are getting better. Men have more brains than they used to. Soon they'll get up and stretch their limbs—they're beginning

52

to do it already. Just watch out. They're stronger than they know." I felt uneasy to hear Krusnayaskov, the communist, talking like this in front of a Turk. There was no telling what he'd say next. And it wouldn't be pleasant if it became known that he was a Russian. After all, that was why we had come this way—to avoid that sort of thing.

But he kept on talking. "As soon as they find how strong they are, just watch out. As soon as they taste fresh water, get into the sunlight, learn to know the feel of muscles, things will begin to happen." He was talking to me now. His silvery eyes were shining. The little Turk was hardly listening. "Don't try to prevent it. The first ones are bound to behave rather childishly, of course. But if you're wise you won't criticize them too harshly. Don't play the prophet. Just do your exercises, keep trim, don't let the fat creep up on you. Don't make up your mind about anything yet. Just keep in readiness." He was looking at me while he talked, at my eyes, my hair, my ears, my neck, my hands. He went on and on, in a silky oratorical voice. "The trouble, you know, isn't with the men. It's with the things they've done, the things they've built up and now outdated. They're spoiled, I tell you. They've got to forget it all and start over again. They've grown stale with the past, the barnacle years have grown heavy and hard on men's backs. Scrape them off, that's the only thing.

"Don't you ever feel the people getting ready for something? Slowly, slowly, like a volcano underground? Huge crowds in the poor quarters of the big cities, in the thousands of squalid villages, out on the dry plains, along the shores, up in the mountains? They're working up to something. But they need control, they need cruelty, even, to guide them." His face grew dark and shining with excitement. He no longer resembled in the least the restrained and elegant young man who had found me in the inn garden at Trebizond. He had transformed himself completely. A Protean creature, like those iridescent tropical fish that change their hue according to their varying emotions. "They're struggling up toward the light, accumulating energy, sharpening their teeth and claws. There won't be any stopping them when they know the taste of blood; soon all Asia, and Europe, too, will be like Russia." I looked across at the little Turk. He looked very bored, his eyes were half closed.

Finally we reached a high plateau, and in the distance we saw dark Erzerum. We passed a caravan of two or three hundred camels, ornate and terrific with the ceaseless sound of the bells.

Then we arrived in the city. And as soon as we entered the streets I felt that we had made some stupid, ghastly mistake. How did we ever get here? How had it all happened? Scavenger dogs were scuttling through the ancient narrow streets, and we came upon a diseased beggar squatting in the middle of the pavement. He shrieked at us, and as we passed he lifted up his shirt, performed an obscene gesture, and cursed us wickedly with the signal of the evil eye.

7

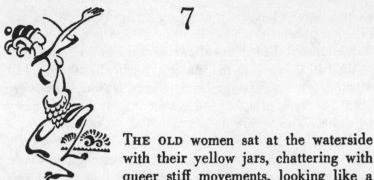

THE OLD women sat at the waterside
with their yellow jars, chattering with
queer stiff movements, looking like a
group of tough and garrulous birds. They were almost outside of humanity by now. God knows what they talked
about—insane little bits, raggedy odds and ends of life,
gray pieces of nothing. Their breasts hung down like flat
leather patches and their hair blew like straw in the sharp
November wind. They were hideous, they were mindless,
they didn't have anything left out of life, anything at all.
Some children were playing in the refuse, faces green and
sullen. Still, they seemed to be happy, tugging at one
another gently, putting their arms around each other. One
of them had short little arms like flippers, with gangrenous
hands growing out at the elbows. But no one seemed to
notice, no one seemed to mind a bit. In the distance rose
the oil-tanks, and along the foothills the row of silvery
power-carriers, great galvanized skeletons.

On the bridge stood the tramps, the quaint ones, the
beggars, the unemployed, all of them watching and waiting. Two well-built youngsters with heavy lips were crying
down at the girls who were washing their linen and wag-
gling their great hips to and fro on the gravel shore below.
There was an old man with one eye, a bleak young man
with a beard, a fat man with a blue derby. They all looked
watchful and yet preoccupied, curled up deeply within a

private shell of hatred and fear. Underneath the bridge little gray water rats were hustling to and fro.

We crossed the bridge—Krusnayaskov and I—and went to the baths. We were led into a gaily tiled bathroom full of shining brass jugs and bowls. Three fat old Turks were squatting there, grunting and gazing at their dimpled hairy paunches. There were no steam baths, no hot rooms as I had expected. Merely a shallow pool, and a fat brown boy who went around lustily scrubbing backs with a long brush.

I felt weary and limp when I stepped into my trousers again. We dressed, crossed the courtyard, and opened the gate that led onto the street. And at that moment two uniformed men slid up to us. "We are sorry," they announced in a sleek degenerate French, "but it is necessary to arrest you on behalf of the Turkish government."

The first three days we spent in a large room with twenty-eight other men. They were all political prisoners; many of them, I suspected, were communists; "agitators," as they were called, of collectivist sympathies. There were several Russians and several Armenians. Krusnayaskov appeared quite calm. He never even suggested that he was sorry to have gotten me into this. I too was, of course, labeled a communist; not, as I had dimly feared, a smuggler, a dealer in narcotics. But it did not take me long to realize that the latter would have been a far less serious offense. No use protesting; no one believed a word, no one even listened. There was nothing to do but wait.

And in the meantime; well, it was terrible during those first three days. All of them needed a bath, of course, and some of them needed far more than a bath. One man had typhoid and another dysentery and a third one gonorrhœa. The air was fœtid. We were allowed to go to the latrine only twice a day. And as for the food, it was unspeakably wretched. We wouldn't have been surprised to discover that the meat was the flesh of hyenas and that the vegetables came out of the Pontic swamps.

Many in this room, I learned later, had died, were dying, were going to die; either from sickness or in the executioner's yard. There were three guards; one of them, a fat little man from Elizabetopol, grew quite friendly with me later. He would tell me tenderly obscene jokes and bring me uneatable sweets wrapped in blue lead foil.

There were men with catalepsy, he told me, with erysipelas, all sorts of worms, tuberculosis, syphilis, eye diseases of a tragic kind, and many saddening things that the exposure and the dirt and the malnutrition had slowly grafted upon them. In a neighboring room were the narcotic patients. We would look at them by standing tiptoe on the bench and peering through an iron lattice-work. They were always quite motionless; heavy-lidded men, lying on rags upon the cold stone floor, muttering and mumbling away. They looked oddly distant, like trees caught in a sack of fog. More than an iron lattice-work rose between them and us. They were living behind a permanent veil. Once or twice some one called to them. But they didn't answer. There was no use trying to get near them; they were far, far away.

At night I'd hear them whistling and babbling dimly, the sound of a little stream deep in a lonesome valley. Sometimes only a thin whine reached us. I thought about them a good deal; they fascinated me. Where were they going, I wondered, and what sort of happiness was this? Did it lead to anything more real? Was there any station beyond the poppy-fields? Perhaps it was they, after all, who faced life squarely, and we the evaders. And so on.

One of them was whimpering incessantly. "He'll die soon," said my guard from Elizabetopol casually. "Next week maybe." And that's just what did happen, but it was an event so trivial and inconclusive that not a single person could possibly have noticed the difference. But still, that's what tragedy is, of course. The things no one else knows. And if I'd had the chance I might have wept a tear or two.

 Then four of us were placed in a separate room in the tower. This was better. There were Krusnayaskov and I, and a soft-voiced Dutchman, and an old lizard-eyed Armenian who never opened his mouth. It was a nasty room, but it might have been worse. There was at least a window high up in the wall, and we could look into the courtyard and beyond, out across the black bridge and the river; we could, that is, if we took the trouble to climb up there and sit clutchingly on the narrow ledge.

The Dutchman was a tall phlegmatic man with glasses and a checkered vest and a red goatee. He spoke French, too. "How did you get here?" asked Krusnayaskov, oddly antagonistic and yet curious at the same time.

"Well," said de Hahn genially, "no one ever knows exactly, you see. . . . I took the train from Tashkent. I'd been in Tashkent, which is a great and learned city, collecting manuscripts. A tedious business, but I got them cheaply, and two or three were priceless, real finds, things on which a loving lifetime had been spent.

"On the train, after we'd left Bokhara, I saw that I was being watched. I took the boat to Baku when we arrived at the Caspian. I slipped down to Azerbaijan with my precious manuscripts, but now that I'd shaken off the Russians, the Turks got after me. God knows why. At Kars they stopped me. But it wasn't the manuscripts they wanted. They took those, merely glanced at them, and threw them in the brick oven. They were polite about it all, I'll grant them that. I'm not blaming them. They probably had to do it. They aren't bad at heart. Well, that was a month ago. 'Why am I here?' I asked them. 'What do you want with me? I'm not an enemy of Turkey! I'm a friend of Turkey!' But I'm still here. And I'm still waiting."

❧❧❧ And while we waited there was nothing to do but talk. Both the Russian and the Dutchman were great talkers. But the old Armenian never said a word, except for little grunts and belchings that meant "Thank you," or "Beg pardon."

Krusnayaskov talked and talked. His imagination habitually ran riot, but he always spoke with great calmness. Only, at certain moments which I grew to recognize and dread, his face would blush and his eyes would shine. "There's no use giving up," he'd say; "don't let up while you're here. It's the same here as everywhere else. Life's got a lot of little assassins watching you all the time. They see everything you do, everything. There's no fooling them. Be handsome and clever as you will," he said pointedly, "there's no getting around them. I've felt them near me. Do you know what I mean?" I nodded.

"And if you do the rotten thing, by and by they'll get you, whether it's in the prison house or the grand hotel room. They'll haunt you." He was quite serious; he wasn't talking nonsense at all. "You become afraid of things. I've known it. You start by looking at some simple object—a chair or a clock or a water-jug—and quite unexpectedly it will frighten you into a frenzy. You begin to see faces and shapes, a warning finger. You won't feel it, it will be painless, but gradually they'll fasten themselves onto you like leeches and suck you dry. You'll still walk around, but you'll be dead and dry. You'll be a ghost. Look about you and you'll see that I'm right. Think it over. You'll smell like a corpse, and after a while you'll look like one too. I've seen it happen, just exactly that."

His voice grew sharp, staccato, like the crack of a whip. I remember his words very clearly. They helped me to understand certain things later on. "God knows," he said, "most people never really get face to face with the truth, with the way things really are. At the first little hurt they go whining and gobble up the next puny little philosophy that comes their way. You know they do! Usually it's a stillborn sentimental one, if they're stupid and like prettifications. And nothing will shake them out of it, not even suffering or death. They grow blind, simply because it's easier and cozier to be blind.

"And the worst thing is this. We could forgive them, bless their stupid hearts, if the truth were really the nasty thing that certain others would have us believe. But they're wrong, too. Truth doesn't bear private grudges—that's the big thing to remember. Truth is the real thing, I'm telling you, and pretty thrilling when all's said and done. You needn't look the other way. She's not a bad one. There's nothing indecent about her. She's the only thing that isn't indecent. Don't you agree?

"She's like a giantess," he said, talking quite calmly, his cold beautiful eyes shining; "clumsy in her way, as we all know: and you can't really expect her to be fair. You can't expect her to be watching you all the time; things are too complicated for that. She's busy enough as it is. She'll shriek at you if you go too far, to be sure; she'll breathe at you while you're sleeping and it's all over. You'll have entered the nightmare phase, the epileptic trance so to speak, once and for all. Yes, she can be dreadful, there's no denying it. But don't condemn her. Maybe she's reaching beyond, trying to crease out a bit of something in the years to come, or coughing up a fishbone that's been bothering her for a decade or two. And there you are."

⚔⚔⚔ De Hahn talked about other matters, very different matters; about picnics, about love, about women. He had his moments of philosophy, too, but it wasn't a brittle chromium affair, it was a decidedly wistful thing, rather quaint and old-fashioned. That's why he and Krusnayaskov never really got along. They didn't fight, but still I could see the hatred there.

He told me about his beloved, Ursule, and how he loved her, how she loved him. They had met at a picnic. They weren't married yet, true; but they would be. He would be very happy and she would be very happy. For, whatever happened, she would always love him, deeply and sympathetically. She'd forgive him anything. She had often said so.

Once, in the middle of the night, he came over to me and woke me up. He put his arm around my shoulder. "I'm lonely," he said; "I've got to talk." And he started in. He told me about his earlier sorrows. He'd been married six or seven years ago. "A blond little Swabian with cheeks as red as an apple." He'd been smoking a cigarette which the guard from Elizabetopol had smuggled in for him. He smoked it to the very edge, then killed it between his fingers. "It was sad. We had two little babies, both boys. They looked just like their daddy, the little rascals! Bright, both of them, and fat! Oh, it was sad! She died suddenly of something wrong inside, you know, a woman's malady, down here"; he laid his hand across his belly. "And a week later the nurse left the children in the kitchen one morning, and when she came back they were burned up, all black and dead. . . . The nurse was very unhappy about it, too, poor woman." But his thoughts turned back to

Ursule an instant later. "A fine woman, intelligent, too; no gadabout, no flibberti-gibbet; a real woman with a real mind. She'll make everything good for me. We'll go picnicking together, in boats, on bicycles, in a little motor-car. We'll be happy." But somehow I felt all along, through all this, that something wasn't quite real with Ursule; that there was something a bit wrong there, something disillusioning and pathetic. One couldn't help feeling sorry for him, the mild, optimistic soul. He couldn't believe anything wicked of the world. It was depressing, really, to hear him speak, disturbing and really sickening. Finally he ran his fingers through my hair and patted me on the back. "You're a good boy." There was an expression of real sweetness in his eyes, a tender world-loving and man-loving look. I could see it only ever so dimly, through the darkness, but it was there; I could feel it as well as see it. It's a look like this, the accident of a moment that will make you love some one for the rest of your life. It's the only thing that can be trusted.

Then he lay down again and a minute later he was snoring.

✳✳✳ We talked about God, about man, about creation, love, hatred and death. But the smell of excrement and sweat and sex was ever-present; it seeped into even the most earnest discourses and made them seem absurd and pitiful. It seeped into our clothes; we could never shake it off. And it seeped into our minds as well, so that after a while all we really thought of was food, comfort, and relief from desire. Never, certainly, did I see so bawdily displayed the difference between love and lust. We lost all interest in God, in love, and even in that lingering and approaching shadow, death. They became things remote and impersonal, oddly enough. They loomed watchfully outside our room, like the Pontic Chain, the Euphrates, and the Black Sea. Not far away, perhaps, but hidden from us by this loathsome brown wall.

≈≈≈ Well, time passed. December rolled by, and then silent and hateful January day by day. It grew whiter and colder. Flakes of snow clung to the window pane and made the room seem even darker than it was. The place wasn't heated decently, naturally enough, and at night we huddled together under the same blanket stained with sweat and semen, sleeping with our arms around one another like lovers.

We even stopped talking. Krusnayaskov lay brooding on the bench, gentle de Hahn walked to and fro, creating patterns with his path across the black rectangular stones. We took turns sitting at the window, making the frost melt on the outside by blowing against the pane or placing our cheeks against it. Whenever something was happening outside, the one at the window described it to the rest. Even the little Armenian joined in. He wasn't a bad fellow; he had his little whimsies, but all in all he tried to be as inoffensive as he could. His chief idea was clearly to have us forget that he existed; simply to fade away. Life hadn't been particularly generous with him. He was deeply, deathly ashamed of himself.

Soon after Christmas a girl, bundled up in a knitted black coat and carrying a hot brass kettle, started passing each morning through the prison yard. Steam would rise from the kettle into the cold gray air, and our mouths watered. Soup for one of the prisoners, probably. Fifteen or twenty minutes later (once or twice it was an hour) she'd go back again with the empty kettle. Then one day she stopped coming. Either he'd died or he'd gotten out; or maybe she was sick or faithless. We used to argue about that, imaginatively but brutally; trying, I suppose, with this silly masturbation to reconcile ourselves somehow to this mess of a place.

On the other side of the bridge, in the middle of the one block we could glimpse, stood a bordel. We could see the yellow rays of light slanting out of the lower windows, and the lights upstairs going on and off all night, and the men going in and coming out again. We were dying to get a view of one of the whores, but we never did. Perhaps they stayed there all day long, or perhaps there was a back door which they used. The only woman we ever saw coming out was a fat old hag with a limp, cane in one hand, basket in the other.

Every night shortly after midnight the dogs would gather on the bridge and start to howl. Sometimes one of us waited at the window even after midnight, watching the lamplight falling on the cobblestones, listening to the dogs and now and then a bawdy laugh from an upstairs window, hoping wildly for a glimpse of a naked woman or, for all that, a man, at one of the lighted panes.

Then there was one grayish place near the baths where the degenerates gathered. Down along the shore, in the shadow of the bridge. We could see them there, hovering in the darkness in nervous pairs, coming and going pointlessly. They looked like dark petals fluttering about under the bridge. We grew vaguely excited, sitting in this prison air and wondering what they did, these sorrowful wretches. They too were caught in a trap. Nothing to win, nothing to lose. They'd be willing to do anything for you. After it grew very cold and the shore lay white with snow they ceased to come.

And I'd sit there and think of Hermione. Rather fatuously, I'll concede. Of my lovely Hermione, of the twilight on the little beach which looked as if a candle were forever being held next to it, of the smell of her hair, her loose white dress, the oblique slope of her breasts as she lay sideways on the sand. I'd grow breathless thinking of what lay hidden under those silky folds, of the smooth skin, the soft curving hollows, the tender pink details, the slant of her hips upraised, the moist little curls. Sometimes I could almost feel her beside me, and I'd reach out my hand and run it along the cold stone, remembering and hoping.

Memory: a miraculous and omnipotent thing, if you only stop to think about it. A. lighthouse in the mind, rising from the level sand beaches and the spotted ocean rocks, looking across God knows what invisible and unconjecturable depths; a man-made thing, creator of hope and fear, a recognizable bit of something amid the uncontrollable things all around you. It was here that I learned how memory can keep the diseased heart beating; and how faithful it is, how silkily cruel, how pityingly treacherous. Not beautiful, precisely, except when striving to penetrate that enormous fog; and then, touchingly human thing that it always is, as beautiful as anything can ever be for us.

8

ONE DAY at the prison latrine I sat down beside a young Armenian who'd been imprisoned in mid January. Going to the latrine twice a day was the great, the truly exciting moment we always looked forward to. There was a pretty good view to be had from this iron bar on the edge of a small cliff: that's all there was, except for a flat roof overhead that leaked when it rained. Down over the city we'd be looking when we sat, and out toward the hills in the west when we were standing. There'd be the morning sun on the snowy city and the hills beyond, or dusk traveling in lengthening shadows from roof to roof, darkening the wet streets, turning the hills to blue. Or far off, beyond the foothills, the Pontic Chain; a grim and hopeless wall it appeared from where we gazed. But no worse than the hideous structures below us, brown and weatherbeaten things, so quiet from this place that there grew a feeling in me of absolute isolation, as if the stony city were broken and dead, and only I and the waiting guard, hating one another, were still alive.

This place was the closest we came to freedom. There was a dreadful excitement about these brief visits, moments for breathing freely even though the air we breathed rose from the vilely littered slope and the loathsome eye of the guard was on us. It was a place, I learned gradually, for a sad sort of relief, for the interchange of ambiguous notes and crude drawings, for hidden meanings, for code-words, for glances and assignations. In January snow came and covered the refuse below us and ice sheathed the iron urinal. The guards cursed us obscenely if we kept them waiting in the cold.

The young Armenian was a nervous unlikable lad, square faced, long nosed, oily skinned. His black hair was fine and silky, like a woman's. He grew a curling silky beard in a very short time, and thick black curls sprang up from his breast where the shirt hung open. His name was Karakelian, and he spoke to me in a broken German the first time he saw me.

"How many years did the buggers give you?"

"I don't know," I said, "not long. It's just temporary, you know. A misunderstanding."

"Uh," he grunted ironically. "Temporary. A misunder-standing." He seemed annoyed by my easy-going attitude.

"How many years for you?" I asked as pleasantly as I could.

"A hundred and one." He paused. "Are you German?" he asked curiously. I told him no, that I was an American but had German blood in me. But he didn't seem to be listening. He was glancing furtively at the guard.

"Have you got lice too?" he whispered. Yes, I said, and as he started to confide something else the guard behind us nudged him unpleasantly with the rifle. "Hurry up, or I'll do it again, in the same place!" he shouted, and my friend hastily buttoned his trousers and trudged away through the slush.

Several days later I saw him again for a few minutes. "The bread they gave me today was black," he said as soon as I stood beside him; "absolutely coal black!" He was very excited about it. "And hard as a rock!

"I tell you," he went on with great grief-stricken eyes, "this imprisonment all boils down to one thing. Terrorism. Cruelty. Sadism. Do you understand what I mean? It's vile, from start to finish." He whispered some shocking words concerning the practices among the guards.

"Patriotism," he said, morosely. "Pfffh! I hate it. Yes, I'm a patriot if by patriot you mean one who would like to see his countrymen, others of his race, well fed, well clad, well housed. But, good God! If you mean detesting those who believe differently, or insisting that your land is the only decent land, ready to think the worst of any-one with a differently colored skin, or hair, or costume, or God—well, then I'm no patriot, but a patriot-hater; and I'd like to see all the patriots in the world condemned to hell fire." He spoke with passion but in hardly more than an excited whisper, for fear that the guard would over-hear. The guard had taken a dislike to him, and never allowed him more than just barely enough time. And there was something rather exasperating about him, really. He always gazed at me in a very intense and disconcerting way, and once he reached across and tapped me softly on the arm.

The next time I saw him he had news for me, exciting news. "I've seen your cell-mate," he whispered, "and I know who he is! Krusnayaskov, isn't that the name? Feodor Krusnayaskov? . . . Yes, I knew it. I can tell you something about him. Or maybe you know? No?" He was very excited. It was snowing, I remember, and the snowflakes clung to his hair and beard.

"He was well known in Daghestan a few years ago. A violent communist, a secret agent, so to speak, a terrorist. Only nineteen or twenty, but feared by all, I can tell you. He killed the prisoners with his own hand, sometimes by pistol, sometimes by knife. And he'd watch them die. I saw him in Baku doing it! That was six years ago, but I remember. He'd watch until they were dead. Then he lost interest in them as soon as they flopped softly on the grass. . . . I remember that pretty girl skin of his, and those little eyes!" Big flakes of snow hung from his long eyelashes and lit upon the hairs that curled up toward his neck.

"Hurry up!" shouted the guard. "You hairy pimp! Telling dirty stories?"

"He's a frightening one, this Krusnayaskov," added the Armenian hurriedly as he tucked his purple shirt in. "He's got second sight. Everyone feared him. That's why they sent him out of the Caucasus. He can guess things in advance—like all the terrorists—and he's hard as steel, no pity at all. A nose like a bloodhound, and hates even his friends; even when he loves them. Watch out. The only thing he really loves is death. Or rather, dying. . . ."

"Hurry up, you perverted bastard!" shouted the guard.

I didn't see him any more after this. He'd been getting hysterical, my guard told me. A paranoiac, and quite unpredictable in his actions. He was going to be sent to another prison. He told the wildest stories, said the guard, all of them grossly exaggerated or downright lies. He'd hanker for a listener, that was his way, and then he'd go plastering one's ears with these disgusting tales. Had he spoken to me, too? No, I answered.

There were bad moments, of course. Moments of immense despair, twilight delirium, really dangerous periods when control would go seesawing and dreadful things were said. The leaning toward sexual viciousness grew softly powerful. Restraint went to the winds, quite naturally. There was no point assuredly in behaving like a prig. You couldn't hide anything, even if you tried. And most of us didn't try. There's a certain pleasure in admitting the worst, the most shameful. It was all a shabby and unsavory viciousness, though, harmless perhaps, but grotesque, fantastic, full of whimsies. One could see the hidden things cropping out, the secret indulgences of the ugly ones, the shamefaced displays of one's boyhood, the flair for high signs and double entendres, newfangled varieties of onanism, ingenious little tortures, odd competitions of one kind or another. We'd see the pimple-faced prisoners in the yard vamping the turnkeys, knowing that all they'd get would be a painful kick in the crotch. Or one of them would watch with fascination while another plucked the lice out of the seams of his trousers. It went on and on.

I began to experience certain striking dreams at this time. Not nightmares, precisely, for nothing very terrible ever happened, no prolonged flights or descents from high places or fear of animals, as in my childhood nights. But everything—even the most ordinary objects—a bit of paper or a lock of hair or a piece of wire or the slowly expanding pupil of an eye close to mine—all these were touched with a sinister quality. The feeling was that of everything about me playing the rôle of a spy, even beloved friends and familiar landmarks, even the best-known, best-loved parts of my own body. After one dream came another, different always yet always similar. Impossible to remember them all. They left me exhausted and profoundly disconcerted. It was an hour or two each morning before I could shake off the peculiar languor which such dreams induced. It grew more and more difficult to vanquish this growing stupor, this timorous flight from reality. But I knew that I'd have to keep on trying at all costs. I'd have to keep on the daylight side, no matter what happened.

✻✻✻ Finally they took away the old Armenian (Miskranian was his name). He'd been getting strange lately. Losing all restraint, showing himself off very unpleasantly, whispering revolting things at night. His face had grown hairy and canine. We'd found out in the meantime that he had killed a Turkish soldier at Kaesarea the summer before. We couldn't quite conceive of this, but of course there are many things that seem beyond comprehension until, in a flash, one really begins to understand the shapes of evil.

The special guard came into the cell. "Monsieur le Commandant would like to see you." We all sat at attention, our hearts beating like mad. We knew what that meant. "Me?" said the old Armenian in a piping voice. The guard nodded, smiling amiably all the time.

"Just a moment," whispered Miskranian. He was like a schoolboy about to be whipped. He looked from side to side helplessly. Then he followed the guard, avoiding our gaze and mumbling apologetically. Feodor and I glanced at each other, but we didn't say anything.

That was the last we saw of the old Armenian. We strained our ears as we sat there, waiting to hear the pistol report. Finally we heard it. *Click.* Then a pause, then *click* again. That was all. The really horrible part had been the way he left us, so shamefacedly, so very alone. He knew that we hated him and were glad to be rid of him. None of us had much pity left. There was always physical intimacy, yes: but as the bodies drew closer the spirits shot apart. Love had no more of a chance here than a tear dropped in a desert.

Only once could we see a man killed. This was in the big courtyard, after a gigantic snowfall. Perhaps the executioner's yard was too deeply under snow. It was a glistening day, clouds moving like rosy-skinned swimmers through the sky. Two guards led out a dark young man with long curling hair. He was blindfolded and walked with an exaggerated and demented clumsiness. They had to drag him up toward the wall. Then one of the guards put three bullets in him, and he fell. A few minutes later a third guard led a girl in a heavy green shawl across the snow toward the body. Sweetheart, presumably, or wife. It was strange to see her hurling herself on him, burying herself in the snow beside his body, creeping about on top of him like a cat and whimpering softly. Finally they led her out again. It was quite melodramatic, and yet at the same time singularly empty and unreal, as if none of them really knew what they were doing, or had the slightest idea of what was behind it all. A puppet show, no more.

Things were beginning to happen more swiftly. It was late February now. Very gradually the snow was growing less, and subtly reasons for anxiety began to put in an appearance. Better food, for instance, and the gentler ways of the guards.

One day the special guard visited us again. He was a powerfully built man, slim-hipped and erect, but quite bald. "Monsieur le Commandant desires to see you." We sat motionless. He was looking at de Hahn. Wretch that I was, I sighed with joy when I saw that it was not I.

De Hahn rose. Silently he reached into his pocket and drew out a small roll of Soviet bills; then he took his gold watch from his watch pocket, and a golden ring from his finger. These he placed in my lap and then, still without a word, went gliding out after the guard. Krusnayaskov sat quietly, playing with his handkerchief, slipping it in and out of his sleeve.

I listened agonizingly for the pistol report. But all I could hear was the blood throbbing in hammer blows deep in my ears. And yet, in this very sickness there was a feeling of inconclusiveness; as if to say, this isn't the end, you'll see him again; this isn't the way he'll die.

❧❧❧ Well, to make matters brief, the end for Feodor and myself came just a week later. It had been a brilliant day, almost warm. The sun had set. There was still a golden haze over the blue hills. The lonely men were beginning to gather at the bridge again.

My friendly guard from Elizabetopol came in with our supper. Krusnayaskov scarcely looked up. He'd gotten very silent lately, interested in nothing. He was growing positively colorless. Pimples were beginning to cover his fine delicate skin. A very strange young man, impossible to describe. I felt quite uneasy about him.

The guard brushed past me as he went out. "They're coming for you," was what I thought he whispered. "Jump at the third bridge." But he mumbled it hurriedly and I couldn't be sure. It was terrifying, of course, this slight uncertainty. Had he really said this? "Jump at the third bridge. . . ." I grew more and more uncertain, until at last I thought he might have said something totally different and quite meaningless, like "Watch at the dirt road," or "Thunder on the bird cage," or "Don't forget their eyes." I told Feodor, of course. But naturally he couldn't help me. He just sat there and looked at me, as if my fate were on a different planet from his. He had changed, and instead of a personal magnetism had come something lightless and impersonal; growing like a geranium plant white in this constant darkness. He seemed far away. It occurred to me that both of us might be going together. But there was no telling, one couldn't be sure of anything here, ever. I wanted to put my arms around him, but I didn't dare.

"Jump at the third bridge. . . ." Well, if that was right, at least I would be taken away. I wouldn't be shot in the courtyard. I was shocked suddenly to find that I'd never seriously considered the possibility of being shot. Never. Even after Miskranian, even after de Hahn. And even at this moment I didn't really think it possible. There existed in my mind some emergency valve, some lucky little channel through which terror could escape quickly and secretly. Only in my sleep had it ever really bothered me. But sleep is a different existence, and one can hardly dare to speak about it, it is so far away and so exotic.

✠✠✠ Half an hour later the special guard came. "Monsieur le Commandant desires to discuss certain affairs with you."

I rose mechanically.

"*Both* of you," said the guard. Krusnayaskov rose. We followed the guard.

And this was what happened. We were taken out to the gateway and handcuffed. There we were ordered into a motor-car, the two of us in the back, two guards in the front. The one on the right, the one who wasn't driving, was my friend from Elizabetopol. "Where are we going?" I asked. But no one answered.

The sky was slate-colored now, and the moon was already silvery and exact. We drove across the bridge, through the town, then over another bridge at the edge of the city, then across the plain for four or five miles. It felt unbelievable, staggering, to be moving through open territory again. The land looked strange and newly discovered.

My eyes were aching as I riveted them on the purple road ahead. Tears gathered on my lashes, tears of suspense, I suppose. Krusnayaskov was quite calm. I didn't dare speak to him and I wondered what he was planning to do. I felt a little afraid of him. My fat guard was sitting in front of me silently. I saw the creases in his brown neck, the stubble of his short black hair, the grayish ridge of his collar. What, I wondered, was he really like? A traitor? Or an angel?

"Where are you taking us?" I asked as we drove past the oil-wells. My voice sounded very peculiar, hoarse and passionate.

There was a pause. Then, "Not allowed to give information," mumbled the driver, and he glanced quickly at the guard beside him.

The road sloped downward and we entered a leafless wood. It was dark now, but the moon was swiftly rising. The road was spotted with mushroom shadows. Our handcuffs shone like fine silver bracelets. All four of us were silent. Each of the guards had a gun lying across his lap, catching the moonlight.

I grew uneasy; quite unreasonably horrified, for some sudden reason. My heart beat icily, like a dreadful little hammer pounding away at my sanity. I leaned forward, hands hanging between my knees.

And then, on the floor below my knees, I saw a small glimmering object catching the moonlight. I stared for an instant, wondered, hoped. Then I reached down and picked it up. A small key. I nudged Krusnayaskov, and with a tremendous silent caution we unlocked our handcuffs and slid them under the seat. Neither of us said a word, breathed even a sigh. We hid our hands between our thighs and looked straight ahead. My feeling toward the fat guard, that kind one from Elizabetopol, was suddenly for one moment one of real love, a heartbreaking devotion to someone I'd never see again.

And then came the river. I heard the sound of flowing water long before I saw the bridge. Then I saw the marvelous water glimmering through the trees. I took the Soviet bills out of my pocket and placed them on the seat. Through the branches I could see the low gray bridge.

The road curved gently. Little hollows full of snow appeared on either side of the road. The long wooden bridge was straight ahead of us now, and we saw the river clearly. I was surprised, for I had expected a small rippling stream; but this was a wide and silent river, and the sound of water that I had heard was only a brook that trickled riverwards along our side.

We reached the bridge, and my fingers were slowly twisting the handle of the door. Krusnayaskov sat stiff and quiet. The car slowed down gently as we entered upon the bridge, and the logs clattered as the tires bounced over them. I waited. We were driving through clear moonlight now, everything was shining. We passed the middle of the river, and now we were approaching the opposite shore. Krusnayaskov wasn't moving, he was like a statue, lovely and silvery in the moonlight.

The car was already beginning to gather speed again. It leaped nervously, as one of the logs beneath us gave way a little, and it swerved toward the edge of the bridge. I opened the door with a jerk, hovered for an unforgettable moment like a diver, then jumped. All I could feel was the metallic air gliding through my clothes, and then almost imperceptibly the cool air merging into cold water, and my body straightening out, slowing down under the knifing water, rising gently again.

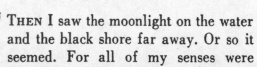

9

THEN I saw the moonlight on the water and the black shore far away. Or so it seemed. For all of my senses were numbed, nothing was close and real. My hands bound tightly together and pointing across the water, my legs almost senseless with cold but still bending and unbending rhythmically, the water icily exploring my body—none of it felt real, and for one paralytic moment I was sure that I was gliding away into another sphere of sensations.

Then I saw the black bridge overhead and the ripples widening around me. I began to feel the cold water plucking at my nipples, tugging downward at my belly, and then a spasm of real pain in my temples and another one in my lower centers, warning signals calling me into action against this rat-toothed water.

Finally I reached the shore. At the exact moment that I collapsed in the sedge grass I saw another figure emerging stiffly and slowly, like a marionette, from the glassy inlet.

And then I saw the snow gently beginning to fall through the night air and myself moving without sound through the white flakes. Moving through the flakes as through a veil, it was; struggling to awaken and see again with clearness, recognize myself again, look at the world with sensible eyes.

Strange, strange to be walking again free through a vegetable world. But what a strange world, what a mysterious world. No sort of welcome at all, nothing except this white mystification, white flakes falling through the darkness. I walked and walked, legs rising and sinking again as if they were plowing through a quagmire. My feet looked far away; yards below me, at the bottom of a cold and spotted pool.

Then I saw Feodor at my side.

"Hello, Feodor."

"Hello."

I trudged on, feeling suddenly elated and warm, no longer afraid. Everything seemed natural again.

"How do you feel?" said Feodor.

"Very well. And you?"

"Well enough. It was you I was worrying about. You're better now?"

"Oh, I'm well. Strong enough to walk. It's snowing, isn't that strange?"

"Yes," said Feodor, "it's going to be quite a big snow. Tomorrow morning everything will be white."

"It will look very beautiful, won't it?"

Feodor didn't answer.

"Isn't it rather late for such a heavy snow?"

"No. There will be snow for another month. For all of March. And perhaps in April."

"Where are we going, Feodor?"

"I don't know."

"Somewhere, surely?"

"Yes, somewhere surely, my friend."

We were climbing a hill now, walking betwixt the slender black tree trunks up and up. The trees were still leafless. Every now and then a twig would give way and a delicate garland of snow would fall down in front of us or across our shoulders, feather silently.

At the top of the hill we halted. It was snowing more

heavily now. My numbness was leaving me and I could feel the heat and cold alternating in my body, caressing me first the one and then the other. I was beginning to feel very feeble; as if I were a cloud moving through clouds.

"Look," said Krusnayaskov.

Down in the little valley through the tree trunks I could see a light. No bigger than a glowworm, flickering on and off as the twigs swayed gently to and fro.

So we started down the hill again, deeper into the tranquil forest. Now we lost sight of the distant lamplight, the trunks grew heavy, the night was so black that we could scarcely see the falling snow. Not a sound; only the fine snow, the smoke of our breath, the closer web of darkness.

And then we saw it again suddenly beaming forth through the snow. The snowflakes glittered like silver, the tree trunks shone like glass in the lovely ray of lamplight. Breathlessly we threaded our way through the trees until we saw the slant of light from the window falling on the white ground, and the shimmering rhomboid of flakes as they slid past the window.

Krusnayaskov paused at the window. It was a small hut, and this was the only window we could see. Snow had obscured the panes. He moved the palm of his hand across the glass and looked in. Then he said: "Come. It's all right, quite safe." I came up behind him and looked in. There was a heavy wooden table, and a red cloth on the table, and a copper lamp shining in a big circle on the red cloth. Everything inside the circle gleamed with a rich orange polish: the brown cognac bottle, the cheese in the wooden bowl, the empty coffee-ringed cup, the brass platter with the knives and forks upon it. Outside the circle of light the rest of the room lay indistinct and blue. A chair, a bed, three logs beside the hearth, embers dying in the hearth, an old man sitting in the chair beside the dying embers.

"Come," said Krusnayaskov. He knocked quietly at the door.

No answer, and again I glanced in at the window. The old man was sleeping. He hadn't moved.

Krusnayaskov knocked again, more loudly.

But still the old man didn't move. I could see his nostrils moving gently with the slow breath of sleep.

I looked out into the white forest again. A silvery path of light led from the window panes into the thicket, the tree trunks shone like silver glass, the twigs were silver lace, the snow was a silvery powder: a lovable man-made forest it suddenly seemed to be, built for dolls and birds. Gone was the terror, gone was the remoteness and the giant shape of time.

Krusnayaskov knocked very sharply, three times.

The old man shifted in his chair, shook himself, extended a hand into the air as if he were trying to grope his way out of slumber. Then he opened his eyes and sat up, alert.

Krusnayaskov knocked again, more quietly.

The old man rose, listened at the door, then called softly, "Who's there?"

"Two travelers," answered Feodor very calmly. "May we warm our hands and dry our feet?"

The old man paused beside the door. He looked with a troubled and helpless expression at the door, at the window, at the fire. Then he drew the bolt back and opened the door.

It was fine in that warm room. We placed two logs on the fire and took off our wet clothes. The old man watched quietly from the table. We sat down naked on the floor in front of the flames, feet raised toward the warmth, and drank Erivan cognac and ate goat cheese.

"Where do you come from?" asked the old man politely.

"Erzerum," answered Feodor.

"But you didn't walk all the way from Erzerum?" said the old man.

"Yes, we did."

"Through the snow and the darkness?"

"It was light and clear when we started."

The old man paused. Finally he asked, "Where are you going?"

"That," answered Feodor, "we do not know yet. What towns lie straight to the north?"

"None; only a few small villages you will find north of here. Kars to the east and then Russia." He looked sharply at Feodor. "It isn't Russia you want to go to, is it?"

"Oh no," said Feodor smilingly. "Not to Russia."

The old man drew his hand over his beard. He seemed embarrassed. "But why did you leave Erzerum?"

Feodor looked at him and smiled again. The snow had melted in his hair and it was dripping slowly down his face, down his flat white breast, down his slender hairless belly. He stretched his arms. "We didn't like Erzerum, to tell the truth."

The old man grew silent. A moment later he rose and walked into the next room. I could see Krusnayaskov growing alert; his gray eyes looked steadily at the fire.

Then we heard the old man saying huskily as he re-entered the room, "You must leave."

"Not yet," said Krusnayaskov in a pleasant, chatty voice. "Wait till morning."

"No, you must leave now! You have escaped from Erzerum. You are spies, I know it. I don't trust you. You will hurt me." His voice rose painfully and slid into falsetto. "You will hurt me! How do I know you won't kill me? Quick, go away, go away!" He swung toward us and held a pistol out in front of him. The firelight rippled across his face and made him look like a grotesque wooden doll.

Krusnayaskov rose and walked toward him. The old man stood paralyzed. "Give me the gun," said Krusnayaskov. He reached out and took it from the old man's hand. Then quite calmly he knocked the old man sharply on the head with the butt of the pistol and caught him in his arms as he fell. He laid him gently on the floor next the wall. Then he returned to his place at the fire, poured himself another goblet of Erivan cognac, and ran his fingers lazily through his long moist hair.

"He isn't dead, is he?" I asked.

"No, no," he replied in a soft conceited tone. "There was no reason for killing him, you know. . . . But he'll lie there till morning." He leaned back and closed his eyes. He looked happier and more serene than I'd ever seen him. He was always handsome, of course, but now he looked almost like a god.

But he wasn't sleeping yet. I watched the red firelight on his quiet, haughty face, the secretive lips, the long lashes, the curls sharply gleaming now that they were dry again; and on the hard square breasts, on the round muscles above his hips, on the delicate hairs curling around his thighs, on the long fine serpent muscles of his legs.

He had come to life again. Within an hour his personality had grown once again sharp and intense. I'd almost forgotten what he was like. Nor, for all that, did I know now. But, like a plant left white and bloodless in the cellar and then returned to sunlight, he was growing alive, quivering with color and secret energy in front of this red fire with the snow falling on the huge white hills outside.

He had grown white in prison; his hair had grown long and limp, his skin pale, his eyes dim and colorless.

But already he had changed. It was almost terrifying: I thought of the poor Armenian's words at the latrine, the whispered warnings. What truth could there have been in all that? What, indeed? And I looked with wonder at the hair curling and crisp, the luminous ruddy skin, the face bright with conceit and inwardness, the lips half open and shining like gold.

And yet remote as ever. I tried to put my finger on this essential quality in him that made him so elusive. Icy, bound within himself; if you touched him you ran the risk of being either burned or frozen. Either the one or the other, and there was, after all, little difference. Still, for this very reason, he shone with a strange and terrifying loveliness, a cold, cruel, inhuman loveliness. And yet, I thought: if I could only grasp the secret there, if I only knew one or two things more, I would understand. I would see him clearly, he would grow close and warm. That had happened before, often enough. Perhaps it would happen again.

Now and again in the course of the night I would wake up and glance at the shape of the old man beside the wall, dim and ugly in the dying firelight. He didn't move all night.

And in the morning he was still there. "You don't suppose he's dead?" said I.

"No. He'll wake up in a few hours. Just leave him there. We can't run any risks. We're criminals, you know."

So we took the rest of the cheese and the cognac and slipped into our dry clothes and stole two fur caps and some gloves out of the old man's chest. And so started off across the hill, northward.

The hills grew higher as we progressed. The snow had ceased; it was only a few inches deep where we walked. "But wait, it will be deeper in the valleys by Kars, you will see," said Krusnayaskov. He never smiled, but I knew that he was feeling very happy and proud.

10

WE WALKED about thirty miles that day. All day long the sun shone on the white snow, dazing us and burning into our eyes and setting our temples beating painfully. I finally had to close my eyes and walk half blindly. Toward evening the snow grew blue and shadowy. A tall hill rose to the left, and very dimly through the dusk we could see the wolves restless upon the slopes; a shifting gray shadow on the hillside.

When the first stars appeared we heard the tinkling of a bell in the distance. We reached a road, and at last we saw coming toward us a sleigh drawn by two black glistening horses. We raised our hands and shouted. The driver came to a halt, gradually the bells stopped tinkling. A lean, wolf-like man, the driver was, wrapped in expensive furs. Krusnayaskov murmured something that I could not understand. Then he said, "Come on; get in; he'll take us to the village." The beautiful horses began to move again, the bells began to tinkle.

There was a charcoal fire burning in the inn, and a great long table in front of it, and beside this a bench covered with wet black coats. The peasants were sitting on the floor in front of the fire. Armenians, most of them. They smelled like wild animals, stale and acrid. The rear end of the room was a barn, and three cows were lying there, chewing softly in the darkness. Bits of hay and cow dung lay scattered about and filled the room with a good pastoral smell.

We sat alone at the end of the table and ate the rest of our cheese and drank the last few drops of cognac. Then we lay down on the floor. We were so tired that we slept solidly until the morning. Then the fat porcine Armenian who kept the place chased us out. We stepped cheerfully into the sharp white sunlight and could hear him grunting damply behind us like a pig that is waiting to be fed.

The snow was deeper here, far deeper. Sometimes it came up to our waists, even along the road. Feodor was reluctant to follow any road for more than a mile or two. He seemed to know the country well, and as we drew close to Russia, "Better," said he, "to follow our own path; trust me, you won't get lost."

"We're going to Tiflis?" I asked him once, to make sure.

"Yes."

"Is your home in Tiflis?"

"My home was in Tiflis."

Now and then a cart or a sleigh or a motor-truck would carry us a few miles. But never more than a few miles. Either they said, uneasily, "Now we must let you off; we can't take you any farther; it isn't safe"; or Feodor would say, "Now you must let us off; it wouldn't be safe for you to take us any farther. . . ."

Through the forests to the west of Mt. Alageuze we made our way, and then across the desolate river Arpa on a small country bridge at midnight; and we were at last in Transcaucasia; in enormous Russia. Soundlessly we set foot on the pale forbidden shore.

The next day we entered the city once called Alexandropol and now called Leninakan. A bleak and icy place in the middle of a plain. Strangely empty it seemed; but the nasty clamor of the radio met us on street after street, and once we met a herd of people coming out of a moving-picture house. Dark ragged people in dark ragged clothes; lazy, remote, peculiar; people marching unseeingly out of one dream into another. Out of the fake dream into the real dream, out of the anæsthetic into the hysteria. Some rubbed their pale city eyes as if they'd been sleeping; others sank wearily upon the stone stairway that led down to the littered street. They chattered aimlessly and stared at us as we passed. One of them was drawing exaggerated shapes on the wall with a piece of chalk. They all looked very frightened and secretive.

A truck drove us from Leninakan for twenty miles into Georgia. The driver was a wistful white-lipped Circassian and he flirted with Feodor as coquettishly as any girl until we finally cried "Farewell." Then we walked slowly for ten long miles or more across the sea of snow.

Like waves the snow lapped northward against the Georgian hills. We crossed a plain until before us high black tree trunks rose like a cliff breaking this ocean. The sun was setting, and as we drew closer the sea turned into a glittering blue, the cliff into a shadowy purple. From the middle of a cliff we saw a plume of smoke ascending. And soon we sat in the lighted inn and gazed through the frost on the panes at the straight dark road to Tiflis.

The room was full of Russians; almost no Armenians here. Now and then I understood a stray word or two, but that was all. It was easy, though, to see what they were like: sentimental, obstinate, lovable as a dog is lovable, terrific liars and exaggerators beyond a doubt; arguing and arguing away without a glimmer of reason, full of religion still, poor souls, even though there wasn't any religion allowed them. In fact, they really didn't know what they wanted; they hadn't the slightest idea of what might be worth having. A rat came scooting across the floor; some one hurled a glass at it, it turned over daintily and lay bleeding, and in another minute everyone had forgotten about it.

Some girls came in with bowls of fruit. They tittered huskily when they saw the dead rat. But then they, too, forgot about it. There it lay, sloe-eyed, slim-fingered, yellow-toothed. A real Oriental with a growing look of uncontrollable evil in its posture—the delicately curved fingers, the fat, blood-stained paunch. The broken glass lay shimmering all around it.

The girls were damp with the thick humid air; dark stains ran down their backs and across their armpits. They whined like cats as they passed the oranges and figs and dates, and they smelled like cats as well—stagnant, selfish.

"What are they saying?" I asked Krusnayaskov and nodded toward the jibbering peasants.

"One of them says he has a new son, three days old."

"Yes?"

"Another says his mother died yesterday."

"Which one says that?"

He pointed.

"He's the only jolly one in the whole room!"

"Yes, he says it's a big load off his mind; she was sickly and quarrelsome, and besides she was a whore."

"Well, what else?"

"They want to kill the Armenians."

"Yes?"

"They also want to kill the Germans."

"Yes?"

"There can be no peace, they say, until the capitalists are killed."

"Yes? What else?"

"In America, says that one by the stove, the capitalists are chaining their laborers together and making them wear striped clothes; they're whipping them and starving them and shooting them dead."

"I think he must be exaggerating."

"No, no. If you say that you will be guilty of capitalist propaganda." He spoke very blandly; I couldn't tell whether he was joking or not. "The American proletariat, he says, is ready for a revolution. He read it in yesterday's paper. It has already begun, he says. San Francisco has been destroyed by the proletarian army, Chicago is in the hands of the armed revolutionists, the fat capitalists with their high black hats are being killed. Soon they will seize New York and control the Hollywood films."

"I don't believe a word of it."

"Oh yes, it's true. I shall give your name to the authorities at Tiflis if you don't believe it. I shall accuse you of capitalist propaganda!" Surely he was joking, I thought. But he wasn't smiling at all, he looked very sharp and confident.

Strange fellow. A communist, and yet he constantly troubled me by his lack of real humanity, even a spark of it; by his unrelaxed inward gaze. He seemed to be living in a jungle full of mirrors. And yet a wonderful man in his way, brilliant, capable of a terrifying degree of self-denial.

And I felt very close to him. Not a feeling of love, pre-

90

cisely, nor even of friendship, nor even of comradeship. But of a secret interdependence, a closeness that I couldn't quite comprehend.

"You are a communist, Feodor," said I. "But do you love your fellow men? Have you even the slightest feeling of warmth for any of them? Any of them? I don't believe it."

He stared at me. "You may think it odd," he said with conceit, "but I do. I love them all. In my own way. I feel a small electrical flash of love go out toward anyone I am in contact with, no matter who it is or where. I become interested in him. I may not show it, my friend, but that is the truth, nevertheless. I wish to guide, control, cure. I am a good communist."

I realized suddenly why he was so strong, so full of endurance, so dangerous, and why I was afraid of him. A fanatic; not very far from being quite mad, in fact. And still very brilliant, an over-developed mind that resembled a hothouse orchid, closer to genius, really, than anyone I'd ever known. He thought of himself, I was sure, as a sort of perverse god. That was all he truly believed in. His own perverse and godlike self.

Charcoal braziers were brought into the dark room. Most of the peasants left; a few lay down on the floor and went to sleep. Once there was an outcry, a quick fist-fight in the glowing twilight, a resounding volley of accusations, counteraccusations, denials, obscenities. "What is it?" I asked. "One of them says the other forgot to pay him, and so he tried to steal it." "Pay him for what?" "I am not certain." It was all a game. You had to be on your guard all the time, against everyone, against everything. The craftiest and most watchful always won.

The lights were extinguished; only the braziers still

gleamed. Outside the moonlight on the early March snow, snow covering everything, deadening all sound. Once I looked through the window and saw, but could not hear, a solitary man passing on horseback, blue snowlight on all sides. And indoors the black shapes lying around on the floor; and the dead rat, grinning terribly like a Chinaman, attracting the flies with its slow black bleeding.

11

WE FOUND a shaggy horror-eyed Georgian to drive us into Tiflis. Past ruined hamlets, disused well-houses, flattened forests, empty barns. Once we drove through a long wooded plain in which stood two old Georgian castles. Sadly ruined they were, with the sun shining on the wet gray stones and the fallen roofs.

Then Tiflis at last, as the night came falling. Dark under the great cliff, a quiet and poverty-stricken city. The cobblestone streets were wet and dark. But now it was beginning to snow again and the walkers moving through the snow seemed hardly alive at all. Thin and ugly people, all of them, coarse-featured, thick-lipped, savage-eyed. Waiting for something, hungry for something.

We walked down a long narrow street and finally came to a black stone house set back among some withered trees. "She will like you," said Krusnayaskov. "My mother is always interested in my friends. But you will please her particularly. You are her type."

He opened the door and walked into the lamplit kitchen. A woman rose from her place beside the tiled oven and stared at him. Her face grew wild with consternation, with hysteria, with love. Without a word or any sound she hurled herself on Feodor and covered his face with kisses.

She was horribly fat. She flowed in all directions like a bowlful of rising dough. There was no stopping that surge of flesh, that flood. Her arms flowed around Feodor: she seemed positively to be swallowing him, like a huge amœba surrounding its prey.

Yet her face was full of a soft restrained beauty. Not the pure beauty of inexperience, rather the beauty of contemplation or suffering; an Eastern beauty rather than a Western beauty. I could see where Feodor resembled her: the eyes, the lips, the nose: but standing beside him, in spite of her richness of curve, in spite of his lean aggressive body, it was she and not he who appeared the more masculine.

They spoke for several minutes in whispers. Now and again one of the two glanced in my direction. Then he put on a great astrakhan coat that hung beside the door and left without another word.

She came up to me. "You are his close friend," she said in French. "You are, in that case, my friend also." She spoke with a cold theatricality, and I had the feeling that she was addressing not me but some imaginary audience seated behind me in the room.

She sat down beside the oven again. "Be seated, if you will be so kind. He'll be back soon. In the meantime, I desire to speak to you." A bowlful of almond paste and a carafe of red wine stood on a small table at her side. She poured me a small glassful, and then a larger glassful for herself. She kept reaching over and nibbling at the sweets.

"I am his mother," she said, "but my name is not, as his is, Krusnayaskov. My name is Zuronova. I married a second time, you see, and a third as well. Life has not been easy. I have no illusions. I may as well be frank. I have no ideals. Ideals are for young men, like my son. Ideals give him dignity and ferocity. They may possibly give him happiness. Do you think so?" I said I didn't know. "Well, in any case they are not for me. I am a practical woman. But in spite of this I must confess that life has not been easy. It has not been happy. I have never been happy." She reached over and plucked another sweet out of the jar. "Have you ever been happy?"

"Yes, I think so, Madame Zuronova."

"Have you felt certain of life, I mean? Have you forgotten about death, have you stopped toying with the idea of death, have you ceased regarding death as inevitable? That is what I mean."

I felt puzzled, of course. I didn't know the answer. I racked my brains, but all I could mutter was, "Well, I have found happiness by enjoying the present and forgetting the future, now and then."

I heard a faint sound over my head. It might have been the sound, I thought, of a mincing footstep upon a heavy rug. Then I heard the delicate tinkle of a girl's laugh— once, twice, a tantalizing little sound, and then quiet again.

"Ah yes," said Mme Zuronova placidly. "You are a boy, you can do that. But an older man can't. And no woman ever can, I assure you. She must think of love, and when you think of love life becomes uncertain and perilous and never wholly, confidently, contemplatively happy."

She belched vigorously and poured herself another glassful of wine. On and on she went. "I don't pretend to be better than other people," she said, gazing through me at the dark brocaded wall. "Not in the least. Don't misunderstand. I have my deceitful side. I'll play a trick or two if it will help me, or help some one I love. But of course, you know, there is only one person I love or shall ever love until I die. . . . I've done cruel things. I've felt regretful afterwards, now and then. But one mustn't take things too seriously. Things get pretty shabby if one hasn't learned to laugh, even if it's only a laugh of disgust. Women learn to do that. They have more sense of humor than men. That's why they kill themselves more rarely, and are happier when old."

The snow fell against the panes and melted, the green curtains moved softly in the draught. I looked at her closely in the flickering lamplight. Did I say she was beautiful? No, she was not beautiful. She was ugly, I now realized; devastatingly so. Moles hung from her face, her neck was one with her chin—a series of folds, ten, twenty of them, with a moist efflorescence lining each. Her eyes were circled with blue, and disquietingly intense. Unseeingly intense, metallically intense, like Feodor's. Her hair was short and curly like a man's.

She wore an old red-velvet gown, threadbare and spotted by the over-richness of her flesh. Her huge breasts shimmered and fluttered through it like waves. And she smelled; distinctly; a mingled odor of cloves, of citron and of venison. It grew overpowering, hypnotic almost.

A mountainous woman full of power. But full of self-deception, a sentimental romanticist, and very selfish. I was growing a bit afraid of her.

"Ah yes," she said, "one must laugh at things. Otherwise they become heavy, drab, nauseating with sorrow. All perspective goes, your eyes grow bleary and begin to focus inward, all that's left of your mind is a sticky bit of a thing, like a ball of wool that's gotten bunched up and odorous from being left out in the rain. I have no illusions. I want truth."

Again I heard the tripping sound of footsteps overhead, and then again the porcelain laughter. An unpleasant sexual sound.

Her face was mask-like with fat. When she turned toward me I had the feeling that it was a mask gazing at me, and what face was behind it, if any at all, I had no way of knowing. None, except that I felt the gaze upon my face like the cold flat side of a knife.

"I shall tell you some things," she proceeded, "about Feodor." She poured herself another glassful of wine.

"He is a strange man. He is very loyal. And he is capable of deep love. But he shows it in strange ways. Sometimes he is very cruel. So much so that you may think he hates you. But you will be wrong, for it is not hatred but love that causes him to be cruel.

"And he is very lonely. Never, never has he confided in me. But I know him better than he thinks. I know, for example, that he is a virgin. I know it. He has never allowed any one to touch him. Fanatically pure. Purity is sacred enough with him to justify blood or death. He has always been like that, and so was his father."

She leaned back. The snow stood heaped on the window ledge and the lamplight shone upon the falling flakes. I could see the haggard trees rising through the snow, and beyond these the low garden wall. Once more I heard the sound of laughter from the room above, and then a low man's voice, and then the laughter gently subsiding into a hum of love and a still more eloquent silence.

Her eyes were closed. I thought for a moment that she'd fallen asleep. But she hadn't. Her fingers reached toward the almond paste, and again she spoke across the flickering shadows, eyes closed and eyelids glistening. "He is your friend," she said, "remember that. Forgive him for what he does. I like you and therefore I shall tell you this. You must forgive him. For I believe that he is planning to have you arrested. . . ."

Was I dreaming? Was she mad? The wine had sent my

brain swimming; I could no longer be certain of anything.

And I grew afraid. I felt sick at the pit of my stomach and peered through the window without at first knowing precisely what it was that had so suddenly frightened me. Then I knew. It was not what Mme Zuronova had just been saying to me.

It was this: through the glitter of snow, down there beside the tree, I saw Krusnayaskov. Motionless, black in the astrakhan mantle, quietly staring up toward the window. Into my eyes he seemed to be staring. The snow was hanging on his cap and his fur coat. Then he turned and disappeared in the shadow of the house.

I began to shiver. There was a wind blowing through me; I felt like an empty room with all the windows shattered, terror blowing through, no comfort left. That was how I felt, consciously and distinctly. The thought of an empty room rose before me vividly. Mme Zuronova was sitting quietly, eyes closed and nostrils glistening.

Then fear broke into hysteria. I rose, I tore the lantern from the table and hurled it on the floor, I broke the window pane with a blow of the fist, I leaped through the jagged glass upon the suddenly darkened ground. Then I ran toward the wall, pulled myself over it, and stood for a moment in the shadows edging the cobbled street.

A few yards down the street two tall men were talking together in a low voice. Then after a moment they separated, the one in the cape disappeared around the corner, the one with the fur cap walked slowly across the street and toward Mme Zuronova's house. The street was empty again. The great desolate trees rose over it silently, glistening in the lamplight with a wonderful glass-like delicacy. Far away I could hear a child crying.

I ran along the shadowy wall, then crossed the street, then up and down the wintry alleys of the city until I found myself in the white windy country again, lonely and free once more.

❧❧❧ I slept in a ruined farmhouse that night. The next two days I walked southward along the white valleys, sleeping at noon in huts, in ditches, in sheltered copses, walking again in the night. Once I saw in the distance a large gray city. An hour later I met a fat red-cheeked man walking, as I was, steadily southward across the pasture lands and the barren fields. He told me that it was the city of Erivan I had just been passing. Then he pointed to the southwest. "There lies Mount Ararat," he said, "and yonder the three nations join. Turkey, Russia, Persia." A golden mist lay far over the tremendous empty land. We walked together quietly for several hours.

We passed Alageuze, high in a cloud and beautiful. The snow was melting, but it still shone painfully in the sunlight until at last blue dusk covered the countryside. This was steppe country, barren waste lands with only a village here and there, many miles apart. "It's the land where men go murdering," said my bald red-cheeked companion. "More than any other place in the world. And naturally enough, for if they don't kill, then they are despised. So they learn to kill, and they learn to revere the killer."

Once I stooped to drink at a well, and there in the shallow water, beneath the reflection of my own face, I saw the swollen dark face of a dead man. His face looked huge and idiotic with desire.

"You are eager to reach Persia," said my companion as we walked side by side through the snowy twilight. "I am also." Then he told me that he was a Nestorian priest and that the Soviet authorities had thought him dangerous; for that reason he had been imprisoned for two years. Then, while being transferred to another prison, he had escaped. "If we are careful," he said, "I think we can reach the river. Then we can cross easily enough into Persia. It is done frequently, and I have been informed how it is done. Oh, this is a terrible and cruel land. Cruel like a boy that is testing his growing muscles." He was an unpleasant-looking man—a great paunch, soft white hands, a face like a boar's. I could understand how people might think him dangerous. But for the moment, I felt sure, he was my friend.

We grew hungry and tired. We slept in a disused well-house, and the next morning we tiptoed past a shabby farmyard and I leaped over the fence and caught a chicken. I twisted its neck round and round. Still it kept on fluttering, and I could feel the gulping movements of its throat and the soft warm push of its blood. Slowly it grew gentle and limp, and when we reached the woods we built a fire and roasted it. It was a tough, savorless bird, but we devoured it like a pair of foxes, savagely and silently. Then we hurried southward again.

❧❧❧ The clouds grew darker above the hills down toward the border; a ripple of peach-colored light flashed briefly beyond the misty hills and then was gone. I tapped my companion on the shoulder and said, "How far is it now?"

He rose and rubbed his eyes. "Not far, I pray to God." And then when we had climbed to the top of the hill we could see the river below us, very quiet and dreamy.

"That's it," said he.

"The Aras?"

"Yes."

"You're sure?"

"Yes."

That was Persia a mile away, then, that bleak undulating land beyond which the sun had set. "Come," said the priest, "we must be very cautious now."

On the field near by the cattle were still munching, and now and then one of them plunged across the pebbly brook that cut the hill in two. We walked past the bushes and along the estuary down to the dangerous shore.

A mile or so below us was a big wooden bridge. Cautiously we crept along the shore until a small promontory hid the bridge from us. Here, on a rocky ledge above the pebbles, lay a heap of debris, ashes and charred sticks. Stealthily my Nestorian priest gathered some sticks and set fire to them; the flames leaped up through the darkness, the water flickered with their light. We waited five minutes, ten minutes, and stared into the swiftly increasing darkness. The mist was growing heavier.

Then out of the foggy dark a rowboat came moving slowly toward us. We could hear the beating of the oars and the whining of the oarlocks long before we could see the oarsman himself. A shabby, saturnine sort, an Armenian, that's what we shortly found him to be—the kind that's been revoltingly frightened into something negative, into a sort of half-living. He sidled suspiciously up to the Russian shore and muttered something to the Nestorian. The Nestorian muttered back across the smoke and the fog. The Armenian muttered something else. The Nestorian answered, and drew some money out of his pocket. The Armenian motioned to us, and we stepped into the boat.

Slowly we moved across the black water, ripples gliding

away from us into the fog, bubbles glimmering for an instant and then lost. Nobody spoke. Persia was now a slender black line that wound through the fog like a sea-serpent. Before we landed the darkness had grown certain and complete, and all we could see was a small light upon a hillock.

I trailed my fingers in the water. Coldly the river flowed through them. Three long ripples ran off obliquely toward each side, three arrows pointing toward Persia. At the tip of each arrow I could see the diamond breaking through the darkness, the reflection of the solitary light on the shore. And then a tree rose in the way and not even the pin-point flame broke the darkness. Everything was empty and alone, silent except for the beating of the oars.

We landed and the Armenian led us to the refugees' hut. A woman gave us some hot coffee and told us the way to the Tabriz road. A tiny melancholy thing she was. She smiled, but it was a timid and uneasy smile. Her eyes were black, bottomless black, with misery. She told us how she had once had five sons and a husband. All of them, all six, had been killed by the Cheka. All six of them, she chanted, all six. But there was no bitterness or hatred in her voice, merely a supine whimpering hopelessness. Nothing was left for her, she wasn't alive at all.

In the morning we started off toward the Tabriz road. A weary, dreary no man's land, nobody belonged here, it was merely a place for hiding and waiting. We passed a strange village that scrambled high among the crags, houses hanging over the edge like birds' nests. At last we reached the road.

Kurdish shepherds and their flocks were marching along the road toward Marand. We walked with them, and after much dusty walking we reached Marand.

My Nestorian priest had taken a liking to me and was feeling very jolly. "We'll have a celebration," he said. So we went to the best inn in town.

Bearded men were playing a game with dark-blue cards, eating eggs and garlic and drinking vodka. They drank like whales; it was staggering to watch them. It seemed unbelievable that their bellies should hold so much food and drink. Now and then one of them would step outside the door and we'd hear him whistling and making water resonantly into the empty flagons. Then he'd return and start in again.

A young Circassian with perfumed hair was playing on a three-stringed zither and an old Tartar was beating a drum. They sang, in high nervous voices, and tears came to their eyes as they sang. Beside them sat a refugee from the hills of Ossetia, a great bull-like man who watched them with a face full of grief. My priest spoke to them and soon we were all friends. We all felt very happy again and began to laugh with joy at one another.

The Circassian told us of his sect, the secretive worshipers who trod toward eternity along a path strewn with the corpses of their enemies. "We must be warriors. We must kill unbelievers," he said in a delicate gesturing way. "And finally we reach the path leading to the heavenly castles. Our mothers love their sons to be killed. If they are killed while robbing their neighbors or murdering their enemies, that is the greatest honor they know and they rejoice. Our girls would rather have us brought home dead than returning from an unsuccessful expedition. We are the proudest and strongest and handsomest of the people."

"I once fought in a battle with the Turks," said the

great man from Ossetia hastily. "I killed three men. My father cut a young Turk through from head to foot with his sword. Straight down he came with the great sword; cut him right down the middle; straight through, from the tip of his head right down through his belly and his sex. I remember. I saw it. I was there. And I saw him pluck the two sacred parts out of the blood, first the right one and then the left one, and he fried them at a fire and ate them. He was an old man, and this he said would give him the power of a young warrior. Never will I forget that. My father squatting at the fire on the rocky plain after the battle was over, crying that he would be a young man again. Far away the Turkish women were carrying their men from the battlefield. They cried like wolves all night long, all night long. Never can I forget it, the women crying and the dead Turk in two halves and my father swearing among the rocks that he would be a young man once more."

"And was he?"

"Ah no. He died a month later, in another battle with the Turks."

"As for me," grunted the old Tartar, a driveling wolf-faced ogre of a man, "I am one of the order of the Khlystys. I belong, that is to say, to the heresy of the Flagellants. There are very few left. Very few have remained faithful to the laws. I am one of the few. The laws are very profound and secret, and I have remained faithful to them."

"You have?" said the Ossete.

"Yes, absolutely and forever," moaned the Tartar.

"I'm inclined to doubt it," said the Circassian.

"You're an idiot," cried the Tartar. "Always and absolutely have I remained faithful to them."

"Well," said my Nestorian priest, "how can we believe you if you don't prove it?"

"Oh, oh!" groaned the old Tartar, and nodded his head three times in a troubled way.

"Yes, how?" cried the Circassian. "Prove it. Tell us."

The old Tartar closed his eyes and told us. Not as interesting as we had presumed, but still. . . . Never to marry; never to serve an orthodox master; to remain alone and poor; to be humble; to be so humble in fact, to fear pride so deeply, that sins must needs be regularly committed as a sort of purge. Debauchery in the name of purity.

"What did you do?" said the elegant Circassian with wet half-open lips.

"Many things in my young days. But, oh, I am old now, I want quiet, I am through with sin, I am through with purging, I want peace."

"But what did you do?" tittered the Circassian. "If you can't even tell us that, how are we to know that the whole thing wasn't a preposterous lie from start to finish? Come, tell us."

"Many things." His face, eyes closed, shone serenely in the lamplight. Beautiful it was, the deep ridges, the brooding lines, the lines of exhaustion, of bewilderment, of dreamy anger, of a fulfilled heterosexuality—beautiful and venerable they made his face. "We stole sacred objects and gold, we burned barns, we killed cattle, we ravaged the fields."

"What else?"

"We played the spy, we frightened the children, we brought dissension into happy families."

"What else?"

"We corrupted the young, we disillusioned the aged,

we made love seem a shocking and shameful disease."

"What else?"

"We betrayed each other."

All of us sat back and closed our eyes. More garlic was brought, the glasses were refilled with vodka.

"My people," said the Circassian, at last, with glistening eyes, "are the wealthiest. The steep hills of Khevsuria and Kakhetia are full of gold and diamonds. But it is a secret. No one tells. We are too proud and too wise to desire them ourselves, too wise and too proud to give them to anyone else."

"I know a city," said the hairy Ossete in a low, tremendous voice, "deep in an inaccessible valley. Only a rope leads from the cliff down to the city. Once you are there you can never leave. It is a place of refuge for sinners. Everyone becomes virtuous and happy there, because good is called evil and evil is called good."

"Where is that city?"

"In Azerbaijan."

"Where in Azerbaijan?"

"I may not tell."

"We believe you are lying," said the cunning Circassian.

"It's on the border near Daghestan, high in the hills," cried the bull-like man from Ossetia.

"In my heaven," wept the old Tartar, "there will be no gold, no sinners. Every warrior will find what he desires. He will find fair boys and fair maidens, whichever he prefers. Many and many of them, all of them voluptuous and willing. Everyone will be happy with love." He put his arms around the Circassian and kissed him tenderly on the lips.

We all felt very sorrowful now. No one spoke, the three-stringed zither and the drum lay silent.

So we left Marand at the end of a row of oxen, my Nestorian priest and I, and proceeded toward Tabriz. Once we passed a corpse caravan. A sleepy moonlit procession it was, with the dead ones wrapped in black felt and roped upon the shaggy horses. There was a very tall man in gray who was leading it, and the priest asked him, "Where are you going?"

"To Kerbela," said the tall man in an unhappy voice.

"That's far away, very far."

"Yes, the bodies will begin to smell very badly as we go southward. The felt will fall to pieces. It will be very unpleasant."

"I should say," said the priest. "My lad, how can you bear it?"

"It is a saintly journey. They wish to be buried near the grave of the great Imam Hussein. Then it will be easier for them to enter Paradise. I have made it easier for hundreds of them to enter Paradise. I too will some day be buried at Kerbela, I hope." He was a haggard man, wild-eyed in the moonlight.

"I wish you luck, then," cried the priest, and as we passed we caught a whiff of the air that floated amongst the dead ones. Terrible, but it would be far worse before they reached Kerbela.

And so we finally wandered into Tabriz one rainy day. An ugly narcotic city, full of insolent Tartars, and the priest left me at nightfall without a word. Perhaps, thought I, I'll never see him again; I'd gotten to like him, his red and startled face, his sly and cynical ways. But the next morning he returned to the hut where I'd been sleeping. "Where were you?" said I.

"Ah well," said he demurely, "we're all human, my lad."

"Visiting the girls? Playing the flute?"

He smiled and lowered his bleary eyes. "No," he said. "You are wrong. You are innocent, I can see that."

"I think not," said I naïvely.

"Oh yes, you are an innocent boy. I am sure of it."

And so we started off toward Kazvin together in a very jolly mood.

12

But in Kazvin we quarreled. We came to a small hilltop inn at the eastern edge of the city, gardens on one side and vineyards on the other. There we sat until late in the night, drinking the fine Kazvin wine, chatting and joking. "Good night to you," said my priest at last. "I'm going visiting." "It's very late," said I, "for a priest to go visiting." "You don't know where I'm going," he cried angrily, his boar-face shining and his white hands fluttering. "Yes indeed I do," said I, "and it's very late indeed for a priest to go out whoring or worse." And he stormed out into the night, and when I woke up the next morning he was gone. And I never did see him again.

So I stepped out upon the road and looked eastward into the fertile country and then westward into the big city. Out of the fog of the big city came a caravan, and then a motor-truck, and then another truck, and then another. I stood beside the road, but none of them would take me. None, until finally a wild-looking young man in a shaggy coat came riding up in a cart behind two shaggy bullocks. "Teheran?" I cried. He came to a stop. "Teheran?" said I. But he shook his head and shrugged his shoulders. Never mind, thought I quickly, and climbed in beside him, and off we were.

Slowly we drove along a thin winding road through the rich valleys, northward toward the huge blue hills. Now and then we stopped for water. He never opened his mouth. There was nothing to be done; he couldn't understand a word I said, no matter what I tried. Where he was going I didn't know. But he had a kind and comforting face. Never mind, thought I, this is pleasant enough and I'm in no hurry.

So we drove on and on until night. The stars came out, and my silent friend stopped to fasten two little bells on his bullocks. On and on, tinkling upward with the foothills, closer and closer to the dreamy blue peaks of Elburz. At last he came to a stop beside a well and stepped out to make water. He drew a large crust of rye bread out of his shirt and gave me a piece. Quietly we stood there and munched and looked out over the darkening waves of land. Then he unfastened the bullocks, drew a blanket from the back of the cart, lay down on the grass, drew the blanket across him, closed his gentle, stupid eyes and began to snore. The bullocks wandered slowly to and fro, tinkling and grazing with a profound peacefulness, and finally I lay down among the tall grasses beside the well and went to sleep, too. Once or twice the cold woke me up and I'd see the bullocks lying silently in the middle of the road and the blue hills rising toward the starlight.

❧❧❧ The next day we climbed up the Elburz hills, and far behind us I could see the huge expanse of land which we were leaving. I felt a little bit nervous now. "Teheran?" said I to my companion, but he shook his head and gazed peacefully ahead. There was nothing to do but go on. And after all, I was feeling happy enough.

We passed some men in white felt coats, gaunt hairy mountain dwellers. At noon we stopped beside a hut, and a kind old man greeted us with a smile, while three women with rings in their nostrils and anklets below their scarlet trousers bustled about and brought us tea. They set the great copper ewer before us and then watched us quietly from the fireside. The old man grunted; my companion muttered his thanks. And that was all. No one spoke a word, and soon we started off again while the old man and his three women stood at the doorway and stared after us.

The land grew lonely, mountain flowers appeared on the slopes. But no cattle, no pasture lands, no villages any more. Once we met some mules loaded with rice being driven toward Kazvin by a slender man in a blue jerkin. He and my driver greeted each other loudly. But they didn't stop to talk, and up and up we rode until at last we reached the top and looked down into the huge valley below. Lovely and green, patterned with silvery threads of water, and to the northeast a great rocky throne towering against the sky. And below us the thick dark forest, the deep fog-covered forest full of secrets. I could see in the blue shelter of the trees snowy shapes still gleaming, a bowlful of snow left in each cool hollow for one or two or three more days. Far to the north, I knew, lay the Caspian, and my heart beat more quickly with the loneliness and remoteness of the beautiful lands below me.

Down into the dark forest we rode, into the cool black caverns under the great trees, into the cool scents and rippling sounds of the leaves high over our heads. We stopped at a small spring that shone pure as an emerald among the ferns and mosses, and my driver leaped out and lay flat on his belly and drank. A clumsy, big-boned fellow he was, with his buttocks swelling out under the tight patched trousers. Then he rose and looked at me and smiled, drops hanging from his shaggy eyebrows and his thick hairy lips. He looked very pleased and I knew he was nearing his home. I knew it by the silent contentment that I felt growing in him, the confidence in his posture, the gentleness in his eyes. He began to sing—a slow repetitious song without beginning or end. It became very monotonous after an hour or two.

On and on through the black woods. The wheels passed soundlessly over the dead leaves and logs of many northern winters. No small plants grew here. No men to stain the shade and the secrecy. Only the black trunks rose leafless high above our heads until, dimly and remotely, they flowed outward in shadowy waves and hid the sky. Under these waves we rode and rode.

The forest grew thinner as the land grew more level. We passed a field hidden among the trees, and then far in the distance we saw a shepherd and his flock among the hillocks. And beyond, following my driver's gaze, I could see the square brown huts of the village which I knew was his home.

The inside of the hut smelled like incense, rich and ancestral. In the neighboring room I could hear the women laughing as they churned the butter and polished the copper vessels. "My boy," said the old patriarch, "you needn't be afraid here. We will feed you well. For three days we will feed you. Then you will take the voyage southward with my son. He will drive you into Teheran. You will be safe with him; he is a loyal and obedient son." His voice had a 'cello sound, a rich, serene, vibrating sound. A stern and beautiful old man, long-lashed, long-bearded, long-fingered—a true aristocrat. Over his silver curls he wore a black skull-cap and in his black leather belt a big silver knife.

"Thank you," said I.

He gazed sadly out across the fields.

"Are you the only one here who speaks English?" said I.

"Yes," he replied. "My daughter speaks English, but I am the only man."

"How does it happen that you and your daughter speak English?" said I.

He glanced toward me for a moment. Then he gazed across the rye-fields again with a look of deep regret. "Once," he said, "when I was stronger than I am now, a woman came from England into the Valley of the Assassins. 'Why have you come here?' I asked her. 'Because I wished to,' she answered in my own tongue, 'because I am curious and adventurous.' And so I fell in love with her, and she taught me to speak English as she did, and she told me much about this England which she loved. She stayed with me two years. Then she went away again. Ah, she was a noble and beautiful lady! Warm as a woman, keen-spirited as a man."

"She never came back?"

He shook his head. "But my daughter is her daughter as well."

"How long ago was this?"

"Twenty years ago. Then, as at this very moment," said he—and his voice was slow and defiant—"the white doves flew across to our homes. Nothing has changed."

In the dark kitchen I could see the women moving. I could see their hair glistening across their backs, their arms shining in the firelight, their white teeth gleaming as they smiled. Outside at the doorway a shepherd was making love to a brown-skinned girl. I could hear their happy whispers and happy laughter, and then I looked at the patriarch's dark angry eyes watching the doves fly over the fields.

"Do you think that you will ever see her again?"

◇◇◇◇◇◇◇◇◇◇◇◇◇◇◇◇◇◇◇◇◇◇◇◇◇◇◇◇◇◇◇◇◇◇◇◇ 113

"Oh no," he said in a voice heavy with irony and discontent, "I think not. But I don't know. I know nothing. I am a very ignorant man."

"I believe you are a very wise man."

"No, you are wrong. I am a very ignorant man, a passionate, foolish, ignorant old man who understands nothing." His voice was low and uncertain, and I could see in his eyes a look of deep disturbance, what or why I couldn't tell. Hopelessness, perhaps, the look of a captured and exhausted old man who has failed to make his peace with life. The very thing, indeed, that gave him also so profound, so persuasive an air.

Later I sat in the doorway and watched the lights grow bright in the windows along the winding village road. The shepherds in their sweaty blue jerkins were flat on their backs in the clover, the workers of the field were washing their great brown arms in the stream, the young ones were sitting in the trees and making love among the foliage.

A bright-haired girl came walking along the road toward me and sat down by my side. She smiled. "I know who you are," she said bashfully.

"Who?"

"An Englishman," said she.

"No," said I. "But I speak English."

"I speak English, too. See, I can speak to you. But no one else can, except my father. And he is old and will die soon. Then there will be no one who can speak to you except me."

"But I won't be here long," said I.

"But you must stay here!" she said. "You will be unhappy in any other village. No one will talk to you or listen to you, because you speak English."

"I could go to England or America, you know. Or Australia or Canada."

"Oh no," said she lightly, shaking her head so that her golden earrings trembled, "those lands are at the other end of the world. Don't go there; they are too far away. Stay here."

Her hair hung over her shoulders. I could smell the sweet young odor rising from it, and the clean young scent of her body. She turned and smiled at me through the dusk, and when I took her hand in mine she looked away again and stopped smiling, but her warm hand stayed in mine.

How can I tell of the next three days? How can I say what they were when I do not know? The real remembrance lies in a momentary fragrance, a turn of the head, the slow lowering of an eyelid, a blade of grass or a drop of water coming to rest against the skin; any of these, all of these, and many others too small and secret to comprehend.

"Tell me about the great cities," said she, and on each side of her head shone the red tulips, far off hung the waterfall like a motionless silver coil from the mossy ledge. "What sort of men live there?" Her gray fanatical eyes looked sharply at me; not a gentle, womanly gaze, nor was the fine healthy smell of her body a womanly smell. "What do they do there if there are no sheep to herd, no fields to plow, nothing to grow, and no animals?"

"They build houses, ships, motor-cars, roads; they make clothes and books and jewels and little round things that will tell you the time of the day without looking at the sun."

"Why?"

"Because they want these things."

"Are they happier than we?"

"No; less happy."

"Why are they less happy?"

"I don't know," said I, "but I am convinced that they are less happy."

"That is very strange," said she, "if they do all these things in order to be happier, and then are less happy after all."

"Yes, it is becoming more and more strange; not even the wise men seem to understand it."

And then, lying beside the pool with the drops still caught motionless on her shoulders and thighs, the goats far down beside the stream, the hawks hovering high overhead, the eagles crying, the silver trout leaping among the pebbles, the breeze rustling through the ravine up into the hot dry valley, her strong sunburned breasts rising and falling with her breath. And in the lazy afternoon, sitting under a tree, the boys and girls whispering and sleeping beside the fields, the old women gathering the mushrooms, the trees in blossom, the thorny briars red and fragrant, the brass jugs standing beside the well. All of it joining, all of it shaping a whole, man being man, woman being woman, nothing there to suggest those others who are far away or unhappy or unoccupied or dead.

"I wish to visit the cities," she said, "Khorramabad or Abbasabad or even Kazvin, but my father says they are wicked. Is that true? Are they wicked?"

I thought for a moment. "Yes."

"Tell me," she said, suddenly interested. "Why are they wicked? What do they do that is wicked? Do they lie, or steal, or kill?"

That was exactly it, said I, and they did it on a very elaborate and subtle scale. The bigger the city and the more people lived closely together, the more they desired to lie, steal, and kill.

"What else?" said she. "What about the women? Are they wicked, too?"

"Some of them, I suppose."

"Are they beautiful?"

"Some of them; very few."

"Much more beautiful than I?"

"No, none of them."

"You are lying to me!" she cried. "I don't believe you!" But she was blushing, her eyes grew soft, her lips parted.

"Do you like them? Do you make love to them if they are beautiful?"

I plucked a sprig of wild thyme and drew it along her neck and through her hair.

"Come," she said, "you must tell me. Tell me. Tell me."

The fourth day came and I stepped into the bullock-cart again and said farewell and thank you to the old patriarch. He stood unsmiling in the doorway, his knife glittering in the sun.

"Farewell," said he, "be happy."

"Farewell," said I. "Where is your daughter today?"

"Ah," said he vaguely, curiously, "she has gone off to her cousin's for the day."

My heart fell. "Say farewell to her for me, then."

"Yes," he said. He opened his mouth as if he were going to say something more. But he didn't. He remained silent. Once again I felt the strange anger deep in him, the hatred for the outside world; for its power to reach deep into the heart, to shatter all calm, to poison what was long striven for and built out of a real suffering and the seclusion of years. And he hated me.

As the cart climbed slowly up the hill I turned and waved my hand, and he waved back.

But as we left the fields and passed the well I saw her running toward us from the copse. We stopped. "Good-by," she cried, and leaned her head for a moment against my shoulder—the shy, restless, and uncomprehending gesture of a boy. The curve of her brown shoulder shone with sweat. "Good-by."

"Maybe I'll see you again. I'll come back."

She nodded her head, but I knew that she didn't believe me. "Good-by," she said with a peculiar coldness, and turned with the pitcher on her strong gleaming shoulder back toward the well. I looked around after we'd started up toward the forest again. There she stood, gazing into the well, with the brass pitcher beside her glittering in the sun. But she didn't glance up toward us at all, she didn't wave good-by; she looked quiet and indifferent as a statue until the black trees came rising between us like a wave.

So we rode silently on toward Teheran for two long days, my big-buttocked driver and I. The Valley of the Assassins and the Throne of Solomon faded behind us, the plains grew dusty and stony. We passed small villages full of sunburned hawk-eyed shepherds, and old women spinning, and old men squatting beside their hideous dogs, and girls bathing themselves on their thresholds, thinking of their lovers, preparing themselves for marriage.

Once, after we'd reached the road toward Teheran, we saw a caravan bound for the south. When we drew closer I saw that it was a corpse caravan; the same one in fact that I and the Nestorian priest had passed a week or so ago. I recognized the long black bundles and the tall anæmic man whose face was so eloquent of the merchandise of death and salvation. I wanted to speak to him, but I could not, nor would I have dared. The stench was very bad indeed; it fluttered and licked at the sunlight like a cat's tongue. Long after we'd passed the caravan we could still detect the smell. The dreadful inglorious dead, it was, making their animal presence known across the land, still weeping tears of disgust and shaking a tremulous finger of warning.

And so we entered Teheran at last by the Kazvin gate. He drove me to the bazaar and there nodded farewell. I nodded back and groped for some way in which I could express my gratitude. But before I knew it he had left me and was disappearing down the long dusky colonnade. I was alone. I had spent all of four days and four nights with him, but I knew no more about him than I knew about his two bullocks. Like a good-natured, uncomprehending animal he moved among the shadows and finally was gone. There was a message I had wished to give him. But I had forgotten, and now that I remembered again it was too late.

13

So I wandered through the labyrinth of sunlight and shadow in the bazaar, watching, smelling, hearing, touching. I saw the long serpentine threads of sunlight sifting through the shade and fingering the booths of the jewel merchants; earrings, anklets, bracelets, neckbands, headbands, amulets, talismans; tooled leather from the southern ports, varnished metals from Indo-China, glittering worthless stones from Ceylon, vermilion and magenta silks from Tashkent, blue velvets from Bokhara, green rugs from Syria, great rippling shawls from Kashmir—no longer fresh, any of them, all of them spotted and stained by the wet seasons or the touch of hands. And beyond these the sweetmeats, clotted syrups soft in the sun's rays, raw spices, dark granular honey, dried citron and figs and dates buzzing with a thousand little golden flies; caskets and bowls and ewers and medicine-bottles twisted out of blue glass; strangely shaped receptacles of iron and bronze and copper; salves and perfumes sickening the nostrils. Something false and pathetic about it all, as pathetic as the faces that hovered over them like moths.

The great shadowy vault rambled on for miles. Everywhere I looked were little stalls, some of them hopelessly shabby and covered with dust, and the sellers beside them dead-seeming except for the quick black eyes that watched and watched. There was a dreadful sense of anonymity, as if this indeed were the world of men reduced to its lowest state of hush and relaxation. The whole place had the air of a sexual dream, quite tragic. Life was slow; each movement was tentative and gradual—a deep sea setting, and the air an oppressive and isolating element. The women moved laboriously, like ferns under water, and were constantly hiding their faces. They too were lonely, but, unlike the men, they could somehow bear it.

I walked into the sunny street and along the Lalezar. A different world suddenly. Far off, indeed, I could see the minarets and the tremendous blue-domed mosque, and beyond these the snow-capped shape of Mount Demavand. But at my side I saw the new steam tramway and the new hotel and the new cinema theater and the new motor-cars. Thoroughly Western. All the show of activity and hurry and restlessness. But something was wrong. There was something very disconcerting in all this. Under all this hurry and chicanery lay a hint of something else. I could see it reflected in the tall well-dressed man with a cane and a monocle who was crossing the street, in the half-starved boy staring through the bars of a cellar, in the old man fingering the pustules on his feet, in the two fat women hurrying down the alley with invisible faces.

I reached into my pocket and pulled out a crumpled slip of paper. "Marie de Chamellis," it read, and below this, "Teheran: till May 1," and in the corner, almost illegible, the scribbled address. I stopped the dark man with the cane and the monocle and showed it to him. He stared at me, suspiciously and then meretriciously. Then he smiled and told me the way. I was very shabbily dressed and unshaven; so I told him that I was lost and hungry, and he gave me a five-kran piece and wished me luck.

✄✄✄ I was led into a large room full of silk and sunlight. I sat down and waited.

Yellow damask covered the walls, and along the great screened window lay a row of cushions. On each side of the window was a golden bowl full of hyacinths. The sun entered the room through an ornate copper screen; on the floor it lay, a great glittering square full of circling patterns, a live thing, sensitive and trembling. Through the screen I could see into the garden, and I could see the bright fresh rays of the March sun trickling through the leaflets and drifting like honey across the gravel and toward the tall thin trees beyond the fountain.

Then the yellow curtains parted and Mme de Chamellis entered. I was surprised to see how very sad she looked. I hadn't remembered her quite so fragile and austere as this. She smiled coldly. "It was very kind of you to come."

She walked over to the window where I stood and looked out. "Yes," she said—and already in that one word there was something reassuring—"the garden is very handsome, isn't it? But first you must meet my sister. She is quite ill, but I know she will wish to see you. Come."

I followed her through several curtained antechambers and found myself in a dark, hot room, faintly and unpleasantly odorous and very ornately furnished. In the center stood a large canopied bed. Beside it sat a girl reading softly from a yellow-backed French novel, and on the other side stood two men, one a slim black-haired fellow whom I instantly disliked, and the other a colorless man somewhat older. Three sword-like rays of sunlight pierced the tall green hangings and cut across the room. I could see the lifeless dust swaying in their path. Very still the room was, except for the murmuring of the gray-eyed girl. And a curious feeling of absent-mindedness pervaded it, as if all four of its occupants were thinking intensely of things far outside and were living not in this room at all, but in an uneasy flight toward something more real in past or future; people loosened from the present, unhappy in their age.

"Madame la Comtesse," I heard Mme de Chamellis murmuring; "Monsieur le Comte. Dr. Ainger. . . ." I stood beside the bed and gazed down. A face like a mask, quite lifeless and expressionless except for the eyes peering with an amazing keenness over the blue-gray pouches which hung above and beneath them. Her mouth was only a scarlet line, her neck a labyrinth of wrinkles, her hands two porcelain claws, her hair an artificial scarlet mass of curls, a great wilted peony. But her eyes, as soon as she saw me, grew narrow and brilliant. "Ah, my young man," she whispered excitedly, each syllable setting the wrinkles of her neck aquiver. I had to listen very closely to hear what she said. "I am still deeply excited by life; it still sets me trembling. You must forgive me. The mere presence of youth, my dear boy, makes my heart beat more quickly."

The others were watching her expressionlessly, as if she were performing a familiar series of antics. They merely stared. None of them smiled. None of them bore the unmistakable look of affection.

"Tell me, my pretty friend, what do you think of life?" Her eyes shone with malice and insinuation. They moved constantly, forever on the alert for something new, forever eager to see a flicker of animal beauty in a stranger. In those two pitiable eyes there still hovered more life than in all the other faces in the room. "Tell me. I am very curious. Have you any ideas at all fit to whisper into an old lady's ear?"

"Yes, Madame la Comtesse," said I. "But they don't hang together very well. For example . . ."

She listened for three seconds with an almost painful look of concentration. But she didn't wait to hear the rest.

Her hands shook with nervousness. "Then tell me," she cried softly, "what do you think of death? Are you afraid of it? Does the mere word set your finger tips trembling and unsettle your stomach?"

"Not yet," said I thoughtfully. "After all . . ."

"No? Oh, my delightful child, I shudder at the years to come! You'll be a wrinkled thing, everything hard and alert about you will become limp and wretched. As for me, look at me! Look! I'm terrified! I admit it. Death terrifies me, absolutely. I shan't live much longer. A week, perhaps a month. All of these people try to deceive me, but, you know, I see right through them." Her hands fluttered toward the group toward the window, and she whispered something that I couldn't understand. "I know it," she went on. "But it's only a matter of days in any case. And still, the thought of it makes me quite dizzy." Her voice grew whimpering and lifeless. She raised her shoulders above the lace coverlet, her hollow shoulder blades appeared, and with an expertly subtle motion she shook the silky gown loose from her shoulders. The wrinkled armpits appeared, the line between her breasts sloped mournfully down into the mass of pink silk. She was very, very far from beautiful. Not age, but discontent and the anxiety of desire, had killed whatever loveliness she'd ever had.

"And what," she cried softly, "do you think of women? And of old age? And of love? I know, I know! I can see it! I frighten you, don't I, my dear? You think me mad. Very well, I am mad." She spoke in a very low, soft voice, and the excitement was slowly dying out of her eyes. "I know it. But there are times, nevertheless, when I can manage to see very clearly. I am hideous and absurd, but now and then I still contrive to get an idea of what's going on. We know more than any man, we women, believe me. We alone understand love. We know that the sickness of life passes, the desire for death evaporates, the desire for life goes, too; all that's left is what the body remembers. You call it resignation. But it isn't resignation. It's habit, that's what it is. And love's gotten to be a frightful habit with me. But look at me! I'm still alive, I've survived somehow!"

The curtains parted and a little Arab boy with curly hair and thick lips entered; he might have been a Negro, except for the precision of his features and the elaborateness of his glance. He brought in a tray with two glass bowls, a small bottle of red glass, and a small pointed cylinder out of silver. He placed it on the table beside her and bowed.

"Hassan," she whispered to him, and took his brown boy's hand in hers. "You lovely boy, you naughty boy. . . ." She ran her fingers through his curls and placed his fingers on her lips. "My little darling, my lovely rascal. . . ." Her eyes grew narrow with tenderness. He bowed shyly and departed.

She turned to me again. "My lovable friend," she said —and her lips parted in a desperate fearful smile—"always remember this: there's a good deal of love in human nature, if you only know where to look for it. In everyone, I swear. If there weren't they'd be dead. Thinking alone gets you nowhere, but if you've lived you know that life's a degrading and nightmarish affair, and there's only one thing that gives it any meaning, and that's the existence of love. Remember that. Promise me, my young man, that you'll remember that."

I nodded my head.

"Promise," she cried.

"Yes," said I.

"Say it. Say that you promise."

"I promise."

She smiled. But it was a quick private smile, not intended to be seen, and very touching. I glanced toward the window and saw the sleek young comte staring at me with cat-like eyes. A flash of hatred, lasting only a second. I looked back at the old comtesse, leering and plucking at the lace of the coverlet.

"Good-by," she whispered. *"Au revoir! Au revoir!"* Her eyes closed. She lay there, absurd and artificial as a wax doll. As soon as she closed her heart to us she became comic again, ridiculous. Seen from the outside, she was a laughable creature, like everyone else in the world; pompous, decaying, mad. Seen from the inside, even if only for an instant, she grew like everyone else into a tragic and terrifying shape. That's the only difference between laughter and terror. Man resides in a shell of absurdity. It's the thing hiding inside that gives us shivers.

Mme de Chamellis led me out through the curtains again. Then she led me along a dark corridor at the end of which a ray of sunlight carved like a scimitar across the stone. I followed her. She walked very handsomely, her posture was proud and erect. Still, I wondered, why should she have taken me to meet the old comtesse? I could suspect, but I couldn't be sure.

The marble pillars on each side of the gravel path led out upon the garden itself. A garden of trees, a garden with no flowers at all except a judas tree in flower and, deep in the green shadows, a peach tree from which the last petals were falling. A blue-tiled channel of water ran winding among the slender tree trunks, and at its end, more than half hidden by the trees, stood a small ruined pavilion. Very quiet and very melancholy it was, once we'd stepped out from the sunlight into the shade. Hassan stood leaning over the pool, playing with the silver fish.

As soon as he saw us he ran off among the trees and disappeared.

We sat down beside the fountain. "It's really an accident," said Mme de Chamellis, "that you should have found me here. I had planned to leave for Burma almost a month ago. But of course it was impossible. I cannot leave quite yet."

"How long will you be in Burma?"

"I expect to stay in Rangoon for two weeks, then visit Mandalay. Then I go to China."

"And then?"

She brought her hand up to her chin. The fingers were long and beautiful, the fingers of a disappointed and austere man rather than a woman's. She paused for a moment. Every gesture, every word that she uttered, suggested a secret strength and determination. And yet, in her eyes I could detect an odd, momentary indecision, a gleam of human weakness peering through the dark forest of resolution and order. "And then," said she, "I shall cross the Pacific. But don't ask me any further. The deeper one looks into the future, the more unhappy and unsound one's mind becomes. For the time being I stay here." A thin book bound in soft white boards lay on the bench beside her, and her fingers ran nervously to and fro across its surface.

"Death is a terrible thing," she said at last. "It is a specter discovered by man. Nature didn't intend us to know death so intimately. Death breeds hope or despair in us, one of the two. Dreams, theologies. We weren't meant to know that life comes to an end. Animals are far happier.

"Even when I was a child the thought of death terrified me. I would wake up at midnight and burst into tears, and

I'd creep through the dark corridors toward my mother's room and crawl into her bed and she would comfort me. But I could feel *her* trembling, too; I knew she was even more afraid than I." She spoke very slowly, and her hand moved in strange stiff gestures through the air.

A gray bird flew out from the trees and fluttered at the edge of the fountain. For a moment it came to rest on the blue-tiled rim. Then it sprang over the water again, and we could see the silver fish passing in and out of its quivering shadow on the bottom of the pool. It circled happily through the glittering paradise of spray, cried once, twice, three times, then flew up into the dark foliage again and was quiet.

"Everything must change constantly, must strive for the moment that follows," she said in a troubled, hesitant voice. "It's all a process, a becomingness, all of it. Poetry moves us because it reflects and holds captured one moment of human striving. That is all that true poetry can be—the arc that a drop of water builds in the air. All poetry, everything that moves us with its beauty, all love and all mortal wisdom, are merely a process, a reaching forward of man's pathetic little mind into the next moment."

"Yes," said I, happy and excited.

"Yes," said she bitterly, "but, alas! it is the simplest things that are most difficult to remember. How man can be thrown off by a bit of complexity! The unhappiness of being a miracle; yes, that's what's wrong with us all. We are wretched, all of us. Look into our eyes and see. Watch your city-dwellers and see whether they are happy." She looked into my eyes for the first time and smiled. The breeze was blowing through her short thin hair. Suddenly she looked young. "It was very kind of you to come. It has given me much pleasure. But tell me, where are you going now?"

"To India," said I, "on my way to Japan."

She nodded. "When are you leaving?"

"I don't know," said I. "Tomorrow, I suppose."

She rose and walked back toward the gravel path. "Dr. Ainger is flying to Meshed tomorrow morning. I shall ask him to take you. From there you might go with him south to the railway at Duzdab, and then into India. Later on you must visit me, if you can, in Rangoon."

"Thank you very much," said I.

"He is on his way to Malay. I admire Dr. Ainger very much. He has been both generous and kind to my sister. A brilliant man."

And at that moment he himself appeared in the portico. There was a sharp and febrile look on his pale face.

"Dr. Ainger," said Mme de Chamellis, "my young friend is flying to Meshed with you tomorrow." Dr. Ainger looked at me curiously and nodded his head.

14

WE left Teheran at dawn and flew straight toward the tremendous misty region from which the light was beginning to rise and spread. Our pilot was a silent anxious-eyed German, incredibly tall and thin. Ainger and I were the only passengers.

I kept looking at Ainger, sitting beside me. I didn't know what to make of him. There was something ascetic and almost savage in his face. And still, whenever he glanced toward me his eyes carried an oddly personal look, as if he were still seeking, in spite of a deep disgust with the world, to enter the minds of others and to see what human nature might after all have to offer.

At first the land below us was still wrapped in a blue veil. Only the great white peak of Demavand to the north of us rose above the shadow into the area stained by the morning sun.

But soon the veil grew dappled. Bits of yellow mist shifted restlessly across the foothills, and here and there a hillock rose suddenly into the sunlight and faded from blue into pink. We flew high over the weird gorges, deep black scars in the empty land. To the south lay the endless bogs, still silvery and phosphorescent with the moistures of the night. And to the north lay the snow-spotted foothills. On the sunlit altitudes vast triangles of snow were still lying, and these now pierced the gray morning like diamonds.

Slowly I grew to dislike the thin, hawk-like face at my side. We couldn't talk, of course. The roar of the motor was giving me a headache. I was freezing, and nausea was beginning to bud and spread in my belly like an evil swamp plant.

He wore a pince-nez, and across his cheek ran a slender brown scar. Now it was almost invisible, now it grew dark and distinct. I couldn't understand it at all. It looked like a malicious sign, rising and subsiding with the beat of the blood. A fine network of lines covered his face. A dry bird-like face it was, aquiline and keen-eyed. His hair looked tufted and feathery. He didn't look at me at all; his eyes were almost closed. Almost, but not quite. I knew he was wide awake, staring straight ahead as if he were gazing into a mirror, searching for something neither on earth nor in sky. I began to hate him. Even when I looked out into the clouds I could feel my dislike of him growing and growing.

The sun shone clear and strong, the clouds flew into the distant west. Far below us the hills and valleys grew distinct. The eastward slopes turned yellow and glistened, the westward slopes changed into sterile brown.

Now and then we could see a cluster of round-roofed mud huts, or a flock of sheep like pebbles upon the hillside. Once, far to the south, the white dome of a mosque appeared for a minute, and beside it the fine mosaic of city buildings. "Abbasabad," shrieked our pilot. But a moment later it had already disappeared mysteriously into the brown empty slopes.

Once three great hawks swept past us out of nowhere. Down, down we could see them falling with tremendous speed, until at last they were gone, close to the earth and hovering no doubt over the staling flesh of a camel or a mule.

It grew warmer, and very gradually my irritation left me. I looked at Ainger again. He was staring absentmindedly up into the sky. I could see in his face something that had eluded me before—longing. Longing for what I couldn't tell, but the thin lines of desire were there. It is strange how a feeling toward another man rises, bursts into flame, subsides. There is only a certain amount of fuel in any given relationship. Draw a line between any two creatures. There is only so much energy, so much love or hatred, shall we say. Use it up swiftly and it's gone forever. Nurse it along and it will last almost indefinitely. I had learned that before: Krusnayaskov, the Nestorian priest, good old Papadopoulos, the dying countess; there's a flash, it lasts a few minutes or days or weeks; then it dies and there's nothing real left, only the suspicion of a shell, the pathetic flutter of ashes, the merest bit of an echo deep in the cistern when the sound of a familiar name is dropped into the darkness.

The air was growing strange and uneasy. The plane began to rock gently like a rowboat. Suddenly the pilot began to raise the plane, and we crawled up and up until we could see nothing of the world below except a labyrinth of browns and grays. My nose and ears and eyelids and lips all began to ache desperately. The air felt like a sort of quicksand, sponging at us, trying to suck us out of the plane. A thousand tender little leeches seemed to have fastened themselves upon my skin. The whir of the motor grew constantly more violent.

The sun faded, clouds suddenly covered the earth. The air grew damp and little drops of moisture settled on our skin and on the glass and the leather.

The motor was sputtering badly. The pilot shut the throttle and switched off the engine. We were low again, not more than two thousand feet, and now he put the nose of the plane down and then swiftly up again, gliding lower and lower across the flat misty country. Everything was very silent. I could almost hear Ainger breathing.

We lurched violently—once, and again, and a third time. Now we knew that there would be a crash. The pilot didn't move, but just sat, as we did, quietly and in suspense. We rocked gently for a few moments, and then for another moment we seemed to glide straight over the earth and gently up again. Low brown rocks rose into view at our sides, and already we could see the glimmering edge of the brush rising into the gentle rain. The pilot was sitting motionlessly in front of us, leaning forward toward the windshield.

Then it happened. At first only a long silky tearing sound, then the crash of the body against hard rock. The tail of the plane skipped up behind us. There was a little screech. And then it was more quiet than ever; no sound at all except a momentary delicate grinding of metal and rustling of grass beneath us.

Ainger and I climbed out. "Are you hurt?" said he.

I shook my head. "I don't think so." Actually I had only a slight bruise on my right arm. "You?"

But he didn't answer. He was staring at the plane and at the pilot inside.

One side of the undercarriage had collapsed; and the plane's right wing was bruised.

"Look," said Ainger quietly. "He's dead."

I looked. The pilot's long thin body had collapsed like a blade of wheat in the wind. His head was bent over his knees. A metal bar had broken through the side of the cockpit and lay bent across his lap.

Ainger leaned over and touched the metal bar. It was rigid, but it had not entered the German's body. Not enough in any case to have caused death, even though it pressed closely against the dead man's thighs. Ainger turned away and stared across the land. It was still raining slightly. But even while we stood there the rain seemed to change into an elusive mist, and slowly the rocks and hollows around us emerged into clear view. Everything was gray and glistening.

"You wait here," said Ainger. "Build a fire as soon as the sun comes out again. You'll find food in the plane." Suddenly he was a stranger again, a man whom I knew hardly at all, an alert and capable city man. "As for me, I'm going to walk back in the direction of Abbasabad. . . . You'd better stay."

"Abbasabad?" said I.

"Abbasabad's probably a good fifty miles away. Maybe more. But there may be a village nearer."

I didn't remember seeing any villages between Abbasabad and this desolate plateau. But there might have been, of course. "Shouldn't I go along?" said I.

He paused, and looked westward toward Abbasabad. "If I find some one I'll send after you, of course. For the present, I think you'd better stay. . . ." He turned toward me again, like a gaunt indifferent bird, and stared at me without expression.

"I'll see you again before very long," said he. Then he turned away.

"Good-by," said I. "I'll wait here." I sat down and watched him finally disappearing among the endless brown hillocks.

15

THE CLOUDS parted, the sun appeared once more. In less than a minute all the moisture seemed to have been sucked back out of the earth. The wet glimmer faded from the rocks, the grasses grew sere and mottled again.

And it was hot. Unbearably so for a few minutes, until the air grew dry and light again. Even after the sky had become solidly blue once more, some faint oppression remained hanging in the air. High overhead I saw three hawks circling. I could see their shadows in the hollow declivity at my side, twisting and turning like strange creatures under water.

I sat down on the brown gravel. Alone in the middle of enormous Asia. But, thought I, this isn't solitude; this isn't real loneliness at all. The whole sun-stricken country seemed alive, each pebble shone with vitality.

I walked toward a small mound not far from the plane. I didn't want to be near the plane itself. It terrified me. It looked like a great clumsy bird shattered upon the rocks, its tiny head folded forward, nothing left to it at all, dead and hollow with fright.

I felt very thirsty. I stood upon the hillock and looked all around. To the north, the haze of the hills and the remote forests; to the south, the glistening salty stretches; to the east, endless brown earth; to the west, endless brown earth. Below me on my right a serpentine path ran through the mounds and the boulders. It was a dried-up river bed, cracked with the spring sunlight, shimmering like copper dust.

I walked down toward the tufted shore. Everything was dry. Not a drop.

But then I saw in a dark hollow a little red gleam. Yes, there among the shadows of the rocks a few drops of water were still waiting. Waiting to be sucked into earth and air until nothing was left.

I lay down flat and leaned over the little red pond. The water smelled like corroded lead. I drank, and I could feel it gliding all the way down into my belly like a slim warm snake. I looked at the water again and I could see tiny red animalcules floating in its hairy recesses. I began to feel sick again.

I started to rise, but a delicate weariness tugged at me and held me back. So I turned back and lay down upon the smooth brown river-dust and closed my eyes.

Physical uneasiness can instil odd thoughts into the mind—thoughts frilled up in all their elaborateness, in all the bizarre intuitive fullness of a dream. I thought for a few seconds that I was dying, was on the very verge of death, was almost dead. "Are you afraid of death?" I could hear the old countess whimpering through the perfumed curtains: "What do you think of death? When do you want to die?" Dimly I could hear her voice continuing. "Think about death," she whispered, "think of these thousands of creatures, here in Teheran, here in Persia, here in Asia. Moving across the sand, living in mud, crawling through the alleys of the dark neglected cities, dying in the reeds beside a river without a name, living and dying with nothing, not even a scrap of paper to state that they existed; dying and living, living and dying, the two processes growing faster and faster as our world grows older and staler, now almost as indistinguishable as the colors in a revolving wheel. Where's the one? Where's the other? Here's a living one that's dead, here's a dead one still alive, a living one's dead life slowly dying, a dead one's living death slowly dying. What can you make of it? Anything? Anything at all?"

I was feverish, of course. This is what I thought—that for a brief while I actually had died, that for a few seconds I was dead, had entered the darkness, was experiencing the first throbs of a dissolution about to spread inside me as at the sound of a gong. And then, there was a confusion of signals. Something went wrong at the switches, some misunderstanding occurred, some slight error on the control boards. By the merest accident I slipped back into life. I was alive.

But everything exists forever, nothing ever vanishes completely. Each second goes off into space and is held there forever, traveling and spreading with unalterable speed, the sight of it now reaching Betelgeuse on an unbelievable arrow of light, the tiniest ray of it now filtering through the circles around Saturn. Somewhere now is flashing the sight of Hannibal crossing the Alps, of Xerxes passing into Asia Minor, of the first ape-man rising out of the green twilight of the swamps. And somewhere, I thought, I am still dead. At some point in space a million miles away a flash of light is now carrying me outward caught in the momentary state of death. And now ten thousand miles farther. And now still farther. Somewhere I am still dead, thought I, and I'll carry the thought of that with me for the rest of my life.

I opened my eyes. It was growing dark already. A mile away across the waste I could see the plane leaning upon the rocks like a huge moth, wings brittle in death. Now I felt really and profoundly alone. It was a new thing;

I could never have imagined it. It was as if I were wearing a mask, or were made out of wax, or were growing scales instead of skin. My body was beginning to feel unreal. The fading light on the dead stalks two feet away might as well have been the gleam of a star in the deep heaven.

I turned and looked at the dry river bed. High above it, passing slowly through the gathering dusk, I could see faint shapes passing westward. The shapes of the newly dead. A regular caravan of them. There they were, the dim astonished spirits moving out of their old life. To hell, or to heaven? There was no telling. Some looked stiff and virtuous, others limp and degenerate. Some appeared to be overwhelmed with delight, others bleak with detestation. Most of them surprised me; they were people of a kind whose existence I should never have suspected. People who had spent their life in some sort of hiding. But now they had to move into the open; they couldn't hide any longer: women with their hair shaved, hands clasped in prayer; others without eyes, horribly fat, the capitalists of the spirit; others dead of starvation, with faces like lamps in a forsaken alleyway; others hideously, exhaustingly insane; a few with faces made wonderfully expressive by lust, revealing every possible variety of degradation and decay; the unemployed ones, dead without hope, eyes not knowing where to look for mercy and mouths wide open in a voiceless, grief-stricken shriek of accusation; several quite rigid with solitude, men like dried trees, arms raised in supplication—cripples and suicides; those dead in battle, lips pressed together with a sudden devastating understanding, eyes bleeding; four or five with eyes exquisitely tender—they were the protected ones, the stupid ones, the lucky flower-like ones whom life hadn't touched; and finally the children, with hard malicious eyes and bodies beautiful as ferns. More and more of them, more and more thickly they seemed to pass, now like a herd of dark slender animals, now like a great funnel of fog swiftly expanding. Then they grew hazy. The sky grew darker. Soon they would be gone, soon it would all be over, none would be left. None at all, nothing, not a trace.

When I opened my eyes again the sky was dark, the land was hidden in a strange flickering shadow. Firelight. And high above me, the usual stars. Then I felt my body moving gently, and when I looked again I saw that I was lying on a couch and that a dark bare-chested man was gently massaging me.

When he saw that I was awake he stopped and looked at me questioningly. He murmured in a rich low voice something that I couldn't understand. I stared blankly. He murmured something else. Still I didn't answer. Then he said, in a broken almost incomprehensible accent, "Perhaps Englishman, speaking English?"

I nodded. He looked pleased.

I raised my head and glanced around. I was lying on a rug outside a tent, and beside this tent stood another tent, and beyond this a third one, large and elaborate. I could see slender tree trunks shining in the firelight, and lying on the grass in front of the fire four great spotted dogs, jowls resting between their paws.

"Very sick," said the big brown man, "very sick." He shook his head sadly. "But better now, much better." He nodded his head.

I breathed deeply. "Did you find me?" I asked him.

He looked puzzled for a moment. Then he smiled and nodded again.

"And you brought me here?"

He thought for a moment. "No, camel brought you here."

I pointed at the tents. "Your home?"

He smiled again, a great white-toothed rich-lipped smile. Sweat was dripping from his bearded chin and his eyebrows. "No, not home." He nodded toward the largest of the tents. "Prince Ghuraguzlu he go hunting here."

I could see naked sweating boys passing back and forth in front of the fire, carrying pots and dishes in and out of the tent. A fierce-eyed old man in a huge white turban was squatting beside the fire, stirring and stirring away in a big black bowl.

"Do you serve Prince Ghuraguzlu?" said I. He nodded. "What is your name?"

He looked embarrassed. "Rama Singh," he replied, gazing downward. His eyelids shone like satin, his lashes cast long slanting shadows on his cheek bones.

He must have brought me several miles, thought I. We were in the hills, the earth smelled rich and mossy, the larch trees were rustling in the hot night wind.

Presently Rama Singh rose and walked into the big tent. A minute or two later he reappeared. He leaned over me. "Feeling better?"

I nodded.

"Prince Ghuraguzlu desiring to see you."

He put his strong male-smelling arm under me and helped me to my feet. Then he led me slowly into the tent.

Prince Ghuraguzlu was lying on a couch. Only a single candle was burning in the tent, and at first I didn't see him at all. Great tiger and panther hides were lying on the ground, and in the corner a little bare-breasted girl was singing so softly that I could scarcely hear her.

"Come, my friend," said the Prince gently, "I should

like to speak to you. I understand that you are an Englishman."

"An American," I replied modestly.

He glanced at me. "I thought so. You don't look like an Englishman." His voice was clear and melodious. The candle-light was slanting dimly across his damp body, fell on his thin brown thighs, lit upon a wisp of hair here and there and left his face in darkness. He was smoking an opium pipe. The air was hot and stuffy, odorous with the twisting opium smoke and his gradual perspiration. The heavy silk hangings were moving very gently.

"Tell me how you happened to be lost here." I could see his face now, very faintly. It was of an astonishing fineness. His eyes glittered with curiosity. "Be seated, my friend."

I sat down on a panther rug and began. "This morning we left Teheran . . ."

"No, no," he cried gently. "Begin at the beginning. Tell me the whole story. Where were you born, for instance? What interesting things have happened to you? Don't feel timid. Tell me everything, everything."

So I told him. Presently the little brown girl stopped singing and fell fast asleep on the black fur rug in the corner.

 I stayed with Prince Ghuraguzlu for two days. On the third day the tents were taken down, folded, loaded on the backs of the camels, and we started off toward Meshed. "My home is in Meshed," said the Prince, "and I shall take you there. You may stay as long as you wish. As long, that is to say, as you interest me." He smiled demurely.

We passed through the Kavir, that huge Persian quag-

141

mire. The camels were forced to wade through long stretches of liquid mud, through waterholes, across sharp stony patches, and occasionally, as we approached a village, across wide muddy canals. We passed two mule caravans, and after we reached the regular Teheran-to-Meshed road we met numerous post-carriages and motor-trucks passing both ways. Now and then we saw single donkeys under terrific loads of grain and fagots, and twice we saw Junker airplanes flying high overhead.

We stopped at tea-houses and ate sardines and biscuits and drank dark tea. Everyone was smoking opium. Old men sat in the shadows, nursing their sore feet and grumbling. The innkeeper would make a great fuss when we arrived, but everyone else looked dull and discontented and lazy. We spent the night in a serai outside Nishapur. Everywhere, accompanying us as inevitably as the tinkling of the bells, was the smell of sweat and of opium. The heat kept me weary and feverish all day, and at night I was forever dreaming ominous and frightening things.

Slowly we crossed the salty lands toward Meshed.

16

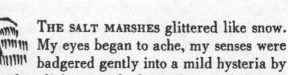

THE SALT MARSHES glittered like snow. My eyes began to ache, my senses were badgered gently into a mild hysteria by the icy flicker of sunlight upon the lands that rippled away to the left. Thin and contemptible thoughts shot in and out of my mind; bits of irritability, splinters of suspicion, of jealousy, of detestation, of loneliness, of wicked understanding. Everyone around me and everyone I'd ever known appeared to me during these three hours in a glassy unpleasant light. And I swore to myself that I'd keep clear of them all. Watch them if you wish, so I muttered to myself: but don't let them toy with you, don't let them wriggle their way into that part of you that matters. Be alone. Be strong. Be proud. I glanced at Prince Ghuraguzlu and decided that he was an effete, a doomed man. He was wearily wiping the sweat from his forehead with a black kerchief.

We stopped beside a pool under a mulberry tree. Three veiled women, grotesque, bat-like, fluttering things with hidden eyes and sharp white claws, rushed out of a mud hut with tea and sherbets. But the tea tasted like ink, the sherbets had begun to ferment. We motioned them away and they watched us silently from their doorway while we rested and scratched our backs in the shade of the mulberry tree.

Then we crept over a glittering hillock and the holy

city appeared suddenly among the mountains. Not in the least spectacular, for such a sacred and remote place; quite calm, oddly colorless, as if an immovable fog had been slanted down upon the smooth hollows from whose midst its minarets arose with feathery delicacy. Not until we came nearer and nearer, and the pure blue of the minarets and the gold of the greater domes grew vivid at last in the clearing air, not until then did it look convincing, look truly like a place that had anything at all to do with men. And even then, something impressed me as a bit singular; somehow apocryphal; as if all the filthy little urchins whom we now encountered outside the gate, and the veiled women above the gate, were guarding with their tittering and bickering and leering the entrance to something we hadn't been expecting: the entrance to another time, shall we say? rather than to another place.

. But it's odd. That, of course, is what one feels on approaching a new thing; timidity, mystification, a sort of poetry and surprise which presently evaporates more or less forever. More or less, I say, for possibly it is this first feeling of remoteness and mystery that is really the closest to the truth; and now and then one can't help gliding suddenly and startlingly back to this first feeling, especially at those dusky moments when one's touching the very things that are closest. One wonders. One doesn't quite understand. But of course the truth is that the intimacy and closeness were all an intricate hoax, an ingenious dream, a subtle but half-hearted mirage.

That is what I thought once I'd entered the city. And so I concluded: don't be strong; don't be alone; don't be proud; it's your only chance ever to understand anything at all. Be fragile, be tender, humiliate yourself, and let the discoloration of dream close in on you. Do that, and oddly enough you'll remain healthy; you'll be yourself; you'll discover the best way to live in this particular most fruitless and tantalizing of possible worlds. The reality becomes a cruel dream while the dream fades into a tender man-made reality.

It was Muharram, the month of mourning. People wandered wailing into the streets even while we were entering them. They tore their hair, they prostrated themselves on the dry rutted alleyways, they scratched aimlessly and absent-mindedly at their flesh until they bled and had to weep with pain and excitement. "Sometimes they die, just out of sheer despair," observed Prince Ghuraguzlu. "It's the holiest possible sort of death, of course."

An hour after we'd arrived a wind went whistling through the streets and drew in its wake a soft gray rain. Black tents of mourning were set up, black carpets were laid out, black banners fluttered mistily on every side like crows fluttering to a halt upon the eaves.

But the rain didn't make any difference at all. The streets remained as crowded as ever; we could hardly thread our way through the dark, spiritless clamor. Everyone cried "Zoh! Zoh!", tom-toms were beaten incessantly, dervishes sat in the cellar stairways and foamed at the mouth. There was no end to the self-torture and the wailing, to the bloody faces and the weeping eyes. Several there were that looked really sick; gray in the face and uneasy. A scattered few, however, looked happy and seized the festive opportunity for eating sweetmeats and drinking fruit sherbets, as well as something else in long green bottles. Some of them were already drunk and boisterously crying "Zoh! Zoh!" along with the rest of them and turning somersaults in the bazaars.

And the rain, discouraged, fled. The wind disappeared, the banners hung limply, the sun began to play with the glimmering wet domes.

෴෴෴ Prince Ghuraguzlu took me straight to his home. Disappointingly shabby from the outside, I thought to myself. Gray, forbidding, streaked with the drippings and droppings from the rain gutters.

But then he led me through a dark hallway into his garden. The sun was out now and raindrops were hanging from every conceivable place—from the yellow roses, from the lips and ears and finger tips of the sorrowful statues, from the rusty railing around the fountain, from the white dove's wings, from the black hyacinth-jars beside the pool.

"This is very pretty," said I.

"Oh, no, no, no! Ugly!" he said, smiling at me with shining eyes. "I have a much prettier one in Teheran. Very much prettier. You would think so, too. Much more modern. With chromium-plated chairs in the latest European manner, and gray leather cushions from Vienna." He smiled slyly.

He walked up to the fountain and allowed three, four, five drops to fall upon his finger tips. For a minute he stood motionless, expressionless. He looked very spoiled and rather feminine. His lips had a natural pout to them; they curved softly but perceptibly downward. His forehead was wrinkling, and his painted eyes took on a sulky look. Bored and haughty. But also unhappy. There was something both hopeless and imploring in those finger tips outstretched beside the coruscating arcs of the fountain.

He turned to me. "How happy are you?"

"Happy?" said I. "I don't know. Contented, at any rate."

◇◇◇◇◇◇◇◇◇◇◇◇◇◇◇◇◇◇◇◇◇◇◇◇◇◇◇◇◇◇◇◇◇◇◇◇

"But happy?" He was flicking the drops from his finger nails. "That's what I wish to know. And I'll tell you why. . . . I think you are Asian at heart. It shows in your eyes."

"And you think . . ."

"A true Asiatic is never very happy. Because he desires nothing that he can see or touch. He looks forward to nothing in this life, be he a Mohammedan or a Buddhist or a Hindu or a Confucian. Or a Christian. He has given up hope in life."

"But I haven't given up hope!" I said anxiously.

He gazed at me. "Yes, you have. Soon you will believe in a God."

Two very pretty girls with long golden chains hanging from their ears stepped into the garden with lacquer trays. Mocha coffee in tiny blue cups, and candied citrons and pistachio nuts. One of them carried on her arm a black satin robe, and this my host now took from her and hung around his shoulders. Then he sat down. He looked very wretched. "Yes," he said, running his fingers along the silver line of embroidery on the cape, "I too am Asian, alas! You may recall that I said that the mourners sometimes die out of sheer virulent despair? I too shall probably die, sooner or later, out of despair. A slow despair, however, a long and terrible ennui."

"And that is Asia?"

"Asia . . . well," he said, "the thing about Asia is its vagueness, really. There you have it. Despair is perhaps too definite and startling a word. Allow me to enlarge. There is a sense of people searching for something over long centuries; not finding it precisely: never being quite sure: growing absent-minded: beginning to forget what they were looking for, to forget that they were looking for anything. . . . Do you perceive?"

I nodded. He didn't take any of the sweets, and so I was taking them, one by one. They had a strange roseate taste about them.

"At the moment they are being disturbed. The West has sneaked in." Behind him went the lazy, silvery drip-drip of the fountain, weaving through the air like a swarm of fat honeybees. "Europe and America have entered, like one chemical poured upon another, and bubbles are arising. Things are changing. Life is fastening itself on death. But death is fastening itself on life, too. And there can be only one ending. The Asiatics know. They are no fools. They are past fear. . . . Indeed, what have we to fear? Death? Nonsense! We've made death a part of our lives. We've woven it straight into our lives. Everything we do, just look at it closely, look again, and you'll see that death's right there, running like a silver thread through the pattern. . . . Do you grasp my meaning? Or am I being too figurative?"

"No," I said. "I grasp your meaning. I understand. But there is still one thing I wish to know. . . . Why do you call me an Asiatic? Do I have death, too? Do you detect the silver thread?"

He looked at me out of the corner of his eyes. Then he smiled blandly. "No, no. Not that. I said that you were an Asian merely so that you would feel that I am your friend. I wish to be hospitable. . . . But," and he smilingly puckered up his lips, "I suspect that you are a very vain man."

He led me into his library now, a large and beautiful room, but very dark. Most of the books were in a script that I could not read. Some of them were in manuscript, very handsomely colored and illuminated with gold and silver. But there were many Occidental volumes, too, sumptuously bound in various leathers, tooled and inlaid, some of them even jeweled. The sunlight from the window slanted diagonally across them, and I could see that the light of years had faded all of the volumes on which the sun was now resting. Those above had remained dark and lustrous, the golden lettering still luminous and exact.

I looked at the titles: Catullus, Persius, Juvenal in pigskin; Seneca, Lucretius, Pliny in vellum; Montaigne, Pascal, Ariosto in full calf; Bacon, Burton, Browne in black morocco. "But I never read them," said Prince Ghuraguzlu regretfully. "They are too exhausting, too pretentious, too energetic. I myself prefer," and he smiled sweetly, "poems about roses, nightingales, kisses. Omar, Hafiz, and so on, you know. Even Firdausi."

I smiled back at him. "Where did you buy them?"

"In Cambridge," he said. "They were very expensive. I think the bookseller cheated me. Oh dear, dear! I am always being cheated." He sighed reminiscently.

He turned to me suddenly. "But you," he said, "you are my friend. I am afraid you will think me very rude. . . . You need money?"

"No, no . . ." I began.

"Yes, yes!" he said. "You do!"

"But really, I can easily . . ."

"You do need money! And I shall give you some."

"My dear Prince, I couldn't dream of . . ."

"Please, please! The thought of your starving would make me wretched. I couldn't bear it." He reached into his pocket.

"You are much too kind, indeed you are, and I don't know how to . . ."

"Please!" he said sternly. "For my sake! My peace of mind! There you are. . . . No, put it in your vest pocket. . . . There are so many thieves. . . . I can't even trust my own servant boys."

Then he said, "Come. You must meet my wife." So he

led me by the hand to another courtyard, a larger one, already tufted with bits of April green and flat bowls full of jonquils. There was a pool here, too, shaded by two lemon trees, and around the pool four women were squatting. He led me to the youngest one, a mere slip of a girl and very lovely. She had kohl painted in huge circles around her eyes; the tips of her fingers, the palms of her hands and the ends of her toes were all painted a bright golden color. "This is my young wife," said the Prince.

I bowed and smiled. She gazed at me like a statue. She looked very much like a doll, a delicate porcelain doll without any life of her own. The other women were shifting to and fro, smelling like wilted flowers, pompous and fanciful. A servant appeared while we were standing there, and placed a trayful of opium pipes on the paving beside the pool. We watched the women, each painstakingly placing the pellet in the round porcelain bowl, and then, as they began to smoke, their eyes growing distant and ornate.

When we were leaving them, four old men bowed and entered the twilit courtyard. One of them carried a covered tray, another carried a basket of bottles, the third carried two large embroidered bags, the fourth carried a little green notebook. "Who were they?" I asked the Prince as we walked slowly along the dark hallway.

"Those," he replied, "were the seller of sweets, the seller of perfumes, the seller of silks, and the seller of local gossip."

"Well, good-by," I said at last, pausing at the doorway. The street lamps were already being lit, one by one.

"Good-by." His voice sounded curt and constrained.

"You've been very kind to me, Prince Ghuraguzlu."

"Nonsense. . . . Kindness. It's only a word. It doesn't exist really, I swear it doesn't. All that exists is favoritism, or fear. And sometimes they just look like kindness. No,

◇◆◇◆◇◆◇◆◇◆◇◆◇◆◇◆◇◆◇◆◇◆◇◆◇◆◇◆◇◆◇◆◇◆◇◆◇

I'm not kind. You have been a good listener. I like you. Therefore I appear to be kind. But it isn't kindness at all. . . . Well, good night."

"Good night, Prince Ghuraguzlu. You've been exceedingly kind. . . ."

He sighed. "No, no," he said. "Good night, my friend, and a happy journey."

"Thank you, Prince Ghuraguzlu." I lingered for one more moment at the darkening doorway. Then I shook his hand. "Good night."

"Ah, good night." His eyes shone happily, his voice was once again soft and cordial.

ＸＸＸ The next morning I found a slender young Baluchi who was driving a truck through to Quetta. Yes, he said, there'd be room for me, too, if I felt sufficiently inclined to pay. The only other passenger would be his uncle, who was very old and very thin; so that there'd surely be room for three in the front seat.

"How much?" I asked.

He paused, shading his eyes from the glaring morning sun. His skin gleamed like gold, shone like satin. He was a dirty lad, his hair was a curly mass, vaguely bluish with oil and dirt. But there was a real elegance about him, a fine, delicate profile, long melancholy eyes, heavy shining lids, long-lashed.

"Twenty krans," he said, glancing at me out of the corner of his eyes.

"Very well," said I.

"But that will take you only to Birjand," he added quickly.

"Aha," I thought, "I've let myself in for it again." I pondered a moment. "How much for the whole journey?" I asked shrewdly.

"Fifty krans," said he, "for the whole journey, from the beginning to the end. All the way."

"What is your name?" I asked.

"Ahmed," he replied thoughtfully.

"Well, all right," I said at last.

"But," he exclaimed, "you must pay my poor old uncle something too. Twenty-five krans for him. That is not much. He is a very thin man and needs much food. . . ."

I walked about in the caravanserai. We were only a stone's-throw from the Russian border and from the Transcontinental Railway. So there were all sorts of strange people lying about, fuzzy blue-veined mountainous-looking people with long knotted beards. Fast asleep, all of them, in their sweat-drenched clothes. There were a few camels lying beside the trough, and three or four lorries waiting outside. All of them, including the camels and the lorries, looked sulky and apathetic even in their sleep. Even though their glistening eyelids were closed, one could be sure of what a slow, fierce look lay there beneath them.

Soon my satin-skinned boy came running up to me in a great state of excitement. "Sir, there's cholera."

"Cholera?"

"There's news of cholera raging in Samarkand and in Bokhara. It is approaching. It has crossed the border. Two cases of it in Meshed already. It's moving southward at a great rate. Very dreadful."

"Well," I said, "perhaps it's just as well we're leaving tomorrow, in that case."

"Yes," said he. "But you must pay me!"

"I'll pay you half of it tomorrow, when we leave."

"But you must pay me more than you said! There are so many people wanting to leave Meshed. I am in great demand!"

"You scoundrel!" said I. "How much?"

He smiled. "No, sir. No, I'm not lying about the cholera. One hundred krans for the whole journey, everything included, even my poor thin uncle. Yes? No? Yes?"

That was exactly half of what my generous prince had given me. "You're a little thief," said I. But there must have been something disarming in my voice, and he was quick to see it. He looked at me with a sly grin which almost imperceptibly grew soft and bashful. He lowered his eyelids. "Sir, yes, sir. Tomorrow, sir?" He danced across the courtyard, drank hurriedly at the fountain, and disappeared. But what was it, what could it have been, in his eyes, his voice, that made me feel so suddenly uneasy? What gave me that brief little fit of the terrors as I stood there hesitating? A fear for myself, here, now? And yet not only for myself here and now, but also for all these others, Persia, Asia? Something was wrong, yes, something had frightened me.

But only for a moment. Beyond the fountain fell the blue shadows of the arches and the pillars. Calm and steady they fell on the sunny cobblestones which with the years had begun to rise and fall like low waves in a lake.

We left Meshed deep down in its hazy valley and started upward toward the hills. Past Muhammad Mirza, where the snow and ice still shone like taffeta in the April dawn. Past the roadside stations, the deserted tea-houses built out of mud, past the frosty, misty hollows of salt. Ahmed's lips were pale with the cold, and the old uncle tucked his finger tips into his long white beard to keep them warm. He remained silent, absolutely silent, from the beginning of the journey to the end. Not once did I hear him say a word. Now and then he groaned gently, or grunted or belched or sneezed. But all attempts at verbal communication he had surely dismissed as vanity years and years ago.

The high desert past the Muhammad Mirza Pass gleamed with the blue frost. A metallic sort of atmosphere, and I could taste the sulphur in the air as we chugged uphill. An icy wind came up just as the sun flashed out across the blue pebbles.

But cold all day long. Higher and higher till we passed Turbat-i-Haidari. Then down, very slowly. And late at night we camped in a hidden valley thick with fog. I could see Ahmed and the old white uncle moving back and forth among the stones like people on a frothy beach. There might have been miles of ocean beyond them, for all I could see in this hazy darkness.

17

A WARM damp hand caressing my forehead awoke me. "It is morning, sir. Come, come, we must be in Birjand before dusk." The sun was out already, the little valley was warm and clear.

Ahmed stripped and dove into a stagnant salt pool while the old uncle proceeded to fry something sweetly odorous over a fire. Sleepily I watched the thin smoke rising straight into the Persian sky, up and up. And then out of the red pool came Ahmed, lithe as a snake. Laughing and dripping with watery sunlight, he ran up to dry himself at the fire. His skin was almost hairless, his buttocks were smooth as satin. He squatted beside the flame and the salt dried in thin white veins across his nipples and over his belly. All the rest of the day the smell of that mineral pool hung on him.

We started off across the empty valley. Once, as we stopped, we glimpsed behind the brushes a dead man lying among the stalks. There was a long pink scar across the shriveled skin which the dew and the fog had washed clean of blood long ago. His empty hands were curved, looking for something to hold, and the huge questioning eyeballs seemed to be looking for something too, for one more illusion perhaps

The next day we met more traffic. Motor-trucks with Baluchi drivers bearing rugs and asafœtida from

India; others overflowing with pilgrims bound for holy Meshed; and one or two mule caravans, slow and wistful as the clouds above them.

We passed the whitened skeleton of a camel and saw some jackals far off across the plain. The sun was blazing hot, terrific; a thick, unwholesome atmosphere shimmered in the vales as we descended toward Birjand.

Birjand was a desolate and filthy city. The central street was a deserted river bed, yellow with dust and pockmarked with the bubbling heat. Out of the distance some vultures came wheeling and circled over the hideous buildings until we left. And the people were hideous, too. Two old women in green rags were the first ones we saw, and then a blind man, and then a tall, sleek man in a Homburg hat who watched us like a weasel as we slowly plowed through the sand.

"I don't like this place," said I. "Do we have to spend the night here?"

"Yes," said Ahmed. "We always spend the night here. Always. It isn't such a bad city, sir. I can show you one or two places where we can go and . . ."

"Never mind about them," said I finally. "I don't want to hear any more about them." But he'd already told me everything about them, of course.

We had hardly entered the city, though, when we realized that something was wrong. The people didn't notice us at all; they looked frightened and shadowy. A peculiar darkness hung over the streets—the inexplicable accompaniment to the sorrowing human spirit that somehow the atmosphere of a place always contrives. Ahmed sensed it right away. He knew what it was without being told. He remained quiet as he drove along the wide central street. Then he said, "Cholera."

And instantly we could see it all. The shapes at the door-steps were not sleepers, the bundles of clothes in the street were not for sale. A smell of rot everywhere. All of the people tense and dry-eyed; merely frightened; not struck into any sort of activity or to pity or to tears. Like rag dolls one and all, carrying these heavy sacks between them, clotted with inertia.

"Let's get out," I said.

"But, sir," said Ahmed, "we must sleep here."

"You're mad. We're not sleeping here, you idiot."

"We always sleep here, my old uncle and I. Always." The old uncle looked straight ahead and ran his claws through his beard.

"We're not sleeping here." And then very angrily I said a few more things, and before long we were driving up the slope that rose from the gray city. A mile away from the city Ahmed stopped. There was nothing I could do. He would go no farther. He insisted on sleeping here, and before I could say anything he was already rolled up in his blanket and pretending to be fast asleep. A strange, obstinate fellow, and I never really understood him.

I looked down on the desolate place below. People were washing themselves at the stream, and farther down I could see them bathing the dead bodies and then stitching them up in the black sacks. From there they were carrying the dead—on their backs, in bags, on stretchers—into the dusk beyond the hollow river. A crazy little procession; it resembled some odd sort of obstacle race, slowly moving in silhouette along the banks.

I could guess what would happen. They'd bury their dead in the shallow earth near by. Then they'd unbury them again when the worst was over and wrap them up in black bags with ropes, and they'd carry them on mules to the fœtid sacred places far away—Meshed, perhaps, or Kerbela, or Babylon. And others would grow sick and die along their path.

A shabby little woman was bustling among the dead that lay waiting on the slope. She was holding a gray veil in front of her face with one hand and in the other she was clutching a small bag. I could see her very clearly, for the last ray of sunlight was shining straight upon her. Up and down she crept, a luminous little ghost, stooping now and then over a body, peering, fumbling. Then she scuttled down the path like a ferret and disappeared.

In the city the mollahs and the mushtehids were trying to exorcise the demon by marching round and round the walls. Once they paused to kill a goat and chant a prayer; then the interminable procession continued, and the ceaseless mumbling of words from the Koran. Stray townsmen joined the procession. Hopefully, no doubt. But they were spreading the sickness, and in another day or two many of them would be dead. And no one would know why, no one would understand at all or even try to understand.

I could hear the crickets at my side, and the old man snoring, and Ahmed gasping in his sleep. And far below the mourning over the dead. "Allahu Akbar," the mourners chanted. I could hear the words from where I sat. "Allahu Akbar, Allahu Akbar." Louder and louder, then dying out. Then torchlights in a new place, the chanting from a new direction, from north, south and west. To the east lay the desert and the mountains.

❧❧❧ We were off again at dawn, still southward. We stopped at the tea-houses for food during the next two days. Sometimes they gave us meat, sometimes vegetables. But filthy and odorous, whichever it was. Hourly it grew warmer as we drew nearer to the Gulf, and we sweated in the day even though we froze at night. I could always smell Ahmed beside me—a bad smell if he'd been eating meat, a good clean smell if he'd been eating vegetables.

We went through Sarbisheh, a village of mud huts, many and many of them, with round roofs like beehives. The air over the houses trembled with the late April heat and the black roofs seemed to arise and swell and quiver like gigantic blisters.

"It's too early to stop," said I. "Let's go on."

"There is no other place for miles, sir," said Ahmed. "Sir, we always stop here, my old uncle and I."

"It's too early," said I. "Why stop here? Come, let's go on."

"That will be three krans more, sir, if we go on. Three krans?"

I took three krans out of my inside pocket and gave them to him.

We drove on and on, through the real desert. It was after sunset when we reached a long shallow lake. Two tamarisks stood on the yellow clay shore, nothing else, not a single blade of grass. The rest of the shore was as flat as the lake itself. We stopped here. "But watch, sir," said Ahmed. "Bad place. I have seen two camels lost in the wet sand here. Don't walk in the wicked wet sand!" I was flattered and pleased and surprised by his solicitude. The water was smooth as glass, but there were white ripple marks along the blue slimy shore as delicate as the lines on a moth's wing. Far out over the lake some birds were flying, barely visible through the dusk.

We stretched our blankets on the warm sand and drank from the canteen. Then we lay down under the tamarisks.

Ahmed lay on his belly, chin resting on his palms, and gazed at me. "You are a strange man, sir," he said quietly. "Not like the Englishmen or the Europeans." The old uncle lay huddled under the other tamarisk. We could hear him snoring, and now and then a bird fluttering waterward over our heads.

"I am not an Englishman or a European," said I. "I'm an American."

"But they are even worse!" sighed Ahmed. "Aren't they?" he added hesitantly. "They have no god!"

"How do you know that they have no god? Who told you?"

He thought he had offended me. His voice grew silky. "Oh, many have said that, sir, but perhaps they were wrong. Have they a god, after all? Tell me. . . ."

But of course I couldn't tell him, since I didn't know. "Look, Ahmed," said I, "do you believe in a god?"

"Sir, there are different gods for different people, aren't there? Yes? And I believe in a god."

"Do you believe in Allah, and in Mohammed his prophet?"

"Yes, sir."

"In Buddha, too, by any chance? What do you think of Buddha?"

"Oh, I know that Buddha exists, sir, since many people believe in him. But I don't believe in him, you see. He is not my god."

"And what about Krishna?"

"Krishna is like Buddha."

"And Christ?"

"Christ is like Buddha. A fine god, but not mine." He rose and brought a long bottle from the back of the truck. Then he lay down again. "Sir," said he with a certain elegance, "here is wine for you."

"Thank you, Ahmed," said I. I was touched.

"Two krans, sir? Please?"

It was a very strong sweet wine. We continued to talk

about god. Then Ahmed told me stories about the bandits of Baluchistan, and before the bottle was empty his syllables began to tumble weirdly across each other. "Are you afraid of the bandits?" said I. I was feeling tipsy, too, though most of the bottle had gone to Ahmed.

"No, no," laughed Ahmed. "I know them too well! They are foolish, crazy men. I know many of them. I have several cousins that are bandits. They are very stupid. Oh, sir, how stupid they are! Fierce, but how stupid!"

The moon was out and the air was growing sharp. The lake looked icily smooth.

"Sir," whispered Ahmed, and I could smell his breath across the shadow of the tamarisk, I could see his eyes glittering like stars. "How much will you pay me to be your servant? Two hundred krans, sir? . . . I will be a good servant. I will do everything. Two hundred krans?"

I began to laugh. "But I need no servant, Ahmed."

"One hundred and eighty krans, sir? I will do everything. I will travel with you to America. . . ."

"But your poor old uncle!" said I. "Would you leave him?"

Ahmed simpered. "Oh, sir, he is not truly my uncle at all!"

"Oh, Ahmed, I don't need a servant at all! I wouldn't know what to do with you!"

"One hundred and fifty krans, sir? Oh, *please!* I will love you always. I will be your slave. I will do everything."

"Nonsense!" said I, laughing softly.

"One hundred krans," he whispered unpleasantly.

"I don't want you, Ahmed."

"Oh," he sighed, "I am not pretty enough for you? Is that it? Do you wish some one younger and prettier? . . ."

I rose beside the tamarisk and made water toward the

stars. I was feeling dizzy and irritable. "Oh, sir," wailed Ahmed stupidly. "Shut up!" I cried. He rose and stood beside me and made water toward the moon. "Very well, sir," he said. "Very well. I will never love you again, sir." His voice was unnaturally quiet and constrained, his eyes were hard with fury.

The land grew wild and frightful as we traveled toward Duzdab. The desert was as desolate as a plateau on the moon. Once we got stuck, and Ahmed had to pile twigs and brush under the rear wheels to get out again. Once we drove through a narrow gully, steep cliffs on either side that almost met over our heads. We crept across a sunken quagmire six miles wide: foot by foot we plowed through the soft slimy bed, and when we reached firm land again the sun, high and hot a few miles back, had disappeared, the great Sea of Sand was in shadow, the moon was rising again.

We drove on another hour, and then Ahmed and his sad old uncle stopped at a tea-khané to quench their opium thirst. I waited outside. Peculiar music came from the lonely hut—two strange instruments and a voice even stranger. "What was that noise in there?" I asked when Ahmed reappeared.

But Ahmed was very quiet and aloof. "Lovely sad songs," he replied absently. "Lovely songs about love and sadness."

It grew chilly. "We cannot reach Duzdab tonight," said Ahmed. So we stopped at a tamarisk grove and built a fire. Far away we could hear the jackals howling.

"Without the fire," said Ahmed stiffly, "the jackals would come and eat you. But I shall protect you, sir."

"Thank you, Ahmed. Perhaps I'll give you another kran

for that." But he remained cool; he refused to smile. And when I wandered down the road a way he did not come along as usual, but sat down on his blanket and slowly with a dark mystifying gaze began to undress.

He was fast asleep when I returned. Tucked so deeply in his blankets that I could see only a few black curls. And soon I was asleep, too.

Or rather, almost asleep. I could feel the frosty touch of the night against my cheeks and my eyelids, I could hear the embers hissing and singing softly, and far away the weeping jackals.

And then I heard another sound, or so it seemed. I opened my eyes, and there was Ahmed squatting nakedly above me, staring at me wildly, right arm raised against the starry sky.

I could see the flash of the knife catching the moonlight. I sprang. My arms moved upward. The cold soft side of the knife slid gently along my left forearm, and with my left I caught Ahmed by the throat. Then I shook my blankets free and pinned him to the ground. He wasn't strong and he hardly resisted at all. The knife dropped promptly from his hand when I twisted his wrist into the sand.

"Ahmed!" said I.

He remained quiet.

"Ahmed!" I repeated. "I'll kill you for this!"

I could feel his warm brown chest rise and fall with sobbing, I could see his lips working and the tears glittering on his eyelashes.

Suddenly he burst into a loud fit of weeping. "Oh, sir, sir!" he cried. "Oh, forgive me, forgive me! I shall be good forever!" The night was cold, but sweat ran down his forehead and glistened on his shoulder blades.

"Look, my brother," said I, very sadly. "Sit up. Tell me what's troubling you. Maybe I shan't kill you, after all."

He sat up. I held the knife in my left hand, and with the other slung the loose blanket over his shoulders. "Come, tell me."

He kept on sobbing quietly. I could feel his body trembling with fear and wretchedness. He put his hands up to his eyes.

"Come, Ahmed. Behave. Stop acting."

He looked at me. "Oh, sir, I am very sorry, I am a very evil man. Be my friend, sir, and I will always be good again. I will be your slave always. . . ." He began to sob again, and buried his head in my lap. I could see him peering at the knife in my left hand.

"Very well, Ahmed, we'll be friends and shake hands." His hand was wet and tremulous. "Now lie down and go to sleep, you evil man. Behave, or I shall kill you, I swear!"

He lay down and closed his eyes. And so did I. But I couldn't go to sleep. I felt the knife cool against my hip deep under the blanket, and strange thoughts went racing through my head. The moon looked like a silvery knife, the stars were the tears of the wicked ones, the tamarisks were the fingers of those tortured by desire, the earth trembled softly with remorse.

And finally it was dawn, and the hills grew red, and the air grew warm.

18

AND PAINFULLY we plowed southward through the dawn and the red hills and the warming air toward Duzdab. In the middle of a muddy blazing plain we found it—a muddy, blazing town, horrible, poverty-stricken, restlessly but aimlessly busy. It was here that the railway began. And though Ahmed had promised to drive me on to Nushki, I decided in the course of the morning to part from him here. "Ahmed," said I while we were standing in the caravanserai, pouring water over our heads and eating bitter oranges—"Ahmed, I think I shall leave you here." I looked at him out of the corner of my eye. "Good-by."

His eyes grew sad. "Here, sir! But, sir, I am driving on to Nushki!" His voice widened into a wail. "You are going with me to Nushki!"

"But I have changed my mind, Ahmed."

"Oh, please, sir, you must drive on with me to Nushki. I will feel very lonely if you don't drive with me to Nushki. . . . I will behave like an angel, sir, and I will drive you there for five krans less than I said . . . Sir? Please? To Nushki. . . ." His feet performed an anxious little dance on the black paving.

So we left Duzdab and came presently to Mirjawa. This was the frontier between Persia and Baluchistan. I sat wrapped up in a filthy black cape and Ahmed loudly addressed me as "Brother." And the guards, who all appeared to know Ahmed well, smiled quaintly and allowed me to pass. Some women watched us from the yellow tower and coyly waved their delicate dark fingers at us.

"Who are they?" I asked Ahmed. "Why are they in the tower?"

He explained that they were Zoroastrians. During a period of menstruation lasting seven days they were regarded as untouchable and were very strictly locked up. Food was sent up to their tower rooms in pulleyed baskets. "And you shouldn't even look at them, sir," said Ahmed.

Slowly we crossed valley after jagged valley. Baluchistan was less monotonous than Persia and much fiercer. The very land looked war-like. The men we met, the Afridi tribesmen and the Baluchi shepherds, were dark magnificent animals who scowled at us and never uttered a word. We saw the old women drawing water with long black poles, and their daughters tilling the fields. But the men did nothing; they sat sulkily at the roadside, weapons in hand, or shuffled lazily across the fields with the sheep, black ringlets and gray capes blowing in the desert wind. Waiting, waiting, like everyone else, for approaching bloodshed.

One or two disconsolate villages. But mostly stones upon the wild wasted areas. And before I knew it, hour following hot hour indistinguishably, it grew dark again, and with the darkness suddenly cold.

We stopped and built a fire. I looked at Ahmed's face captured in the red firelight. The gentle puzzling lines of his face now gleamed with wickedness. The long lashes and the curling hairs on his temples looked like those of a whore, deliberate and enticing. And yet in that very quality there was a sort of innocence; freedom from a sense of guilt; ignorance of the man-made gulf between bad and good. "Well," I said at last, "this is my last night with you, Ahmed. Tomorrow I shall surely take the train."

"Where?"

"Where? Wherever I can. Nushki, for example."

"There is no train at Nushki, sir." He was behaving very sulkily. Not at all his usual self, and he'd hardly opened his mouth all day long.

"At any rate," said I, "I'm going to bed now. Good night." Secretly, in my heart of hearts, I didn't want to take a train at Nushki at all.

"Good night, sir." He stood and watched me roll up in my blanket.

"Well?" said I. "Aren't you going to bed, too?"

"I can't go to bed yet, sir."

"Why not?"

"I'm not sleepy, sir."

"Come, better go to bed."

"I can't, sir; I'm too awake. I will walk." He looked around, up at the sinister foothills toward Afghanistan.

"Very well. Good night, Ahmed."

I closed my eyes. But I kept watching him through my lashes. He walked off and disappeared among the rocks. I waited. But he didn't return.

The moon was rising again, and far away on the rising pasture land I could see with jewel clearness the black peasant huts and the sloping stone-spotted fields. Three white goats browsing, still as tufts of snow, caught the frosty moonlight. Nothing could have been more peaceful. Close at my side the embers were still glowing.

Later, several hours later it must have been, I heard him return and lie down softly. Through my eyelashes I saw him peering at me. He drew the blanket about his body without undressing, and even after he'd lain there quietly for ten minutes I knew that he wasn't asleep; I heard him shifting furtively to and fro, and the uneven moth-like flutter of his waking breath kept me awake as well.

I gazed northward again toward the foothills. Here everything looked bright and secure; the three white goats lying quiet two miles away and the white moonlight on the near-by stones and the remotest mountains.

Everything bright, secure and quiet. But then, through eyes that were heavy with the desire to sleep, I saw three of the stones shifting, changing shape, casting suggestive shadows. . . . A dream? I looked again. The stars were brilliant and motionless, watchful eyes counting up serenely the good in this huge world on one side and the bad on the other; calm, trustworthy, all-seeing guardians. The Milky Way glittered with their watchfulness.

But the stones? Yes, they were moving, those three. Not slowly now, but quickly, appallingly: I could hear the sand grinding beneath them almost as they rolled toward me. Ah, they weren't stones at all! No stone could run so swiftly and bend so gracefully. I sat up. I cried with surprise. I shouted "Ahmed!" But in another moment the bandits were on me. I felt their hands warm and smelling faintly of women and cattle pressed hard against my lips. Then their knees painfully against my loins and my hands tied swiftly and silently.

In spite of everything, I went to sleep at last. And when the morning sunlight awoke me I saw that I had not been dreaming. With sorrow I saw my guardian sitting at the door of the tent and gazing at me vacuously. When he saw that I was awake he turned and called to some one outside.

Another man appeared. A tall saturnine man clad in sheepskins, skin cracked with sunburn, teeth white as a fish's belly. He too gazed at me with an empty curiosity, and then came up to my side.

I tried to sit up. But I couldn't, the ropes were holding my arms, wrist against hard wrist. I could only roll over clumsily. I must have looked very sheepish, for the newcomer laughed like a child and then squatted smilingly at my side.

He looked at me carefully from head to foot. Then he said, quite amiably, "Money?"

My lips were swollen and bulbous where they had gagged me. "It's yours," I lisped, "you can have it all."

He looked questioningly toward the other. The other one came up and mumbled something. Then he turned to me and said, "Speak to *me*. I speak English and Russian. . . . Then I tell *him*. You understand? He knows only that one word in English—money." He smiled.

"You can have all my money," I repeated. "Only," and I tried to speak as pleasantly as I could even though my lips were bloody and throbbing, "you must let me go, of course."

He stared at me. Then he smiled. He mumbled again to the tall saturnine man who was squatting at my side. The saturnine man nodded. Then they walked out of the tent together, silently.

🙰🙰🙰 They freed my wrists and ankles and allowed me to sit beside the door. I could watch them shooting the dice under the dusty trees and the big-breasted women moving duskily inside the huts.

Mine was the only tent, and it grew nightmarishly hot under the black canvas as soon as the sun rose high over the hills.

A dark-blue heaven, no single cloud. The sky was almost

like a night sky, so dark against the blazing stones. The rays of the sun had an edge like a dull knife: I stretched my hand through the doorway into the golden out-of-doors; it pierced, it stung. Only the grasshoppers and the locusts went leaping up and down the path. Every tiny sound was sharp and metal-perfect, like the sound of wires moving in the wind at the touch of sand against a copper kettle. And with things seen and smelled it was the same. Each sunny blade of grass a fine pin-prick, the tent smell sulphurous on the tongue and eyes and nerves.

I could feel the sweat trickling down my back and running from the armpits down to the hips. Drops hung from my lashes, I could scarcely see, and the whole glittering world swayed and quivered.

A skeleton of a man in a great white cape crept past my doorway. He was carrying a long club and a gourd shell full of water, dervish fashion. Every now and then he dipped his fingers into the gourd shell and tossed the drops upon his forehead. He leered at me savagely as he passed. A penetrating yet unseeing gaze, as if he were looking through me as through glass down corridors scarcely human; the dangers of seeing too profoundly. His eyes were like the hollows in a skull, empty and desperate; no life left in that desert of a man except the quiver of heat across the dry sands.

Soon my guardian reappeared with a small red bowl balanced on the palm of his hand. "Soup for you," he said, and placed it politely on the ground beside me.

Then he squatted in the twilight beside the doorway and watched me.

But just as I was about to taste the oily mess the doorway flapped in a sudden gust of wind and a brisk tattooing sound flickered across the tent: all in a moment, and in another moment the air was filled with locusts, locusts swung idiotically against my face, fell on my lap, dripped nastily into the soup. The path outside was covered with their glimmering bullet bodies. My eyes ached from the brittle peppery touch of their wings and I could feel one, two, three of them clinging like syrupy bread crusts in my hair.

Quickly my guard closed the flap of the doorway. The tent was dark and silent now. I could scarcely see him squatting once more upon the ground two yards away.

The soup had a sweetly acrid taste: five locusts were floating hypnotically in the grease. I set it aside and began to feel sick. "I can't eat this," I said.

My guardian kept watching me. Half shyly, half expectantly, like a naughty boy watching his elders. Black curls hung wetly from his skull cap down into his forehead. Dimly I could see the perspiring eyelids and the wet lips, lips forever ready to burst into a smile, I felt sure; but timidly so, and the smile was never quite fulfilled. He didn't trust me, naturally enough. There was a questioning look in his big black eyes.

"I can't eat this soup," I repeated.

He looked at me sympathetically, almost sadly. He leaned over and fished out the locusts with mud-black finger tips, one by one. Then he smiled at me. "Now it is good again."

But when I didn't take it he said, "Some other soup?" and then, "Bread?" and then, "Water?" I nodded, and he went and fetched me a jar of lukewarm water.

I asked him to pour it slowly over my neck and my shoulders. Then I cupped my hands and washed my hot face in it. I felt more comfortable now. The locust storm was over; it was quiet again.

He sat down beside me and began to ask questions.

"Have you ever been in New York?" he asked with great seriousness.

I nodded.

"Is it a beautiful and wealthy city?"

Both wealthy and beautiful, I replied; but only in spots; not everywhere; very much of it ugly and poor, in fact.

"Beautiful golden domes?" he asked. "Like Ispahan?"

"There are some fine silver domes, and one or two golden ones as well, I think. Taller than those at Ispahan, I am sure, but perhaps not so beautiful."

"Is it a learned city?" Like Shiraz?"

I hesitated. Well, I said doubtfully, not really very learned. Less learned than Shiraz, perhaps. About as learned as Teheran.

He sucked at his lips. Then he glanced at me through his lashes and smiled.

"Are there handsome people there? Soft-breasted women? Strong warrior men?"

"Well," I sighed, "the people are disappointing, to be frank with you. There lies the actual weakness of the city. They are really rather ugly. There are exceptions, of course. But most of them are soft and ugly and selfish. And they are always pretending."

He looked very disappointed. "Then I do not wish to go to New York."

We talked and talked till late afternoon. The sun descended slowly, slowly the heat grew bearable. He told me about his family and about his fellow bandits. "They are very stupid," he said. "Much stupider than the Persians or the Americans." He lay stretched out on the ground with his toes in the circle of sunlight at the doorway.

"They are cruel, though," he said. "They treated their

prisoners with great cruelty when I was a boy. Now they are afraid. But they would still like to be cruel and torture their prisoners. . . . They would like to torture *you*, I think, you are so young and limber."

"Do you think they will?" said I, rather anxiously.

He shook his head.

Once, he continued, they used to club their prisoners to death. Or they would strip them and burn the sacred symbols on their backs and their bellies. Or they would mutilate them, castrate them, perform cruel amputations. "The women would watch from their doorways and shout with happiness." And they would be imprisoned in loathsome cellars, vermin-infested and full of the smell of excrement and wounds.

"All for a bit of ransom money?"

"Oh no, not for the ransom money. All for pleasure. It is so boring here, you see, we long for excitement."

"And cruelty is the only excitement you can think of."

"Ah, it hurts us too sometimes to be cruel, to see the blood flow from a fine young man. But the sight of blood and death is a good thing for us all, says my grandfather. . . .

"Are you an American Indian?" he asked suddenly, as if an idea had suddenly occurred to him. "They grew strong through torturing and watching the blood flow and other men die. I have been told about them by my grandfather."

"No, I'm not an American Indian."

"But you are dark, almost as dark as I. You don't look like a white American. Your skin is smooth and dark, your lashes are long, like my own. You are much like an American Indian. You watch and watch; no one ever knows what you think; you look strong and passionate and sly. Yes, I think you are an American Indian." He smiled pensively.

I told him no, but he wouldn't believe me; he only grinned at me in a cynical manner, as if to say, "After all, it is nothing to be ashamed of, you know!"

Then he said, "Tell me, are you a happy man?"

I nodded. "Most of the time."

"Yes. I knew it." He stared at me absent-mindedly. Then he said: "Do you often feel passionate? Do you have great passionate dreams? Very often? Every night?"

"Not quite every night," I replied modestly.

"I do," he replied very seriously. "Every night. Very passionate. I am very uneasy about them."

"Perhaps you ought to get some women," I suggested.

"Ah, I have tried that too. But it doesn't help. Nothing helps. It is very sad and troublesome!"

I looked through the doorway and saw the shepherds coming home with their flocks and the old women in the twilight kneading the bread. They all looked very indifferent and very stupid. The women were just bundles, nothing more than bundles, some fat, some thin. There were smaller bundles, too, all of them thin, children that hopped about in the dust like crickets and stared at me with sad and serious eyes. But even so, it occurred to me, handsomer and more alive than the people in big New York.

"Do you wish," whispered my guardian, "that I help you?"

I nodded earnestly.

"I will help you to escape, if you wish," he said, still lying motionlessly on the ground. "If you tell, I will kill you, of course. And of course you must give me your money—all of it." He stared vacantly up at the black ceiling. The sunlight was slowly creeping along his brown hairy leg as it sank lower and lower into the western desert. And there was a wind arising, setting the tent atremble, blowing the dust through the door.

◇◇◇◇◇◇◇◇◇◇◇◇◇◇◇◇◇◇◇◇◇◇◇◇◇◇◇◇◇◇◇◇

"Yes," said I. "I'll give you everything. It isn't much, though." I reached into my shoe and pulled out the rest of good Prince Ghuraguzlu's money. A hundred krans it was. "Here," said I. It didn't occur to me to deceive him.

He sat up and looked at it. "That is all?"

"Yes."

"You swear?"

"Yes."

"Not another kran?"

"I swear."

He took it. Fifty krans he slipped under his shirt, the rest he handed back. All very casually; he didn't even trouble to close the flap over the doorway. "You may keep this."

"You are very kind." I was touched. I felt sick and feverish still, my stomach was still turning treacherous somersaults, my temples were throbbing. Yet for a moment I felt truly happy. "Thank you."

He peered at me through his eyelashes. "Now will you always be grateful to me? Will you remember me?" His voice had changed suddenly, shy and soft like a boy's.

I nodded.

Later I said: "Tell me one thing, Mostafa. How did you know I was passing through?"

He hesitated. "Some one told us."

"Who?"

"I must not tell you. You might do him harm."

"You don't wish him to be harmed?"

"No. He is my cousin, and I love him. Some day we shall visit New York, he and I."

"In spite of the ugly, stupid people?"

He smiled gently. "You are deceiving me! The people in New York are very beautiful, I am sure! And how can they help being wise, in such a big and complicated city?"

The wind grew stronger. The black burlap flapped madly back and forth like a great crow's wings. The sand beat on it ceaselessly, and soon after nightfall the sand changed into rain. I could hear nothing but the wind and the rain, see nothing but the surging waves of burlap over my head. Alone in the wilderness, I thought; but I knew that Mostafa was thinking of me.

There was a clap of thunder, and then the curtained doorway parted and Mostafa entered. His hair hung in black icicles down to his shoulders, his wet cheeks shone in the flickering light of the oil-lamp. A gust of wind came in with him and slid like a serpent past my feet across the sandy floor.

He stood beside me. Raindrops fell from his head and his arms into small puddles. The oil-lamp hissed.

"Where will you go from here?"

"I don't know yet. Wherever anyone will take me. Toward India, eastward, toward Calcutta."

"Why are you going to Calcutta?"

I paused. How to explain? How, how to explain, even to myself? "I am on my way to Japan."

"Why do you wish to go to Japan? Japan is a crowded country, full of hairless little men that have no souls."

"I have an uncle in Japan. He is very rich, and if I behave nicely to him I may some day have more money than I have now."

Mostafa gazed at me quietly. Then he said, "Yes, you are an American. I am very disappointed in you. I thought you had a soul, but now I see that you have no soul, after all."

Outside, the storm was howling like mad; great slabs of it were rolling and tumbling out of the hills. The sides of the tent billowed and coughed without stopping, and the little oil-lamp continued to flicker sorrowfully. It sent thin golden tongues licking at Mostafa's chin and ears. He drew his hand slowly across his face.

"Yes, but what is a soul, Mostafa? How can I believe you if you don't tell me what a soul is? Possibly you don't even know!"

"Yes, I do know. My soul is the part of me which no one else can touch. It is secret, like a diamond hidden inside a hard stone."

"Has everyone a soul?"

"Oh no! Fewer and fewer! That is the way the world goes, fewer and fewer have any real lonely souls left, fewer and fewer are happy. There are too many things to do now in the world; no one has time to be lonely and discover his soul, and therefore no one can be happy. I know that this is true. There is nothing to be done about it. My father has told me this, and my grandfather, too. They were very wise, both of them, and I know that this is true." He drew his hand across his face again, and his eyes wore a troubled look. We sat quietly for a moment. Then I asked:

"Where should I go, Mostafa?"

"Join a caravan or a truck to Quetta. From there to Peshawar. From there to Lahore. From Lahore the great road across India to Calcutta."

"Quetta first?"

"Yes. . . . Look"; he motioned me to the doorway and lifted the curtain. I peered into the raining blackness but I could see nothing, nothing except a few raindrops flashing across the lantern's solitary ray.

"Look," he said, and pointed down into the valley. "I shall set fire to the tent. That will be your chance to escape, and no one will dare to blame me. Then you run past the well and across the field toward the ravine."

"Yes."

"Then along the ravine."

"Yes."

"It is only two miles from the ravine to the caravan road. Two large tamarisks stand at the side of the road. You will see them surely."

"And I would find a caravan?"

"Yes. There are fewer caravans each year, but you will find one tomorrow morning, I think. Tell them you are my friend. Tell them you were sent by Seyed, the wise man."

"Who is Seyed?"

"My grandfather."

"Is he still alive?"

"Oh yes! He is the leader of the tribe. He is eighty-six years old, but still a great and powerful man, full of wisdom. A son was born to him a week ago. He loves me the best of all his grandchildren, and I love him the best of all my ancestors." There was a sudden extraordinary sweetness in his voice, his handsome eyes were glowing with adoration. "It is good for me to love him."

He raised the oil-lamp and held it over the bed. Meditatively he gathered the cushions and sprinkled them with oil. "Now," he said hoarsely, tenderly, "farewell." And he set the lamp carefully upon the couch. The flames sprang up, the place grew bright and warm in an instant.

Mostafa was gone. I ran down toward a clump of bushes and turned to watch the fire. The tent was flapping heavily and a slim blue flame was creeping through the doorway.

The rain had stopped, but the wind continued strong. I ran past the well and down toward the singing ravine.

I sat between the two tamarisks and watched the sun rising. I was wet, cold, feeble. "It's going to be a hot day," I thought: not a breath of wind was left in the place. "And I'm going to be sick," I thought. The land looked strange and terrifying. Not far away lay the white bones of a bird; beyond these, rocks; and beyond these, that voluptuous, sleep-feigning giantess, the silent range of hills.

And then out of the silent hills came a sound of bells, the same sound I'd heard one night at Trebizond.

And finally I was riding slowly eastward into the morning sunlight with a camel caravan that was loaded with petrol crates bound for Nushki. Two Afghan guides and a Persian soldier were in charge of it. Tall, burly men, proud and silent, the Afghans; the Persian was a small, delicate fellow, and he spoke to me in a swift flamboyant French. "I too was once lost here," he said. "When I was young, handsome and adventurous."

We passed two or three tribal villages, grim, secretive places protected by a square mud wall and a watch tower at each corner. Here and there along the road lay camel skeletons, whitened by the sun and glimmering in the sun, and once after we had left Dalbandin one of our own camels wearily folded her front legs under her and, hind legs still upright, closed her disillusioned eyes and prepared herself for an illusionless death. The two guides transferred the crates onto another camel, and so we left her. "She was very very old," explained the soldier. "We expected that she would die today."

The blue misty mountains forever watchful toward Afghanistan: the black rocks, strangely veined, some of them brilliantly glistening and obscenely shaped, rising one after another from the waves of sand: and the waves of sand, now yellow, now gray and hideously spotted with black pebbles, now almost black with a lava-like dust. Once we stopped at a tamarisk grove beside an empty river bed. Blue-green and silvery the stricken trees rose through the waves of heat. Over the dunes it hung, this crystal inescapable sea of heat, and the tufts of grass rose here and there like hairy submarine vegetables. The sand was moving southward with a great slowness, there was a low whining sound to it whenever a breath of wind came down from the north.

The Persian was chanting to himself incessantly. Finally I asked, "What is that poem you are singing?"

"From the Shah-nama," he said in a pleased effeminate tone. "A very beautiful poem. I know it all by heart."

"What is the story?"

"It tells how the lovely Princess Rudabal let down her hair from a tower so that her lover, Prince Zal, might climb up and make love to her."

"I like that story."

"Ah yes," he said anxiously; "it is a tender story. But dead, dead. The world has changed. How well I know it! Men are no longer loving and compassionate."

"We have the same story in the West. But they have different names, of course."

"What was the princess's name in the Western story?"

"Rapunzel."

He pursed his lips. "An ugly name."

"But a beautiful princess."

"I doubt it. No Western women are beautiful. They are coarse. Like men. No gentleness, no patience. Men should be warriors; women should be angels. That is the only way."

Finally we reached Nushki. At Nushki I joined another caravan, a small donkey caravan which was carrying brushwood up to Quetta. Turbaned, filthy, long-coated men these Baluchis were. The Afghans were far superior—erect and proud, with their beards dyed red and their boots fresh and glistening. But the Baluchis were a sorry, cringing lot, not to be trusted.

With these I arrived at Quetta. Here I fell sick. For two days I lay in the inelegant hotel bed, plucking the lice off my body and sprinkling gray water over my forehead.

On the first morning an enormous girl came up to my chamber with a jar full of water. She set it on the floor beside me and smiled, very sweetly. Then she said something that I couldn't understand. Then I said something in English, and repeated it in French. But she didn't understand, she merely simpered. We got along very well after this, and she brought me fresh water every two hours. Once she rubbed me with olive oil, another time she brought me some wine, and my only regret was that she should, with all her amiability, have been so very ugly. Great smallpox scars on her face and a body as pendulous and clumsy as a cow's. But a tender, forgiving spirit, nevertheless.

I drove onward to the north on a big native truck loaded with wool and cotton and three exuberant Afghans. It grew very cold soon after we left Quetta. Hilly at first, a region full of shaggy tribesmen who carried on an insane and incessant guerilla warfare. We could see them slouching among the rocks with guns on their shoulders. Once we saw a man standing thoughtfully on the edge of a deep ravine, gazing into the sun; and then suddenly the sound of a gun, and the flight of the body downward, graceful as a diver or a speckled hawk, until he was lost in the perpendicular shadows of the abyss. A wild volcanic-looking country, jagged and serrated, red with what might well enough have been either blood or heat or long rusty neglect.

And then the long sandy wastes lining the Indus. Now

and then an oasis. We stopped at Dera Ismail Khan, a grassy place full of lilacs and parrots. It snowed here during the night, and in the morning the lilies and the lilacs were fringed with snow until the sun came out full and strong.

Then northward with the spring into Kashmir. Past valley after lovely valley, shepherds and their flocks moving across the greenery in the day, men squatting by their hillside fires in the night. Soft-lipped boys with enormous turbans shrieking at us from the dark alleys, black-lidded girls with roses in their hair bringing us ices. And finally we reached Peshawar, and again I was alone.

19

A BOY led me to my room; a dark and shabby place if there ever was one, full of amazing little smells.

"Sahib desire anything else?" He hovered by the door, a dark bow-legged creature with eyes inflamed and sorrowful.

"No."

He stuttered with surprise. "But, sahib. . . . Can arrange thing for sahib, anything sahib prefer. . . ." He coughed.

"No."

"Sahib come down later to the dancing-room?" His dhoti fluttered moth-like in the shadow of the corridor. He coughed again; a quick porcelain sound.

"No." This was merely curiosity, I felt sure. He merely wanted to watch the strange young foreigner, to hear him talk, see him wash, and so on—possibly even see him undress. The sight of a naked Occidental is a thing that never ceases to amaze and fascinate the Oriental.

"Sahib wish me to bring some one up?" He spoke in the same soft dragging voice, without inflection. "Up to the room? Pretty girl, or if sahib prefer maybe . . ."

"No, and get out. . . ." I began to wave my arms violently at him, and he fled down the corridor like a limp and ineffective bird, whimpering softly.

The smell in the room was vile. The hotel lavatory adjoined my chamber, and in the wall I could see great brownish stains where the moisture had worked its way through the stucco. The lavatory itself was only a little wooden turret pinned on the side of the building, reached by a ramshackle stairway running up from the courtyard. The smell invaded my room both through window and through wall. The only way to get a breath of decent air was to open the door leading onto the balcony. But there was no screen and the mosquitoes promptly entered in battalions.

The sun had just crept behind the dome of the big mosque at the end of the street. Below, the shops were sinking into a silky shadow, and the people were coming out of doors, looking around, creeping to and fro like hungry jackals. They were depressingly silent, and through their bearing and their movements a shabby sort of resentment trickled out into the open, uneasily infecting the air. None of them were smiling; all of them looked thoroughly distrustful. But above all they looked hungry; not for food, but for something else. They were looking, watching, gazing. A regular tribe of gazers. Their faces were like the staring faces of flowers, already wilting, turning very slowly first one way and then another. No life except that of watching constantly the secret doings of others, no emotions except those that entered through the eyes. Their eyes were big and shining, dreamy, beautiful, oddly intimate.

I could see the bazaar of the coppersmiths softly striped with shadow. Older men with green turbans were squatting there, and younger ones with smart mustaches and collyrium-painted eyes were passing slowly—Moslems most of them. And Afghans, filthier and far cruder in build and feature than the rest; smooth and expressionless

Hindus sailing very lightly through the archways; curly-headed Jews with nobler features than the others, but that inescapable leer of self-pity in their lovely eyes. Under the balcony sat several shaggy old men, eating opium or smoking their charas, every one of them coughing almost incessantly, adding an irritating undertone to the stale and weary noises of the street. "Chah, khach, kukha," they went morosely; "chah, khach, kukha"; and now and then a pair of salmon-colored eyes turned upward unseeingly toward the sky.

A man in white at the corner was selling taffy. Another one was limping away with two pink doves on his arms. At the entrance to the bazaar sat three filthy beggars, and two slender Arab youths meandered past them, closely side by side, hips touching and hands clasped. They too, proud though their bearing was, were spoiled like all the rest of them; the clear straight look was gone from their beautiful faces, their gait was consciously graceful and elaborate, their eyes were sensuous but melancholy.

I felt profoundly listless. Something about this place absolutely sickened me. Nothing in particular, merely one of those periodic spasms that remind one like a cancerous pang that there's trouble brewing in the world, something we'd better be afraid of. Just a quick twinge of something for which there isn't any word. We all know it. It comes like a sultry breath and fouls the landscape suddenly into something alien and unpleasant.

I went back in and threw myself on the bed. The odor hadn't left, the mosquitoes came buzzing, and worst of all I only too soon recognized the loathsome familiarities of the bedbugs. Wearily I got up, placed the four legs of the bed in four little tins of water which I found on the wash-stand, and then went scrupulously through the bedclothes, murdering whatever I saw. The mattress I tossed on the

185

floor. Then I lay down again. But it didn't help. I felt more and more wretched, and peculiarly restless as well.

⚘⚘⚘ And so I got up again and stepped out upon the balcony. The evening was closing in on the city, caressing into being the one thousand and one little sins for which it was so elegantly famed. A fresh breeze came rippling across the roofs, one by one the lights went on, somewhere a radio was beginning to blare wickedly. A rustling undertone of whispers and hurrying footsteps rose from the winding streets below.

Across the alley from my hotel stood another hotel, far more pretentious and almost clean; outrageously expensive, no doubt—for Westerners, at any rate. As I stood there sniffing at the city smells a light was turned on in the room that faced my own. I could see two figures, a man and a woman, moving about behind the screens; once or twice I could see them, coming together and kissing. Then there'd be a cackle from the woman. I could actually smell her perfume from where I stood. Presently the man parted the hangings and stepped out upon his own balcony, which was no more than ten yards away from mine. He was wearing a blue brocaded dressing-gown. He stood there watching the half-lit street, smoking a long pipe. Then he turned slowly. What could it be, the glint of his hair, the suggestion of a smile, the gentle motion of his arm as it bent and then straightened again? . . . Something, certainly . . . And then the lamplight from the doorway fell across the russet goatee and the checkered vest beneath the robe. My heart leaped, all my listlessness was gone in a flash. The light gleaming across those slender black lines on the white flannel made me happier than I'd been for weeks, all in less than a second. "De Hahn!" I called, "Hans! It's you! It's you, I knew it was. . . ." I grew speechless with delight and surprise. I remembered all the things he'd told me, all of them in that brief pause during which he turned and looked at me. I remembered the way he'd left us, and I also remembered Ursule, whom he so loved and who so loved him. He stood and looked at me, silently and motionlessly. I grew worried. Well, it *was* he, wasn't it? Or wasn't it? Surely it was! Suddenly he shouted joyfully, called my name, moved his arms up and down. "Come on, quickly. . . . Here, jump across, can't you? By God! this is a fairy tale. I can't believe it at all. . . ." I couldn't jump, but I ran downstairs and up again and there he was at the door, the light full on his lovable ruddy face. Yes, it was he, and a moment later he had his arms around me.

"Tell me, tell me, what happened?" I shouted. "You're alive! I can't believe it!"

And finally he told me. "Well, I was lucky, I'll admit it. I've always been lucky. I can't complain of the way life's treated me, no sir. . . .

"Here's what happened." He leaned back, gesturing with his pipe like a bandmaster. I could hear the lady rustling away with her silks and satins in the bedroom. I hadn't seen her yet, and of course I was very curious indeed. Was it Ursule, the faithful? Well, I'd find out before long. "You see," said he happily, "it was all a big mistake, this business of locking me up. And they knew it, as I found out later. But they couldn't afford to admit it. They couldn't afford to set me free. There'd be trouble, apologies, reimbursements, and so on. So the best thing, of course, so they decided, was simply to eliminate me and forget all about it. Shoot me. And that would be the end. Well, I can't blame them.

"As for me, I thought fast. I'd kept my Turkish money with me, and this—there was a good lot of it I can tell you

—I pressed into the guard's hand. 'See what you can do,' said I. He squeezed my hand just to show he'd caught on, and 'Fall down,' he whispered, 'when we shoot.' So I did. The guns went off, but all that happened to me was a bit of a bruise on the elbow where I fell." He chuckled.

"Well," he continued in a tone of delighted reminiscence, "presently my guard comes along and drags me off, strips me, sews me up in a burlap bag. 'You'll be all right,' he whispers in my ear through the burlap. 'Just keep still.' So he puts me in the sleigh (there was a big snow, remember?) and goes driving away toward the cemetery for the poor outside the city.

"I was freezing to death in my burlap bag, in the meantime. 'How much more money have you got?' said he as soon as we hit the country road. 'Nothing,' I wailed, 'not a penny.' He thought it over. 'How much can you get?' 'I don't know,' said I; 'Let me out! I'm freezing!' He laughed and drove on, bells ringing merrily.

"Well, I was ready to howl with the cold by this time. . . ." But at this point the curtains in the bedroom doorway parted and a lady entered the room. "By God!" cried de Hahn, "you haven't met Ursule yet! Well, there she is. But you two practically know each other already. Well, well! It's almost unbelievable. . . ."

She was tall, beautifully built, and moved with a lovely subdued sort of grace. But her face was lean, sharp, peaked. And yet, in spite of that, very handsome. She smiled and reached out her hand without a word. As for me, I blushed like a bride. I'd heard so much about her and imagined so much more—maybe that was the reason. She was better than I expected, I'll confess. Rather glittering-looking, no rough edges, and a quick, intelligent look in her eyes.

She went up to de Hahn and folded her arms around him. "Put on your coat, dear," she said very softly. "By God!" he cried, "You're looking fine! All dressed up for our guest!" He smiled blissfully at me. "You're coming along with us for dinner, right away. Don't you dare refuse. . . . By God! I'm happy tonight!"

The café was full of smoke, full of men, full of rich masculine smells. Afghan chieftains in brilliant trappings tramped in and out—big hairy men covered with shawls, turbans, burnous, multicolored capes, tassels of silver and black, jewels dripping from their ears. They moved with a self-conscious swagger, roared instead of laughing, shouted instead of talking. They made the room seem violently overcrowded, and drank sloe gin in great resounding gulps.

"Well, as I was saying," proceeded de Hahn, Ursule and I listening raptly, "it began to sleet. So there I lay while he ran into the inn to get a drink of cognac. He was torturing me on purpose, the degraded bastard. Still, he'd saved my life. I've no right to call him names. There I lay, waiting and waiting. It was getting dark. I was sure I was dying. I began to wish that he'd shot me dead, after all. The sleet trickled on me through the burlap, stinging my poor buttocks like red-hot needles.

"So I worked up my last ounce of strength and wriggled and twirled toward the back edge of the sleigh. Finally I plunged off, right into the snow. It felt good, I can tell you, positively like a warm blanket. I squatted there quietly in my burlap bag, not daring to make a sound. And a minute or two later he comes out, as drunk as the Grand Llama, and tumbles blindly into the sleigh. 'Feeling any better?' he yells without turning around, and drives off. The thud of the horses' hooves and the tinkle of the bells fading out in the distance was music in my frozen ears.

"I began to yell. 'Help, help!' And in another minute out came a woman and cried, 'Who's there?' 'It's me,' I groaned. 'Where?' 'Here in the sack!' 'Who the devil,' said she, and walked up to me and kicked me gently. 'Let me out,' said I, and she took a knife and cut the burlap. Very cautiously she peered in. I looked harmless enough, I'll wager, even though I was as naked as an eel." I glanced at Ursule. She didn't seem to be listening any more. She was tapping nervously at the edge of her green wineglass.

"It wasn't an inn at all; it was a home, and this was the guard's wife! That's what she told me as soon as she'd rubbed me down and set me in front of the fire with a blanket over my shoulders. A fine wench; no false modesty. 'What a joke,' she said, and laughed. 'He's a fiend, that husband of mine,' she added, 'and I wish he were dead. . . . Do you know what he does? Sees me once a fortnight, and do you suppose he even kisses me? Not he! That city's corrupted him, I'm sure of it.' I kept smiling at her sheepishly, happy and grateful, but still a trifle uneasy.

"Well, to make a long story short, I got out of her clutches too, finally. But a terrific job it was, let me tell you. She'd gotten a man, you see, and she meant to keep him. She wasn't particular, either, poor soul. Almost crazy for want of a good night's love, I guess. . . ."

Ursule glanced at me rather sharply, then lowered her eyes. She had long black lashes, like a young Arab's. She looked at me once, twice, a third time, as if there were some thrilling secret between us. The third was a rich, slow look. I could almost feel it running across my cheek like a piece of satin. I could feel myself blushing. Restlessly she turned around, glancing here and there, her hands playing with the crimson tablecloth, running her fingers along the edge of the wineglass. She was striking, dashingly handsome, there was no denying it; but somehow not quite the type I like.

"You'll come with us, won't you?" said de Hahn. And I confessed to him that I had no money. "The devil take the money," he replied with energy. "Who cares? Forget about it. I've got enough. . . . Everybody's thinking of money. One long succession of extortion, that's what the world is—bribery, hush-money, usury, prostitution, blackmail, beggary, theft. Everything's for money. Let's you and me forget about it." I never knew quite what to believe when he rambled on like this, getting tangled up in the jungle of his imagined world, with me sitting in a treetop like a puzzled monkey and not knowing where the path lay, not knowing what was real and what was unreal. For where, after all, did he get all this money which he so loathed? How did he always contrive to have so much, how could he afford to be so generous? Shameful thought. He had a heart of gold, didn't he? Wasn't that enough? What did a few exaggerations matter? Or even a bit of unscrupulousness here and there? Well. . . .

Some dancing boys came gliding into the café, limber as snakes and nastily drunk, every one of them. They fluttered and swayed. The Afghan chieftains grew jealous and quarrelsome. The place was rapidly becoming bawdy.

"You'll come with us to Leh," repeated de Hahn gaily, "won't you? Of course you will! It's settled, then. It'll be a superb experience. Right up into the Himalayas— fancy! On the road to Tibet. The big picnic that I've been looking forward to for months! But before we start we'll have a little picnic in Srinagar, eh? How'd that be?" He was drunk. Ursule peered at me eloquently, as if there were a definite secret understanding between us. I felt like a cat being stroked, very gently and expertly, and something inside me began to purr. And still, at the same time, I began to feel a little bit uneasy about it all. Here I was, sitting in a warm wine-scented room, growing soft and drowsy. But I could hear the hounds baying at the end of the bazaar, and the delicate drumming of long red finger nails upon the table, and the lisping of the wretched ones from the unlit corner of the café.

I looked across at de Hahn. He was fast asleep, lips puffing and eyelids sagging, but a blissful, tender look on his face in spite of everything.

20

BEHIND us we could still see the waters of the Jhelum sliding under the seven bridges of Srinagar. In front of us lay the Dal. Boats everywhere, everyone smiling, everything sunny. The mountains above us sparkled as if they had just emerged from the chrysalis.

"Are you happy?" said de Hahn.

Ursule nodded.

"Are you happy?" said he, turning to me.

"Yes," said I.

He smiled. "They're happy too," he said, glancing toward the four Kashmiris who were boating us up; "too stupid to be anything else." They sat there staring at us, the four of them; the father, a fierce black-bearded man who stank like a wolf, and two brothers and a sister— pasty-faced Mongoloid-looking youngsters, built like gods. The two boys poled, while the other two sat on their haunches and stared at us cunningly, wondering how much money they would presently be wrangling out of de Hahn. The girl looked like a gypsy, rings in her ears and long streaks of dirt across her face and down her yellow breast. She sat pouting and sighing all afternoon. I could see her watching the lean brown legs of her two brothers, tense with strain and bright with sweat. Slowly growing stale and wretched, she was, and badly in need of a lover.

Silently we slid through the glassy water. Lilies and ferns and tall new grasses covered the shore. Lovers were sitting there, arms about each other. Others were singing and laughing, still others were leaping naked out of the moss into the water. We could see their arrowy brown bodies flashing through the air, the splash of drops in the sunlight, the wet brown faces smiling through the ripples.

On the opposite side of the lake rose the Shalimar gardens. Iris and wild rose lined the watercourses, and beyond these the poplars and mulberry trees, each leaf crystal clear. And beyond these, terrace upon terrace, the gardens themselves, the rocketing cascades, the towering hedges, the marble basins, the iron railings, all gleaming with water and sunlight. And beyond these, the corridors of rock, the real Himalayas, the channeled mountains fading into their own clear winter a hundred miles away.

All around us flashed the little boats and the big boats —men with huge turbans sitting with their arms around their knees in each one, and then they'd take off their turbans and their heads were smooth as lacquer, their lips full and soft, their eyes coal black, both hateful and tender. Some of them smiled, some of them sat quietly with closed eyes.

We came to a fine shadowy bank, all covered with iris, and there we landed. Ursule spread the napkins and laid out the forks and knives. Then she opened the basket and pulled out a great roasted duck, and a big white cheese, and a big bottle of wine. "Ah," cried de Hahn happily, "now I am back in Leyden again, the days of my happy youth! Only we had no mountains in Leyden. Merely a windmill or two, and a couple of ganders coming up and asking for crumbs."

"Now, this matter of happiness," said he, after we'd finished the duck and the cheese and the wine. We lay back in the soft grass and looked up at the mountains, feeling full and contented and the least bit tipsy. De Hahn folded a napkin across his face to keep out the sun. Ursule lay down under a lilac bush, eyes and teeth and new silk stockings all flashing in the dappled sunlight. Her black hair rippled and shone like the hair of a wild beast. "It's not so simple," he went on, belching softly. "You say you're happy, both of you. But I know better. You're not. Not a bit. . . ." On and on he went till at last he fell asleep.

Ursule turned toward me and smiled.

And so, after an hour or so, we got up and tickled his nose with a reed. He blinked. "Time to go back," said I. He grunted, and the three of us walked sleepily back to the water's edge and called to our boatmen. They'd been dozing off, too, out there among the lily pads, and now they spread their great brown arms and poled closer to the shore.

The nap had put de Hahn in excellent spirits. "Ah," he sighed, "but it's fine to be with people whom you love! We do get along well, we three, don't we? I love both of you, both of you love me. Isn't that so? Isn't that so, now?" He ran his fingers through his hair. He still appeared a little bit drunk, and his eyes looked big and affectionate.

"The trouble is, people don't get close enough together. Intimacy, that's what we all need. Understanding, sympathy. We ought to know one another's little vices, every single one of them, and forgive them. That's the only real kind of friendship and loyalty. Isn't that so? Don't you agree, now?

"Tell him about your family, my pet," he continued, tenderly taking Ursule's hand in his own. Ursule smiled. "Or shall I? You should have seen them!" He turned to me.

"Incredible," he said slyly. "Unique. They came from Tours, and finally dissolved in Bagdad. How they got to Bagdad I don't know. That's where I first met my darling, in Bagdad, isn't it? How lovely she looked! How old was she?"

"You know perfectly well," she said. "Twenty-one."

"Twenty-one. But you looked like fifteen, my lovely dear. Fresh as a pomegranate. But her sister! You should have seen her, a painted big-buttocked thing"—he moved his hands in eloquent curves—"and the look in her eyes! Well, I'm not attracted to that type, thank God. Forgive me," and he winked drunkenly at Ursule, "but I'm sure you share my sentiments, my pretty one, don't you? Well. And her brother! Pffh! . . . Moved like a butterfly. He didn't walk, he danced, he flew! A nauseating specimen, though I must admit he always behaved very nicely indeed to me. . . . But I'm a fool to talk like this. I loved them all, every one of them. I love everybody." He ran his fingers up Ursule's bare arm, up past the shoulder, down under the armpit. "My adorable dear," he whimpered, and she trailed her long red finger tips in the water and glanced up at the Himalayas.

Finally, when the sun had slid behind the peaks and the whole vale day drowned under a sea of shadow—even though the sky was still azure, each cloud still summery white—we entered Srinagar again. Through bridge after bridge, past the shrieking boatmen and the women beating their linen upon the blue rocks. Down by the tall sedge grass some Kashmir lads were lying motionlessly. Dark furtive eyes they had, and soft insinuating voices. Two of them shouted at us shamelessly. A few years more and they'd tint their eyelids, grow shrewd and treacherous, travel eastward and become dancing-boys. That would last about five years. After that they'd become valets or barbers or petty silk merchants, and possibly marry. Or of course they could become *saddhus,* and wander southward with cow dung in their hair.

On the opposite shore bird-eyed old men, hands like claws and faces like furry beaks, were following a Muslim priest. They gathered and then washed themselves in the tributary water at a broken marble basin. Then they took their shoes off and prayed in unison, heads bent toward the turquoise dome on the southwestern shore. Overhead, some big jackass birds, come freshly northward from the Ganges, were wheeling about and about.

And then some screaming beggars, sellers of silk, of horses, asses, ponies, of pottery and cutlery. De Hahn grew sad and talkative when he saw all this. "Well," he lamented, "what can one do? What can one do? Move with the multitude, go to war with them, catch their diseases, pray with them, hate with them, sleep with them, get hurt with them, sit right in the middle of the huge stinking crowd and let it push you about, paw you, lip you, cling to you, trample on you, kill you? Where does it get you? Consider a moment. A ghastly spectacle. You remain alone. You can't get inside the rest. They can't get inside you. A million little spirits each with its own peculiar tastes, hopelessly far away from one another. Nothing to be done about it, now or ever.

"The hidden people," he sighed. "They're the ones that I keep thinking about. The ones that crawl away into their hiding-places and only peer forth now and then when no one is looking, to get a bite to eat maybe, or, if they've got the nerve, to go and beg for a snatch of darkness and a piece of loving. Everywhere. Thousands and thousands." He was very melancholy. He was, after all, a pathetic and lovable sort. He'd see at a glance the secret shabby places in you that you'd been trying so hard to hide, but he'd like you the better for them, he'd forgive you anything. And yet he never got anywhere; he was, in a word, thoroughly inefficient. And still, in return for his childish, forgiving disposition, one couldn't help wishing him the best of luck.

But in the meantime Ursule had been holding my hand, ingeniously caressing the palm of it with her index finger. I closed my eyes as we passed under the sixth bridge. I thought pantingly of how I'd be tiptoeing to her room that night, when de Hahn was deeply and alcoholically asleep. The thought of her black hair hanging over my arm; her lips, large and warm; the rays from the street lamp glazing the wet tip of each breast and the curve of her belly and her thighs; delicate hidden secrecies I had barely glimpsed the night before; all this made my breath come short and heavy, and my brain go spinning like a top.

❧❧❧ We left Srinagar by caravan in the early morning moonlight. We had breakfast at the hill station, and then passed on toward Ganderbal. After a few miles dawn suddenly sprang up into the grayness, and then came feathery shells of gold rippling across the clouds around the mountain peaks, and then on the sides of the mountains and the trees and the valleys deep down at our side.

But before long something dark and heavy crept into the air. The donkeys flattened their ears and a surreptitious look came into their great eyes. A green gloss settled on the valley. And in another moment, just as the path took a sharp steep turn around a cliff, down flew the storm. It thundered across the darkening hollows, it rolled and crashed in the distant precipices. Before I knew it I had a hailstone in my eye, and when I opened it again I saw a flash of blue lightning blazing across the entire range, revealing for three seconds tall jagged peaks previously unsuspected. Then the hail came down heavily, the donkeys came to a disconcerted halt. Ursule shrieked, de Hahn cursed bloodily.

But the hail stopped after a minute or two and what came instead was a great gush of water, rain as thick as a waterfall. The coolies ran up with strips of canvas to cover the baskets and our heads. Nervously the donkeys kept lifting their hooves as the water carried the sand and shale away from under their feet and flushed it all down into the canyon.

"How far's the next station?" shrieked de Hahn.

"Oh, five miles," shrieked back the head coolie, who then consulted hurriedly with one of his colleagues. He shouted again, a moment later. "Maybe fifteen miles, sahib."

De Hahn called him a filthy name. But it didn't matter, for the storm departed as suddenly as it had arrived. The rain stopped, the thunder rumbled away like cattle down a distant street. The darkness broke in half, sunlight fell through in two, three, four huge shafts. "Look!" cried de Hahn, happy again. "Isn't that magnificent! Look at it!" All the rocks were still alive with raindrops lit by the sun, a hundred crazy rainbows were chasing one another to and fro in the big valley below us. The coolies stood gaping grayly at us, their black bangs dripping down over their noses, their trousers dark and sagging.

All of us were soaking wet. But we made our way somehow down the slippery path toward a cedar-speckled meadow, and there we got off and shook ourselves like wet dogs. "Come, come," said de Hahn. "We'll all lie down in the sun and let our clothes dry. That's the only thing to do." So we crept behind a boulder and stripped, and hung our linen on the cedar limbs. It was warm, but we still shivered a bit; I could see de Hahn's teeth chattering as he sat down nakedly on a round white stone.

So there we lay, breathing the wonderful smell of the wet cedars and the wild mountain iris, shivering a little bit. De Hahn began to tell us stories about his school days in Leyden, about his fat great-aunt, his fat schoolteacher, his fat pet goose, his fat little girl cousin. He could be very amusing if he chose, and very charming.

And I'd look at Ursule's lovable white body that gleamed in the sunlight like wet marble. Her eyes were closed and she seemed to be asleep. The coolies peered at us whimsically, then sat down beside the donkeys and played cards.

Our path ran along pebbly meadows, rivers, cascades, steep luminous ravines. We stopped and had tea in a pine grove late in the afternoon. At nightfall we reached Sonamarg, and slept in a rest-house under a great black cliff.

Then we came to the Zoji Pass and the great hills began. We crept precariously past slopes that were bright with teeth of ice and tongues of hanging snow. These were the real Tibetan mountains we were approaching. We could see them ahead of us, above us; barren, yellowish, spotted with boulders, and here and there a farm or a deserted bungalow. We met two caravans, one a group of pilgrims traveling from remote Kashgar to Mecca, another a group of handsome tradesmen from Leh bound for Srinagar with a supply of Chinese silks, Tibetan shawls, jewels from the Turkestan, furs from Siberia. In Srinagar they'd exchange these for European haberdashery and leathers, and for Indian spices.

We rode on to a huge sandy plateau. "Kargil," said the head coolie. Here we changed horses again, and started off toward the kingdom of Ladak. We passed several Buddhist shrines, and we knew by the very looks of the land that this was an austere, religious, ceremonious and secret country into which we were traveling. We passed great ruined castles one after the other, and an old monastery guarded by huge statues of black stone. We passed girls grinding barley and pressing oil while they squatted on the flat roofs of their houses. We passed the ruined town of Kharki, dead, so our coolie told us, for three hundred years, dark and quiet except for the jangling and flickering of the iron lamps as the secular spirits stumbled nightly over the flagstones where they'd been sinning centuries before. There was a ruined castle high above it, and not far away a lamasery, with caves for the monks built into the cliffs and staring at us like blind eyes.

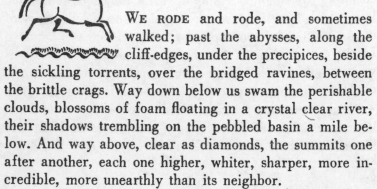

21

WE RODE and rode, and sometimes walked; past the abysses, along the cliff-edges, under the precipices, beside the sickling torrents, over the bridged ravines, between the brittle crags. Way down below us swam the perishable clouds, blossoms of foam floating in a crystal clear river, their shadows trembling on the pebbled basin a mile below. And way above, clear as diamonds, the summits one after another, each one higher, whiter, sharper, more incredible, more unearthly than its neighbor.

I couldn't keep from thinking high thoughts here. They're huge, these hills; that's how my mind got started. Huge and old, immensely so. But is there anything still older? And what is age? What is time? Ah, time's a huge and endless thing; everything shrivels up with terror when you stop to think about time. In the twinkling of an eye these Himalayas will be worn away, will go tumbling into dust or go gliding away into fog. And as for the temples, the paths and sanctuaries built by men, the houses of wicked delight or of saintly suffering, alas, when all's said and done they'll be no more than a silly momentary sigh in the night.

We passed the ruined temples of Basgo and followed the Indus until we got to sNye. Near sNye we stopped and visited the Yellow Hat Monastery. "You will be permitted to enter the rooms of the Incarnate Lama," hinted our coolie when he slyly suggested that we should go. So we went. It stood on a steep rock, a shabby forlorn place covered with dust and rust and lichenous decay. The monks were very talkative, very dirty, very insolent. They plainly expected bakshish, and after de Hahn had slipped them a bit of something they grew perceptibly more cordial and proceeded to show us their secret passageways. These were covered with curious frescoes and lit dimly by bronze lamps, but otherwise quite dull and ugly. Finally they took us to the haggard commonplace rooms of the Incarnate Lama, and here they brought us tea and sweets. They were served on a black embroidered shawl, in vermilion china dishes that were dull with the dust of weeks. "But where is the Incarnate Lama?" we asked. Oh, he'd left them long ago, many years ago, they said, and shrugged their round shoulders. Where had he gone? They didn't know. Was he dead? They thought it likely. They looked very bored.

We didn't care for the monks at all. They were slovenly and effeminate. They began to giggle like schoolgirls when I burnt my lips with the hot tea and then spilled the rest of it over my knees. A great fat one brought me another cup, wagging his finger at me and shaking his hips. Rubbish and filth were lying about everywhere. We saw one or two of the older monks busy with their little prayer wheels. But the young ones all lay around in the sun, gossiping, telling jokes, teasing one another. The garden was going wild, yellow with weeds and peppered with rat holes.

🐾🐾🐾 We pitched our tent that night on the edge of a shady pine grove, and built a big fire. We three sat on one side, and the coolies on the other, grouped among the tree trunks like wolves. They sat there quietly all evening. Now and then I'd see a face grinning stupidly in the firelight, or the firelight falling on a sleeping figure. Or

I'd hear them talking in gruff monosyllables, or lapping loudly at their soup, or one of them tramping off among the pines to make water, or one of them tittering at a whispered joke.

De Hahn took a long sip out his bottle and proceeded to grow very chatty. He was worrying about the monks. "It's like entering a jungle," he said; "a frightful wilderness. That's what it is. These queer plants all around, crowding the sunlight out, sapping the brightness out of the air, making strange faces and swaying from side to side. Very sad. They grow into queer shapes and get hopelessly tangled up. And the time comes when they forget that it's sunlight they need. That's when the rot sets in. Before long it's too late to save them.

"They're beyond hope. Sometimes it almost seems that they'd rather go under, lose their grip, get twisted and lost in the neighboring branches that come twining this way and that. And give way one inch, just one single inch, and the new ones will rush over you like a flood. You won't ever see the fresh air again. The only consolation will be that you're not the only one. You'll never be the only one. But you'll be alone just the same."

The fire was flickering softly. All around the glowing embers lay gazing at us with soft red eyes. The three of us were lying in front of the tent, winking at the flames, Ursule in the middle, and every now and then she'd turn and peer at me tenderly across the darkness.

"They're really searching for love," de Hahn continued in a melancholy tone, his pale asexual eyes gleaming sadly. His fingers were fondling the empty bottle beside him. "We all know that by now, of course. And it's no wonder, considering how few dare openly ask for it, how few know it when they see it, how few even know what it is they want, how stiffly and timidly they grope about. No wonder if most of them get lost on the way. No wonder if it all ends in waste, in sorrow, in a big agonizing muddle of silliness." He sighed. "They're so lonely, I weep to think of it, I tell you."

❧❧❧ "And still," he said later, opening his eyes again and staring at the dying embers, "maybe they're lucky compared with the rest of us. They're lonely, yes, their life grows queer like a twisted jungle orchid. Admitted. And very sad, too. But what about us, those of us who're caught in a net by a civilized society like innumerable sardines and dragged out upon the shore? Well? What do you think about that?"

There was a fine smell of pine rolling over the rocks like a fresh mountain stream. Impossible not to feel vigorous and carefree here. What did those troubles way down below us, miles below us in gray mechanical cities— what did they amount to, really? Look at them from a distance and you can see them in a philosophical light, you can argue and draw conclusions and enjoy yourself thoroughly. You've forgotten completely that little nocturnal wind, that malignant breath flowing out of the city's mouth and creating unlucky exhausting dreams and making the poor unemployed think of suicide every solitary night. That was what de Hahn said. "Oh, we're worse off than those perverts in the monastery, don't deceive yourself. They know what's happening, at least. Take everything away from them that you can and they've still got a little bit of something left. Enough to keep them this side of madness, at any rate. But not we newer ones. Take away our clothes, our food, our liquor, our quaint sexual pleasures, our fatiguing little conversations and our loathsome excitements about this and that: what's left? A hollow thing, like one of those silver Christmas-tree ornaments, with no more blood or warmth. Let the snow fall and we're cold as ice, let the wind rustle the branches and we drop and shatter for once and all. Nothing's left, because we never really believed anything, we never rose above the world of objects, we never deep down within us were alive. It's the age of inversion, the negative age. We're changing into tremendous plants, and soon we'll be breathing carbon dioxide instead of oxygen, at the rate we're going. Mark my words." He grunted unhappily and turned over on his back. And soon I was asleep, too, dreaming of prayer mills and inaccessible peaks and men with monstrous, miserable eyes who kept running after me, asking peculiar questions in voices almost too faint to hear.

Ursule tapped me on the shoulder and woke me up long before dawn. The first thing I saw was the giant range to the north all covered with snow and the snow all covered with starlight. Then I saw her leaning over me. "Listen," she said in a tense, subdued voice— "listen to me, listen." It sounded like the hissing of the pine needles. Her eyes were black as coals. She looked singularly lovely, her face like satin and her hair rippling down over my neck, hiding the sky behind a black dewy cataract of curls.

"Listen," she whispered. "You've got to go. I just heard him talking in his sleep." She nodded toward the limp disheveled form at her side.

"Well?" said I.

"He knows what's been going on."

"He does?" I still didn't know what she was talking about.

"And what's more, he's angry. Absolutely furious."

"What about?"

"What about! You know very well what about! Really!" Far off I heard a mass of gravel tumbling noisily down the slope toward Tibet. De Hahn turned over on his side and grunted.

"He's got a pistol in his pocket," mumbled Ursule after a moment of suspense. "You'd better go. He'll kill you, I tell you. He knows what's been going on."

I leaned back on my elbows and began to shiver a little.

"You don't want him to kill you, do you?" she murmured slowly. "And me too, maybe? Don't you love me? Can't you ever think of some one else? Must you always be so selfish?"

I shook my head. I felt dizzy and alarmed.

"Well, you've got to make your getaway. Right now. Don't you see? Don't you see?"

There was a soft wind going through the trees. I could see them trembling. I could almost feel them trembling. I could almost feel the earth on which I was lying, and the deep places beneath the torrents and deep down crevices, all trembling softly. I looked at Ursule. She was gazing at me with a tender look, but she was trembling, too.

"Now, look here, Ursule . . ." I began. But at that moment de Hahn shifted over to his other side and grunted again. I was growing nervous. He grunted a third time, resonantly.

"Well, good-by," I said, and grabbed the coat on which I'd been lying and the two shoes at my side. "Good-by, my dear, good-by."

Her mouth dropped open, her eyes yawned. "Oh, take me, too," she whined softly. "Here, wait, wait. . . ."

But I was already skipping down toward the black path, setting the gravel rolling, still tipsy and misty-eyed with sleep.

❧❧❧ I didn't know anything at all; my mind was pure of thought; all it could grasp was the gray sky parting overhead like a huge moth opening its wings; nothing else, until slowly the greater peaks came into view, the stars disappeared, and the mists went rolling.

I was alone and it was very quiet. I listened painstakingly, like a man's fingers groping in an unlit room, to make sure that the silence was absolute. Yes, it was absolute. I turned my head slowly to one side and then the other. Not a murmur anywhere. It was as if I had been buried in ice, frozen still, everything stiffened and quieted.

I tried to go to sleep, for delicately I was growing aware of a nasty biting feeling in my left hip. But as I was beginning to doze off I heard a sound, a low buzz, steady and quite unexplainably frightening. The sound of time, I thought to myself, time, rolling past, and the world turning on its tiny axis.

And again I thought of time. These hills, yes, they were pretty old, there was no denying it. But the space that went dripping from their sides like a spring from a bare rock, that was older yet. It was like a well; way down inside it one could be aware of the shapes still moving. The roar of the saber-toothed tiger had hit against it and rebounded from it; and before that the croaking of the first toads; and before that the bubblings when the continents rose out of the sea and others sank into the sea. And even that wasn't real age. Real age was silence. Real age was way before that, when light separated from darkness, and before that. No well as deep as that could be imagined. Drop a man's thought down that abyss and it would go *pop*, evaporate, fade into nothing long before it got halfway down. The voice of humanity would be like a little bell, exploring wistfully deep in that huge cistern. I could hear it tinkling and tinkling, ever so faintly.

Suddenly I began to feel calmer. The pain in my hip was growing less. I rolled over on my back and stared up at the sky. But instead of the sun and the clouds what I saw was a kind dark face gazing down at me.

The old man ran his fingers softly across my forehead. His face was incredibly wrinkled, and a few long white hairs hung down over each ear. They rippled silkily in the morning wind. All he wore was a long leather tunic, a belt around the waist, and hanging from the belt a little bronze bell. Each time that he moved the bell went tinkling.

He put his arm under my back and lifted me up. "Thank you," I said, still dazed and uncertain.

"You are very fortunate," he replied. If I hadn't been still lost in dreaminess I should have been surprised. He spoke an exotic but pure and beautiful English. He spoke it somehow as if no one else had ever spoken it; he made it his own language, and pronounced it in strangely clear and lovely tones. "Did you fall?" he asked. "Yes," I said, "I think so."

"It is fortunate that I should have been passing," he said, and even his most casual utterance sounded peacefully and profoundly certain. "Solitude can be very sad for a young man." He helped me get on my feet, and then we started down the slope, quite slowly. He must have been very old, yet he walked with ease and grace. His bell went tinkling constantly, a pathetic little sound in this huge valley.

WE CROSSED a bed of gravel at the foot of the slope down which I'd gone glid‧ing helplessly some hours ago. Then we crept down a steep ledge, he first and then I. He held me as I stepped down to the ground, and his arms felt hard and delicate as ivory against my chest. Then we waded through a snowy ravine and up along a pebbled place, past frowning cliffs and overhanging ledges, all of them desolately bare and dripping with icicles. It was misty here, and we had to walk with great precaution. Neither of us spoke.

Finally we reached a narrow path, and this wound up‧ward into the sunlit regions along the side of the hill. The abyss lay below us, two feet away, a thousand feet straight down through an apricot-colored fog.

We came to a Buddhist rest-house when the path reached the plateau, and here we halted. It was a foul hut, torn and decayed by the weather, full of the smell of death. The old pilgrim chanted some words from the Upanishads, and then turned toward me suddenly and ad‧dressed me in a voice of extraordinary gentleness.

"It is very easy to come close to dying, but it is only rarely that one dies on such occasions. I have traveled from the sacred mountain over there," and he pointed across the clouds toward a snowy peak to the east. "Three days ago I sat in the ice for many hours. I thought I might die. I waited and waited." He paused, and I begged him to go on.

"I saw the familiar circle of white light as I sat there. This was shortly after midnight. At that time I thought that I should probably die, for I could feel my bowels hardening with the cold. Soon the circle grew faint again and disappeared, and I saw a pure darkness attached to no shape or form. This was a state beyond sleep. Presently I awoke from this state. I was still uncertain at this moment whether I should die or not, but shortly afterwards I realized that in all likelihood I should remain alive. My legs were covered with ice, and ice was dripping from my hair and piercing my shoulders." His voice was very soft, almost sorrowful, but his eyes shone brightly with excitement and joy.

Soon we started off again across the rocky plain. An old Buddhist nunnery stood on the slope where the westward hills rose again. "From there, my boy," said the old priest, "you will be able to join a caravan bound for Srinagar." And at noon we reached the long stone stairway that led up to the black portals.

He took me by the hand and we walked up the long stairway side by side. I turned and looked at his face. It was not by nature a handsome face. The skin looked hard and inhuman, more like the bark of a tree or the surface of a rock than the face of a man. Sun and rain and spiritual sureness had hammered his face into purity and permanence. There was no telling how old he was. He might have been forty or a hundred.

"Why did you become a monk?" I asked him.

"I do not quite know." He turned his silky bullet-shaped head toward me and stared at me with the beautiful eyes of the introvert. "I always desired that. There was no doubt at any time. There was no other possibility."

"Why did you desire it?"

"The usual life was not intended for me."

"Why not?"

"I was both too strong and too weak for it."

"For marriage, you mean? For children, families, all that?"

"I was not fitted for those things." We'd been climbing over a hundred steps, but he wasn't panting. He moved as if he were treading across water, rising on the waves. I was very tired indeed, breathing heavily and sweating weirdly.

We sat down on a bench at the nunnery gates. Great streaks of sunlight came through the iron bars, and far below us slants of sunlight came sliding through the crevices between the peaks. The plateau appeared to be shrouded in snow, but while we watched this fog grew thin and spotted, and sleek rows of evergreens, fingerlike stretches of pebble and soil, and two swift and silvery streams began to shine through.

He told me several anecdotes; little incidents in his life, some of them quite pathetic and others quaintly amusing. Only a month or so ago, he said, some robbers had attacked him on the road. The first time this had ever happened to him, he added, the provocation being a small leather bag in which he was carrying a certain relic from one monastery to another. "I deceived them very cleverly," he said, eyes twinkling. "I lay down quickly in the Yogi posture. I pretended to be passing into a Yogi contemplation. I lay there for a long time and muttered to myself. Then I looked out of one eye, very cautiously. There they were, all five of the robbers, lying in the same Yogi posture, their temples resting in the palms of their two hands. Quietly I rose and walked away. I looked back at the bend of the road and they were still lying there and praying, gentle innocent souls that they were." He chuckled softly, and ran his fingers through the five or six long white hairs of his beard. "Impermanence, evanescence, misery of evanescence." The words occurred to me suddenly out of a remembered conversation. Then I looked at his face again, the elusive light in his eye, the sorrowful lines, the ghostly whiteness of his hair. Everything he said sounded vague and unreal; deprived of almost all significance, of all poignancy. His voice had an airy quality about it, as if the words he was uttering were merely rejoining their element, floating back to their parent air; and things happening were scarcely more than raindrops falling out of the air upon vast rocks. Even death, I realized, would be to him a minor incident, like the turning into a new path or the glimmer of moonlight breaking through the fog.

Two nuns came out through the portals, carrying a body between them. A dead nun, my companion explained to me. Slowly and clumsily they waddled into a small barley-field behind the nunnery. There they disappeared from sight.

"Where are they taking her?"

"Into the field."

"For burial?"

"Oh no."

"To be burned, then?"

"Only the holiest of the lamas are burned. No, she will not be burned." He paused, and seemed to be thinking of something else.

"But what will become of her body?" said I.

"They will cut her body into small pieces. Then the

vultures will come and devour the pieces. That is the regular mode. It is clean and effortless, and sufficiently spiritual. No one is unhappy about it."

"What happens to the body is of no importance?"

"No," he replied. "What happens to the body is of no importance."

"Not even terrible sickness or complete destruction?"

"No, nothing that happens to the body matters."

"But," said I, "why do the fakirs mortify the flesh, sit on nails, rub cow dung in their hair, starve themselves and so on?"

"They are Hindus," he said bashfully, "and I am a Buddhist. We are worlds apart. They, too, long to be free of the body, but they seek a very different way."

"Tell me," said I, "why would you rather walk in the mountains than in the cities?"

He smiled. "We are all selfish. What I seek is peace and purification for myself. I think that is the wisest way. I have thought about it much. In Asia we believe that selfishness is the only way to gain peace. Selfishness by prayer and contemplation. Each one must find the secret for himself, after much suffering or little, as the case may be."

After a while the two nuns returned. They were very sunbrowned and very wrinkled; their heads were shaved and their garments were a filthy spotted gray. But their faces, which I now saw for the first time, were what most struck me: cynical, energetic, thin-lipped and button-eyed with cruelty. They'd found a certain calmness, yes; but it was clearly in hate that they found it, not in love. Perhaps that made the calmness more secure. At any rate, they spared themselves the chance of bitter disappointment. They had an acid twist to their lips, a dried-up look, and they looked more like bald-headed crows than like women.

I caught a whiff of them as they passed: a dry, sulphurous smell, mischievous and secretive.

❧❧❧ Toward nightfall a caravan passed the nunnery on its way to Srinagar.

I almost wept with gratitude when I said good-by to the old ascetic. I remembered again that he had saved my life. "Good-by," I said. He nodded solemnly, and turned stiffly back toward the portals.

❧❧❧ Finally the caravan reached Srinagar. In Srinagar I was sick for three days. Then I went on to Jammu by truck. I had very little of de Hahn's money left in my pocket, and this I resolved to save. So I began to walk from Jammu to Lahore. I didn't know how far it was. No one could tell me. "Half a day," suggested one man; "Ten days," suggested another.

But as I was walking along, hot and dusty but not unhappy, idly watching the yellow butterflies, a fine motorcar came alongside of me and a pair of soft black eyes peered questioningly out of the window. Then I saw a fat brown Hindu face, and two fat smiling lips.

"Englishman?" said the driver in a high tremulous voice.

"No," I shouted. "American."

"Oh," he said, and paused reflectively. He looked at me closely. Then, "Come," he said amiably, "I shall happily drive you."

"Thank you," said I.

"Where are you going?"

I thought quickly. "Well," I replied, "I have nowhere to go, actually."

He stared at me with surprise. "Then I shall happily

215

drive you to Badrapur," he said after another moment's consideration.

So I got in. "My name is Hamadullah," he murmured with an air of bashful self-importance. "I am the secretary to the Maharajah of Badrapur. . . . And you?"

23

IT WAS late afternoon, almost sunset, when we entered the driveway that led to the palace. The sunlight sifting through the leaves and across the lawn made everything seem hazy and unreal. Everyone we passed was asleep, or almost asleep. Two fat boys lay dozing under a flowering bush beside the tennis-court, hands clasped over their round bellies, scrawny bow-legs spread far apart. Under a green umbrella beside the pool sat a dignified old man sipping absently at a tall blue glass. This I learned later was the Diwan.

We drove past a large pool on which two swans were floating, and suddenly, as we rounded a clump of willows, the palace came into view. It was amazing, dazzling, incredible in a setting at the edge of the jungle. An enormous building of white stone, quaintly studded with balconies, turrets, porticos, archways and colonnades. In front of it lay a formal garden full of little evergreens clipped into the shape of birds. An old man in a slovenly dhoti was slowly and sadly raking the gravel walk. Everything looked neglected. Bits of plaster were missing from the façade; here and there a pillar was cracked. The marble pergola was discolored and spotted.

Hamadullah came to a stop at the edge of the rose garden. Beside the pool in a hammock lay a dark, heavy man in white. Near him in the shade of a palm tree sat a brown boy reading aloud from a book. The heavy man looked up listlessly when Hamadullah approached, and then glanced at me. Hamadullah addressed him with considerable elaborateness, I thought, and affectation. He answered monosyllabically and expressionlessly. Could this, I wondered, be the Maharajah? He kept glancing toward me.

Hamadullah walked back to the car, smiling. Yes, it was the Maharajah. "He desires to speak to you."

His Excellency's face was far more distinguished on close view; his lips had a soft disdainful curl, his skin was heavy and oily, but his features were amazingly delicate. "You are American?" he said. I answered that I was.

He paused reflectively. "Are you a happy man?" he asked.

I nodded.

"Do you like people?" He hesitated. A worried look crossed his face. "Do you think there is good in people?"

I nodded again, rather vaguely.

"Ah," he grunted. "There are several things I wish to discuss with you. Your misfortune is, for me, a fortune." He smiled charmingly. "You will stay in the guest-house." This was an order, not a request. But I was more than happy to obey. His eyes glittered, and he waved his hand as we departed; beautiful eyes and a gesture oddly graceful, oddly eloquent. Then he closed his eyes and the boy continued reading.

❦❦❦ Some one had evidently tried to Anglicize my room as much as possible. There were a few dusty books —*Trilby, Uncle Tom's Cabin,* and one or two by Rider Haggard; also some old copies of *Punch.* And also a small piano, discarded, I suppose, by the palace, and a dusty photograph portrait of Edward VII on the wall. There were silk curtains hanging in the doorway, and over the

218 ◇◇◇◇◇◇◇◇◇◇◇◇◇◇◇◇◇◇◇◇◇◇◇◇◇◇◇◇◇◇◇◇

arches of the veranda some heavy cocoanut mats. A spacious, pleasant place. Outside, the palms were stirring gently in the late afternoon heat. A slender young native lowered the jalousies and sprinkled them with water.

I was tired, and lay down on the bed. It wasn't very comfortable, and I glimpsed two enormous pink scorpions on the ceiling; these disconcerted me, and there lurked in my mind the thought of a cobra coiled between the sheets.

Nevertheless, the next thing that I saw was my young native's face, eyelids gleaming and forehead moist, close over mine. "Did you sleep well, sahib?" I nodded.

"There will be dinner in an hour," he said. "Do you wish a bath? . . . Do you wish a massage?" Yes, said I, I thought I might.

"You have fine strong muscles," he observed presently; "and you are not hairy, like most Europeans."

I said, rather shyly, that I was an American.

"Oh, it is all the same. America is in Europe." I expressed uncertainty about this, but he was quite positive.

I asked him about the Rajah. "He is still fairly young, isn't he?"

"Not very young."

"He seems to be a kind and intelligent man."

"Oh yes," he said vaguely, "very kind, very intelligent."

"Is he an able ruler?"

But he didn't grasp my meaning. "He is going to buy two airplanes," was all he had to say.

"What is your name?" I asked.

"Akbar."

"There was a great king called Akbar, wasn't there?"

"Yes. But he is very dead now." I glanced at him. My Akbar, certainly, was very much alive. His eyes glittered, his brown arms rippled and gleamed as he moved them back and forth.

The Maharajah was wearing a handsome waistcoat of light-blue silk and silver embroidery, and over this a long white robelike garment. The others wore dinner coats. Akbar had supplied me with one, too, but even so I felt out of place and ill at ease.

The dining table was grandiosely arranged. There were silvery laces, black drinking glasses, silver statuettes, black glass candlesticks. Many of the dishes were of silver. "You think it is extravagant," said the Maharajah later on, "to have silver plates? But no. You are wrong. It is economical, for they never break, and they last a very long time. Sometimes the cook steals one or two, but not very often. It is a great saving."

There were puris, vegetables cooked in ghi, baked fruits, a baked capon dressed in silver leaf, a boiled pineapple garnished with gold leaf and pistachio nuts. The laws of caste were apparently not strictly observed by the Maharajah. There was champagne and port; and later on a choice of liqueurs.

The Maharajah was a glutton. He gorged tremendously. But always with a look of utter weariness, complete satiety; he was, after all, a true aristocrat. I looked at him carefully. His mouth was haughty, but it was soft and depraved as well: his lips were like petals, delicate, droopy. Most conspicuous were his great glimmering eyelids, and his little black eyes slid to and fro beneath them like marbles. Though they were small they were sad and very beautiful eyes. From a distance he looked fat, piggish, gross. But actually his features were of an amazing precision and subtlety. His hands fluttered nervously, hungrily. Very spoiled, he appeared to be, and full of whims. I was a bit afraid of him.

Then there was the Resident, the Burra Sahib, a lean and sunburned man, whose pince-nez flashed ambiguously in the candlelight. He was a keen golfer, full of anecdotes which he related in a dry but suggestive manner. There was the Assistant Resident, the Chota Sahib, like the Resident an Englishman from Oxford, also wearing heavy glasses, but fat and gloomy and silent. And there was a man introduced as Colonel Biscuit (or so it sounded), an old man with lovely manners and a magnificent goatee. He was even more quiet than the Chota Sahib, and left directly after dinner.

The Maharajah, the Burra Sahib, the Chota Sahib, and I played bridge in the music-room after coffee. I played miserably, and my partner, the Chota Sahib, grew very sullen. The Maharajah grew a little bit more cheerful. Cigars were passed around, and the Maharajah took one. A little boy came skipping in with a silver lighter on a lacquer tray, and the Maharajah pompously lit his cigar at the flame. But after two or three puffs he dropped it furtively, and the little boy picked it up when no one was looking and then skipped out again.

During this uncomfortable game of bridge the Maharanee put in a brief appearance. She wasn't in purdah. She wore high-heeled slippers, but the rest of her costume was native. A large transparent veil hung down from her head and was fastened between the knees. It was an exceedingly graceful costume. She herself was rather heavy and appeared to be somewhat older than the Rajah, for there were gray lines in her hair. She might have been his sister; she had the same eyes, the same lips. But she looked like a very modest, gentle person, and very shy. A pet animal followed her into the room—a tame cheetah, a lovely, graceful creature that licked her hand with a rough magenta tongue and flicked its long nervous tail incessantly. Now and then, the Maharajah told me, the cheetah would be hooded and leashed, then whipped and starved for several days; whereupon it would be sent, with the men following on horseback, to chase a herd of black bucks. It grew very ferocious indeed on these occasions; it would sink its teeth in the victim's throat, moan wildly, lap the hot blood. For the next few days it would behave unmanageably. But gradually it would grow calm again as it was now, and lick the Maharanee's hands with a great show of tenderness.

Soon the Maharajah grew weary of bridge, even though he was winning, and asked me to sit beside him. He sighed. The broadcasting station at Bombay, he complained, had very poor programs, and as often as not they were unintelligible. What was he to do about it? As it was, the radio was most disappointing. Unfortunately I had nothing to suggest. Should he get a phonograph, he asked, the new kind that turns over the disks itself? He was seriously considering it. I agreed that that would be a wise thing to do. Provided, of course, that he had a good set of records. Records? Oh yes, disks. Well, he didn't have very many, but he could order all the latest ones from Lahore. American ones especially, he added politely.

And now regarding an airplane. It was necessary to keep up nowadays. Yes, I likewise thought it was. Well then, which kind did I recommend? And should he get one or two? Two might be wiser, I said: one for himself, very handsomely upholstered and stylishly outfitted with the latest devices from Berlin, and another for emergency purposes. He thought this over; he seemed to be pleased with the idea, but he said no more about it.

"It is a strange thing," he said presently; "I have always wished to write poetry, but I have never done so. Do you like poetry?"

"Yes, now and then."

"Do you like Milton? Tennyson? Hardy? Victor Hugo?"

"Yes, I like all of those fairly well."

"Only *fairly* well? Whom do you prefer to these? Masefield? Longfellow? Alexander Pope?"

"Well . . ."

"Oliver Goldsmith? Poe? Amy Lowell?"

"Depending, of course . . ."

"Anatole France? Walt Whitman? Oscar Wilde?" He looked at me with a sardonic sidelong glance. "Baudelaire? Lamartine?"

"Yes; but of course . . ." But he wasn't interested in what I had to say.

"I am a very nervous man," he said unhappily as he rose. "Often I feel very, very nervous. I was a delicate boy, sensitive. I should have been a great poet, I think. I have read very many poems, you see. I read a poem whenever I am unhappy. Sometimes they make me more unhappy, sometimes less unhappy." His eyelids dropped heavily, his lips were a bit moist. He seemed to be very sleepy.

"I suffer very much, you know," he added.

"All great poets have suffered very much, Your Excellency." I couldn't help saying it. He looked tremendously pleased, his cheeks grew dimpled and glowing, and I felt a little bit ashamed of myself.

"I have always been a poet in my heart. Many people have said that. I write poems, now and then, especially after I have been suffering."

"Oh really! I should consider it a very great honor, Your Excellency, to be allowed to read some of them sometime."

His lips curled softly with vanity and self-contemplation. "They are very musical," he sighed.

"I am certain of it, Your Excellency."

"And very deep and sad, very difficult to—how shall I say?—to comprehend. . . ." His voice was growing very soft and narcissine. "Like Lord Tennyson."

"May I see some of them, Your Excellency?"

"Ah . . . We shall see." He closed his eyes. "Perhaps. It depends."

"Good night, Your Excellency."

"Good night, and loveliest happy dreams."

"Thank you. Good night. . . ."

"Good night. . . ."

Before I went to bed I stood on my balcony and looked across the silent lawn toward the lily pool. There were three willow trees nodding over the water, and beneath one of them I glimpsed the white garments of two servant boys. The water was absolutely still, a sheet of mercury under a chilling half moon. From far away came the toneless melancholy cry of a bird, no bird that I knew, some unidentifiable Indian bird. Overhead were long thin clouds floating toward the south, whitened by the moon. They too seemed frightening and unreal, moving in sleep.

And then, as I lay in bed in the darkness, I could hear the jackals howling. And as soon as they grew silent I could hear the celluloid rustling of insects—moths, flies, crickets, katydids, locusts, termites, beetles, worms—in the ceiling, in the walls, in the floor. I wondered whether the two scorpions were still there, and suddenly I grew deeply disturbed about the possibility of a cobra in my bed; I could almost feel the dainty flicker of its tongue against my instep.

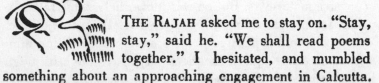

24

THE RAJAH asked me to stay on. "Stay, stay," said he. "We shall read poems together." I hesitated, and mumbled something about an approaching engagement in Calcutta.

"Oh, disregard it. Stay; to please *me*," he said coyly. "One week, two weeks, a month. *Please.*" His eyes looked melancholy and anxious. Yes, said I, and he walked absent-mindedly down toward the rose garden. I wasn't sure whether he was pleased or not.

I grew to know the people at Badrapur better, bit by bit. There was the Burra Sahib, for example. He told me many things about the Rajah, some of them quite shocking and no doubt highly exaggerated, but always with an air of great triviality, as if these indeed were mere nothings to what he could say if he chose. A subtle and malicious man, the Burra Sahib. I liked him very much.

"In his younger days," he stated benignly, "the Rajah used to have regular little orgies from time to time, you know. That was before he married. Twenty or twenty-five years ago. Fireworks, charades, contests of one kind and another, elaborate dances. Men dancers, painted and quite naked except for a veil and a big golden headdress, and many golden bracelets of course. The veils were generally removed during the dance. But these lads were so apt to be treacherous, thieving, capricious, tiresome and spiteful, that only in rare cases could His Excellency bear to have them around for any length of time. I thought them all disgustingly spoiled, not even particularly handsome. But there is most certainly no accounting for tastes."

He also told me about the Rajah's son, who was now at Oxford. Prince Sharavaji had already smashed up three expensive motor-cars. But he was, nevertheless, his father's pride, for he was living very gaily at Balliol, was on the Varsity XI, and expensive professionals were drilling him into an excellent squash-racquets player. A delightful boy, Prince Sharavaji. Handsome but quite small, and very alert and mischievous by nature. The Burra Sahib had things to say about Hamadullah, too. Hamadullah, it seemed, was already wealthy with the misappropriations he had contrived as head-steward. The Minerva in which he drove about was his own. Now and then he would disappear suddenly, for two days, three days, four days; and then return very polite but a bit worn. Possibly he had a mistress in Bombay. Possibly. But the Burra Sahib had no difficulty in imagining several more sinister possibilities which were far more likely. The day would come when he and the Rajah would come to blows. Hamadullah was a designing fox, treacherous to the last degree, incredibly selfish. Sooner or later the Rajah would discover this. Hitherto he had disregarded all hints. But it couldn't last much longer. "Hamadullah is an absolute devil," said the Burra Sahib; "don't have anything to do with him. Keep far away from him. He'll do you no good. His hold on the Maharajah is most deplorable. I disapprove of him highly. Keep away from him, my boy."

As for Hamadullah himself, he was behaving in the most amiable possible fashion, it seemed to me. There was no one for whom he didn't have a smile. He was a rather silky man, not undistinguished, with beautiful manners. He dressed with punctilious care and cleanliness; he wore his dhoti very gracefully, on his bald head a tiny turban, and a thin band of paint across his forehead, the emblem of his caste.

I also met the Diwan and the head bookkeeper. The Diwan was a tall thin man with a face wrinkled and ridged like a relief map of the Himalayas. The eyes were only two horizontal seams. He looked, like the Maharajah, utterly weary, utterly jaded; but unlike the Maharajah he suggested certain resources of the mind, a self-sufficiency behind that Himalayan face. He was the Rajah's most loyal servant, so the Resident told me. And Hamadullah was furiously jealous of him, and the Diwan in turn despised Hamadullah.

Mahmoud, the head bookkeeper, was a fat, officious man, quite thoroughly detestable. A pimp, too, I was given to understand. If I should ever desire anything along that line, he would be more than happy to supply it, whatever my tastes. He was perspiring constantly and his clothes were fœtid. It surprised me that he should have been allowed at all in the palace.

🦋🦋🦋 Then there were my two guest-house servants, Akbar and Iqbal.

Akbar was obstinate, I found, but intelligent. He showed me all around the palace—the swimming-pool, the billiard-room, the library, the gymnasium, the roof gardens, the hothouses, the garage, the stables. It was all very luxurious, very ornate, full of gilt and lacquer, mildly discolored by the dampness. Scarcely restrained, yet oddly elegant, perversely so, like the distinguished Hindu whose hands and lips suggested things which no Westerner would care to admit. He also showed me the Maharajah's racehorses and the delightful gray-eyed elephants. There were three elephants, each with two Mohammedan keepers, a driver and a feeder. The Maharajah's favorite, Baba, was at this moment being bathed. She lay down on her side, allowed herself to be sponged and scrubbed, sprayed water all over herself, and then, with a quixotic gleam in her eyes, all over her keeper. She was trembling with delight. Later we saw her whisking herself with a bundle of hay. Once, long ago, said Akbar, she had broken into the sherry cupboard outside the kitchen and had gotten vulgarly drunk. She had pranced about, plucking flowers with her trunk, hurling missiles at her observers with unfailing aim. Finally she calmed down, rubbed her trunk gently against a banyan tree, then ambled back to her stall with a sly victorious leer.

Akbar was very ambitious. "I shall not stay here always," he said. "I wish an education."

"Could you take me with you?" he went on. "Back to Europe? I wish to go to an American university."

"But you're married, Akbar."

"Oh," he said airily, "she can wait till I get back. I don't love her any more."

"What do *you* think of the Rajah?" he asked me once. And then, "What do you think of the Ranee? Do you think she is beautiful? Is she more beautiful than American women or less beautiful?" And then, as he warmed to his subject, "Do you like fat women better, or thin women? . . . Do you think the Rajah is too fat? . . . Do you think I am too fat?" Then he told me about his past amours, quaint and shabby little affairs, not very pleasant. After a while I stopped listening. Akbar could be very much of a bore.

Around his neck he wore a string, and at the end of that a little bag. This was a talisman against evil spirits, he told me. What was in it? He hesitated; a bit of rice, he said, and the testicles of a cat, and some hairs from a wild boar, and a few wrinkled roots, and one or two other things. He wasn't sure.

"At night," he explained, "men become wicked. But after they fall asleep, the wickedness leaves their bodies, it goes out into the dark air, and all these wicked spirits join together and hang over the houses where people sleep, and float in past the cocoanut mats, and bring the bad dreams with them. Then the people suffer and do wicked things the next day. But if you wear a talisman you are protected."

"And you have therefore never done anything wicked, Akbar?"

"Oh," he said shyly, "when I wish to do something wicked I do not wear my talisman."

Iqbal was my chamber-boy. He made my bed and cleaned my room. He was very young, hardly more than thirteen or fourteen, but he was already shadowing his eyes with kohl and beginning to look out for himself with subtlety and surmise. He had long black lashes, glistening black eyes, and was as graceful as a girl. His skin was very much darker than Akbar's. He had a weakness for golden ornaments, which looked pleasing against his mahogany skin, and he always wore a moth-eaten cap of blue velvet embroidered with gold. A gift from Hamadullah, he explained.

He was very mischievous, a rascal, a regular little thief. Once I caught him stealing my comb, which had an ornamental golden rim along the edge. I sent him away. "And don't you come back again," I said, "or I'll tell the Diwan."

He looked very pathetic and lonely as he walked away. But he did come back presently, with tears in his eyes. "Forgive me, sahib. I have been very wicked."

But two mornings later my golden watch was missing. I had my suspicions, of course. And then when Iqbal appeared to make the bed, I saw the telltale fob peering out from under his jacket.

"Come here, Iqbal."

"Sahib?" He looked very surprised, and cast an involuntary glance toward the doorway.

"Come here, Iqbal."

"Oh, sahib," he cried, and threw himself on his knees. "Oh, sahib, forgive me, forgive me!"

This time I whipped him, and said that I most certainly would tell the Diwan. But after this he was very faithful and well-behaved. He began to imitate my mannerisms, and to follow me around the palace gardens whenever I went for a walk. He would ask me questions, like Akbar, in a timid, husky voice. "Where is America?" and, "Have you many concubines, sahib, when you go back to America?" and, "Will you go back to America soon?"

But there was no privacy with him about. No matter what I was doing, there he was, peering at me with his glittering, truculent eyes. But I was used to this sort of thing and didn't mind.

Once he related to me the most exciting thing that had ever happened to him. It appeared that he and his older brother Ahmed were quarreling, some years ago, about a pet monkey. It was Ahmed's pet monkey, but Iqbal wanted it. Ahmed struck Iqbal. Whereupon he, Iqbal, seized a knife and struck it into Ahmed's side. Ahmed died several days later, and Iqbal was thoroughly spanked. He told me this in a rather sad voice. I wondered whether he was lying. Probably not. I could understand, looking at his pretty

◇◇◇◇◇◇◇◇◇◇◇◇◇◇◇◇◇◇◇◇◇◇◇◇◇◇◇◇◇◇◇◇◇◇◇◇◇◇◇

face, how people, both men and women, young and old, might forgive him a good deal.

Once he rowed with me in a little green rowboat with green satin cushions out to the island in the middle of the great pool. There was a marble pavilion on the edge of the island, guarded by a row of little marble elephants. Above the pavilion and the elephants stood several orange trees, and behind the orange trees a shrine in the midst of a flower garden.

There were large pink lotuses around the steps into the shrine and in the doorway. Inside were candles burning, the smell of patchouli, several little golden statues of Krishna, Rama and the rest of them. I didn't like the smell of the incense and walked down the stairway toward the water. But here too there was a vague smell of patchouli and of decaying flowers. Through the orange trees, through the motionless green twiglets dripping with dew and spider webs, I could see the marble balustrade of the pavilion running along the water, and the dark-green water below covered with lotus pads; and the two white swans motionless in the water and the two inverted swans in the glassy surface below them. All of it as unreal as a child's dream. What could I feel, there, except what was unreal? An unreal melancholy, an unreal regret for lost childhood, an unreal feeling of peace and absolute seclusion.

But it was too unreal to be consoling. My thoughts grew feathery, dream-like, all against my will. I grew drowsy, lascivious; my reflections grew sultry and far-fetched. Soon I fell asleep, smelling unripe oranges and incense. In my dream it appeared, among other things, that the oranges had dried out, had turned hollow and metallic, had changed into little bells.

When I woke up I saw a thin old man ambling to and

fro in front of the temple, absent-mindedly ringing a small bronze bell. He was wearing a light blue tunic. When he saw that I was awake he came limping up. "Good day," he said.

"Good day."

He craned his neck, his sharp eyes peered at me questioningly. "Pardon, I do not hear well."

"Good day," I repeated, more loudly. He smiled. Then he spread his fingers daintily and rang his bell some more.

"What are you doing?" I shouted.

"Oh," he replied airily, "some praise of religion, love of Krishna and all that."

I liked his casual manner. I asked him about religion, Krishna and all that, and finally about transmigration. He sat down beside me and rested his chin in his palm in a pleased and leisurely way. His face was a labyrinth of wrinkles.

"Oh yes," he said, "we all believe it. We die, you understand. Well then. Let us assume that we have been slow, impractical in life. So we must change. We become a rabbit. Now we are quick, full of energy, but you might say too afraid. Very well. We become a tiger. But alas, now we are too fierce. So we become a cow. It is very fine, of course, to be a cow. And so on. Finally the god-like in us is opened little by little, like these lotus buds. Do you see? And after thousands of years the world will be god-like and perfect. All will be god-like perfection and god-like unity. Do you see?" He looked at me with great earnestness and then broke into a soft intelligent smile.

Then he ambled away again and disappeared in the temple. I saw him only once after this, hurriedly and from a distance. He had been scolded on this latter occasion by the Diwan for some bit of negligence, and was walking past the kitchen, weeping silently into his spotted blue sleeve.

Iqbal had been playing by the water, making pebbles skip, catching frogs and turtles, and so forth. He came up to me now with a bunch of flowers—wild arum lilies, geranium, heliotrope. "For you, sahib," and he placed them in my lap and leaned against my knees. The edge of his velvet cap was wet where his forehead was sweating; his eyelids shone; there was just the beginning of a downy shadow on his wet upper lip.

"I want to be with you always, sahib," he murmured. The little hypocrite, I thought to myself. But I felt flattered, nevertheless.

He put his sticky little hands around my arm. "You are strong, like a god," he said softly. "Are all Americans strong?"

Then he placed his black forefinger on a long ugly scar on my left arm. "Did you get that in a battle, sahib?"

"Yes. In a great bloody battle."

"And that streak of white hair in the middle of your head," he said, smiling softly, "how did you get that?" He had an odd precocious look on his little brown monkey face.

"In another battle."

"Oh," he laughed, "no, no!" He placed his cheek tenderly against my knee. "Oh, sahib, you are so strong and limber. You have a face like a boy's but a smile like an old man's! Your face is so smiling and loving! You are like the water, your voice is so low, you smell so good and so deep and so far away. . . ." I began to feel very pleased; I could feel myself purring like a cat.

As soon as we returned to the mainland he ran off with three of the kitchen boys. They all skipped down the bamboo path toward the bathing-place, giggling loudly. About me no doubt, I thought peevishly. The humid heat had given me a headache.

🙣🙣🙣 Hamadullah met me on the guest-house veranda. Would I care, he asked, to go driving with him?

First we drove down toward the town of Badrapur, and through the filthy clamorous streets. Hamadullah had to ring a bell and blow his horn constantly to clear the way. *"Hai! Yenwela!"* shouted some street boys running along at our side. *"Hai! Yenwela!"* There was one barefooted policeman in the middle of the town, but he blinked his eyes wearily at us and did not move.

We left the town and entered the flat open country that stretched southward toward the jungle. We passed a syphilitic priest thumping his gong, a saddhu beating a tom-tom, some naked boys bathing in a muddy stream, some old women making bricks out of cow dung. It was very hot, very dusty, and we had to drive very slowly to avoid hitting sheep, pigs, bullock-carts, cows. I began to feel quarrelsome and uncomfortable.

25

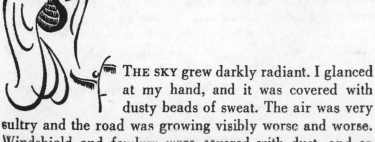

THE SKY grew darkly radiant. I glanced at my hand, and it was covered with dusty beads of sweat. The air was very sultry and the road was growing visibly worse and worse. Windshield and fenders were covered with dust, and so were Hamadullah and I. The tall grasses hissed against the tires.

"We have taken the incorrect turn," sighed Hamadullah; "I am profoundly sorry." We crossed a dry river bed, and signs of civilization were gradually disappearing. Far off to the left lay the gray furry edge of the jungle. "I suggest," said Hamadullah, "that we proceed to Pandrapore. There we can rest. I think there will be a storm. I am profoundly sorry. Please forgive me!"

A warm wind arose. Dust went swirling along the road. The grass flattened upon the plain and across the swampy places we were passing. Laboriously Hamadullah drove the car through a sandy stretch, and then forded a shallow stream which was now only a thin trickle winding between vermilion rocks. And just as the first drops of rain began to fall the road took a sudden turn and we saw the village in front of us.

"This is Pandrapore," said Hamadullah, "and it is, as you see, a very shabby village. We are all ashamed of Pandrapore. No one ever visits it. It is going to the dogs."

The village ran along on either side of the road, with the dry brown rice-fields radiating from each side in irregular unfenced rectangles. There were a few acacias and laburnums sending forth a thin cascade of yellow flowers, but beyond these nothing except the low windowless dwellings out of cow dung squatting in the brown earth, uniform and dead.

The villagers jumped up as we passed, assuming quite simply and amiably that we—Hamadullah, I, and the Minerva—were creatures superior to themselves. They peered, they whispered. Out of one door two naked little boys were watching us, out of another a cow. It was not uncommon that a cow lived in the same room with a Hindu family.

As soon as we reached Pandrapore, the rain crashed down on us with the noise of a hundred drums. Where dust and brown fields had extended two minutes ago there now was a bouncing of raindrops, a rough muddy sheet.

One of the villagers—a dignified old Mohammedan—led us to the largest of the houses, his own home, distinguished by gay decorations on the walls, pictures of elephants and parrots done in whitewash. The Minerva was left in the middle of the road, with a blanket over its hood.

"This is bad," said Hamadullah in deep sorrow. "The road will be a big bog, the fields will be lakes, and since we are not frogs we shall have to stay here. I apologize for my stupidity; I am very much ashamed. It was most unforgivable of me. Please, please, forgive me."

❧❧❧ And he was right, for the next morning, although the sun was already peering through holes in the clouds, there was nothing around us but a gray quivering mass of water where the road and grassy swampland had been, a shallow pond full of quixotic bubblings, sudden whirlpools, eddies that lasted only one capricious moment. The rainfall during that hideous insomniac night had been constant and tremendous. This was the result. We were caught. There was nothing to do but wait for the road to emerge again. And wait we did, for three days.

Our Mohammedan host was very kind. He gave the hut a fresh coat of mud as soon as the sun came out; brought fresh straw for our beds, a pot and a pan for whatever strange ablutions we should wish to perform, and tried pathetically to feed us well. But he was also very curious. Each morning, and each evening as I went to bed, I could see him peering surreptitiously to see what might be seen. I could see that he was very much interested in my clothes. He asked questions constantly until Hamadullah ordered him to be quiet. But he was a gentle, submissive soul, and felt highly honored to have the motor-car standing in front of his hut.

The rice-fields were all glittering mirrors now, and before long the bullocks were sent out, the men were knee-deep in the muddy water, and the women marched out in the afternoon, carrying on their heads the day's lunch in great yellow straw baskets, and brass pails full of drinking-water. Everybody was excited and happy. The women were singing and joking, and the older ones squatted beside their huts and made dung cakes. In the afternoon the sun came out clear, and everything shone like crystal.

I got to know the whole village. They were all very thin, their dhotis and saris were shabby and stained, but they were graceful little people, bird-like, delicate, suspicious, quick and quiet, and surprisingly sensitive, anything but clods. There was the man with the cow. The cow was a stupid, obstinate beast, and gave very little milk; but she was sacred, and he loved her. He gave her the best food, and though he was only a thin little rat of a man himself, she somehow continued to look sleek, smug and superior. Doubtless it is this gentle, contented air of resignation in their cows that so appeals to the Hindus; the perfect attribute; and no sin, therefore, is so bad as killing a cow. Strangle your mother, poison your father, slaughter your children—wicked, yes, but forgivable. But killing a cow is unforgivable.

There were two holy men, too. One a Mohammedan, one a Hindu.

"Saddhus?" I asked Hamadullah. "Fakirs?"

"Oh no. Nothing in particular. They are all different, you see, they call themselves this and that, but it doesn't matter. They are all holy, but mad."

Even here the laws of caste were rigidly in force. "Caste is a wise thing," the Diwan had told me, "and if you condemn it, that is because you don't understand it. It gives stability, contentment, resignation, continuity, specialization. In your country there is caste, too, I am aware, but it is too easy to move from one into a higher one. This breeds discontent, materialism. Do you see?"

I understood it more when I saw how vaguely, how casually, these people seemed to live. And the women; not all of them were virtuous, it was true (one of them had tried, very foolishly, to bargain with Hamadullah: for a few annas she would show herself to me, without clothes. Would I enjoy this?), but most of them looked very peaceful, very aloof, and their faces were like their daily existence, spiritual, free of desire.

But times were changing, said our host Ali with deep regret. The girls wanted more jewelry and they wanted to go to Lahore, of which they had heard fascinating tales; and as for the boys, they were hopelessly naughty. Some of them stole, several had run away recently and had started a traffic in opium, two or three were already bitten by venereal diseases. Criminals on the road were growing more common. There were several in the neighborhood, attacking carts, robbing pilgrims, stealing little boys and girls. Even the children were cultivating strange new vices, said Ali, and there was no trusting them any longer. The world was changing. The young ones were beginning to want things, new things, expensive and unspiritual things.

We lived on rice, bread, and goat's milk. A gangrenous little boy once brought us some dried fruits and sweets wrapped in silver foil; but they looked so strange and so unsavory, I could not bring myself to eat them and gave them back. I regretted it, though, a moment later, for he had come happy and expectant, and departed with a sad look on his hideous little face. Various other favors as well were forthcoming. One old Hindu lent us a large white sun-umbrella that clearly hadn't been used for years. We insulted him by not using it. And a young girl with coal-black slanting eyes brought me a chain of sky-blue beads, in the hope, Hamadullah simperingly explained, that I might possess certain magical powers and be willing to arrange that she should have a child before long.

"An odd way to ask it," I said.

Hamadullah tittered. "No, no. Not what you mean! She is married and highly chaste. But her husband is only a hairless boy and she is most impatient!"

✄✄✄ There was a little Shiva shrine at the end of the village, on a small hillock beside the village well. A sacred bull carved out of wood guarded it on one side, and on the other, under a young eucalyptus, stood three small clay elephants. Usually the place was deserted and it wore an air of shabbiness and neglect. Even the statue of the kindly god Ganesh, with pot belly and elephant's head, the god who supervised motherhood and in general stood as the omen of a successful conquest of obstacles—even fat Ganesh had a chipped trunk, his genitals were broken off, ants ran across the creases in his belly, and pigeon droppings streaked his huge elephant's ears.

But now and again, as I watched one morning, natives would come with shamefaced offerings—offerings of gratitude in this case, for the rain had arrived: bits of corn, sweets, a few bedraggled white flowers. One old man brought a small bowlful of painted pebbles, and a dirty little boy came up with a nosegay, pasty and forlorn, tightly wrapped around with grass-stalks. They all behaved like children, old as well as young, bringing their excessively humble gifts with a mingled air of pride and confusion, mumbling a snatch of prayer, perhaps, then walking away and forgetting all about it two minutes later.

But less child-like seemed (wrongly, perhaps) the ceremony of thanksgiving performed the second night after we came. The whole village assembled shortly after sunset near the big well. "You may come, too, if you wish," Ali told me: he and a handful of Mohammedans stood among the trees and watched with an air of breezy superiority the strange proceedings. A lingam as tall as a man had been erected, and it was being showered with sprays of jasmine and laburnum. Later, when it grew dark, torches were lit. There was a glittering of cheap tinsel and a fluttering of stained silk, a stink of stale sandalwood and a rattling of old tin pans. As it grew darker the spirit of the worshipers grew more intense and more vigorous. They cried, they sang, they shouted, they barked. One old man groveled in a heap of hot ashes beside the crematory, face down, bruising and charring his shrunken privacies in the embers. There was a peculiar sexual smell -weaving about through the smell of incense. Farther down, near the black water of the rice-field, stood several silent couples, and also a few animals—a cow, a donkey, a goat. Control had left them all, and a low religious grunt ran through the higher noises like water through the swamp growth. The little boy who had brought the nosegay to Shiva that morning was running back and forth in a noisy naked excitement, clapping his hands and waving a long white feather in the air.

A child had died a few days before, and the funeral took place the day following the thanksgiving ceremony; this was the day before we left. The sun had been shining brightly and the road was muddily visible once more. The old Minerva had, after great trouble, been started again and two boys had brushed and polished the nickel for us.

It was dusk when the funeral procession crossed the fields toward a clump of pines near the edge of the jungle. The child lay on a little bier, dressed in white silk. A holy man sprinkled water from the Ganges absent-mindedly on its dark wrinkled face. Petroleum was poured on the pyre, and the fire was lit. The pine trunks began to shine like pillars in a temple. Far off I could see the flicker of the torches reflected in the rice-fields. Animals approached curiously—two pariah dogs and a cow, and farther off, no doubt, the ever-watchful jackals.

The fire didn't last long. It died down as suddenly as it had sprung up. The holy man approached again. He dipped his fingers in the ashes, then sprinkled some up toward the sky, some down toward the water-smooth fields. The people began to chant gently. "Go away!" muttered the holy man to the departing spirit. "Go away!" sang the mourners in a subdued voice, "go away . . . go away. . . ." No one was weeping, not even the mother.

Their faces were all quite apathetic. Presently the holy man placed the rest of the ashes in a small urn, and they all walked back to the village, chatting pleasantly.

🙚🙚🙚 When we drove off, Ali came up to us and said good-by on behalf of Pandrapore. There were tears in his soft intelligent eyes; but he was an old fox, and I wasn't convinced that they were real.

"They are all children," said Hamadullah as he guided the steaming car through the morass. "Nothing more than lonely and inefficient and unlucky children."

"Yes, they are lonely; they are afraid to be anything else," said the Diwan that afternoon in the palace garden when I asked him about the villagers. "Their feeling of home is very strong, and so is their attachment to their few wretched belongings, and so is the force of habit and surrounding. Rupees are fairly important to them, humility is most important, food is, of course, important, and religion is distinctly important. But actually they are quickest to notice love. That is what touches them all, Mohammedans as well as Hindus. That is what ties them all together, though they would be the first ones to deny it. Love is what they want, but all they ever see is the shabby shamefaced edge of it, most of them. But they keep on hoping till the very end."

🙚🙚🙚 When we got back we found we were just in time. The garden party was to be that very afternoon. The Rajah would have been very upset indeed to have anyone rashly interfering with his plans by being absent. He had been very sulky lately, Akbar told me after my bath. He had accused the entire household, one by one, even the Diwan, of disloyalty, inefficiency, and lewdness.

"And," said Akbar after a meditative pause, "there were reasons. For all three."

"Well," I said, "come on, Akbar, and give me a rub." It felt pleasant to be clean again and to feel Akbar's strong hands limbering up my calves and my buttocks.

26

THE TENNIS-COURT looked very green and velvety. Six little ball boys in blue silk jackets stood at each end of the court to catch the balls as they passed the players, for there were no backstops at all. But there was an umpire's chair painted flaming red, and there were several umbrellas, including a large embroidered one with a golden pole intended for the Rajah himself. A melancholy old man (a Brahmin, for he wore a string around his neck) walked slowly around and around, measuring the height of the net, plucking a bit of clover here and there, stamping out stray flecks of lime with his bare feet. The only others who were there as yet were the fat gardeners in loin cloths squatting on the lawn, chatting vaguely, joking in an aimless depressed manner, snipping the grass haphazardly with little black scissors. Nobody else ever spoke to them. They too, I noticed, wore the white Brahmin strings. They were like the sparrows chattering on the gravel—just a sadly necessary part of the scenery, no more. But even they, I remembered, were many, many degrees higher than the poor Mehtar who swept the dung from the bridle path beyond the big pool, and he, Lord knows, was lucky and affluent compared with certain unmentionable others.

Beyond stretched the lovely lawn dappled with sunlight. There were some parrots in the palm trees, a tame peacock was strutting along the walk, and out under the weeping willows beside the great pool two swans nibbled away at the vermin under their wings.

There was, after all, I reflected as I watched all this—the gaudy little ball boys, the sweeper, the swans—something decidedly troubling about living here in Badrapur. It was almost like an opium dream, not natural, and the imagination was gently lulled into the trite channels of forgetfulness; and these stray bits of misery and evil became unreal, too, merely rhythmic undertones in this soothing swampy melody.

When I first reached the tennis-court no one else had yet arrived. But before long they appeared, one by one, the Resident, the Diwan, the General, the Assistant Resident, Hamadullah, Mahmoud, and presently the Rajah himself with several guests whom I failed to recognize. Later I was introduced to the Bishop of Jodhpore and his wife, Mrs. Squair, and to Miss Elverton, a spinster authoress. They were bores, all three of them, and insufferably smug. The Rajah looked very weary and a bit sad. "I do feel sad," he admitted when I mentioned this to him. "I am losing faith in everybody. Even my closest ones are a pack of wicked jackals."

Two young princes began to play. "Love to love!" cried the umpire, and everyone laughed happily. The Rajah beckoned to me and asked me to sit beside him.

"Love," he whispered to me. "Why is it called that? I have often wondered." But I didn't know.

I looked at him closely. It was like gazing into a pool. Stagnant and deep-seeming, but what made it seem so deep was only the motionless floating of a million green fragments. Nothing profound, nothing harmonious. A bit disturbing and that was all.

He was silent for a few minutes. He seemed preoccupied.

Then he whispered. "Tell me something about your God, please."

"My God?"

"Yes. The American God."

"Well," I said hesitantly, "it varies with each individual. As indeed it should. . . ."

"Nonsense!" he said. "You know that is not true at all. I desire facts."

"But," I temporized, "there are no facts about God, are there?"

He looked annoyed. "Very well," he said with a pout. "If you prefer not to tell me, of course . . . You apparently do not wish to trust me."

Later he said, more gently, "Your God is Love, is not that so?"

But just then Hamadullah came up. He was going to play a set with the Rajah. He knew very well how to play with the Rajah, I found. Hamadullah was no fool. With amazing skill he managed to play the balls high and shallow to the Rajah, so that the latter could stand near the net and smash them viciously, if clumsily, out of reach. This was plainly his favorite, and indeed his only shot. He won the set, 6-1. The guests applauded. The Maharajah looked pleased.

But only for a moment. When he sat down he looked very hot and very unhappy again. He wiped his forehead wearily with a gold-embroidered kerchief.

The English and Indian ladies began to play croquet now, and several brown gentlemen played badminton. The rest talked about the recent cricket match, and the approaching Hunt, and about the ball that was to take place that very night. Ices were served in the marquee, a little native band all dressed in green and gold put in a surprising appearance, and several acrobats performed on a big rug stretched across the tennis-court. Everything looked mild and precise, like a toy scenery, a setting in a marionette show. It was the first day of June, the monsoon was arriving, and in another week they would all go to the Hunt. I hoped that I, too, would be asked to go to the Hunt. There was a heavy green light over everything, each object was unnaturally vivid. The swans, the musicians, the spangled acrobats, the rose-colored parasols, all of them gleamed in the green sunlight as if they possessed an inner light of their own.

When the sun began to sink, Japanese lanterns were brought out and lit. The General's wife sang something by Amy Woodford Finden, and the Maharance appeared for a moment to play "The Happy Farmer" on the viola. The twelve pretty ball boys passed gracefully among us, bearing tall julep glasses and sherbets and almond wafers shaped like tigers and doves. As twilight approached several Catharine wheels and Roman candles were set off.

But all the time I had the odd feeling that something was about to happen; perhaps because the Maharajah seemed so fretful, possibly because the air was so heavy and strange. Once I glimpsed Mahmoud whispering hastily to Hamadullah. But I thought nothing of it, of course. Certainly there was nothing exceptional in that.

But then something did happen. The sun was suddenly blotted out, there was a hissing sound among the trees, the Roman candles flickered and went out. In less than a minute the rain was falling in sheets, lightning was flashing across the sky, great roars of thunder resounded from the jungle. The ladies cried daintily and ran toward the palace with half-opened parasols, and the gardeners gathered the purple cushions, the red umbrellas, and the yellow wicker chairs, the little brown ball boys were sad to see their silken jackets get wet, and rushed helter-skelter up toward the palace kitchen with their trays and dishes.

❧❧❧ The rain had subsided by the time the Maharajah's ball got under way. Everything was running very smoothly, the guests all tried very hard indeed to appear genteel and worldly. Two or three petty rajahs from the neighborhood were present. They were costumed magnificently, far more magnificently than our own Maharajah, in light-blue silks and light-green satins studded with precious stones. The Maharajah stood in the hall to receive. A stream of motor-cars, tongas, rickshas and victorias passed under the main portico. In the Great Hall curtained stands had been placed, and behind these the ladies who were in purdah could listen to the music, and flutteringly parted the curtains now and again to peer at the doings of their men. The Englishmen were almost all in uniform. They were tall and thin, whereas most of the natives, garbed in silks and jewels, were short and plump. The natives all looked very shy, and it seemed strange and sad that they should fit less easily into these surroundings than the gossiping English ladies who were stalking to and fro like noisy pink flamingos. A regimental band from Amjer was playing in the conservatory. The storm was over. Lanterns were hanging over the marble pool, carpets were spread on the wet sweet-smelling lawn, ices and champagne were being served on the terrace above the rose garden.

But the Maharajah himself looked sulky. He looked more than sulky, he looked nervously unhappy. I heard him speaking to the Collector. "I have ordered two airplanes from Calcutta," he said portentously. "One for my own use, with upholstery from Berlin, and one for staff use, emergencies, and so on, you understand."

The Collector nodded his approval.

"One must keep up," added the Maharajah meaningly, and walked off with a grunt.

I thought at one moment that he would come up and speak to me. But he didn't. He looked very strange, there was no doubt about it. For one instant—it may have been only an effect of the slanting light, it may have been nothing more than a nervous prescience on my part—his eyes took on a look of peculiar hatred. That was the last I saw of him.

The storm had left a disagreeable heaviness in the air. The visiting rajahs wiped their brows with purple handkerchiefs. The guards in the hallway looked hot and embarrassed. They wore red turbans, red waistcoats, white wrinkled breeches, but they didn't look right; some were too fat, some were too thin, some were too tall, some were too short. Their legs looked particularly unmilitary. They were all either knock-kneed or bowlegged. One of them kept picking his nose, another was hiccoughing noisily.

As I walked across the lawn toward the pool I passed Hamadullah. He was looking very agitated. "Hamadullah," said I, but he passed without looking at me. I was beginning to feel badly. Everyone was snubbing me. Out on the croquet lawn I passed the Chota Sahib and the Collector's wife. They snubbed me, too. Then I sat down beside the pool and began to contemplate on the uncertainties of life and the vanity of human wishes. Perhaps it was the banana ice and the champagne; something had disagreed with me. I felt dizzy. I began to be sick.

When I returned at last to the palace I saw that something, very clearly, had gone wrong. The ball was over, the musicians had left. The Maharajah was nowhere. Hamadullah, Mahmoud and the Diwan had disappeared. I asked the Burra Sahib. He looked surprised and embarrassed. "His Excellency has retired," he answered primly, and stared at me with curiosity and distrust.

⧈⧈⧈ When I woke up the next morning I was amazed to see that all my belongings had been packed, very neatly, in a little bag and set beside my bed. I noticed Akbar standing in the doorway. He looked very sheepish and a little bit sad.

"Akbar!" I said. "What is the meaning of this?"

"I am very grievous, sahib. You are leaving today."

"Leaving?" He nodded his head. "What's happened?"

It developed that there had been a silly and disagreeable plot of some kind. I never discovered precisely what it was. It all remained forever somewhat of a mystery to me, like everything in India. Hamadullah was leaving, too. He had been the instigator; I was considered to have been involved. It was all very complicated and disconcerting. The whole thing, of course, had gone wrong. And of course there had been accusations, counter-accusations, recriminations, lies.

"Did some one want to kill the Maharajah?" I asked.

"Oh no," said Akbar gently. "It was the Diwan. They wanted to steal him away, I think. . . ."

"But they didn't succeed?"

"No, the Diwan is very well and safe, but very angry."

Where shall I go now, I wondered. But it wasn't so bad as it might have been. Hamadullah was leaving that very day for Calcutta. I could drive with him, said Akbar.

I was regretful, naturally, that I should be forced to miss the Hunt. But it couldn't be helped. I wouldn't even be able to say good-by. Akbar suggested that it would be wiser not to try to see the Rajah. It was most unfortunate, and not in the least as I had planned.

"Good-by, Akbar," I said.

"Good-by, sahib." There were tears in his eyes, unmis-
.akably.

❈❈❈ I saw Iqbal playing with a pet monkey down
by the stables as I was leaving. I waved my hand to him
and called his name. I wanted to say good-by. But when he
saw me he ran away; and a moment later Hamadullah
came driving up to the guest-house.

27

A RAGGED dirt road led from Badrapur to the outskirts of Lahore. In Lahore we met the Grand Trunk Road which led all the way to Calcutta. It was fifteen hundred miles, said Hamadullah, from Lahore to Calcutta. It would take the old Minerva five days. His grandfather had once walked from Jammu to Calcutta, he said, and that was even farther than from Lahore to Calcutta. It had taken him, who was a very pious man, well over a year. He never recovered from this long trip, in fact, for not long after arriving he died of an unidentifiable but dreadful disease which, so Hamadullah had heard, distended the body to three times its size and turned it into a golden pink.

After Lahore came huge stretches of grassy plain; nothing but reeds and grasses, all of a muddy indeterminate color, and now and then fields of clover and vetch. Then, as we approached and departed again from Amritsar, we passed enormous ponds of white lilies, endless fields of roses cultivated for their attar, bamboo groves, cocoanut palms, toddy palms, banana, banyan, mango, mimosa, acacia. Both Hamadullah and I were very fond of trees, and he explained each variety to me with great care. He didn't seem in the least depressed.

We passed Delhi and Agra. As we moved eastward the traffic grew heavier. There were bullocks and bullock-carts, cows, camel-carts, donkey caravans with the drivers lazily smoking their hookahs, American trucks overloaded with boxes and dozing Hindus, and as we approached the towns we met tongas drawn by ponies, motor-cars, bicycles. And then, when we entered a stretch of wilderness again, monkeys on all sides, parrots, and now and then a pretty gazelle.

Hamadullah drove extremely well. He avoided many an unexpected creature, wild, domestic, human, or mechanical, for whom the road was a gathering-place rather than a thoroughfare. He told me about himself, frankly and charmingly. He told me about his childhood, and how he had become a dancing-boy. "I was a very lovely boy," he said lasciviously, "and the neighboring rajahs would borrow me at very high prices to dance for them. I danced for the Maharajah of Mysore and the Maharajah of Udaipur, and for the Gaekwar of Baroda. I would always stay a week or two. Sometimes they placed me into elegant boudoirs, with great silky beds to sleep in. Oh, I had many suitors in those days! I danced very well, I think, sometimes in a long black satin robe embroidered with serpents out of silver, sometimes in stiff and complicated velvets arranged so as to suggest the variable powers of the god Vishnu. And sometimes quite naked except for a sort of veil. In this mystic costume I pretended to be Shiva, the destroyer." He smiled reminiscently. He was really a very handsome and dignified man. Except for his hands, with oddly long fingers which I found repulsive, and an indefinable air of softness about him. Whenever he spoke his words suggested a richly ironical mind, a modest but critical philosophy all his own.

"When I grew older, alas, I grew hairy as well. It was depressing, but it couldn't be helped. It was bound to come sooner or later. One by one my suitors deserted me. I was no longer in demand as the god Shiva. But it is, after all, the sort of disappointment that one can get used to. No one is to be blamed. It is fate. I am quite happy, as you see." It was a poignant little recital. I began to like shifty, hairy, gossipy Hamadullah much better. I wanted to ask him about that final affair at Badrapur, but for some reason I didn't quite dare. Some mystifying little aroma about the whole matter disconcerted me.

ℳℳℳ We passed the swampy places of the Punjab, and palm grove after palm grove. We slept out-of-doors, usually, under our green mosquito curtains. There were hundreds of little villages—all India appeared to be living in villages such as Pandrapore, and presently we approached the huge grassy country by the Ganges.

At Cawnpore everyone was wearing roses. It was the night of some festival or other. Tall dark Pathans were leaning against the filthy walls, with roses in their hands, or roses behind their ears. Girls were walking around with rings in their noses and candle lanterns in their hands. We met a strange man here, a very learned Turkoman from Bokhara who had escaped across the border into Persia and from there had made his way through Afghanistan into Kashmir. He told us many wild tales about Soviet Turkestan, incredible tales about the Cheka, the spies, and so on; many of them were lies, no doubt. He had a hare lip and his face was disfigured by heavy pock-marks, his eyelids were red and scaly, and he also suffered from a strange disease called the *rishta;* everyone in Bokhara had the *rishta,* he said placidly; they drank nothing but stagnant water, and with it the worms that grew and flourished under their skin until the barber drew them out. A hideously ugly man, but very wise and in his way refreshing. He didn't tell us his name and he left us abruptly without a word.

At Allahabad there were thousands of fakirs, feet bleeding, stomachs bloated, loins shriveled; dust on their lips, ashes and cow dung in their hair, their sinister secret odors assailing one from afar. Absurd, puzzled, pointless people, they were, with expressions both profound and devastatingly stupid. People who had found it impossible that they should be happy in this world, and yet sufficiently accustomed to vileness and misery to feel no bitterness whatever. All day, along the Ganges, in the sedge grass or on the paving, sat these wretched masochists, asking no more than that you should give them a crust or spit in their eyes. They tortured themselves in every possible way: self-whippers, sitters on nails, skeleton men, grovelers in dung, devourers of filth, pullers of hair, quaint pinchers and tweakers, contortionists, one or two who bit themselves, one or two who practiced a constant and quite horrifying variety of self-contemplation. Many of them were dreadfully deformed or dreadfully diseased, or both. And beyond them, along the opposite shore, the melon-beds of Allahabad shone tranquil and misty in the twilight; and over these, the scavenger birds wheeling bleakly; and over these, the salmon-colored clouds drifting slowly southward, mile by mile, from the Himalayas.

It was just as bad with them at Mirzapur and Benares. At Mirzapur we saw a saddhu walking across some burning coals, stooping, picking them up and scattering them over his head. Then he began to chant and limped away, down to the sandbanks. We could see him through the reeds, rolling in the water and moaning. There was a loathsome smell of burning flesh in the air: that was as close to anything spiritual as the whole affair seemed to get. Across the road, at the gate of a small weather-beaten temple, stood a *devadasi*, a temple harlot, watching us, loose-lipped and subtle-eyed. There was no telling, assuredly, what these people were thinking, what they were planning to do, where they expected to end up. But apparently there was nothing they weren't prepared to bear, nothing at all.

The Ganges is a very big and very sacred river. Every possible sort of thing happens along its shores, in it, on it, under it, beside it, near it. At Benares corpses were being torn apart and devoured in the water by tortoises. There was corruption everywhere, but all of it so pointless and disconnected that one felt that it was all very far away, vaporous and incomprehensible, merely a simile, a dream. The lingam, the many-armed idols, the pitiless and odorous holy men, the blood and the cow dung and the human secretions that invaded everything, water, earth and air.

At the public urinals in Benares, for instance, which were simply ridges on the river's bank backed by a stained wooden wall, the exhibitionists were to be seen. Hamadullah told me about them. They were the ugly ones whom no one loved, sad-eyed, timid-lipped men, with faces saddeningly inhuman, weazened and furtive. There were many of them, making this place their resort, habitually excited by the smell and the wandering glances, noticing each newcomer with a quickening of the breath but nevertheless repelled by one another. There was nothing else for them; that, of course, was the reason for it all. Inspiring pity and disgust, but terror, too; shabby, indefinable creatures, peering and shifting slowly from side to side like pariah dogs, never uttering a word, unless perhaps a monosyllabic whisper. Lost altogether, quite incurable. There was no mistaking them. The expression on their faces was a nightmarish thing, never varying much.

Two saddhus sat on the burning ghats, as still as idiots,

mud-caked and cross-legged, their monstrous black eyes the only thing about them that seemed alive. "They believe very little, actually," said Hamadullah, "but they do believe that everything is the same everywhere. There are no differences that matter anywhere. It doesn't matter where they go, what they do, how much they suffer, for everything is the same. That is what they believe all their life long until they die."

There was another man beside them, though, who was quite different. He had a face like a fox, big ears sticking up, a reddish face, jagged teeth, an expectant, alert look. He was a syphilitic, but still hoping against hope, perhaps, that there was a chance for him somewhere. A chance, that is to say, that somebody might love him; or at least like him; or at least tolerate him; or at least pretend to; or at least say a kind word to him, not notice his exterior: but it was a very far-away hope by now, almost gone, like a pretty gray bird catching the vanished sunlight and dipping beyond the horizon. But not quite gone, as yet. He was not yet independent, not yet free.

Then there were the daydreamers, sitting under the dusty palms and watching the sunlight on their filthy naked bodies. They were almost the worst of all. All life had left them, all will, passion, desire, except just that one desire to escape into their own secret world, to hide there forever and ever. It gave to their faces a strangely empty look, and yet at the same time a terrible intensity. It was dangerous and dreadful, this life of dreams, because it was at the bottom of all human decay: eyes turned inward; and so limitless in its allures, its varieties, so full of inexplicable gratifications for those whom the world has treated cruelly, for the spiritually unemployed. And, once the path had been entered, there was no turning back.

At Chandernagore there hung, like smoke in the air, an overwhelming spirit of vagueness and apathy. All around the mosques lay the sacred cows, chewing away with a silly, spoiled, egotistical look in their lovely eyes. A guardian of the mosque told Hamadullah how an old woman, who did a business in small rugs, shawls, sweets and spurious relics, had finally sold everything she had, including two old Korans and some aphrodisiac herbs; all in order to buy a coffin for her dead son, who had been lying in a cellar for three weeks, covered with a sack and some sand. She still bickered and bargained each day with the carpenter, the coffin-carriers and the guardian of the mosque, concerning the matter of fees. She didn't want to pay the fees. She would win out yet, hinted the guardian of the mosque with a grin.

Inside the mosque were a few stragglers, two lazy and ill-kempt muezzins, a bored and casual priest. The dignity of religion, I said to Hamadullah, seemed to be gone, all the spirit and freshness were undeniably gone, certainly religion was dying.

"No," said Hamadullah curtly, "you don't understand what this religion is." But it seemed to me that man had lost all spirit here in Chandernagore, that man would have no more of the spirit, that he loathed it and didn't want to hear any more about it. Everybody looked bored to death.

"Asiatics are afraid, you see," said Hamadullah. "Afraid of almost everything. Afraid of life, of death, of Europe, of the mountains and the sea, of God, of love, of hatred, of happiness, of any sort of reality. I myself fear all these things. And so, naturally, we try to run away. That is true of myself, and it is true of all of us. You will have noticed that we are all the same at the bottom. Cowards, but sensitive, and not really selfish."

⁂ Finally, on the sixth day of our journey, we arrived in Calcutta and I said good-by to Hamadullah in the café where we had our last meal together.

"Farewell, Hamadullah," I said to him, "and thank you very much for all your kindness."

He simpered. Suddenly, in the flash of a second, he had become artificial, remote and unlovable. "Very, very welcome. Farewell."

"Perhaps I shall see you again?" I don't know why precisely I said that. I knew that I would never see him again. But still there was something in the back of my mind when I said it.

"Oh, I hope." He was shuffling his feet clumsily, anxious to be off. It seems absurd, but there was something truly heart-breaking in the way Hamadullah said good-by; such strange things moved unsaid beneath the surface, so many things, permanently hidden and unrecognized; pathetic, frowsy, terrified bits of himself.

Suddenly he seemed ugly. And tragic as well. For in the shadow crawling across his hopeless face I could now see what had been troubling me. I could see how wisdom and understanding could weaken a man, could hurt him like a disease, could finally vilify him. No man was safe. In the securest refuge, apparently, some trap lay hidden.

I looked out of the window and saw him waddling down the shrieking street, swaying slightly, looking from side to side. Now he was calling to a passing ricksha and grinning at the ricksha man officiously. And now he was gone.

And now I was alone again. I began to miss my companions. I felt ill at ease, uncertain; like a leaf fallen from a dying tree upon the water, hesitantly afloat upon the waves. I began to think about the past and the future; their interrelation, their interpenetration, their effect on the spirit, and so forth. But it got me nowhere, it didn't help at all. I felt distinctly melancholy. In a strange sentimental manner I began to think about Ceylon.

Hadn't some one told me to visit her in Kandy? Very well, I would take the next boat to Colombo. I could afford it; only barely, but still it was possible. I sipped my tea, which tasted like perfume, sickly sweet. I looked out toward the Bay of Bengal. Far away I could see it, a quiet greenish desert, catching the sunlight in its slow ripples. A big, deep, unemphatic piece of water, but yet compared with India, not so very big or so very deep or so very unemphatic. And upon it, like fallen blossoms, the ships in the sunlight pointing, who knows? perhaps to some happiness mysteriously dreamed of, or undreamed.

28

KANDY was full of noises when I arrived. The elephants were being driven through the twilight down to the Mahaweli Ganga for their bath—pert, delighted creatures, watching us all with wise and malicious eyes. I walked along the brilliantly lit street full of venders and beggars and vociferous curio shops, on to the hotel beside the lake. I knew that I'd find Hermione here. The arcade of the hotel ran close along the sleepy lake, the wavelets lapping and shimmering almost at the very steps. I could hear the cicadas among the bamboo trees.

And there she was, sitting out on the lawn among the lanterns and the palm trees. Two men were with her. All three of them were drinking cocktails. I could hear the orchestra playing in the ballroom and the sharp-tongued women laughing and chattering at their tables. I felt very shabby and out of place.

But I was overcome with delight at the same time. She saw me right away. She looked at me with her cold gray eyes, expressionlessly at first, but then, as I approached, with a gentle smile. "Miss Bariton," I murmured, "do you remember me?"

There was an embarrassed pause. Then they grew very cordial and asked me to sit down. They'd changed, all three of them. Timothy was certainly fatter. His face had grown quite red. "Have you enjoyed your trip?" he asked pompously.

Yes, I replied; most of it.

"You look older, you know."

Things had been a bit wearing in Turkey, I observed, and also in Persia.

"Really?" he said with condescension. "How did that happen? We found things monotonously free of hardship. Did anything really difficult happen?"

"I was usually without money, of course."

"Oh." He looked suddenly bored. Then, on second thought, he called to one of the little brown waiters and ordered a gin sling.

We sat silently for a minute or two. I could see the lean bronzed women in their Worth gowns standing on the half-lit terrace, and the men in their white shell jackets, and a few fat Eurasians, and a Kandyan chief or two in stiff brocades.

Mr. Bariton watched me without a word. He looked very frail and nervous. His face was oddly well preserved —almost, in its contours, the face of a boy. But all life had left it, a thousand tiny veins ran crisscross upon his cheeks, and his eyelids were dry and weary. His hands were like delicate ivory instruments, tattooing away on the arms of the chair, perfectly white and flawless and lifeless. A very elegant man, but sick, dying.

And as for Hermione, she too had changed. At first I couldn't tell quite how. Beautiful as ever, more so, perhaps, since solemnity and resignation had crept into her face. She looked much older. Her eyes were surely the most beautiful I had ever seen—enchanting, full of secrets, suggesting infinite liquid variations of beauty, humor, austerity, pride. "You must tell me about Turkey. We saw very little of Turkey. And nothing of Persia. You really must tell me. Come. . . ." She rose. "We'll go walking." She smiled at her father and at Timothy. "Come."

As we wandered along the path we could hear the natives worshiping at the Temple of the Tooth. We could hear the beating of the drums and the malicious screaming of the conches, and, very faintly, the treading of their naked feet upon the stones.

Yes, she'd changed. Patiently she listened as I told about Erzerum, Meshed and Badrapur. Her exuberance had left her. She walked at my side nervously and self-consciously. I began to feel rather downcast. "And what's happened to you?" I said finally.

"Nothing," she answered.

"Oh, something, surely."

She paused. "Well, perhaps."

"Were you in India much?"

"Yes, rather."

"Where?"

"The usual places."

"Which usual places?"

"Bombay. Delhi. Agra. Calcutta."

"Were you happy?"

She looked at me with a peculiar smile. "You ask such strange questions. Happy? Well, I hadn't thought of it, to tell the truth."

"Don't you think about being happy? Is that it?"

"Not only that." She seemed unwilling to talk. My heart felt heavy, all the delight of seeing her was disappearing, only the dull longing remained.

"What else, then?"

"This, perhaps. That I'm never very happy or very unhappy. Does that seem logical?"

I looked at her again. Her eyelids looked heavy as wax, her hair cold as glass. "You haven't ever been very happy or very unhappy?"

She turned to me and took my hand in hers. It was almost dark now. We were standing on the side of the hill and could look down on the lovely artificial lake with its fringe of palms and stones. The air was shrill with the noise of crickets. "Listen," she said, "and try to understand. I am married. You didn't know that, did you?"

I shook my head.

"You didn't even suspect it?"

I shook my head again. We walked slowly back along the walk. Two Cinghalese youths met and passed us; they were carrying boxes upon their heads and were walking silently side by side, graceful as panthers, smelling vaguely of cinnamon. I could hardly see their faces, but still I could discern the pride and callousness in their half-open eyes.

"Whom did you marry?"

"Timothy."

I had guessed it, of course. "When did you marry him?"

"A month ago. In Calcutta."

"Calcutta?"

She nodded.

"I was thinking of you in Calcutta a week ago. That was why I came here."

She didn't answer.

"Do you love him?" But as soon as I said it I regretted it. She didn't love him; I knew it; she'd never really love any man. And at the same moment I began to feel sick and trembling with desire. She was very beautiful, there was no doubt about it, with that extreme loveliness that seems destined to bring corruption, hurt, excess; which is perhaps as it should be. I could feel the peculiar fragrance of love breathing suddenly through my veins as through the twigs of a willow tree, sweet and disquieting, mischievous.

"Come," she whispered, "let's hurry back."

◇◇◇

But I held her still on the path and ran my hand over her fine silvery hair. She closed her eyes. "You know that I loved you, don't you?" I said softly. "You know it? And you know why?" I pressed my face against her hair and then against her neck. Like a flower she was, cool, orchidaceous, not of my race at all.

🜲🜲🜲 Early the next morning I left Kandy. But before I left I walked out past the Temple of the Tooth and the Garden Temple and the Library. There was a little pond hidden among some gnarled silver-barked trees, and beside the pond stood a very small snowy-domed dagoba. The door stood open and I entered.

An old monk was sitting inside on a sofa of ruby velvet. A very small old man, with sharp intelligent eyes and the delicate features of a statuette. His flowing yellow robe was brushed aside and I could see his bare arms and legs, dark and fragile as the stem of a flower. He nodded as I entered, and I nodded in return. "Good morning," I said.

"Good morning," he replied. "Pray be seated, if you wish. You are more than welcome." Something in his voice and his accent seemed peculiarly familiar. But when I looked again at his cool gazelle's eyes and his wrinkled face I felt sure that I had never seen him before.

I sat with him for about an hour. He told me about ancient Ceylon—Lanka, he called it; about the kings robed in rubies and sapphires, and the thousands and thousands who worshiped all at once on the great terrace of Setavanarama; about the Palace of Bronze with its nine blindingly magnificent stories; and Anuradhapura, the greatest of the world's sacred cities, sixteen miles each way, thousands of pillars of silver and gold now covered with jungle; and about the incredibly sacred Tooth Relic and the incredibly magnificent rites of the Perahera. "On the night of the full moon they go out on a boat. They go up the great river with their sacred swords and sacred pitchers and wait for dawn. At the moment of dawn four of them strike the golden water with their sacred swords, and the others empty the ancient water and refill the sacred pitchers. Then they go back. And finally, late that night, after all the gilded elephants except one have been led away and the devil-dancers have grown weary, all go down the torch-lit path. Here the great priest receives the relic in his silken draped hands from the back of the most sacred of the elephants. Quietly he walks down the path through archway after archway, way down toward the shrine, and finally he fades out of sight, and the music ceases. That is the end. Everyone is happy and serene." He spat at intervals into a tall copper vase, and sat gazing with raised eyebrows at the dappled ferns and the trailing lianas.

"Everyone?"

"Everyone. Even the elephants and all the minor animals."

I asked him to tell me about transmigration. So he explained. "It is not of great importance," he said slowly, "that our spirits move from one creature to another. The thing to remember is that we are all pilgrims, gentle partners, stone, grass, animals, all of us on the same road, in a vast ascending curve, through universe after universe, dissolution after dissolution, higher and higher. Twenty-four Buddhas have come and gone. The last one was the utterly perfect one. But there is still the Lord Maitreya Buddha, the Comforter, who is to come. He is the most deeply adored. He will precede the dissolution of our earth, which will split apart, and the rocks and metals will be slowly purified until all is Nirvana." He spoke in a dull, effeminate voice. Only now and then, in the light in his gentle eyes, could I see a glimpse of the real power of what he was telling me.

A shabby little brown boy had crept down to the pool and now he was furtively placing some wilted temple lilies in a pattern upon a big flat stone. The monk watched him without a word.

"They are already wilted," I observed.

"Yes," he replied severely, "but they will bloom forever in the Infinite Loving Heart. You see, the Lord Buddha said that all would come to him, some by the road of sacrifice, others by the road of action, and the rest by the road of weariness. It doesn't matter. It is all the same." He looked prim and self-satisfied now, as if he had reduced life to a neat, graceful pattern. He spat again into the copper vase.

⚜⚜⚜ The next night I found myself waiting in Colombo for the boat to Rangoon. I walked along the beach beyond the big hotel. The palms rose like great feathers from the sand and I could see the Cinghalese fishermen among them, shining and naked except for a wet bit of cloth around the temples. Some were drawing huge nets upon the shore, others were standing motionless in their skiffs and holding lanterns. Beyond them rose the waves. I lay on the sand for a while and then walked back into the hideous city. And before long I was on my way to Rangoon.

29

WHEN I reached Rangoon I walked straight to the Strand Hotel. "Is Mme de Chamellis staying here?" said I to the tiny bald-headed man at the desk.

He looked into the register. "De Chamellis, de Chamellis. . . ." He looked up again. "No, s . . ." But then he glanced at my clothes and left out the "sir." "No," he said. "I'm afraid not."

So I went to the Royal Hotel. "Is Mme de Chamellis registered here?"

The clerk looked at me suspiciously. "No," he said briskly. "Not here."

I walked two blocks farther and arrived at the Criterion Hotel. "Mme de Chamellis?"

The clerk, a tall sad man, looked puzzled. "Yes," he replied. "Shall I call her room?"

The next day we were sailing up the Irawaddy, the three of us—Mme de Chamellis, Hassan and I. "We'll be on the river a week," said she. "Then we'll sail for Hongkong. . . . Will you go with us?" She looked at me inquiringly. "Yes," she whispered, "you must if you can. Hassan is so undependable; and I do need a man to look after the luggage and all."

We passed the tall new chimneys of the English oil companies, and the golden dagobas fading gently into decay.

It was a brilliant day; everything glittered, everything looked lively and happy. The boat was crowded. The natives, several of them Buddhist monks, lay around on blankets and smoked or slept. Two old leather-skinned monks were silently rubbing one another with olive oil, and a third one sat beside them, smoking his cheroot.

The river was dotted with houseboats full of short-legged sloe-eyed natives. We could see the steam rising from the meals they'd been cooking. On and on we went, passing paint-cracked flotillas and long canoes which were being steered by bronze-skinned Burmese. Now and then we'd pass an old dagoba, and we'd see the small young priests dressed in yellow hovering on the green bank like so many dandelions.

Mme de Chamellis would sit on the shady side of the deck for hours at a time. Twice I peered over her shoulder to see what she was reading. It was the letters of Mme de Sévigné, the first time, and the second time a volume of Racine. I wanted to talk with her, but I didn't know quite how to start. She was very remote and unresponsive, far more so than before. She'd changed. Gentler, quieter. I wondered what had happened to her since I saw her last in Teheran. But by degrees everything grew trivial in her presence, nothing really seemed to matter, contemplations of the past and conjectures regarding the future became mere exercises of the brain. Communication seemed completely without point. And, as a matter of fact, I couldn't even begin to guess what sort of woman she actually was. Benevolent or cruel, happy or wretched, selfish or self-sacrificing: I couldn't have guessed even that. I couldn't even have said whether she was alive or dead, whether something still went on in that heart beneath those undeveloped breasts, or whether she had said good-by to all capacity for grief or love. There was no telling. Her face was a mask, her eyes were two dark cisterns too deep to see the bottom.

While we were having tea together on deck the second day I observed, as amiably as I could, that I hoped that her sister, the Comtesse, was now in better health than when I had last seen her.

She looked at me calmly. "No, I'm afraid not. You see, she died the very next day after you left Teheran." She looked away again. "I thought I had told you."

I mumbled that I was very sorry indeed.

"I am surprised that you should have asked me that," said she. "I thought that I'd intimated at the time that she was dying."

"Well, I had hoped . . ."

She smiled. "Her life had been very unhappy, really. She'd never found what she wanted, never. So that the actual arrival of death was the first taste of calm that she'd ever known, I dare say."

"What did she want and never find, Mme de Chamellis?"

She lowered her eyes wearily. Hassan came up to her with a sheepish smile and sat down at her feet. Gently she ran her fingers through his hair while he gazed at the swampy shore. For a moment she sat quietly. Then she raised her fingers to her forehead in a slow uncertain curve and rested them there. "I think you know," she replied. "Love. Not merely a pretense at it, but the real thing, the real thing."

"Are you sure she never found it?"

"I'm afraid it's a very rare thing that she was hoping for. And I'm sure that she, at any rate, never found it."

"Do you think anyone ever finds it?" I asked anxiously.

"There's no way of telling," she said. "Love; well, what is it?" A peculiar tone entered her voice, part tenderness, part fear, part anger. "Take any two lovers; one is the lover, the other the beloved. Isn't that true? Mustn't it be so? Can it be possible that two people ever love each other to a mathematically equal degree? And if the balance is disturbed, even ever so slightly, then what happens? One becomes a little bit bored, the other a little bit wretched. And the boredom grows, little by little, and the wretchedness grows, little by little. What's to be done? What's to be done except draw a line through it all and try again, and again, and again?"

On either side of the great river rose the ivy-tangled slopes—woolly impenetrable masses of green cut here and there only by the thin copper ribbon of a stream or the round golden thimble of a village temple.

"You sound like a very cynical lady, Mme de Chamellis."

"No, you know that isn't true in the least. But I am, I confess, a materialist." Perhaps, thought I; for I had asked her about love; no, she had replied, perfect love could never exist; but what she had meant was, happy love, contented and successful love. "I can see what you are thinking," she said quietly. "True love, you suspect, does not demand anything in return, it exists primarily in giving. Is that what you were thinking?"

I nodded.

"Yes, you are right," she said. "There are many kinds of love, assuredly; but love in the grand manner is out of date. That much is certain. We know ourselves too well. All that we can feel now with our whole impassioned hearts is, on the one hand, hope, and on the other, despair. Those two. And everything depends on which of the two is stronger."

"Which of the two is usually the stronger?"

"Who is the stronger, the lion or the philosopher?"

The last glimmer of sunlight was still gliding along with

the currents. The boats that we passed still shone, the foam still glittered in their wake. But on each side of us the greenery was slowly building up a dusk of its own.

She lit a cigarette. Two inward-curling spirals of smoke, one gray and the other blue, rose between her fingers. "Whatever you do," she said, "remember this: be faithless, happy-go-lucky. Look ahead of you, not behind you. Be on the side of the lion, not the philosopher. Do you understand? The trouble with me, you see, is that I have never been able to follow this advice." She smiled casually. But I could see in her eyes that she was thinking of something else. Something else was lingering in the back of her mind. She wasn't telling me all that she really knew.

❧❧❧ Mandalay was a hot and tiresome city. Lovely-sounding name, far up the great sacred river, a stone's-throw from the untraveled regions toward Cathay. But the city itself was obvious and ordinary. Only at dusk, when the great wall and the fort overlooking it grew pink and misty, did it relapse into the past and grow suggestive.

We walked through the little park on the shore and sat down on a bench beneath an old bo tree. Above us we could see the gilded carving of the Queen's Golden Monastery glimmering through the leaves. Below us rose the seven-roofed tower of the Arrakan Pagoda. We could smell the incense which fluttered across the entry like a curtain of gray silk, and we could hear the chanting of the evening worshipers. Two sheep were grazing on the smooth green slope at our side, and below, hidden from us by the cat-tails, the mandarin ducks were flapping their wings and complaining.

"I have spoken to Mr. Maung," said she. Mr. Maung had been a fellow-passenger on our Irawaddy steamer. "He has a little boat of his own, and is passing on through the defiles up to Bhamo. He has very graciously offered to take us. He is a lonely man, he tells me, and longs for company."

Farther and farther up the river: where would she finally stop? Asia was acting upon her like a narcotic. Swifter and swifter, deeper and deeper, more and more remote. Her health, too, was suffering. She looked gaunt and nervous. Traveling up the Irawaddy was contriving for her some sort of dissipation, of body as well as of mind. Where would it end? "Bhamo and back"—yes, but once in Bhamo would she desire to go still farther, perhaps? Across into China, over the Salween, up among the gorges?

An old monk in a yellow gown walked past us with a big tray full of flowers. Jasmine and lotus, all of them limp and wilting but still odorous. He stared at us, but with eyes so dead and sightless that I felt sure that he didn't see us at all. His lips were moving silently, a few long silvery hairs were fluttering around his ears. He walked toward the trees beside the pagoda and soon all that was left of him was the scent of dying flowers in the air.

※※※ Mr. Maung was a fat smiling Burman who dealt in precious stones, was very rich, dressed in Occidental clothes with a wonderful Oriental neatness, and spoke English with the same slow pleasure that he might have taken in fondling a ruby between thumb and forefinger. "I fear," he said sadly, "that you will find my boat very shabby after the fine Flotilla Company steamer."

Actually it was a spotless, glistening little thing, with straw mats on the floors and little silver tea-bowls standing in every possible nook. I was beginning to feel very glad, after all, that we were going to Bhamo. The only thing I didn't like was the crew. Surly, squat-shaped men, coarse-lipped little Buddhas with breasts like a woman's.

"But Bhamo is a very ordinary town," said Mr. Maung. "*Very* plain; nothing in Bhamo is worthy of being inter-viewed by you."

"But the scenery on the way is fine, isn't it?"

"The scenery?" he said smilingly, looking out toward the high green slopes past which the river was moving with an increasing swiftness. "Not very fine, I am afraid. Rather plain, rather ordinary. Not like England," he added sententiously, "which is so full of beautiful parks, meadows and church steeples."

"Do any people live here in the jungle? Any savages?"

He reflected for a moment. "Some. Not many. Two or three little villages. But you wouldn't be interested in the people. They are very dull and ordinary people, unfortu-nately, without any desire for beauty or civilization. Quite without imagination."

"But the river surely is very fine, Mr. Maung?" said I. It was so clear up here that I could see the fish playing deep below us, among the pebbles and mosses.

In the middle of the second night on board Mr. Maung's boat I awoke quite suddenly, as if some one had touched my forehead or whispered into my ear. I listened. The motors were silent, there wasn't a sound. No sound at all, except for a faint extended rustling, like a hot wind among the shore grasses.

Then I heard the sound of bare feet along the passage-way, quite unmistakably. And then a little groan—from far away it seemed to come; and presently a soft tapping at my door.

It was Mr. Maung. A pathetic sight, his silk nightgown

swaying softly in the night, his hands fluttering, his face perspiring with dismay. "Oh, oh!" he cried. "A terrible, terrible thing has happened! Mme de Chamellis will be dreadfully angry! I am ashamed, I am mortified!"

I sat up in my berth. "What has happened, Mr. Maung?"

"We are stuck! Deep in the mud!" A strange little light played around his sorrowful face.

"The fault of the crew?" I suggested.

He nodded his head mournfully. "Very, very careless! I should never have hired them. They are scoundrels."

"Fire them," said I sleepily. "Get a new crew."

"But that is the very trouble," he sighed. "I cannot fire them. They have gone, they have stolen all my silver and disappeared! Shameful!"

I agreed.

"What shall I say to Mme de Chamellis? She will think me a very bad host! I am deeply upset . . ."

But our troubles had only begun. Suddenly a naked little figure shot toward us out of the darkness. It was Hassan. He looked very hot and very excited. "Sahib," he shrieked, "there is fire! Quick, hurry, hurry!" He was moving his hands to and fro in front of him and was trembling with fear.

We stepped into the passageway. He was right. The boat was burning away merrily. And not a thing to be done. "Quick," cried Mr. Maung. "We must wake up Mme de Chamellis! She will be furious at me!"

There we sat, a French noblewoman, a Burmese jewel merchant, a whimpering Hindu valet, and I, lost in the reeds on the shore of the upper Irawaddy.

A hundred yards away the boat was burning madly. I could imagine the fine mats, the silken coverlets, the lacquer dishes, the bronze statuettes, all eaten by the flames, turned into black bits of nothing. Poor Mr. Maung!

He was feeling very depressed. "Oh," he wailed, turning to Mme de Chamellis, "my dear lady, I am full of apologies, I am overwhelmed with shame. What shall we do?"

"Wait until morning," she replied. We all sat quiet. Poor Hassan had only a bit of a cloth around his middle, but it didn't matter; all of us were wet to the skin. Mme de Chamellis looked quite terrifying. Her hair hung over her forehead and shoulders like a little black hood, and her wet face shone like ice in the flickering firelight.

Quietly we sat there, until suddenly we heard the snapping of a twig not far away. All four of us heard it at precisely the same moment; our heads turned simultaneously. At first we saw nothing. Then we saw very gradually disentangling itself from the shade of the reeds and the shrubs, a man's naked silhouette. For a moment he stood motionless on the shore between the boat and us, watching the flames.

And then there were two. And then three, and then four. There they stood, watching the wild glitter like fascinated cats. "Natives," whispered Mr. Maung. "Kachins. Dreadful people."

"Shall we call to them?" said Mme de Chamellis.

"No, no," he whispered anxiously. "Don't let them see us! They are rude and inconsiderate men!"

But it was too late. They had heard us. In a single movement they turned and stared straight at us. The firelight was playing on our faces, and it was too late to hide.

They looked surprised. "Speak to them," said Mme de Chamellis. Mr. Maung looked deeply disconcerted.

One of the natives walked slowly up to where we were

sitting. He looked at us carefully. Then he muttered something. Mr. Maung muttered in reply. The big native muttered again. Mr. Maung said something in a very quiet, timid voice. The native smiled.

More and more of them were coming, some of them with torches and one of them with a twenty-two rifle. They stood around us in a big circle, chatting with a great show of amiability and politeness. Small brown men, all of them, their limbs plump and hairless, their eyes narrow and totally expressionless.

Mr. Maung sighed. "Come," he said in a tone of systematic resignation. "They will lead us to their village. From the village we can reach the road to Tiebaung tomorrow. From Tiebaung we can ride to Bhamo along the caravan road."

"But why can't we just wait here," said Mme de Chamellis, "and take a boat in the morning?"

"They are very hospitable," he replied in a faint voice. "They insist on playing the host."

So we trudged along a wet leech-infested path for half a mile, preceded and followed by the flicker of torchlight on wet brown limbs, brown faces and black hair. And finally we reached the Kachin village as dawn was beginning to filter through the trees.

30

THE BOYS extinguished their torches, and high overhead we could see the freshly gilded leaves emerging from shadow. Women were squatting in front of the huts, nursing their sad-eyed babies and preparing rice. Their faces were white with powder; hideously fat short-legged bodies, but finely shaped hands and features. Not one of them ever smiled.

Mme de Chamellis was led to one hut, Hassan and I were led to another. Mr. Maung had mysteriously disappeared. "Where is Mr. Maung?" I asked Hassan while we were sitting in the odorous twilight of our room. He shrugged his shoulders. "I cannot tell, sahib, but I think it is bad for Mr. Maung. They do not like Mr. Maung." He had gotten over his excitement entirely. He lay on the floor in a drab vacuous sort of fear. Tired for one thing; I remembered how his thin wet arms had trembled among the reeds during the night.

"And your mistress?" said I. "What are they going to do with her?"

"I know nothing, sahib."

"And me?"

"I know nothing, sahib."

"And you?"

He began to whimper softly. "I am afraid for myself, sahib."

We could hear the women bathing their children in a

great leather bowl near our hut. The mothers were silent, the babies were silent; timid rabbit-eyed creatures, born with a fear of the wilderness, knowing just enough to keep still. Mournful little faces they had, still expressive enough to reveal a desire to discover more about life. But their mothers had gotten over that long ago. Their faces expressed nothing, no desire, no understanding, no love, no anxiety, nothing at all.

Once, as I was lying on my back about to fall asleep, a little man crept silently into our hut and stood beside me. I hadn't heard his footsteps at all, but somehow I knew him, half in dream, to be standing suddenly beside me. I opened my eyes and waited for him to speak.

But he didn't speak. He stood at first, then knelt beside me, staring oddly at my face and body. An ugly fellow, stocky and muscular, well past middle age; there was a bright look in his eyes, a mischievous, prying look, rather terrifying in the present circumstances, to tell the truth.

I waited. Gently he placed a finger on my breast, then removed it. Next he pressed curiously at the tendon behind my ankle. Then at my calf. Then at my wrist. Then at my groin. Then under my armpit. Then behind the ear, quite painfully. I didn't dare move. Finally he rose and disappeared.

Hassan had been watching, interestedly but apparently without surprise. In fact, he looked rather piqued, rather sulky for some odd reason.

"Tell me the truth, Hassan. What do you think is going to happen to us?"

"Oh, sahib," he replied in a low shamefaced voice, "I think they will want much money. Give them much money, and my mistress and you will be allowed to go."

"And Mr. Maung?"

"I think they will kill Mr. Maung. They do not like Mr.

Maung, and Mr. Maung has many rubies with him, in his pockets. I saw them. They will kill poor Mr. Maung and take his rubies."

"And you, Hassan?"

He sobbed. "They will keep me here."

"But why, Hassan?"

His black eyes looked suddenly wise behind their long lashes. "Sahib," he said softly and sadly, like a true Asiatic, "it is sad to be a pretty boy."

I saw Mme de Chamellis only one more time. Toward twilight a smiling old man with snow-white teeth took me by the hand and led me to her hut. He sat down beside the doorway while I entered. She was lying inside on a straw mat and glanced at me wearily when I approached. She looked very unwell. Her skin was gray, dry, pendulous, her eyes were dull and lifeless. She needed cigarettes badly; her hands trembled with nervousness and her voice shook irritably.

"How are you feeling, madame?" said I.

"Sit down by me, please." I sat down. "They want ransom," she continued. "For you and me, that is."

"And Mr. Maung?"

"I'd rather not think about Mr. Maung."

"Why not?"

"The natives detest him. They regard him as a sort of traitor to their race. And of course they want his jewels. At any rate, let's not talk any more about Mr. Maung."

"And they're going to keep Hassan here as a slave?"

She looked at me curiously. "Yes, how did you know?"

"Hassan told me."

She nodded. "Hassan knows everything that is going to happen to him. He is never wrong. Yes, he's to stay here; they won't treat him badly, I dare say."

Through the doorway I could see the naked boys running up from the pond. Their bodies looked oiled, they were as smooth and dark as bronze statues. Their wet hair hung over their foreheads like wet black silk. All of them were chattering softly and smiling—showing their fine white teeth. They looked happy enough. But their faces were hopelessly stupid and violently coarse. Very unlike Hassan, with their shapeless features and pock-marked cheeks.

"Tell me," said Mme de Chamellis, "What is wrong with us, what is wrong with men? You are young and a male; perhaps you know. Why do I feel sad when I think of men? Why have I grown sick and weary of the world?"

"I don't quite understand what you mean, madame," said I.

"Do you mind if I chatter on? Do you mind listening?"

"No, no, not at all."

She looked away again. "My tragedy of course is this. I'm not free of the flesh, I've never been free of it, never quite. I've been a prisoner, and therefore unhappy. Not till you grow indifferent to what happens to the flesh will you lose fear and be happy. Ask those boys outside; they will agree. Ask anyone in Asia. I still fear death. A release, yes. But imagine! Never to be in on anything any more. Think of it, think of it; the end, the absolute end. Oh, my dear boy, I wish that I could have believed in an immortal God."

"You have never believed in an immortal God?"

She looked at me. A suggestive and touching smile crossed her lips for a moment. She shook her head.

"You see, most people are never really put to the test. Nothing ever happens that really places them, identifies them as brave, cowardly, cruel, angelical, or whatever they may happen to be deep down in the secrecy of their real selves. Only once in a great while something will happen that reveals them, as the bones are revealed under the X-ray. Do you see? Life has never really touched my secret self. Very rarely does anything but love touch a woman's secret self, so it seems to me."

There was something odd and pathetically moving about all this chatter. She seemed to be trying, circuitously, to arrive at some difficult point, to be on the verge of a decision of some kind, a rather important decision. I began to feel very melancholy.

"I might say," she said, "that I've really staked everything on one thing—the very moment before death: will I or will I not feel happy and complete at that moment? Everything that I've done or thought has pointed toward that. And now. What does it mean? How will I know that I've chosen the right death? How am I to trust that final moment? Tell me.

"Yes," she continued in an earnest, subdued voice, "that is the thing that is so hard. And on it depends all our peacefulness, our dignity and our pride. Choosing the right life—that is hard but not too hard. But choosing the right death, to feel at that moment that your life has at last acquired meaning. Do you see? Do I make myself understood?" But I suspected that it wasn't to me that she was putting that question, actually.

And then I could feel the atmosphere changing again. It was me she was thinking of again, to me that she was speaking. I could scent this change in her heart across the hot twilight.

"I'm chattering, my boy, to help myself out. It is a sort of medicine. I have never come thoroughly to life. If I had, I would feel quite serene now, possibly. But, you see, no one has ever really loved me."

It was growing quite dark now and I could hardly see

her face. The little old man at the doorway was motioning impatiently to me.

"Good night, my boy. I shall see that things turn out well for you."

"Good night, madame." I waited a moment.

"My darling boy," she said, so hoarsely, clumsily and tenderly that I could hardly believe it was she speaking, "forgive an old lady for saying something sentimental. I have loved you very, very much. I cannot tell you why. Good night."

And that was all. The next morning Hassan woke me up and cried excitedly into my ear. Tears were in his eyes. "Sahib! Sahib!"

I sat up. "Yes?"

"She is dead, sahib!"

"Who, Hassan?" I cried. But I knew who it was already, of course. I needn't have asked.

Hassan drew his dirty fingers across his cheek and whimpered softly.

"How did she die?" I asked, unhappily. It didn't matter, though, how she died. She was dead, I knew it; that was enough, that was the point. I wasn't surprised, but I felt very lonely now.

"Of sickness, sahib."

"What sickness?"

"I do not know, sahib. Of the sorrowing sickness, I think, but no one knows. Every one is very disappointed."

An hour later the old white-toothed man came up and chattered some directions to me in broken English. He gave me to understand that I was free. Things had turned out inauspiciously. They all thought it wiser to let me go. He pointed out the forest path that led to the caravan route, and gave me a tunic, a crust of black bread and a ball of tobacco. I was a little bit surprised, but not very much.

I said good-by to Hassan with a heavy heart. He was sitting beside the pond, tossing pebbles at some monkeys. He looked quite contented.

"Say good-by to Mr. Maung for me, please," I added.

He nodded his head amiably, but suddenly he appeared to remember something else, for he turned away and laid his head upon his elbow.

The heat was terrific. The rays of sunlight sank into my skin and spread there, breeding and expanding like a poison. I walked eagerly along the forest path toward the highway, thirteen miles distant. I was barefooted, and little cracks appeared in my toes and dull bruises in my heels. It wasn't pleasant, but I felt oddly cheerful and contented.

Huge old trees. This wasn't the usual sort of jungle. The gum trees were monstrous pillars, they rose like arrows toward the wrinkled green sky above; nothing else could flourish in their presence. No shrubs at all, and I could look deep, deep into the wood through the black array of trunks. All the little bits of fern, moss, vine, all looked weazened, just temporary bits of decay in the presence of these beautiful and mighty trees.

Once the path sloped downward and crossed a stretch of bog. Leeches and mosquitoes and a terrible vaporous heat all surrounded me in an instant. A few yards of it and I felt sick and exhausted. Then the path rose again toward the dry hollow forest.

I thought about my friends. Love. A simple and time-honored word, to be sure. Fatuous even to think about it. What is the use of saying more than that it can be any of a million different streams leading to some unguessed ocean, some unexplainable meeting-place? A million streams, some well disguised, running through territories ever so cruel, desolate, austere, frightful, lonely, winding away like the Brahmaputra and its three great neighbors through one isolated landscape after another—for real love makes you lonely rather than otherwise, beyond a doubt. No two streams ever really meet, of course. They merely run on with varying degrees of power, fed by many springs or few, into this huge Indian Ocean which remains so thoroughly mysterious to us—since, as soon as we enter it, we dissolve forever. That is the way my thoughts ran as I walked along under the great gum trees.

It grew later and later. I must surely have walked thirteen miles, thought I, when I saw the trees growing dimmer in the distance and the streaks of sunlight among the leaves grow softly red and horizontal. The path went on and on, but no highway appeared.

Presently the trees grew less and a stretch of tangled undergrowth appeared. The sun had set, and a silvery little fog was descending over the foliage. I walked on, and a few yards farther I saw a square pond, edged with broken overgrown stones, and so thickly clogged with lily pads that the water was hardly visible. On the farther side of the old tank I could see some broken pillars and a few bare mounds covered with grasses and pebbles. And hidden deep in the foliage I glimpsed a tall weather-beaten image of Buddha. Very dimly I could see his flat hopeless face peering down through the shadows.

31

I STARED across the root-bound ruins. The marshes were black, the hillocks rose pointlessly. There wasn't a soul in sight. Life had passed southward, northward, westward. At any rate, it had left this place. Wild, neglected, but still uneasy. Something was still troubling it, something was wrong.

Yes, something was wrong. But what? Something was insane, lightless, unconquerable. The forces making for the destruction of man. Danger. Danger was still hanging in the air and floating over the stagnant water and those black hillocks beyond all doubt.

But what could it be? Gradually I could begin to suspect. Here, in this empty place, one thing became clear and disturbing: something about man had changed, and in that change lay the danger to the world the way I loved it. The great revolutions and changes begin actually where they're least suspected—at the edges of civilization, in the small and secretive places where real wretchedness and disillusionment have a chance to grow undiluted and unrelieved. There was a hint of it here, in these beautiful sad ruins. They hadn't given up yet. They would still see man brought low.

I could imagine the walls of the old Burmese city rising again, as if they were glass, and through them I could see the people, all of them. Caught in every conceivable posture of malice, gluttony, avarice, despair, madness, delight, intoxication and prayer. Some of them in strange disconcerting couples, others in groups of three, four or five. And many of them solitary, twisted and degraded, with the green light out of the jungle throwing faint shadows across their faces.

And now the conspirators were lurking in the wood. It was growing hazy, stars were appearing overhead. There was a sense of breathlessness, savage expectancy, plotting. The woods were full of the enemies of man. The swamps were thick with spies. What were they after? What did they want? What was the trouble with the whole business? Why, after all, couldn't life go on peacefully and continually? There was no telling, yet.

The fog lay over the path like a web catching the moonlight, as if it were melting snow. The path grew wider, and suddenly it turned. I saw a clearing in front of me, and in the middle of the clearing two buildings, one large and one small.

The large one was dark and bare; it looked like a half-hearted village church; there was a bit of a steeple on it and a large double door in the middle. The small one was surrounded by a little garden and a light was shining through the window. Great white moths were fluttering in the ray that slanted through the panes.

I walked up to the door. But just as I was about to knock, the door opened and a tall man formed a shadow in the rectangle of light.

Even though his face was in darkness, I could see his eyes looking sharply into mine. He had a long black beard and wore a gray robe that reached almost to his ankles. He waited motionlessly for a moment, then said something in what sounded to me vaguely like Spanish. But I couldn't quite understand. I wrinkled my brow and shook my head.

Then he spoke again. This time I understood. It was in Spanish. "Are you lost?" he asked.

I nodded.

"Where are you going?"

I was looking for the caravan route to the south, I explained.

"The one to Mogok?"

I nodded.

"You took the wrong turning, my friend. Come in, spend the night with me. Tomorrow we'll put you on the right way." He held the door open and I entered.

It was a shabby little bungalow. A kerosene-lamp stood by the window, and beside it lay open a great double-column folio. I glanced at it later and noticed that it was in Latin. The words "Confessionum S. Augustini Liber Nonus" ran across the top of the page.

A brown woman lay on a bundle of mats in the darkness on one side of the room, and two girls on a bundle on the opposite side. "My wife and children," said my host. They blinked their eyes and gazed at me, but said nothing.

We sat down at the table and he poured me some tea. "Tell me what has happened to you," he said. And I told him about Mr. Maung's boat, and the natives with the torches, and the death of Mme de Chamellis, and my journey from the village through the woods.

"Yes," he said, quietly, "that has happened before. Once, two or three years ago, some wealthy Belgians were captured by the villagers not very far from here. They were held for ransom. But there was some misunderstanding. So they were killed."

"Why do you live here?" I asked presently.

"I am a priest," he said. "That is my church out there." He smiled. Then he said, "Come, I will show it to you."

So he took the lamp in his hand and led me out through the hot moonlight to the dark little church. He opened the door and went in. It was very bare. At the farther end stood a box with a cloth over it, and in front of it five rows of benches. On the wall facing us was printed in chalk the legend, "The Eternell God is thy Reffuge." Dust was lying everywhere. On the floor under the bench nearest the door a little Burmese boy was sleeping soundly.

"Who is that little boy?" I said.

"Oh, one of the villagers from near by. His father whips him, so he comes to sleep here every night."

I looked for a moment at the worm-eaten rafters, the spider webs on the wall, the stains on the altar cloth.

"Do many natives come to the church?"

He drew his fingers across his forehead. He was a very handsome man. There were gray hairs among the long heavy black ones on his head, and his face was wrinkled by experience. But his eyes were very young and keen. "Not many," he replied. "I help them when I can. I love them, and they visit me whenever they are unhappy or puzzled. I do whatever I can."

"Do they come to the church regularly?"

"Oh no. Only this little boy, who sleeps here every night, and my wife and daughters. They listen to my sermons every Sunday."

We returned to the bungalow without waking up the little boy. "Wait a moment," he said after I had seated myself at the table again, and he disappeared in the garden.

After several minutes he reappeared with a freshly killed pigeon in his hand. He sat down opposite me and began to pluck it.

"My name is Pereira," he said, "and I was born in Lisbon. I had a very wealthy aunt who loved me a good deal. She planned to leave me all her money. She was very devoted, but also very spoiled and stubborn. One night when I was fourteen years old she caught me making love to the kitchen girl out under the orange tree. So she burst into tears and told me to leave, and I have never seen her since. I was not very wise at that time, you see.

"So I ran away and led a wild rascally life in the streets of Portugal and Spain until one day a kind English priest picked me up in Seville and took me with him. He too was very fond of me, and I grew to be fond of him as well. I traveled with him for two years, through Italy, Egypt and Arabia, and finally we came to Burma. He built the church that you have just visited." He rose and placed the pigeon in a pan and sprinkled it with salt and pepper. Then he stepped behind a curtain and I could hear the pigeon beginning to sizzle away over the fire.

"He died a year after he got here, of malaria. I was grief-stricken, and for a long time very lonely. That was twenty-two years ago. For several years I was very unhappy. I married five years after he died."

"Was he a wise and good man?"

"Very good, and—yes, wise also in his way, I believe. But not strong."

Later he brought in the pigeon and we ate it together. It tasted bitter and hard, but I was very hungry. My host looked pleased and friendly.

"Are you happy now?" I asked him.

He looked at me keenly with his deep intelligent eyes. Then he nodded his head and smiled.

🐦🐦🐦 The next morning he told me how to reach the caravan route. It was only two miles away. Toward noon I met a mule caravan, and with it I traveled southward amid the jingling of bells and the shouting of the strange-eyed muleteer and the hot smells rising from the road. We passed several villages. Women were digging everywhere, very lovely women. But what they were digging for I never discovered. Rubies, perhaps.

Finally we crossed the Mannaut River, and from there we rode south to Momeik and Mogok. At Mogok I took the river boat to Mandalay, and several days later I was again in Rangoon.

❁❁❁ An hour after I had arrived in Rangoon I glimpsed a familiar face driving past me in a bright lilac-colored Packard car. "Mr. Maung!" I cried. "Mr. Maung!"

He leaned forward and asked his chauffeur to stop. I ran up to him. He was, after all, a very kind man. He seemed really pleased to see me again. I was an Occidental, of course, and that made a great difference. But he behaved very gently and very generously.

He gave me new clothes and took me to dinner at his house. Silver bowls stood everywhere in the big room where we ate—great silver bowls and little silver bowls, bowls of Chinese tea, bowls of cold meat with sauces, bowls of strange salads, bowls of ice. We ate and ate. There was champagne, and after dinner a choice of liqueurs.

After that the lights were turned off, two tall candles brought in, and the dancers appeared. I sat beside Mr. Maung on an enormous green cushion. He looked very much like an image of Buddha—thin-nosed, tiny eyes, a soft womanly look about the mouth.

The dances were quite silly and pointless. The dancers were squatty little creatures, not at all supple and graceful like the Indians. Their gestures looked stiff and monotonous, and there was a look in their faces that I found strangely unpleasant.

"Where are you going now?" said Mr. Maung, after

the dancers had left and the pipes had been brought in."

"I don't know. I should like to go to Japan."

"Japan?"

"Yes, Mr. Maung."

He sighed.

"Tell me, Mr. Maung," said I, "what happened to you in that village where we were captured? I was very worried about you."

He was silent for a moment. Then he said, "First I arranged that they should free you. The next night I bribed my guard and escaped to the river."

I was very much touched. "Thank you very much, Mr. Maung." He sighed again.

"Don't go to Japan," he said softly. "I dislike that selfish little Japan."

"Where shall I go, then?"

"I can procure you a job in Rangoon. Or near Penang." He looked at me eagerly.

"What is the one in Rangoon?"

"Would you disdain to be my valet, my dear young sir?" He looked away again, rather shyly and self-consciously.

"What is the one near Penang, Mr. Maung?"

"Oh, that one. I have a friend, a doctor in one of the villages. He has requested me to send him an assistant. His previous assistant died of fever. It would be most unattractive, I fear."

"I think I should like to go to Penang, Mr. Maung."

"Really?" His eyes opened wide. "You surprise me deeply, my young sir."

"It would be very kind of you."

"Very well." His eyes closed again. His face looked moist and pathetic in the flickering candle-light. "I shall write to Dr. Ainger tomorrow."

"To whom?" I exclaimed.

"To my friend Dr. Ainger, who desires an assistant near Penang, my young sir."

❦❦❦ The little brig took four days between Rangoon and Penang. Now and then we would glimpse the shore of the long peninsula, green and flat.

I lay out on the high poop, naked in the sun, hearing the cordage creaking and tugging above me and the water mumbling below. It was very hot. Now and then I saw a shark gliding curiously alongside, then disappearing like a flash.

Soon after dawn one morning we reached Penang.

32

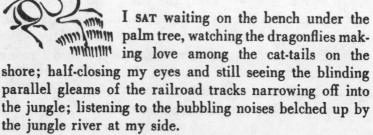

I SAT waiting on the bench under the palm tree, watching the dragonflies making love among the cat-tails on the shore; half-closing my eyes and still seeing the blinding parallel gleams of the railroad tracks narrowing off into the jungle; listening to the bubbling noises belched up by the jungle river at my side.

I was alone. I waited five minutes, ten minutes. The gnats had discovered me and came swirling wildly round my head. I stepped for a moment into the sunlight to escape them. But that was still worse, much, much worse, even a moment of it. The sun went tonguing at my limbs and even through my shabby white helmet, so that a second's contact with it was enough to make me dizzy. I stepped back under the shade of my palm tree and resigned myself to a slow death by insects.

Through the drops hanging from my eyelashes I gazed down the empty road. At last I saw a cloud of reddish dust slowly rolling toward me, and in the midst of it I glimpsed the long-expected ox-cart. It came creaking up toward the railroad tracks and stopped in front of my palm tree. Out hopped an ulcer-bitten Tamil who straightaway began to gesticulate and jabber, pointing at the road, at the sky, at a sore in the bullock's neck, at a pretty little girl who sat in the back of the cart with nothing on but a long striped skirt. Yes. I understood. He'd been delayed, and he was very sorry. I got up beside him and we started off through the dust.

We followed the river for mile after mile, now and again losing sight of it as it plunged into a mad orgiastic growth of jungle, but usually near enough to hear the frogs and to see the coppery glimmer of water through the foliage. Several times we skirted tremendous mangrove swamps thick with day flies. And once we passed a great terrace of open land still yellowish where the cane had once been glowing; a ruined plantation—twigs were already twisting their way through the wooden shed beside the road, and the orchard on the other side was nothing more than a tangle of lianas.

My driver, once he'd started off again, didn't open his mouth. But the little girl in the back kept chanting to herself, repetitious and unmelodious tunes without beginning or end. I turned around and looked at her. She stopped singing instantly and stared at me with huge black eyes. Slowly, like candle-light springing up in a darkened room, she began to smile. And then when I turned around a second time, a few minutes later, there she was lying, barelegged, peering at me lasciviously. The third time that I looked at her she was lying in the most voluptuous imaginable posture, and I turned back again quickly. But the thought of her lovable cinnamon breasts kept tantalizing me, and I couldn't keep from stealing a glance every now and then, even though my silent, sinister driver began to leer at me disconcertingly. Each time she grew more intimate in her little displays, more inviting, more entrancing. I felt restless and excited. She was as fresh and firm as an unplucked apricot, and her hair shone like blue satin in the sunlight.

We reached the swampy parting of the river as it was

beginning to grow dark. My driver got out and walked toward the shore. There was no sign of a boat. He looked upstream and then down the hazy lavender stream. The only people we saw were two old Malayans gossiping in the shade and watching us with furtive pig eyes.

My Tamil exchanged a few swift words with them and came back. He looked abashed. "Boat!" he said, and shook his scrawny pin-head. The two dessicated Malayans were watching us quietly. He pointed toward the river, then opened his hands in a gesture of resignation and apology.

One of the old Malayans came up. "No boat tonight," he explained somewhat mournfully. "Boat gone." He made deprecatory gestures to indicate that we'd been too slow, that the boat hadn't found it convenient to wait. "Tomorrow," he added with an optimistic grin.

The little Tamil girl was gazing at me coyly from the bullock-cart. Dusk was dripping like gray moss from the trees all around, and even while we'd been waiting there the river had grown dim, the distances unattainable and mysterious.

They stretched a hammock for me under a casuarina tree and hung a mosquito net from the boughs. It was hot and sultry, not a breath of air, and I took off all my clothes except for a moist pair of underdrawers. The Tamil and his girl lay in the back of the bullock-cart. The bullock lay down on the road.

But I couldn't sleep at all. I watched the fireflies over the grasses, and the cat-tails bending gently at the river's edge, and the streaks of starlight passing very slowly down the oily river. And the sounds—hundreds of them, all different, from the tiny falsetto shrieks among the grasses to a great subterranean echoing, so low that it was barely audible, as if a great frog were croaking in the lilac depths of the river.

And then there was the Tamil girl. I waited and waited, thinking that she might arise and pass by my hammock. But nothing happened; not, that is, until long after midnight.

I was almost asleep, in fact. So that I wasn't at all surprised, indeed it seemed quite natural, to feel her soft warm hand on my shoulder. I opened my eyes. All I could see was the very dim starlight falling through the intricate foliage upon the water. I couldn't see her at all. But I could feel the mosquito netting being slowly raised, and her hands on my belly, and the electrical touch of her hair hanging over my breast. She murmured something—a low excited little sound—and began to tug gently at my arms. She was quite naked—I couldn't see her, but I knew it, nevertheless. There was a wonderful young smell coming from her; I felt dizzy, my hands trembled. Then I felt the mosquito net falling softly back into place. And then the warm, the sweet, the unexplainable touch, the damp caresses, the ripe-plum smell, the marvelous suspense. Everything was very quiet, there wasn't a word or a sigh, nothing, no language at all except that of hand and lip and limb.

The bamboo boat came gliding up the river through the morning mist, and I left the Tamil and his girl on the shore beside the casuarina. They watched silently as I moved waterward; they didn't even wave good-by. Like statues they stood there, motionless, sulky, and at last they disappeared beyond the green curve. Would she remember me? Was she wondering whether I'd remember her?

297

The river was deep and sluggish, and the boat plowed through the water as if it were molasses, with scarcely a ripple, without a sound except the rhythm of the four poling coolies.

It was heavily hot, and the coolies were dripping wet. Presently they took off their loin cloths. Their curling hair glittered like copper in the sunlight, and even their eyelids shone with sweat.

We passed a huge mangrove swamp, mile after horrible mile of it along the western shore. And once or twice on the eastern shore little native villages in the jungle, the men shrieking and singing at us from their huts. Once near a village at a bend in the stream we surprised a group of girls bathing in the shallows. There was still a rose-colored mist on the water, and we could see their golden bodies gleaming through the haze, breasts shellacked with water, water dripping from their thighs. As soon as they saw us they ran laughing up the wooded shore and disappeared. A flock of monkeys followed them with a great fluttering and chattering through the branches overhead.

Gradually the river grew narrower, and toward noon the sun disappeared. A furry curtain of cloud slipped over it without warning. In another instant came the sudden wind, the strange tinkling noise, the smell of roots turned up, the electrical alertness. And then the rain. A terrific roar, a crackling, a gushing, a sudden flowing from everywhere into everywhere. Little torrents flashed down the mossy banks, rivulets trickled along the dead tree trunks.

After several minutes of this we could almost see the river rising. Waters came rushing down from the hills and churning riverward along fresh ravines. Trunks came floating down toward us, and cocoanuts, great brownish clusters of foam, leafy twigs, bits of liana. I thought that surely the boat would sink with all this whirling and whipping and effervescing. I could fancy the pythons slowly gliding down from the floating limbs and the crocodiles rising turgidly from the deep. But the four lean coolies looked unconcerned. One of them presently fell asleep under a sunshade, where he stayed until another one jabbed him with his pole.

And just as we came to a halt, and I saw a fat Malayan on the shore holding a big yellow umbrella, the rain suddenly ended. I could see the last drops rippling outward in the river, and forthwith the water as smooth as a mirror again.

Dr. Ainger was napping, lisped the fat Malayan; he would be up in an hour or so. This sort of weather always made him sleepy and sometimes, he slyly suggested, just a shade petulant as well. I suspected that he didn't like his master. Not a very promising beginning, I thought to myself. The Malayan kept grinning at me creasily. His fat breasts hung like a woman's, bare except for a few long silky hairs that flowed tassel-like down from his nipples.

It was an ordinary sort of bungalow that he led me to—two rooms and a screened porch, with a dispensary and two medicine-cabinets built on at the side. It was shocking to see how slovenly everything looked—stray bits of stained cotton, open medicine-bottles, pills lying on the floor, a reddish cluster of gauze.

But when I saw Ainger I understood. He looked terrifyingly weak; not physically weak—though he was that, too—as much as nervously weak; thoroughly on edge. It wouldn't be easy here; that much was certain. He greeted me without display, there was hardly even the gleam of recognition in his eyes.

We had supper quietly, as soon as he'd gotten up and mixed himself a gin drink. He also took some quinine, I noticed. We had olives, stewed chicken, peaches, milk— all of it out of cans. Giant wasps were hovering over the bowls, and everywhere were ants, ants, ants. But it was pleasantly served, at least, by a very pretty brown girl. A sad and silent creature, and I presently concluded that she was Ainger's concubine. But there was certainly no love here; he was thoroughly indifferent, she listless and doll-like.

Ainger sat there silently, with his drooping mustache, his pointed cheek bones, dry skin, eyes deep in their sockets. I expected him to tell me about what happened after that airplane smash outside Abbasabad. But he didn't so much as mention it. "Well, we're both still alive, aren't we?" said I. But he merely looked at me with scorn and did not reply. Nor did he as much as refer to the odd coincidence that brought us together again.

"Do you like the natives?" I asked, trying to make talk. "Are they good obedient patients?"

He smiled icily. "Not precisely. They're both indifferent and obstinate. They're apt to take a fancy to dying, you know, just like the rest of us. And it's hard to do anything when that happens." He looked cold; he was constantly shivering. There was an ivory precision in his features, beautiful in a fashion, but bleak, petrified.

"They seem to be so carefree," I said. "They look happy. Aren't they happy?"

"Certainly not." He spoke with such exactitude that everything he said sounded convincing and final; no matter how fantastic, how patently neurotic. He was gazing into a mirror that hung from the opposite wall. There were several mirrors in every room, even in the dispensary.

And when he spoke it seemed to be these mirrors he was addressing; himself, in short; and every gesture was reflected, and reflected upon. "They're wretched; they're all unhappy. Ugly with it, ill-mannered with it, sick with it, reeking with it. Unmistakably. You can smell the unhappiness hanging over them, following like a shadow, coming out of their pores like sweat, growing over them like a green rash. That's why nobody likes them. Look at my brown girl and you'll understand. And since nobody likes them they get so that they want to destroy, to poison, to gloat over other people's misery. You'll find out. It's not encouraging. They loathe me, every one of them."

It was getting dark, and the girl lit a lamp and placed it on the table. As it flickered the sharp lights and shadows on Ainger's face moved up and down, left and right. I could see the same face in the mirror that hung opposite him; the glassy face gazing back at the fleshly face. Or rather, it was a mask, it wasn't a face, and the expressions shifted only as the shadows rose and fell. Rather suggestively, though, even if falsely, even if only the illusion of the dancing flame.

"No, you're wrong," he replied, when I timidly suggested that possibly the West had better leave the East to its own devices. "I'm sure. The trouble isn't with the West. It isn't with the East. It isn't with the North or the South, or the white or the black. It's with Man. He's had his day. . . . Just look around. The black, the brown, the yellow, and the white. They're tired and stale, all of them." His voice was weary and tense, like the tense weary skin over his cheek bones, the tense weary eyes. But there was more than weariness in his shabby little despair; it had grown and grown, and now it was licking gently at his vitality. And it was infectious, too. He had given up. Solitude and idleness had done their job. He was no longer interested in others.

"Yes," said he to the mirror, "the world's on the downward path. What's coming is only the last desperate spurt —revolutions and wars and so on. And then the black ages again. Think it over and you'll agree. The real spirit is dying out of this man-made world. It's had its day."

I could hear the noises in the roof overhead; lizards scuttling across the boards, beetles and moths and nibbling things. There were thousands of tiny white spiders all over the place.

A young Malayan entered noiselessly through the netting, and sat down on the floor and began to play on a little harp while the brown girl sang. "Her brother," said Ainger, glancing at me for the first time. "He loves her, and comes to see her every evening." It was hot, and sweat ran down the lad's back and dripped from his chin. I could smell him from where I sat. Ainger lay back on the couch and smoked absent-mindedly. My visit had cheered him up a bit, had placated him, perhaps. I could imagine without effort how nasty he could be.

Finally the boy got up and walked out quietly with his harp. The girl followed him. Both of them were quite without expression, quite unsmiling. I could see them tenderly kissing good night, the two lovely, shining creatures, on the dappled path that led toward the village. But Ainger wasn't watching. He'd fallen asleep, and grim fat Mat Lela, too, was snoring noisily out in the porch hammock. I took off my wet clothes and went to bed.

But not to sleep. The jungle noises again. Leaves rustling, crickets chirping, monkeys bickering, frogs grunting; and rustling little pursuits across the shingles; glidings, whimpers, whines, laments, love calls, death calls, chirps of exasperation or delight. But so constant, so confused, that there wasn't any use trying to follow up one tiny fragment of joy or pain. And as soon as I got used to listening to the sounds as a single thing, inevitable and endless, they stopped bothering me with their pathetic intricacies and I fell asleep.

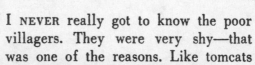

33

I NEVER really got to know the poor villagers. They were very shy—that was one of the reasons. Like tomcats they were, gliding soundlessly into sight and then out again. Haughty, filthy, secretive creatures. Nothing repelled them, absolutely nothing, and it was puzzling that such subtly and silkily shaped bodies should harbor no mind at all, should feel at home in a verminous mess of ashes, excrement, dead leaves, and dead animals. I'd see them pick up dark, damp objects from the ground and put them in their mouths. But, miraculously, their bodies lost nothing in loveliness from day to day; their skins stayed spotless and metallic, their muscles long, lean, bird-like. Some of them were quite weirdly beautiful. But like plants —supple, thermotropic, alien.

On hot days I would sit at the river's edge and watch them. Mothers would come to the shore and cover their babies with a coating of red mud, to keep them cool and safe from the swarming gnats. Then they would sit down at their side and gracefully sprinkle water upon them to keep the mud damp; and now and then would run their own long hair through the water and then let it flow down between their breasts and over their backs.

The lovely adolescent girls would lean against trees with half-open lips, aching for love, and the naked boys would swim swiftly across the stream and back again and then lie panting in the grasses; or they would go to sleep in the shade, dreaming visibly of love. They were very affectionate, all of them, and quite without any feeling of shame. Sometimes a boy and a girl would disappear in the greenery on the opposite shore, and then reappear, always happy and smiling. Fortunate beyond words, they had as yet found nothing on that joyful side of life to frighten them and drive them into an Occidental sort of despair.

"But they don't live long, of course," said Ainger. No, for they lived much too swiftly and carelessly. Their beauty wasn't the sort of thing that could possibly last or possibly limber up into any sort of graceful decline. They worked terrifically, for one thing. Most of the young males worked on the neighboring camphor and teak plantations. One of these plantations was run by a wealthy Englishman who had come down from Tenasserim. He lived in his bungalow with three brown wives and a dozen daintily tinted children. A dirty, unshaven scoundrel who ruled over his men like a mad rajah. All they did was work. If they didn't work they were punished, they were outlawed, they were starved. Now and then they would get hold of something to drink, and there'd be wild orgies in the camphor forest, noisy bloody affairs that frightened the small silent women in the villages. This was what started some of them on the downhill path. Others grew angry when their pretty wives or pretty daughters or pretty sons were taken from them; but they promptly lost their jobs if they grew unpleasant about it. Naturally. Once a slender-hipped young laborer came to the house for some medicine. Both he and his wife were sick. They had "sores," he explained. "I had them from her," he said, "and she had them from a white man from Singapore, and now everyone is getting them, even the children. And once we get them, there's no getting rid of them. Can't you help us?"

There'd be spiders hanging from the food and worms in the cereals. Centipedes a foot long, corrupt and undulating creatures, would curl up in my trousers during the night and then flow out upon the floor when I stepped into them in the morning. Once I went swimming in a green pool in the forest. When I came out I was covered with leeches, soft and painless things that swelled up even while I watched them. It was hard to pluck them off my skin, for they stretched like a rubber band. They'd come rippling toward me from all sides, through the marsh and over the wet moss, hundreds of them.

Whatever I did, it was weakening. The forces of debilitation gliding forever like eels through the jungle. Even to breathe seemed an act of treachery to the physique.

It kept drizzling for a week. One night there was a storm, an almost lunatic frenzy among the trees, a roaring, whipping, splitting, screeching, gnashing of vegetation. The next morning everything looked green and pulpy, like spinach. And then it would start growing again. Like drooping rubber things being blown up with air. Growing absurdly, fantastically, an absolute orgy of growing. I felt like Tom Thumb, the gigantic grasses and cabbages and ferns and mosses all around me leering vapidly, fumbling about, panting and quivering and reaching supinely. Their voluptuous python roots must have been raging under the earth like mad, wheezingly sucking up the moisture with a million nervous tongues.

And then the early August heat, as soon as the dripping stopped—so intense that stepping out-of-doors at noon was absolute insanity. The air was full of smells, horrible with heat and insects. A week of this and I was sick with malaria —fevers and gooseflesh and chills. I took aspirin and quinine by the mouthful.

But Ainger—I didn't know what to make of him. A regular stock villain I'd have said, tall, thin, saturnine, treacherous, callous; an absolute cad. Sentimental and inaccurate, too, and that made it worse, far worse. But every now and then he'd take my breath away by doing some one a kind turn, a real piece of unselfishness, or a phrase that was almost noble. And still, this somehow made it worse yet. It made him a real and competent devil. It added the final stench, the unforgivable intellectual aroma. "After all," he said one night, "it's restful to have you here. You're doing me good, you know." And he began to chatter away about himself.

"Look," he said, coming up to me; he was naked—soft-breasted and pale and hairy compared with the natives; "look at this. What do you think of it? I can't help worrying." It was only a reddish spot on the arm, a sort of eczema caused, no doubt, by the constant eating of canned food; nothing of consequence. "Sometimes, I tell you," he said in a curious penetrating tone, "it revolts me beyond words. Flesh, blood, living bodies and sick bodies and dying bodies. Not the disease. I can face the disease. But the human part of it, the *people*. The *smells*."

He'd talk and talk, gazing at his mirrored self hanging from the wall, and then he'd walk off, a stale flat-buttocked creature; and he'd draw the curtains behind him, and then I'd hear the soft whinnying sounds of his nutmeg girl making mechanical love to him.

Cripples came to the bungalow; naked natives with elephantiasis, with jaundice, with pellagra, with syphilis, with paralysis, with nymphomania, with everything in the world, with nothing at all. They came to him simply to be amused, some of them; or to bask in the private luxury of an examination, the touch of the doctor's fingers on their wrist or their ribs; or possibly to be tortured, to revel in the slow removal of a wen or the delicate opening of a boil. Or simply out of curiosity. My duties were to disinfect, to bandage, to administer pills, and so forth. Many of them began to come to me instead of Ainger.

There was one old woman who brought her little albino nephew to us. He was sick, helplessly pining away. We'd heard about the two of them before. They were always together, they loved each other only; they had no one else in the world. They couldn't eat or sleep if apart; indeed, each of them was only half a creature, shy, insipid, rabbit-like. Ainger knew the boy was dying. And then a few days later he did die. And two days after this the old woman was dead, too. All of it just as we had expected. The natives refused to bury her. They refused to touch the boy's pale body which filled them with distaste and fear. So Ainger and I buried him, while a few yards away the woman's relatives were performing the funeral rites in a suspicious, half-hearted fashion.

Ainger told me about a girl who had come to him, begging to be relieved of her sterility. He'd sent her away, of course. But now she was pregnant. Why? "Well, the oldest man of the village heard about it. So he mixed up a paste. Ground together some rice, the blood of a pregnant woman, some dried camphor leaves, the semen of a handsome fellow who had begotten several children. This was rubbed on her forehead, her breast and her belly. And it worked, as you see." He seemed rather pleased about it all.

The women would come again and again, with their hanging lips, their slender hips, their lovely cone-shaped breasts. They feared and hated Ainger; I could see it in their eyes. But they thought he might help them. And there was an ugly fellow, a eunuch, who came almost every day. He kept scratching and digging into an open wound at the base of his spine and then came waddling up, seeking pity. It was the only way he could get any attention. It was his way of asking for love. His sores stank dreadfully; they were covered with a dirty whitish foam. He was old and silly and his mind worked only at intervals. One day he stopped coming. But no one knew what had happened to him. He'd crept off to some secret cubbyhole, no doubt, for his last moments of loneliness.

There was a man who beat his wife every night. All because she was unfaithful. We could often hear her screaming in the distance.

"Oh, that happens every night," said Ainger when I first asked him about it.

"Is she unfaithful as often as that?"

"Undoubtedly."

"One might suppose that she'd learn, in time."

"Oh no. She *likes* it, you see. She is unfaithful on purpose. And secretly he wants her to be unfaithful. You understand?" She kept howling like a brain-fever bird. He was very strong, she was very slight and weak. Some day he'd probably kill her, said Ainger.

Fat Mat Lela was the only one who remained unvaryingly cheerful. A lovable, cynical soul. He ran errands for us, brought food from the boats, carried prescriptions down to the village, killed the poisonous snakes that crept into the bungalow. Once I saw him sitting by the river, fishing.

"Have you caught anything, Mat Lela?"

"No."

"Did you catch anything yesterday?"

"No."

"Last week?"

"No."

"Ever, Mat Lela?"

"Never," he replied blithely. "I don't like fish. I am happy just to wait." I sat down beside him and he told me about his life. He'd been a bandit once, a spy and a thief. There was something exciting about that, he observed. Not in the danger, not in the profit, but in the subtle form of morality that it induced. Everything was reversed. Good was bad, bad was good, and life was freshened up for a while at least.

"What is good?" he asked after a while. "What is bad?"

"I don't know," said I, "but you know, surely?"

"I have thought of it, many times. Again and again. Good. Bad. Staring at them is like staring at my face in a mirror, the more I stare the stranger my face grows, it is like a face under the water, it flows out and becomes something else. Good and bad, they too flow away from my mind, I know nothing about them, and when I look at them again, lo! they have exchanged places, good is bad, bad is good, and I understand nothing."

He looked with a peaceful smile across the river toward the naked girls in the shadows of the inlet. Now and then we could see one of them leaping out of the foliage, gleam for one golden-brown moment in the air, then disappear in the black water.

"Do you see? I hurt you, shall we say. That is bad. But then I am free of the wicked deed, it has left my mind and body, less badness remains in me. For every man has only so much good, so much bad, so much joy, so much sorrow, of that I am sure. So I am more good. Then you die. I am unhappy, I grieve. That is faithful and kind? Ah yes, but grief brings evil into my body, good and joy have left it, so I am more bad. Do you see?"

"No, Mat Lela."

"You do not? Look carefully into people, look for bad

and good, and you will see." But I knew that he was far more expert than I in this. He was a veteran professional, I merely a youthful amateur. I looked at the crook of his little finger and the soft slant of his lips; and I felt sure that many surprising bits of philosophy were stored up somewhere inside him. His eyes, too, looked very penetrating, very wise, very weary.

Time passed. I'd lie in my hammock listening to the mosquitoes and thinking about the passage of time and time's ambiguous ways. Sometimes it was a constant nibbling terror, sometimes a series of huge percussions, like a row of cymbals being beaten one after the other so that the echo of the two or three past ones lingered onward into the present and already hinted at the future; and sometimes hardly more than a steady rippling wail, like the grinding of sand over which the breakers were continually toiling. That was how it all seemed when I thought of it late at night, half asleep. Both less than real and more than real.

And I'd dream of Hermione again and again. It was a self-induced sort of thing, a kind of masturbation, but still at the same time a terrific passion if I thought of it long enough: so that every night she would grow more unreal, yet more desirable, and every night I would seduce her anew. Sometimes I almost grew mad with love for her, tears would come to my eyes, the whole world would become unexpectedly thrilling and alluring, everything about man would move me deeply; it seemed impossible not to adore the foolish temporary little creature that he was.

But it was all a dream, it wasn't Hermione at all. And still, though I thought of the others from time to time— the girl in the café, the girl in the prison yard, the girl in the bullock-cart, the girl on the river's edge, and so on—it was only she I really desired. It all became very unhealthy, very false, very sapping. The mere night air was enough to set my blood tingling. And even at daytime I couldn't touch a patient's warm brown skin without feeling dizzy.

One night a strange thing happened. The nutmeg girl's brother came and played on his improvised harp, and she sang. They looked very touching and very lovely, the two of them, facing each other: the pyramidal lamplight falling on her breasts and her open lips, playing on his flat nipples and the crease that ran outward from his navel. She beautiful, cold and resentful, he beautiful, cold and sly. Ainger lay in the darkness with a bottle at his side, fast asleep. Finally I turned out the lamp and fell into my hammock and went to sleep too.

And then a warm touch woke me up. I thought immediately of the lovely girl in the bullock-cart. It was so nearly the same thing, it was natural enough that I should. I grew tender and amorous. I spread out my arms, and I felt a hand running softly through my hair. But something was wrong. The breasts I was caressing were hard and flat as porcelain, the atmosphere was tense and florid. I felt embarrassed. I pushed the unfamiliar hand away and turned over. "Go away," I said, and I could hear the soft tiptoeing across the room and across the porch and down the leafy path.

34

As for Ainger, he was growing daily more peevish, slovenly and garrulous. In certain ways he was doubtless a very intelligent man. Passionlessness and disgust had certainly sharpened his mind, there was no doubt about it. But they had removed him from all gentle ways of feeling as well. Closer to reality, perhaps, but farther and farther away from humanity. Even his gait reflected it, even the scar across his face, the pores in his skin, the birdlike tufts of hair, the veins in his eyes, the hiss of his voice. Cold and dry, selfish and solitary as a spider.

"Everything that's nasty here," he said, "well, look around; it's recent, you'll observe, and it's Western. Don't you agree? Everything that's old is going. The temples are being deserted, the fields are rotting, the forests are falling, the old quarters in the cities are growing vile. And why? Because we won't keep our dirty panic-stricken paws off the East! We insist on giving them our stinking progress. Away with the Vedas and the Peace Everlasting. Bring in the Fords and the factories. What's a bit of faith compared to a fresh oil well or a new road? Civilization. Rot. All it means is making money and making things easier for those who've made it and killing the spirit in themselves as well as in everybody else. Kill everything that's brought them peace. Well, we'll see who wins in the end. I'm not so sure, myself. Asia has one or two weapons we never thought of. She can stand a lot. She's got something we can't comprehend." He would go on and on for hours. But the odd thing was that there was no end in his hatreds, and the next night he'd attack the opposite side with equal invective. There was nothing he didn't hate.

There was the war, for example. "The war," he said angrily. "Well. There it still is, reaching slimily out of the past into the present like a rotting tree trunk in a bog. And why? Why, I ask you? I must say, if Providence did feel disposed to experiment on that particular occasion, He did so in a very amateurish and ineffective manner, entirely at our expense. Here we are. Look at us. We aren't so very different, after all, from our brothers, the ones whom a stray bit of lead put under the ground. We've still got skin over our bones, that's the only difference. We can still tremble a little bit. But we're ghosts, really. We're out of date. We're no good. You young ones do well to despise us, though, bless your hearts, I'm not sure that you'll be much happier. The war was enough to cure me of optimism for good. Only a scoundrel would keep his optimism after such a war, or an imbecile. I'm through with sweetness and understanding."

And on and on. "The future!" He spat. "The real and final glory to which civilization is moving! It looks to me more like an insane and horrible blight, crossing one continent after another like a huge swarm of locusts, killing everything alive. That's what your American civilization looks like to me, young man; I hate it. And if I hadn't already given up life as a silly job I'd be terribly afraid of it as well."

"But look here," I said with a vague sort of energy, "you're too destructive. If everything's going to pieces like this, surely you must have some warning to give! Some piece of advice. Be constructive, that's only fair. . . ."

"You're a young fool," he replied. But it seemed to be the mirror he was talking to, not me.

One real trouble with him was that he was more than half dead, and yet for that very reason perhaps paralyzingly afraid of death. One couldn't help suspecting that this fear of death was the real thing in the back of his mind all the time. He always looked secretly afraid of something, and secretly suspicious of everything he touched, ate, sat on, walked over, talked to, listened to, smelled, drank, caressed, made love to. He didn't have a warm spot for anything, anything at all. Once I felt his hand upon my hand, and it was like cold pond water trickling down on me. I couldn't help loathing him, just as the natives loathed him. They feared him, too, but they detested him more than they feared him.

"I'm not going to live very much longer, you know," he said once.

He made everything seem chilly and unreal. Even the natives walked like ghosts whenever he was about. In fact, I felt bewildered from the day I arrived until the day I fled. I'll never know exactly why, since I can't possibly recapture the tone of those three swampy weeks. At any rate, whenever I think of them now they appear as a long, hot, odorous dream. I was green and soggy with inertia, and I didn't even have the spirit to feel sorry for anyone except myself during those muddled last six days. Once or twice the little thought came to me that what had happened to Ainger was beginning to happen to me, too. Well, thank God I got away in time. Though, as a matter of fact, there's still a bit of something nightmarish clinging softly to me like a leech. I try to keep it hidden, but it's there. Sometimes I won't notice it for days, and then suddenly it will begin itching a bit and the landscape and the people suddenly look different, smell different. When it gets strong I feel as if I were buried underground. But actually, now I come to think of it, I'm always aware of that shadowy alien bit of something waiting for me around the corner. It isn't me, but it's fastened to me like my shadow. It's the threat of what I'll be like if I ever muster up the nerve to stare straight into things.

꩜꩜꩜ One day a woman came up, holding a baby in her arms. It couldn't have been more than six months old, but it was a dreadful antiquated-looking thing; face rough and wrinkled, great swellings on the legs, and all over the body a plum-colored sheen.

I watched Ainger's face. It was unpleasant to see the change in his eyes; sweat went trickling down his temples, his lips trembled wetly.

And that was the beginning of the plague. The mother died twelve hours later, and within another twelve hours the rest of the family was gone, too. After that it went through the village like a fire. No one knew what had happened, what was happening, what would happen next. The constant bubbling sound of mourning rose from the village, and after a day or two of that a silence even worse.

The strongest man in the village fell with it; he grunted with pain, grew apathetic, wished only to be left alone so that he could die in peace. And that was what they all wanted. Merely to be left alone like animals, to be allowed a solitary death. There he lay surrounded by a sickening stench, his great brown body turning gray, swelling and decaying. The buboes were very painful. If they burst in time, there was still a slight chance. But if the pus penetrated as far as the lymph glands and the blood, death was never more than a few hours away.

The natives would cover the boil with a rag, pour salted

water on it, and then press down vigorously with a hot iron. Painful, but once or twice it really seemed to help. There was a danger for the doctor, too, Ainger observed; if the patient coughed and a bit of saliva were to light in the eye or be inhaled, that would be the end.

And another bad thing was this: when the patient died, the vermin emigrated and infected all who were near. The corpses were thrown in the swamp and in the river; there just wasn't the time or the energy to bury them all. Once a swollen body was dropped into a well outside the village at night. The next morning people came to drink from it. They didn't discover the body until several had already drunk the fouled water. Then one of them saw it huddling down there in the greenery. All of these that drank died the very next day.

No one understood it at all. At first they were alarmingly resigned. They had no conception of how to protect themselves, how to avoid infection. All they did was hope and pray and weep. The mothers who wept over their dying children, the children who caressed their dying parents, all of them died the next day. A girl's lover died, and she hurled herself on his naked blue body. A woman died, and her husband carried her quietly and tenderly down to the river, kissing her breasts, her neck, her thighs. There was one very fat woman, an absolute mountain of flesh, who could hardly move; her husband died, but she remained stolid—possibly she didn't understand, possibly grief lay too deep for outward expression. But the following day all four of her children lay dead at her feet, and now it was a different story. A long uninterrupted wail floated up from her hidden throat, she rubbed her hair slowly with filth, she shook with grief. We could see despair traveling outward through layer after layer of flesh, dripping off finally with a futile agonizing whimper. Then she lay quiet, and before long she too was dead.

One skeletal old man with rheumy bloodshot eyes tried to exorcise the unfathomable nastiness from his dying daughter. He tried every possible device. He built a fire, rubbed her with heated roots, spat on her, made water on her, bit himself in the arm and bled on her, covered her with ashes, and finally laid a dead serpent across her neck. But when he uncovered her again she was dead.

Many of them believed in witches. They implored the birds, whom they particularly suspected of wicked powers, and sang prayers to the water rats. Some of them went into trances. Once or twice it really seemed as if it had helped. A pregnant woman was strangely saved, a dying boy recovered miraculously. It was all done gently and with reserve, and the village was very quiet. Sometimes it appeared unbelievable that the place was vile with the plague. People kept walking softly down the path toward the river, they passed back and forth among the palms, and now and then a fire would flare up silently in the middle of the night.

All this time Ainger was growing more and more nervous. But he didn't explode, it never came to a head. I could see it fluttering constantly in his temples like a little insect, and I couldn't bear to look at him after the first two days of it. All the reality had gone out of him, all the vitality. What was left was stale, with a quivering, dying smell about it, like something that had better be hidden, something on the other side of the wall. After all, there had been a certain dignity about him. But now there was only a slender serpentine aliveness remaining in the ugly body which was really no longer a part of him.

On the third day the people grew restless and resentful. They no longer came to the bungalow, and they seemed

afraid of Ainger. On the fourth day they grew visibly
hostile. One man came to the house and cursed him, and
Mat Lela suggested furtively that I should leave. "No good
here. Better go quickly." Some of them, in fact, had mistrusted Ainger from the very beginning. "Why should he
help us?" they seemed to ask themselves. "Why should
he want to cure us without reward? Very strange, and we
don't trust it at all." Now these same ones suspected him
of being at the bottom of the whole thing. They'd always
hated him.

On the fifth day three men walked up to the dispensary
at dusk, and spoke to Mat Lela. Mat Lela silently shook his
head at them and pointed toward the river. Ainger and I
watched from the porch. We saw the men push Mat Lela
aside and tear open the door. A moment later we heard a
great shattering sound, and when we came running out toward the dispensary we saw that they had broken all the
medicine-bottles, torn all the gauzes, spilled all the serum.
The place was littered with bits of glass and dark-brown
liquids. Ainger stared, and then began to smile.

On the morning of the sixth day—the sun had
not yet risen, only the faintest pearl gray was beginning
to hover on the tips of the palms—Mat Lela came to my
dark bedside and woke me up. "Come, come," he whispered; "hurry, hurry."

"Why? What's happened?"

"Quickly, master."

"Is some one dying?"

"No, master," he implored softly. "I'm thinking of
you."

I looked toward Ainger's bed, but Ainger wasn't there.
"Where's Dr. Ainger?" I asked.

Mat Lela thrust my trousers and shoes at me. "Please,

master, quickly." His voice was a nervous whine. He was sweating violently with excitement, and his fat body shone in the darkness like a lacquer idol.

"Well, where's Dr. Ainger?"

"Must not worry over Dr. Ainger, master!"

I was excited, too, now. For I saw through the palms the glimmer of distant torches; and then the torches themselves emerging from the thicket—one, two, three, four of them. I hurried out, and as I passed the porch I thought I saw some one lying on the floor. But I wasn't sure. It might have been a bundle of clothes, of course.

Mat Lela led me pantingly by the hand down the path to the river. Then along the river toward a small grassy place on the shore.

"Wait here; boat will come. . . . I love you, master." His eyes were red with terror as he said this.

"Where's Dr. Ainger?" I asked; but Mat Lela had already disappeared in the woods again, and I was alone.

And then I saw the strange salmon-colored light flickering in the water and against the foliage on the opposite shore. I turned around, and there were the flames shooting high above the palms, the sparks spouting skyward, the gray smoke joining the gray dawn. It lasted three or four minutes, no more. And then only the slowly blossoming smoke.

A minute later I felt a warm hand on my shoulder. It was Ainger's brown girl. She leaned over me and placed a small leather bag in my lap. I knew that this contained Ainger's money—a good deal of it, too; I could feel the paper and the coins through the pigskin. "Where's Dr. Ainger?" I asked her.

She sat down beside me on the grassy edge, dangling her feet in the water. She was hot and out of breath. Even at that moment I couldn't help wanting to touch her lovely skin glistening in the morning haze; I wanted to do it more than ever before. But I was afraid of her.

"Dr. Ainger dead." Her expression was precisely as always, melancholy and remote. I didn't know what to say. My head was still foggy, and for a moment I thought she was lying. She seemed to be waiting for something, rather sullenly. Once when I glanced at her out of the corner of my eye I noticed that she was trembling gently.

Presently she rose and left without a word. And about an hour later the river boat arrived.

 I HAD just enough money left when I arrived in Bangkok to buy myself a fine new suit and a pair of fine new shoes and a fine fawn-colored hat. Just enough, also, to go to the best café in town and order a splendid dinner.

There I sat, tossing the ashes from my cigarette into the little black coffee-cup, when I heard a familiar voice. I looked around. I couldn't tell at first where it was coming from. Then I knew. At a small table behind a great bowl of ferns sat two corpulent middle-aged men. The one facing me wore a pince-nez. There was a fine cultivated look in his pale round face. He was speaking in a very low voice, mouthing his words ironically, a sort of sad half-smile on his lips all the time.

The other one's face I could not see. But the shape of his back and the sound of his laughter I recognized instantly. Perhaps because secretly I'd been expecting to meet him again. I don't know why. But actually I was not in the least surprised to see him there. These coincidences began to appear natural rather than otherwise.

And so, cockily aware of how well I looked in my fine new clothes, I rose and stepped up behind him. "Hamadullah!" I said. "I am delighted to see you again!"

He turned quickly. "Ah, ah," he said. There was a frightened glance on his face for a moment. Then he smiled and looked very pleased. "Oh, I am delighted also, very delighted!" His eyes took on a coquettish, calculating look. "You must meet my dear friend M. Laurentz. M. Laurentz is our French—what is the term—chargé d'affaires?—here in Bangkok. Won't you sit down?"

I sat down. Hamadullah looked rather proud of himself. Probably it flattered him that a well-groomed young Occidental should have gone out of his way to greet him, especially in the presence of another Occidental. "Most delighted," he repeated. "You must tell me all concerning yourself later. I am most anxious to learn. Will you come to my room in the hotel?" I saw him cast a sidelong glance at M. Laurentz.

"Yes," said I. "I should like to." I was very eager to hear the latest news from Badrapur.

"Fine," said Hamadullah with a coy little smile. He actually blushed for a moment.

M. Laurentz was smiling too, sadly and ironically. "Perhaps your young friend would care to attend our festivities tonight, M. Hamadullah?" He turned toward Hamadullah inquiringly. Hamadullah turned toward me inquiringly. I turned toward M. Laurentz inquiringly. Hamadullah was leering with pleasure at my having made so favorable an impression on his friend.

"Yes?" said M. Laurentz.

Hamadullah smiled and nodded.

I smiled.

"Then it's settled." M. Laurentz rose. "I shall see you later, gentlemen. Farewell." He made his way cautiously through the potted ferns. I couldn't help noticing how erect and military his bearing was, how flawlessly he was dressed, how politely restrained his whole behavior was. All of it somewhat in contradiction to the mellow yet tragical softness of his face.

"M. Laurentz is a very polished and diplomatic gentleman," observed Hamadullah benignly. "I am very proud to know him. He has done many kind things for me."

"Tell me, Hamadullah," said I, "what are these festivities you just mentioned?"

"Oh," he replied, "just an informal party at the palace of one of our Siamese princes. Prince Sawankalok. A very delightful boy. You will enjoy it. You must come. I insist, really."

Hamadullah had changed, I decided. He had gained in self-confidence and poise. But he'd lost something, too. He'd lost his freshness, his spontaneity. Something about him had gone just a little bit stale. I wondered what he'd been doing, for he looked very contented and prosperous.

Out in the palace garden rows of colored Japanese lanterns were hanging between the trees, and beyond these two fountains were springing gaudily into artificial light. Behind the fountains and the trees an orchestra was playing American jazz pieces in an odd indecisive way. They sounded unspeakably melancholy.

Indoors, in a great vermilion room, stood the tables. Blue wineglasses, little lights shining through green bowls, nude black statuettes among the almond cakes and candied pineapples. On each side of the glass doors that led into the garden sat young men tending the joss-sticks, and in the corner hovered a tall half-naked man who was working a punkah with a string tied to his instep.

Cocktails were served in the garden. Then the guests all stepped inside for dinner. Everybody was very polite and witty. Some of them were Frenchmen—attached to the French legation, I gathered—two or three Englishmen, the rest of them Orientals. All of them were men. M. Laurentz came up to us and spoke charmingly for a minute or two.

Prince Sawankalok hadn't arrived yet. His health was very delicate and uncertain, said Hamadullah. Also he was very touchy. "You must be careful what you say to him," explained Hamadullah. "Flatter him. Tell him he is both charming and beautiful, and he will be happy."

At that moment the Prince appeared. He was borne in on a richly gilded palanquin by four men dressed in green velvet. He himself was handsomely robed in orange silk and gold. His features were incredibly fine; each movement that he made was incredibly graceful. He sat down quietly at the head of the table and looked at us sadly, without a word.

He couldn't have been more than seventeen or eighteen. And yet there was something devastatingly old about him. Each glance and each gesture was consummate, with the flowerlike perfection of generations. "He looks sad," said I to Hamadullah.

"I think he is unhappy about some love-affair," whispered Hamadullah.

"Whom is he in love with, do you suppose?"

"Oh, one of the boy attendants, probably. Prince Sawankalok, like many of the Siamese princes, was brought up as a girl. That explains why he is so sad, you see."

"I see," said I thoughtfully. "But why, Hamadullah, should he be unhappy just because he is in love with one of the boy attendants? Need he be unhappy, do you think?"

"Oh yes," replied Hamadullah casually. "It will be quite impossible for him to find happiness in love. No one will ever love him enough, nor will he ever love anyone else enough. He is only half alive, you see."

Dinner progressed smoothly and wittily, and finally the champagnes and sweetmeats and cigars were placed on the table. Hamadullah, I noticed, was beginning to be a little bit drunk. "Please tell me about Badrapur now, Hamadullah," said I. "What have you heard from Badrapur?"

"Badrapur? Oh, I am not in touch with Badrapur. Badrapur no longer interests me. I have gone into new fields and pastures." He chuckled.

"Don't you know anything at all about our friends at Badrapur?"

"No, nothing." He coughed gently.

"Is the Maharajah still alive?"

"Oh yes indeed. Very alive."

"And the Diwan?"

"The Diwan has become fatter and uglier, I understand. A well-meaning little man, the Diwan, but really quite impossible. Very stupid and unobliging."

"And Mahmoud?"

"Oh, poor Mahmoud was caught stealing liquors from the sherry closet. So he left. He had his weaknesses, Mahmoud. But never did I think that alcohol would be the thing that would ruin him. Poor Mahmoud." He chuckled again.

"And Akbar?"

"Akbar ran away. He no longer loved his wife; he grew unhappy and restless, and so he ran away. He was a very ambitious youth. He was planning to go to a European university, I believe."

I grew thoughtful. Finally I said, "And Iqbal?"

"Iqbal?" repeated Hamadullah with a puzzled expression. "Iqbal?" Then he began to smile. "Ah yes. I recall. Iqbal was a very naughty boy. He too has run away. He has become a thief."

"But he was so young."

"There are many ways in which one can be a thief, my friend," he replied ambiguously.

Dancers appeared, both boys and girls, and after they'd finished the guests began to leave. I walked up to Prince Sawankalok and spoke to him.

"This has been a very splendid party," said I, "and thank you very much."

He smiled sweetly.

"I envy you a good deal," I added.

His eyelids folded over his eyes like those of a weary bird. The lines in his young face were surprisingly exact, almost like the lines in an old man's face, hieroglyphics of wisdom and sadness. But there was something very young there, too, and it was this innocence that made his face so subtle and mysteriously moving.

"You must be very happy, Prince Sawankalok, with all these beautiful things around you, and your wonderful palace." I was a little bit tipsy, I suppose. But secretly I was hoping that he would say something to me that would make him seem less remote.

He nodded his head and smiled again. "Yes, I love beautiful things." He ran his fingers slowly along the golden embroidery of his jacket. Long, tinted fingers, strange, habit-ridden boy's fingers. "But beautiful things do not make me happy," he added softly. "Beautiful things bring sorrow, not joy. It is better to desire nothing." He lowered his eyes again. "So I have been taught to believe."

And that was all. I knew that I'd never get a real glimpse into that isolated and intricate mind. So I said good night to him.

A few minutes later I said good night to Hamadullah, too, and walked to my shabby hotel. The evening hadn't turned out quite right. Something had gone askew. I felt disappointed and curious.

What is really touching, I thought, as I watched Hamadullah disappearing in his ricksha, is to observe how life affects human beings; how by nature man strives toward something he does not quite comprehend, how he reinterprets each intensity through which he passes into terms of the eternal; in short, his endless desire for the beautiful. But what is terrifying is to observe how life can gradually kill the freshness of this desire in all of us, in the weak and stupid as well as the subtle and experienced, how the beautiful is twisted and degraded, how a desire for the beautiful becomes a frightful parody, an obscene sort of ritual, and ends up by tainting precisely that in us which is closest to the eternal. Be satisfied with very little, desire nothing—that is what Prince Sawankalok had said; a desire for beauty brings more sadness than joy.

I wandered about in the enormous city the next morning. Tiresome, modern, dusty, full of cars and tramways and dingy little Chinese shops and dingy little Chinamen going cloppety-clop in their clogs across the cobblestones.

There were some rich Europeans walking along the better-known streets. They were laughing all the time. They swayed when they walked. The women screamed hoarsely and the men laughed in high thin voices. They were comparatively rich and very spoiled. All of them seemed to have been drinking steadily for several years. They pretended to be happy, but actually they looked distinctly unhappy. They looked afraid. They looked as if they no longer understood anything at all. They were pawing one another all the time, but it was only a pretense, a game. They looked as if they were simply waiting for death. I remembered the natives in the fields and the forests and villages: dead, but waiting for life.

Two old American ladies in my hotel wished to drive to Pnom-Penh by motor. Did I know of a young man, one of them hinted, who would be willing to chauffeur them to Pnom-Penh? Yes, said I. Excellent, said they. So off we went the next morning in a small purple Buick, off through the beautiful teak and bamboo forests of Siam toward Cambodia.

36

CAMBODIA is a haunted country, full of shadows, full of ambiguous little hints of the past. Villages lie scattered through it, hovering behind old trees like huge mushrooms. Time doesn't exist here. Men are born old and die young. And as for love, which is the real thing that makes us think of time and fear time, there's no trace of it anywhere. Look in the eyes of the women, or the idle young men, and there will be no softness visible, no tenderness at all.

Yellow-clad bonzes wandered with their begging-bowls through the groves here and there along the roadside. Serene, without fear. They had ceased thinking of themselves. Fear or melancholia could never bother them again. They looked very lazy and rather sly.

Finally we drove into Pnom-Penh, beside the huge brown Mekong River, and I said good-by to the two old ladies and the purple Buick. I walked to the river's edge and sat down on a barrel and watched. Flat-bottomed boats lay along the shore, and near by stood great baskets of fish—long silvery fish, flat pink fish, gold-and-black fish, bluish serpentine fish. Leaves were laid over them to protect them from the sun. Naked Chinese boys were rowing out into the river in little wooden boxes with pointed ends. They had round heads and stocky brown bodies, and hair like fine black silk. They were forever smiling and laughing, splashing one another and diving into the reddish water. Supple and finely shaped like statues, but their faces were flat and coarse.

September. Autumn twilight. A sad evening haze hung over the grasses and the gravel, and the foliage on the opposite shore looked very far away, very gentle and tender.

I walked up toward the broad street again, through the arcades full of Chinese shops and brownish Chinamen and a few shabby Frenchmen, onward to the large disconsolate French hotel that looked toward the river. A French flag hung grayly over the walk, and behind the pillars, under the balcony, sat the white-clad Frenchmen reading *Le Matin* and drinking rum punches. The setting sun shone fiercely upon the street. Every palm leaf glowed like burning metal, deep purple shadows among the pillars glowed like flames. Everything seemed motionless, caught under glass. My body felt soft with heat, my bones ached and my eyes swam and my temples throbbed.

I walked farther along the glittering street. A lovely little girl came tripping up to me with a basket of thin brown cakes. I bought one. I longed to run my fingers through her hair and over her brown satin neck, but before I knew it she was gone.

And suddenly the sky darkened, and in less than a minute great raindrops began to fall. The passers-by instinctively and wearily moved into the doorways, a fruit-vender ran his little wagon hurriedly under an archway. All the color had vanished suddenly, and I too stepped hastily out of the rain into a sheltered doorway.

But then, to my surprise, the door behind me opened and a lovely brown arm reached out and beckoned to me. I looked into the hallway, but could see only a few soft feminine shapes dim in the cool darkness. I hesitated for a moment. Then I entered.

They were pleasant girls, gentle, sweetly mannered, adroit. And kind hearts as well. They not only loved all men, but they liked men, and understood them, too. There was something oddly comforting in their behavior, they knew so exactly what to do, they seemed so completely content to do it; life was really a cool and carefree sort of thing for most of them. Either that, or their faces were exquisite masks and their behavior a flawless piece of pretense.

They all knew a few words of French. The girl that took me behind the screen spoke very well. She was a tiny little Chinese girl, fresh and blooming as a peach blossom. Her face was the picture of innocence, her eyes and lips the very emblems of sweet inexperience. "You have fine long legs," she murmured while she was rubbing my body with oil. "Like our devils."

"Like your devils?"

"Yes. Whenever I see a man with long legs like these I grow afraid. I think they are wicked. The men of my village all had very short round legs, and they told me that the evil demons with long legs would carry me away if I behaved wickedly."

"Why did they say that?"

"Because they did not wish me to behave wickedly."

A peculiar perfume filled the place. A feminine smell, sweet and oppressive. The boards in the floor were loose and they creaked with every little step that she made. And way down below I could hear the mice nibbling away, scurrying back and forth, busy with their own little intrigues and amours.

"And did you behave wickedly, after all?"

"Yes," she murmured very softly, "because I wanted the evil demons with beautiful long legs to come and carry me away." And so what really distinguished her, like others of her kind, from the less tender majority of her sex was largely an elasticity of mind and an eagerness to face facts. "I dreamed of the devils as very lovely silky-skinned men, wicked and strong and impolite."

"Why wicked?"

"Because they thought only of themselves."

"Did you have angels, too, in your village?"

"No. What are angels?"

I paused. Softly she ran her fingers along my arms. "Tell me, what are angels? Are they wicked, too?"

"No. Angels are the opposite of devils. Very good."

"And weak, and wrinkled, and without charm?"

"I don't know," I replied.

"I don't believe I would like your angels."

"But they are very kind."

"That is without importance, to be kind. It means nothing."

"But, my beautiful girl, *you* are kind. Don't you wish to be kind?"

"You are wrong. I am not kind. Some day you will comprehend that I have not been kind to you. You will wish you had never met me. You will curse me angrily."

"No," said I softly, "you are wrong." I turned over and looked at her face. She looked as innocent and passionless as ever.

"I think not," she said. "I understand men, and I have watched life. Do you see?" She turned away, and I knew, of course, that it was of no consequence to her whether I understood or not. But, very dimly and distantly, as if it were a silvery fish moving slowly deep down in a well, I could glimpse something of what she meant.

She left, and soon I was fast asleep.

When I awoke I heard a loud French voice on the other side of the screen. I sat up and listened. Something about the voice seemed familiar. "No, no, my lovable little parrot. I haven't another centime, not me. So there you are." There was no answer, and the voice broke into a loud laugh. And then I knew who it was. I rose and almost called his name. But then I thought again, more cautiously.

For there was something strange about this continent. In moments of loneliness it conveyed a feeling of indescribable vastness, of territory without end. And yet, in this very nocturnal vastness it seemed for some reason all the more natural that certain things should appear and reappear with an eerie regularity; coincidences, familiar faces cropping up again and again through the nightmare stillness like puppets in a marionette show. Things were beginning to happen more and more rapidly, more and more disconcertingly. Suddenly I felt, quite distinctly, that it would be better for me if I didn't see him, no matter how eagerly I longed to hear his voice, feel the hard touch of his hand. I felt, somehow, that I would be entangling myself, involving myself in a whimsical series of accidents, like a row of dominoes placed upright and then set a-tumbling. If I get mixed up in this, I thought to myself, there'll be other troubles following.

Swiftly and noiselessly I slipped into my clothes and turned toward the other doorway. A girl was watching me from the neighboring room. I tiptoed up to her and very softly asked her the way into the street. She pointed, and a moment later I stood out in the dark warm alley, listening to the soft irregular dripping from the eaves and watching the lights on the river in the distance.

I sighed with relief. After all, I had done the wise thing. And yet there was a little twinge in my heart. Had I no true friend, none at all? Perhaps I was merely selfish, heartless, mean. After all . . .

I heard footsteps on the wet cobbles behind me. Then suddenly I heard some one calling my name loudly. It was too late. Here he was; he had found me in spite of all. I turned, and "Samazeuilh," I said, quietly, "I am very happy to see you again." And then, as soon as I'd said it I knew how true it was. I was overcome with joy. The great hearty voice, the great powerful body, the great indiscriminate face: they warmed my heart; my voice grew hoarse; tears came to my eyes.

"You scoundrel," he cried, putting his big arm around me, "why did you try to run away from me? I was waiting for you to wake up, and then I looked, and you were gone. But the little whore by the doorway told me where you went. Yes. I should knock your head in. Why did you run away?"

"I didn't know you were there," I lied. "And I was shy," I added. And that was the truth. People have a quaint way of trying to dodge behind a corner when they see something they have longed for coming along.

He laughed. Then he pulled my ear painfully. "Owow!" I cried, but I was happier than I'd been for many weeks.

It was still very hot, and we walked down to the river. Slowly the Mekong moved past the shore, carrying odd little lights and odd little shadows along with it.

He sat down beside me on a stone bench and began to talk.

🌿🌿🌿 I had almost the feeling of gazing into a mirror. Get close to a person and you'll never shake him or her off again. He'll be forever hiding in you. Forget his name, forget his face, it won't matter, he'll be hiding in you still; you'll never be the same again. Man is utterly lonely; he'll never be understood by any other creature. And still, he's never quite alone. Inside him, so deep that he can't see or understand, the vague and touching shapes of his past hopes and despairs and all the familiar faces are still shifting uneasily, lying in wait—like an old photograph album, dusty, but still terrifying.

". . . and so I said good-by to her and took the next boat for Singapore. And from Singapore I took the next boat up the eastern coast. That's all. And you?" But I had scarcely begun when he said, "Come, this heat's more than I can bear; take off your clothes and we'll go swimming."

And so we did. Carefully we folded our clothes under the bench and crept into the brown water. It was fine and cool. Nobody was around, everything was quiet. The muddy bottom crept through our toes and up over our ankles, and gently the water slid over our thighs and higher and higher till we could barely tip the soft sand with our toes and could feel the current carrying us slowly southward. A boat passed us. Three dark men were sitting in it quietly, and when they saw us they began to chatter and laugh. But we couldn't understand what they said. Soon they had disappeared in the darkness.

The water smelled stale, half mineral and half animal. But there was a strengthening quality in it and my dizziness left me. It was fine to lie on my back and see the starry water running across my breast and my belly, and watch the clouds grow fiery overhead as they approached the moon.

"Antoine," I cried joyfully. But there was no answer. I looked around. There he was, slowly climbing out on the shore a hundred yards away. I had to swim against the current to reach the place where we'd left our clothes. I felt tired but happy.

Laughingly he stood there on the littered shore, the same young animal's look in his face, the same delighted power in his voice, the same god-like body. He hadn't changed. Bad luck hadn't gotten him down. Some wonderful sort of strength was there that made it possible for him to do anything, endure anything and allow nothing to matter. A will to live, an ability to look at the world warmly yet objectively, a feeling for everything of both love and indifference. Things that I longed for.

Suddenly he cried, "I've been robbed, by God! Not a cent left, not a single penny!" He cursed vigorously. Then he looked at me and smiled.

I felt uneasy suddenly. I reached into my own pockets. Empty, absolutely. The notes that my two old ladies in the purple Buick had given me were gone; I'd been robbed. "I've been robbed too, Antoine!" I exclaimed. But it sounded hollow and unconvincing, somehow.

"Well," he laughed, "we've never been millionaires. We'll survive, won't we? Some people need money to get along, but not you or I. Isn't that true?" He put his arm around my waist. "Look here, I've a few centimes left in my back pocket. That's enough for a drink. Come along."

So we marched along the darkened street till we came to a little tea-house with a lamp burning at the door. "Have you wine?" we asked the fat little Frenchman who greeted us. He winked his eye at us and nodded.

🜲🜲🜲 "Tomorrow we'll leave for Saïgon," said Samazeuilh, running his fingers tenderly around the wine-glass. "Move, move, keep on moving, that's the whole thing. That's the way to survive."

"How will we get to Saïgon, Antoine?"

"Train. I'll show you how it's done. Quite simple and surprisingly cheap."

"Come, come, Antoine," said I primly. "You can't keep this up indefinitely."

He grew quiet for a moment. He was thinking. "I don't know," he said. "The main thing is to keep alive. Think of the moment. Live in the moment. That's the way to be happy. You'll be surprised, my gentle boy, how much you can stand and how pleasant each moment can be." He grew quiet again, and began to hum an old French ditty in a soft sentimental voice. Something of the philosopher there, after all, I reflected. His blond beard and long lashes caught the lamplight. A beautiful man, a strong man, a happy man.

The lecherous little Frenchman tapped him on the shoulder. "Sorry, monsieur, but I must really go to bed now. I need sleep, my wife needs sleep. You understand." Samazeuilh reached into his back pocket to pay. "I'll pay, my lad; I've still got enough to buy you a bottle of wine, thank the Lord, and maybe a bit of love and a nice warm bed for tonight as well." He smiled mischievously. But out of the corner of my eye I glimpsed the bill with which he paid, and I knew who'd robbed me, and I couldn't help feeling sad about the ways of the world.

"It's all very well," said he tipsily as we walked down the hollow glimmering street, "it's all very well to think about the sizes of the stars up in heaven and about these big black distances and all that, and to say that, after all, man is a pretty farcical and despicable little business. Granted. But let me tell you this. Don't let it prey on your mind. Don't let it bother you too much. We're men, aren't we, so let's keep to man's own little standards, struggle the way man's always struggled, struggle against other men and not against the laws of the universe. Your life depends on it. Just remember that."

The street grew narrow, the eaves groped toward each

338 ◇◇◇

other over our heads, stale smells dripping from them, catching the warm night air and breathing it back into our faces like a great sleeping beast.

Antoine stopped outside a little door marked with a cross and knocked. A pretty little Chinese girl opened the door.

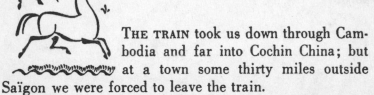

37

THE TRAIN took us down through Cambodia and far into Cochin China; but at a town some thirty miles outside Saïgon we were forced to leave the train.

So we drove toward Saïgon on an ox-cart, over the vast low plain. One great level stretch of mud-lands it was, spotted with jungle and marsh and swamp, netted by the delta of the Mekong. A dreary, steaming, vaporous land. Down in their rice-fields the limp brown laborers moved very slowly to and fro. Here and there we glimpsed coffee plantations and rubber plantations in the distance. But most of it was muddy, watery land, very unlovely.

The peasants in the villages were terribly poor. Rags were all they had to cover themselves with, and their bodies were dreadful to behold. Red-lidded eyes, spotted skins, hair coarse and matted, strange sores on their legs. And in their eyes a look of utter indifference. That was the really disturbing thing. They never spoke at all.

Night fell before we reached Saïgon, so we slept in a small village. Our coolie friend stretched mosquito nettings for us among the trees, and there we lay, listening to the leaves and the villagers near by moving through the shadows. They went wandering by till far into the night, making love in the moonlight that filtered through the leaves and chanting in a strange inconclusive way. Very melancholy it sounded. The men wore very little, and once or twice we glimpsed two figures pale on the ground, and a gleaming thigh or a silvery arm where the shifting moonlight happened to light. It was very hot, and we could almost smell their love-making all around us.

The next morning we drove into Saïgon.

🪦🪦🪦 We walked down the Rue Miss Cavell, Antoine and I, past the very French-looking cafés and on into the wide tree-lined avenues, past the fine white buildings, the fine Governor's palace, the fine cathedral, the fine Hôtel Continental. Now and then we'd hear the noise of a radio coming out of a shop, and everywhere we saw brightly colored sport cars, American makes, most of them—Cadillacs and Chryslers and so on.

Everyone looked very lazy. The coolies looked stupid with opium, the Frenchmen stupid with conceit. They'd be sitting in the sidewalk café of the Hôtel Continental with pomaded hair and cork helmets and white suits. They preened themselves and with spoiled eyes watched their spoiled compatriots promenading. Now and then a fat sleek Chinese merchant would drive by in an expensive motor-car.

We sat down in a desolate little café in the Rue Catinat and Antoine generously ordered a bottle of wine. "No, no; I've got enough," he said, "I'll pay; I've still got a few coins jingling in my pocket. Not many, but enough. They didn't leave you a cent, you poor bastard, did they?" He pulled my hair playfully. And oddly enough, I didn't mind. He was a selfish, merciless fellow, and yet so captivating, so happy and good-looking, that I hadn't the heart to be offended. Even if he'd stolen my sweetheart or my very life away, I couldn't have hated him for it. I noticed two pretty French girls in the back of the shop, peering at us and tittering nervously. Alas, thought I, how little most of us know what is good for us, how cleverly most of us, after all, do manage to snatch at the very thing that will bring us nothing but regret.

I felt very lazy. And for some odd reason I was beginning to feel unhappy. Thinking about Antoine was what did it. "I don't like this city," he was saying; "not in the least. It's smug. Let's leave tomorrow. I can't stand it here much longer."

"But why not, Antoine?"

"I don't know," he cried. "Stuffy. Stale. Stagnant. Don't you see?"

"But what about money, Antoine?"

"We'll manage, my quaint one; don't worry," he replied. He's really a generous sort, thought I for a moment. Then I began to laugh at myself secretly.

"What's the matter with you?" he said. "You look funny."

"I'm laughing at something I just happened to think of," said I.

"Really! Well, I could have sworn you were ready to burst into tears. Well."

"No," said I, "try as I may, I can't bring myself to cry, these days."

He looked at me oddly. It displeased him to hear me talking like that. He thought it was all affectation, nothing more. A moment later he said: "Look here, I'm stepping down the street a way. I'll be back in half an hour. Wait for me, will you?"

And out he went without waiting for an answer. I watched him through the big window. He was following a girl down the street. I leaned out and watched. He sidled up to her, peered at her as he passed, paused, turned, coughed, leered, accosted her. I could only see her back. But a very lovely back it was, slender and suggestive, tightly clad in green silk, a big green hat over her head.

But she'd have none of him. She walked straight on, and spoke to him angrily when he came up alongside. Then she turned around and walked quickly back in the direction of the café.

I drew my head in hurriedly and sat down at my table again. Something about the green lady had disturbed me. Something a bit familiar. I closed my eyes and reached back into my memory. Where had I seen her, what made me so uneasy?

I heard the door opening and started. Was that she? No, it couldn't be; she wasn't walking that fast, surely. I looked furtively toward the entrance. No, it wasn't a woman. Not quite. It was a slender young Chinaman wearing a soft black hat and carrying a basket covered with a yellow napkin. He crept noiselessly across the floor and set the basket on the counter. I saw him glancing at me out of the corner of his eye. I stared hard at the coffee-stained French newspaper that was lying on the table.

Then I looked up again. He was still standing there, leaning daintily against the counter, trying to catch my eye. It made me sick and unhappy to see him there. He was actually quite handsome, almost beautiful, with a fine pure skin and long silky lashes. But he looked unhappy and somehow unlucky; as if he'd lost the knack of regulating his life. What I saw was not the decay of one man, I knew. It was the decay of a whole social order, of a whole method of thinking and living, of a whole system of consolations and philosophies and reconciliations and hopes, built up during long years. There he stood, gazing half in grief, half in love, out from under his soft black hat, smiling dreadfully, fingers trembling.

I turned my back. Presently I heard the door opening again and I knew he was gone, even though I hadn't heard his departing footsteps at all.

Then I heard the door open once again. This time I was really startled. It couldn't be Samazeuilh yet, surely. I turned quickly and looked.

It was the lady in green. She sat down wearily at a table in the dark corner. She hadn't noticed me at all. Wearily she ran her fingers over her eyelids and yawned. She didn't look very pretty.

Then she took off her hat. There was something rather odd about her hair. It was done up in innumerable little curls, and shone with an unnatural gilded color.

Of course. She had dyed it. And suddenly I knew who she was. I remembered the lovely veil of black hair hanging like a waterfall over my head, and the cedars and snowy hills beyond. Yes, she'd changed. I turned in my chair so that I'd be facing the other way. I felt very strange, almost terrified. These meetings were getting to be like the repetitions in a nightmare, stranger and stranger, more and more frequent.

But she heard me. I could feel her becoming aware of my presence, straightening up, hanging a pretty look over her face like a mask. It was too late. I knew that she had recognized me.

"Ursule!" I said, rising from my chair. She smiled, with all the serenity and coquettishness of an instinctive actress. "I'm happy to see you, very happy indeed. You are looking extremely well, I must say. I like your hair that way, really!" I was feeling rather embarrassed, for I knew that I'd glimpsed her off her guard, and it wasn't a consoling thing to see.

But she really looked very glad to see me. My heart melted. She'd been lonely, I could tell—lonely and frightened. "Where have you been, Ursule? My, but this is a delightful surprise; you're the last person I expected to see here!"

"Really?" She sounded a bit curt, as if I'd been insinuating something. "Oh, I've had a difficult time. It hasn't been easy, truly it hasn't."

I told her that I was very sorry. "What's happened to de Hahn?" I asked.

"I was just about to tell you. Well, I left him in Bangkok. I ran away. And there you are. I simply couldn't bear it any longer, that's all."

"But, Ursule . . ."

"Oh, it was dreadful," she cried affectedly, gazing at herself in the mirror on the opposite wall. "He was growing slovenly and conceited beyond words. Talk, talk, talk. He'd never stop, even in bed. He gave up shaving, his finger nails turned black, and would you believe it? he's grown fat. Positively. You should see him without clothes. Soft little bundles of pink flesh here and here and here. Indecent!" She tittered softly.

But then she too had grown a little bit fatter. There were delicate little folds in her neck. Her dress was cut very low and her breasts showed quite plainly under the Shantung silk. Rich and fleshly she looked. She was hot, and there were wet rings around her eyes and wet creases in her hands.

"And so you ran away," said I.

But she wasn't interested in that any more. I could see her energy rising, a new vitality spreading through her like a tonic. "And you, darling?" she said, her eyes big and soft. "What have you been doing? Oh, you were a wicked man to run away from us! We worried so about you. . . ."

At that moment the door opened again. It was Samazeuilh. He looked hot and tired. "Well!" I cried. As soon as he saw Ursule he straightened himself up and smiled. As if by magic he looked bright and eager again.

I watched the two of them. I could see them blossoming forth, exhaling vigorous little perfumes, rubbing their wings, stretching their antennæ. "Ursule, this is my dear friend, Antoine Samazeuilh."

He bowed. "Haven't we met before?" he said facetiously.

She smiled and lowered her eyes. He sat down.

"Will you excuse me for a moment?" I said presently. But they didn't even notice me. So I got up quietly and walked out into the street.

Bearded men were sitting at little white tables along the boulevard, drinking quinquina dubonnet and reading newspapers. Ladies in the latest Paris gowns drove by in long motor-cars with iridescent hoods and chromium superchargers like great silver serpents. At one table an oldish woman in a huge gray hat was sitting and flirting with a young sunburned Japanese in a pongee suit. At another an old man with a monocle was caressing a smartly dressed brown girl with diamond earrings.

Two blocks farther I saw strange yellowish people leaning out of jalousied windows—fat meretricious women, shabby old men lost in an empty dream existence, nervous little girls with grubby, intent faces. On the doorsteps sat the full-grown daughters, passive but alert, some of them beautiful, all of them heavy-eyed with a desire for love.

Just as I reached the café again Antoine and Ursule were coming out. They looked a trifle disconcerted when they saw me. "Well, where have you been?" said he. "We'd almost given you up. Trying to run away, eh?" There was a note of relief in his voice; he seemed pleased that I should have returned in time.

But not Ursule, I suspected. I no longer fitted into her

plans, somehow. She looked very beautiful suddenly; intent, nervous, amorous. She'd fallen in love with Antoine already, poor thing.

"Well, let's get along," said Antoine merrily. So we went to a fine restaurant and had an enormous dinner. All three of us were very drunk and happy. Ursule paid.

"Where's de Hahn tonight, I wonder," said I dreamily as we walked toward the hotel near by.

"I don't know," cried Ursule, "and I don't care! He has no power over me. I owe him nothing. Besides, I know all about him. If he behaves unpleasantly I'll have him arrested, that's what I'll do. He's told me everything, and it's enough to send him to jail for life. A vulgar thief! Receiver of stolen goods. Smuggler of stolen valuables. I'm not afraid of him!" She showed her teeth whenever she was angry. Very fine white pointed teeth, showing under a pair of lovely perverse lips. The street lamp fell full on her face, glowing in her peculiar golden hair, turning her skin into a rich orange color. Never had I seen her so beautiful. There was a marvelous richness in her eyes. She looked very happy.

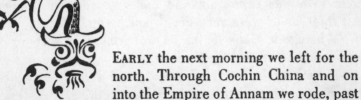

38

EARLY the next morning we left for the north. Through Cochin China and on into the Empire of Annam we rode, past Plan-Thiet, Phan Rang, Nha Trang, Qui N'hon, Binh-Dinh, Quang-Ngai—names that sounded like a parrot calling, or the beating of a tin gong. Across the low blue hills all day, through cool thick stretches of pine trees, past high waterfalls that shone among the low trees rich with a September look. The Chams lived here—men and women of great beauty, dark slender creatures that lived in bamboo huts set high upon poles and reached by a ladder. We saw some of them sitting under black cotton umbrellas, drinking chum-chum, and several riding, clad only in their loin cloths, along the road on bicycles. But whatever they did, it was with a look of aloofness and scorn that they did it. They despised the pale pudgy visitors from the west and the north.

One night we spent at Qui-N'hon. The next night we spent in Huë. A delightful city, surrounded by small French villas and pretty park-like spots, everything green and tidy. The Annamites were proud and elegant little people, dressed in neat black turbans and white trousers and black silk tunics. They mixed freely with the French, never with any air of inferiority or fear, always precise and restrained.

It was very hot the day after we arrived. Even early in the morning the air was dripping with the moist sunlight, and moving through the half-dark rooms of the hotel was like moving through a steam bath.

I walked out upon the terrace and before long Ursule joined me. "Where's Antoine?" said I.

"Sleeping."

"Still!"

She nodded her head.

"Why didn't you wake him up?"

She looked at me blankly. I could see she wasn't listening to me. There was a peculiar secretive look about her face. Her eyes were dull again. Underneath her eyes I could see little crow's feet, and hard, contemptuous lines on each side of her lips. Her hair looked streaked and oily. There was something a little bit frightening about her. She's making plans, I thought to myself; perhaps she's trying to get rid of me, perhaps she thinks I'm jealous. As a matter of fact, I was—a little bit.

"Why did you run away from me that night?" she said after a brief silence.

"Up in the hills? That night?"

She nodded.

"But you told me to run away! Don't you remember?"

"Absurd," she replied in a flat tone. "You must have been dreaming. Preposterous. Why should I have told you to run away?"

"Well, I could have sworn . . ."

"It was rather stupid without you, you know. De Hahn grew very tiresome. He missed you a good deal, I suspect." She was looking at me intently, eyes like tunnels, sending quick little arrows of conjecture out into the sunlight. She leaned over and sipped daintily at her coffee-cup. Then she ran a red silk handkerchief across her forehead. But all the time I could see her looking at me. It's rather exciting to watch people opening out, like a big tropical flower, slowly changing color and shape, displaying whimsies and secrecies never previously suspected or thought possible.

"You're in love with Antoine, aren't you?" said I.

She didn't move, but I could see that I had excited her. Then she said, "What makes you think so?"

"I don't know, Ursule," I answered. Then I added: "But don't think that I resent it, please. I like both of you, I want to see both of you happy . . ."

"I know what you're thinking," she said slowly. "Well" —and her voice rose gradually—"one never knows what's going to bring happiness, never. But then, one's got to try. One's got to try to be happy. I can't just sit back and cry; it isn't natural! I've got a healthy body. The breaks are all in one's favor if one's good-looking and not too stupid. If one takes care not to expect too much." Her voice didn't sound very contented. I wondered what had happened between her and Samazeuilh; not physically, that is, but emotionally.

"Yes, yes," I said, nodding my head.

"Tell me," she said softly after a pause, looking past me at the motor-cars on the street. "Am I still pretty? Tell me the truth."

"Why, of course, Ursule . . ."

"Tell me the truth. I must know the truth. Do I look older?"

"Not a day older, Ursule, really."

"Have I grown too fat? I'm terrified about that. Please tell me the truth, now. Be frank. Don't be afraid of hurting me."

I realized that she no longer regarded me as a lover, not in the slightest degree. She was confiding in me. She was allowing me a look at her secrets. It was touching, of course, but it was a blow to my vanity.

"Are you thinking of Antoine?" said I.

She didn't answer. She looked quietly over the shrubs, watching the autumn butterflies making love on the gravel walk. There were tears in her eyes.

🙢🙢🙢 And then it happened. The most dramatic possible situation, almost ludicrously so. The final touch. The ultimate, the incredible bit of nightmare coincidence. And yet, perhaps, not so very incredible after all.

A long yellow motor-car was driving slowly by. Then it stopped. A tall heavy man with a goatee stepped out upon the walk and looked up at us. It was de Hahn. I got up from my wicker chair and waved. He smiled and waved back. Then he turned toward the white stone stairway beyond the wall that led from the street up to our terrace.

For a moment he disappeared from sight. I heard Ursule utter a faint little sound. Her face looked like a mask, suddenly beyond surprise or terror. I sat down again and breathed deeply.

And then the door from the hotel opened. Out stepped Samazeuilh. "Well, well," he said cheerily. "Here you are, my little love-birds. Up early, aren't you, enjoying the cool morning sun!" I looked at Ursule. She was perspiring heavily. I could see the heat dancing in and out among the coffee-cups and silverware.

He sat down. "Well," he said, "you don't look very energetic, I must say. You don't seem particularly pleased to see me. Not even so much as a good morning. Really . . ."

Ursule and I rose simultaneously. There was de Hahn, standing beside one of the little potted palms at the edge of the terrace. He was wearing a light suit and a white cap, and was carrying a Malacca cane. His face was in shadow.

"Ah, you two," he cried, "how happy I am to see you again!" His voice sounded genuinely tender. "First the one runs away, high up in the mountains, and then the other, down among the rice-fields. Well, I've found you again, that's all that matters." He came up and kissed us, first Ursule and then me. Then he took off his cap and sat down. His face was dripping with sweat. Yes, he'd grown fatter.

"M. Samazeuilh," said I. "M. de Hahn." They smiled and shook hands. "Delighted," said de Hahn amiably.

Strange fellow, thought I. Quite incapable of malice. Apparently everything was forgiven. It seemed so preposterous that I at first couldn't help suspecting a trick. Perhaps he was acting. Perhaps he was merely leading up to something. But no. He was sincerely happy to see us again. It was incredible.

But he'd changed. "Now let me tell you how I found you," he began. "I stopped, quite by accident, at a hotel in Qui N'hon . . ." I watched him while he talked. He looked prosperous and was dressed in great style. But his face had changed unmistakably; he looked lonely and remote; something had happened to him. My heart went out to him, for I still liked him as much as ever. But he'd wandered off, somehow, he no longer looked responsive, his eyes seemed soft and ineffectual.

"Really! . . . Incredible! . . . Well, that was fortunate . . ." said Antoine from time to time during de Hahn's recital. None of us could get more than a word in edgewise. I could see that Antoine was getting the hang of things. He glanced humorously at Ursule and then at me and then back at de Hahn again. The whole thing seemed to amuse him very much.

As for Ursule, she kept smiling in a really gruesome way. I could see little bits of anger and despair and hatred and deceitfulness and love all fluttering around in her mind like confetti. And through it all she kept smiling in this dreadful manner. I began to feel worried about her, and about de Hahn as well.

"We're all going on a picnic," de Hahn finally announced. "I'm going to buy the things, the most delightful surprises imaginable. You'll be amazed! And off we'll be to the park." He looked happy again. "That will be very pleasant," said I. Antoine laughed genially. Ursule smiled.

It was early afternoon when we started off. We drove out to the park in de Hahn's yellow car, and then walked slowly, with the baskets on our arms, down toward the pond.

It had grown unbelievably hot. The streets were ribbons of pure golden heat, and even in the park among the pine trees the rays of sunlight slanted down like flames upon the grass and sand. Big open cars were being driven by sweating Frenchmen slowly along the avenue; straight-lipped nurses with gaily tinted parasols were taking their little girls for a walk; lovely dark concubines were riding by in freshly painted victorias and gaudy rickshas; down by the fountains two little children were playing nakedly in the stone basin. Pines and palms and bamboos lined the path. And everywhere we could hear, hazy and confused as the dappled sunlight, the babble of voices, leaves, water, birds, motor-cars. We passed a fine bronze statue of Buddha in the middle of a green glade, and then a little pagoda hidden among some trees. Once Ursule cried out in alarm as a pretty green snake crossed our path. The rest of us laughed in the superior manner of males; but it was a nervous, uneasy laugh.

39

IT GREW still and secluded as we wandered farther and farther from the streets. We passed through a stretch of thick forest and then along a rocky path that led to a concealed shrine. The steps to the shrine were covered with moss and the sacred little pool was bright with lotus blossoms. It was very peaceful.

Autumn again. The year moving backward once more, its experienced eyes gazing across the territory it has just covered. Sad and nostalgic, like a return to childhood. And exciting and mysterious as well, more and more so as you watch it closely. The season of recognitions and recollections—dead leaves again, the soil already rich with the decays of the spring and summer. A crisp rustling sound everywhere, a sort of warning whisper. What is it saying? What can it be about those swift, delicate syllables that makes us lose confidence in ourselves?

Finally we reached a shady spot under some willows that overlooked the Fleuve des Parfums. Here we spread our napkins while de Hahn opened the baskets one by one with little grunts of pleasure. "Jellied beef broth, yes; two quaint little jars of lambs' tongues; and camembert cheese, soft but not too soft; and pickled pig's feet, tender and pink as your pretty body, my love; and maraschino wafers; and dates from distant Egypt; and two bottles of claret. Is that enough? Yes?" He laid them out in an orderly row upon the grass. They looked very gay and innocent, like a little boy's presents laid out under a Christmas tree.

"Here, my dear," said Ursule suddenly. "I've brought something too. All for you." We all looked at her. She held out a little dark glass toward de Hahn. "Caviar! Aren't you pleased?"

"My darling," he said tenderly, and kissed her on her neck. "How sweet of you to think of it."

"I knew you loved it. It's all for you."

He was touched. He put his arm around her and kissed her three more times. She closed her eyes and smiled.

🙰🙰🙰 After we'd finished the wine we all lay back in the grass and closed our eyes. It was very still. At first we heard nothing except the rippling of the Fleuve des Parfums. Then, very faintly, we could hear the crickets chirping, and far off, across the water, a train whistling as it passed through the valley. And from far, far away, from an almost legendary distance, tiny human sounds drifting down to us from the walled and moated city. Once two lovers in a rowboat passed us near the shore. They looked sulky and preoccupied. "They look as if they'd been quarreling," said Ursule.

"They'll get over it," said Antoine jokingly. "There's one thing that will cure that in short order."

Ursule turned and smiled at him. Then she glanced at de Hahn. He was fast asleep, with a napkin over his eyes.

"Oh dear!" she said. "I think I'll walk along the shore a way. I feel sluggish, I need a bit of exercise."

"Good," said Antoine. "I'll go with you. Do you mind? After all, you need some one to protect you, you know." He winked at me slyly.

So off they went. I watched them through the leaves of the willow tree. They were looking at each other, smiling softly, not saying a word. Then they were gone. All I saw was the beautiful sunlight gliding in and out among the long feathery leaves—gold on the top of each leaf, silver on the bottom, bronze along each twig, metal black on the shadowed trunk.

I lay back and closed my eyes again.

Then I heard de Hahn murmuring sleepily, "Where are the other two?"

"Off," said I, "for a little walk along the shore. They'll be back shortly."

He sat up and blinked his eyes. Beads of perspiration hung on his forehead and his temples. His eyes looked bloodshot, his cheeks were scarlet.

"They just left a moment ago," I added. "They won't be gone long."

He looked at me dreamily. "Oh," he said, "I shan't worry about them; they won't get lost. He is a fine fellow, that Antoine. A wholesome sort, a real man, loyal and trustworthy. And my lovely Ursule . . . well, it hurt when she left me without a word in Bangkok that morning. But what would we all be if we didn't have our whims now and then? After all, she loves me. That's enough, isn't it?" He looked mistily across the water. Three pretty ducks were floating by serenely among the water lilies.

"Two things I've discovered about life," he said, leaning back on his elbows and closing his eyes. It was the posture of a young man, but everything about him—his voice, his eyes, his face,—seemed suddenly old.

"Yes?" said I eagerly. "Tell me, what are they?"

"The first thing is this—loneliness. Man is a lonely creature. It's taken me a long time to make sure of it, and it's been a sad process, I can tell you. I've always instinctively reached out toward people. I'd want to see into them and let them see into me. I'd want to become part of them and let them be part of me. But something always happened. It would never work out properly. They'd resent it if I detected a weakness in them—though Lord knows I loved them all the more for it. And they'd grow bored and contemptuous if I showed them my weaknesses. Always. Intimacy scared them.

"Perhaps if I'd been ravishingly handsome it might have been different. I'd have been the beloved one, not the lover. And they would have longed for intimacy and I would have dismissed it. There's no telling. Being beautiful makes a tremendous difference in one's character, there's no doubt about it."

He lay back again and wiped his face with the napkin. "This is what I think," he continued. His voice now rose flutteringly from his throat; it sounded uncertain and hoarse. "This is what I think: we're all lonely little souls, we've all got to work out our own salvation. We've got to arrange ourselves somehow so that life won't seem too terrifying. Isn't that so? Don't you agree? We've got to build up little ideas, pathetic visions about God and immortality and so on, behind which we can pretend to hide. We've got to close our eyes to the big thunderstorm that goes on all around us. We've got to, if we're ever going to be peaceful and contented. We've got to pretend that life has a point for each and every one of us, that there's a point to each of our little hearts beating like tom-toms in the midst of this endless black jungle."

The sun was sinking. Very gently twilight settled on the reeds, the grassy slopes, the water lilies, the willows. The hills beyond the water grew blue and dim.

"What is the second thing you've discovered about life?" I asked.

His voice sounded hazy and dreamy, like the twilight

over the pond. "The second thing? Let's see . . . well . . . ah, yes. This is it. That you really can't say anything at all about life. You can't be sure of anything at all. That is it. Don't you agree?"

"Yes," I replied, vaguely disappointed.

"You see, sometimes I have the feeling that something's wrong somewhere; that something's slipped by without my noticing, and that there's something around me that I'm missing. I get the feeling that I've made a dreadful big mistake somewhere, that there's some big point about existence that's eluded me completely. I grow afraid. Everything looks as if there were a secret lurking just around the corner that I hadn't in the least suspected. Do you grasp my point?"

I felt strange and uneasy. There was something very disturbing about all this. "Yes," said I. "I understand."

"Things look dangerous. There's a fine sunlight on the green meadow, the windmills look peaceful on the horizon, there are fine flowers along the path, but there's something beneath it that frightens me badly. And I don't know what it is. Do you ever feel like that?"

He sat up again wearily. There was the frightening look on his face of a man who has no occupation—the dull, shifting, sensitive eyes, the soft anxiety of the lips, the signs of loosening control. "Yes," said I, "I feel a little bit like that now and then."

"Asia," he said, and his voice for some reason sounded like that of another man, resonant and desperate—"Asia; yes, it has taught me many things, things that I'll never unlearn. For Asia, my boy, is the final tragic land. It is the last of the five great continents that we come to. Africa is the beginning, Asia is the end. Africa's the land of

358 ◇◇◇◇◇◇◇◇◇◇◇◇◇◇◇◇◇◇◇◇◇◇◇◇◇◇◇◇◇◇◇◇◇◇◇◇◇◇◇

birth, Asia the land of death. I feel her all the time now; she never leaves me, she has fastened herself to me like an infatuated lover. At night I feel her breath passing through the darkness. I feel her in the ruined temples, the forlorn cities, the yellow deserts, the green lakes, the icy mountains, the frightening woods. I feel her heart beating in complete and terrible wisdom. There is nothing left for her, my boy, not a single thing.

"We're all Asiatics," he continued dimly. "We're lost, the race is dying. What's ahead for us except a dark age? What possibly? Straight into deep, deep darkness, that's where we're going, don't deceive yourself. I know it. We're waiting for one thing, all of us. Some of us know it and some of us don't, that's the only difference."

"What is that one thing, de Hahn?" said I.

But he didn't seem to hear me. "Now and then," he said, his voice singularly low, subtly appalling, "I really get a glimpse of things as they are, just a brief clear glimpse. But the odd thing is that during that brief glimpse things are more muddled than at any other time. It's a brief clear glimpse of nothing more than a muddy haze. The certainties and simplicities of life are things that we've all invented ourselves. They did that sort of thing very well in the lovely eighteenth century. The age of reason. Yes, but when reason goes we've got to fall back on instinct. And do you know what instinct is? It's a wild lion roaming through the jungle with blood on his tongue.

"Yes, that's what I see at the end of this sinister tunnel. Darkness. The dark ages coming over us like an ocean. These voices of warning and exhortation and disgust that you hear everywhere, what are they but sighs before the real storm arrives? Man no longer desires reason. He no longer desires order. He no longer desires love or joy.

There's only one thing he wants. Look around. What do you see? Darkness, darkness."

He lay back in the grass and laid his arm across his face. I was silent for a moment. Get close to a man, and in spite of what de Hahn said, he will reach out to you across the invisible barrier. His hopes and loves, but above all his fears, will reach over and infect you, too. Perhaps there won't be any true understanding; but the fear will spread and multiply. Light is a timid and sensitive thing, but shadow grows and expands at the merest suggestion.

"What is the one thing that man desires, de Hahn?" said I. But he didn't answer. So I sat there quietly and watched dusk settling over the pond.

🦋🦋🦋 Like a moth's wing, dark and silent. The ducks had disappeared, not a single boat was left on the water. Finally, after I'd waited for half an hour I thought of looking for Antoine and Ursule, and got up from the ground.

But at that moment they appeared. They looked happy and alert. "You haven't grown impatient, I hope," said Antoine. "We lost our way. Didn't we, Ursule?"

Ursule nodded her head. Her eyes looked dark and clear, her skin looked young and smooth again.

"Has he been sleeping all this time?" asked Antoine, nodding toward de Hahn.

"No," said I. "He talked to me for a long time."

"What about?"

"I forget."

"About us?"

"Oh no."

"You're sure?"

"Oh, quite. No, he merely hoped that you wouldn't lose your way."

◇◈◇◈◇◈◇◈◇◈◇◈◇◈◇◈◇◈◇◈◇◈◇◈◇◈◇◈◇◈◇◈◇◈◇

Antoine laughed.

"Well," said Ursule, "we'd better be going." For the first time she looked at de Hahn. It was a sharp, expectant look, not precisely nervous but rather impatient. "Wake him up," she said brusquely.

"A shame to wake him up," said Antoine. "Sleeping so soundly, like a little boy. What is he dreaming of, I wonder?" He leaned over and called de Hahn's name.

But de Hahn didn't move.

"De Hahn," he cried again. I walked over and placed one hand on his forehead. Cold, peculiarly cold.

☙☙☙ Hurriedly we walked back along the path, past the shrine and the fountain and up toward the palm-lined avenue. It was almost dark. Far off through the tree trunks we could see the lanterns in the park being lit one by one.

We passed an old woman near the shrine, a dry old thing with bright and jolly eyes. She frightened us a little, and we began to walk faster. At last we reached the row of street lamps. In the distance we could see the car.

"Be sure and call the hospital, now," I repeated unhappily. "Don't forget. You can't leave him there."

"Yes, yes," said Ursule impatiently. "Don't fret. I'm the one that ought to do the worrying." Her voice was full of a restrained eagerness. There was a quick little spring in her footsteps as she walked along, and she still had the same bright look in her face. De Hahn's death had shocked her, beyond a doubt; she had almost fainted when we told her, her hands had trembled terribly and her lips had quivered with excitement. But the whole affair was peculiar and disconcerting as well as tragic. Dreadful little suspicions were beginning to take shape in my mind.

I looked at Antoine cautiously as we hurried past the

street lamps toward the car. His face looked serious and puzzled. He didn't look at either of us, but walked steadily along with a basket on each arm.

Then I looked at her again. Each time we passed a lamp her face would flash into an exaggerated brightness; her features would grow brilliantly white, her eyes shone like coals through the black shadows cast by her hat. Each time that I looked at her it seemed that she had once again changed her appearance. She never looked the same twice. There was something rather grand and awe-inspiring about her at this moment; she had acquired stature, poise, depth. And each time after she'd passed the lamp her face would suddenly relapse into shadow again and all I could see was the sharp resilient silhouette walking swiftly under the palms.

At last we reached the car. "Have you the key?" asked Antoine.

"Here it is," said Ursule. So we got in, and Antoine drove us back toward the hotel.

"Wait," said Ursule as we approached the building. "I don't think we'd better go back to the hotel."

"Why not?" said I.

"There'll be trouble about de Hahn. Inquiries, suspicions." She spoke rather irritably. "Drive on to another hotel, Antoine. Please. Quickly."

"But your luggage?"

"There's none worth mentioning."

"You'll just leave it there?"

"Might as well."

"Very well, then."

So he turned and drove back toward the Hôtel de l'Orient. I could smell the scents from the park as we drove along—great September flowers, lilies and asters, the au-

tumn trees, and through it all the larger fragrance of the
night, as if night itself were a black flower slowly opening
and from the lip of each unrolling petal new ribbons of
scent were gliding forth, curling through the branches toward us, caressing us.

☙☙☙ Antoine and I slept in one room, Ursule in another. In the middle of the night I heard him get up and
open the door and creep along the hall.

An hour later he returned.

"Well," I whispered, "where have you been, Samazeuilh?" I felt very angry and disgusted.

"Saying good-by."

"Saying good-by?"

"Yes, my friend."

"To Ursule?"

"Yes."

"Why?"

"I won't see her again. You and I are leaving early in
the morning, alone. So I went and said good-by, in my
little way. She didn't know I was saying good-by, but
that's what it was. I was merely saying good-by."

"Really?"

"Yes."

I reflected for a moment. "Tell me, Antoine," I began.
"I'm a little bit uneasy about all this. . . ."

"Stop worrying. Go to sleep."

"But did you call up the hospital? Is it all taken care
of?"

"Ursule took care of it. Don't worry."

"But are you sure?"

"Go to sleep."

I paused again. "Listen, Antoine," I said after a moment. "You won't leave me tomorrow, will you? You'll take me along? Promise?"

He ran his fingers through my hair. "Don't be afraid, little boy. Go to sleep."

But of course I couldn't go to sleep. Several hours later I saw the gray light falling upon the window pane. "Come, Antoine," I whispered. "Let's go."

40

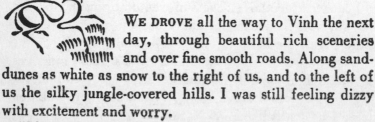

WE DROVE all the way to Vinh the next day, through beautiful rich sceneries and over fine smooth roads. Along sand-dunes as white as snow to the right of us, and to the left of us the silky jungle-covered hills. I was still feeling dizzy with excitement and worry.

"Listen, Samazeuilh," said I, "what do you think will happen? Do you think it will turn out all right?"

He wrinkled his lips and nodded. He looked very healthy and sleek, full of confidence.

"But tell me," I went on with great earnestness, "what do you think *did* happen? It's all very puzzling, you know, and I really can't decide what to believe."

He scratched his chin. "Well, she murdered him, of course."

"Terrible," I said softly after a minute or two.

"Well," he observed, "if there's one thing I've learned it's this, life is neither good nor bad. Life, fate, nature, call it whatever you want, that is to say, the way things happen—all this, I say, has no regard for what we two-legged creatures have decided by a majority vote to call good or bad. That's the truth. I'm not deceiving you. Why not see things clearly? It's not so bad, really, once you get used to it. Rather thrilling, in fact. There's nothing one can't get used to, you know, no matter how frightful. You don't even need to be particularly brave, unless, of course, you're more sensitive than the rest."

It was difficult to believe all this, with the charming man-made lands to the right and left of us shining like lacquer in the sunlight. Small temples under the banyan trees, the roadside red with flowers, great areca palms underneath which the black-toothed Annamites were sitting in their black turbans and chewing betelnut.

I looked at Antoine. The sun was outlining his profile. He was very handsome. I could see the pock-marks, the large pores, the hairs in his nostrils and his ears, but all of them added to the strong manlike look about him. Yes, he was a fine animal, he was fit, he'd survive. I looked at his heavy cruel lips glowing in the sunlight and wondered why I still liked him so well.

❧❧❧ And then from Vinh we went on to Haiphong and Hanoi, and then northward the following day toward the Chinese border. I wanted to get to Hongkong. There were many rivers which we had to cross, some very shallow and wide, on which the Tonkingese families lived in their little sampans. There'd be a matting covering the boat, and a basket for chickens, and poles for the fish nets, and that was all. But they looked far more contented than the people farther south, in the peninsula cities. Water and sunlight were enough to make them happy.

But still, things weren't all they might have been. In a hamlet north of Vinh we saw signs of disorder. And a Frenchman there, a plump goateed officer, told us of unpleasant things that had happened there two or three days ago. There had been a conspiracy among the natives, a Communist sort of affair apparently. Forty of them were arrested, and thirty-three of these executed. The rest of them had been tortured; as an "example to the community": hot coals had been tucked between their toes, long hot needles gently inserted in their ears, strange insects set nibbling away at their genitals. Not very pleasant. The French officer appeared quite placid about it all. "Well, they'll get us sooner or later," he said whimsically. "But in the meantime we shall be forced to make it uncomfortable for them."

We stopped for tea at a little village some fifty miles north of Hanoi. It was late afternoon, and the workers in their umbrella hats were coming home from the paddy-fields. There was an avenue of date palms, and on each side of it a row of straw huts. Everyone looked very healthy and pleased. Below the village I glimpsed a little stream rippling down toward the river through a tangle of palms and ivies.

"I tell you," muttered Samazeuilh as we sat in the tea-house, "the bad thing about existence nowadays is just this, in a nutshell. People become unreal. They eat, drink and copulate as always, at times indeed they still appear quite actual and distinct. But what you see is a mask. That's all; they've become ghosts, they've lost touch with the huge wave of truth, they're out in the stagnant waters. They chant little ghostly philosophies under the weeping willows, they invent a silky little world of their own, and when they look at you they don't see you at all, to tell the truth. There's a strong undercurrent which is the result of weakness and stupidity and grief; it's backwash of experience, and it leads us straight into this green pond of forgetfulness. We're all tempted to enter it with the rest. No wonder so few survive."

"What's the way to survive, Antoine?"

He grunted. "Who can say? Be happy, be happy-go-lucky, and so on. Some of us can, some of us can't. Well . . ." His eyes grew vague and hesitant. He was, after all, more complicated than one might have supposed.

"Have you ever known anyone who survived?"

He shook his head.

Presently he excused himself and went out. "I'll be right back, my boy," he sang from the doorway.

So I waited. But I began to feel uneasy as soon as he left.

And then I heard the roar of the exhaust and when I ran to the door I could just see the yellow fenders and the chromium tail-light disappearing behind the palms on the highway.

So I sat down again at the table. But oddly enough I didn't feel as badly as I might have. I didn't even feel angry. "Good-by, Antoine," I thought. "Good-by. You've helped me in your way; I shan't ever forget you. This hasn't been much of a farewell, and probably I'll never see you again. But you're part of me now, like all the rest of them, and I can't help loving you still."

I stepped out into the sunlight again and walked down toward the stream.

❧❧❧ There was a narrow path leading to the grove. At the end of the path was a gateway, and behind the gate, at the head of a little stairway, stood a small deserted shrine. The walls were of a silvery gray wood, mossy and spotted. From where I stood I could smell the damp rotting walls.

I heard a soft chanting sound. I stepped to one side, and there on a stone platform beside the stairway, hidden among the evergreens, I saw a little Chinaman. He was sitting motionless, legs crossed beneath him, eyes closed, hands folded, chanting—the very picture of serenity.

Then he opened his eyes and saw me. He smiled, quite without surprise. He rose and limped slowly toward me.

He was very, very old, dressed in a black silk cap and a

tight black brocaded coat. Shabby and yet elegant he appeared, smilingly responsive and yet full of precision and restraint.

He nodded. I nodded back across the ivy-grown gate. "Are you lost?" he asked quietly.

I was startled, but still not wholly surprised. He was gazing at me with such certainty and comprehension that nothing he said or knew would have seemed incongruous.

"Will you do me the great honor of making my humble hut your home for tonight?"

I nodded.

He led me back along the path and then down another stone stairway toward the stream. Beside the stream stood a small straw hut. Out in the twilight sat an old woman embroidering a green silken jacket, and not far away a girl and a boy were playing at the water's edge with the ducklings. They were like dolls, eyes like black glass and hair like black silk.

🐦🐦🐦 I fell asleep watching the branches against the sky. Through the window came the scent of the garden. The rotting trees, the overgrown paths, the brambles and vines, the moss beside the brook—all of them fading into a gentle ruin. The same scent of neglect and decay filled the interior of the house. The silks in my little room were all heavily clotted with moisture. A damp dreamy sigh seemed to bind the whole place, both inside and out, into a melancholy harmony. Silvery flickers of light hovered in the darkness over the decaying straw mats and the worm-eaten woodwork. It was all quite enchanting in its way; it was so very quiet and secluded.

A spider crawling across my forehead woke me up in the morning. There was already a patch of bright sunlight on the floor. I looked through the window. It was a fine morning, full of sunlight and dew. The old woman was already sitting in the garden, playing with some silk cocoons which were floating in a bowl of water.

Presently the children came clattering into my room. They laughed happily at me and kept shouting words which I couldn't understand. I knew they wanted me to get up, so I got up. They watched me with wide eyes as I dressed and walked down to the stream for a morning bath. The old woman with a face as brown as wrinkled leather laughed and called a morning's greeting after me.

I walked up the shore a way until I reached a small waterfall. The water poured over a great black rock and split into three streamlets—one spread flatly, went tumbling among the stones, white and foaming, a miniature torrent; another flowed transparently like silk, smooth and green, almost motionless it seemed; the third was only a thin ribbon; it fell over the edge in a graceful arc, descended through a little rainbow of its own, then scattered into a thousand drops just before it reached the shadowy pool at the bottom.

The pool looked cold and deep. I stepped out of my clothes and hesitated at the edge. A warm ray of sunlight fell on me through the pines. It was good to watch the glitter of the sunlight on each bubble along the shore, on the white pebbles, on the ripples pushing their white paws tenderly between each stone, on the frail day-flies that were pursuing one another among the ferns.

Then I heard a soft laughing voice. I looked down the stream. There, sitting among the rocks at a narrow place in the stream, sat the old Chinaman, fishing-pole in hand. "Don't be afraid," he cried, "don't be afraid!"

And then, the plunge into the cool water, the green flow of it past my body, the feel of my muscles growing long and taut; and then when I crept out again and stood among the ferns, the sunlight glistening on each crystal drop that trembled on my skin, the fine warm sunlight making my body quiver with eagerness and affection. Yes, there was no denying it, I was feeling very happy.